SLEEPER: THE RED STORM

SLEEPER

THE RED STORM

J.D. Fennell

THE
DOME
PRESS

Published by The Dome Press, 2018
Copyright © 2018 J.D. Fennell
The moral right of J.D. Fennell to be recognised as the author
of this work has been asserted in accordance with the
Copyright, Designs and Patents Act 1988.

This is a work of fiction. All characters, organisations and events portrayed in
this novel are either products of the author's imagination or are used
fictitiously.

A CIP catalogue record for this book is available from the British Library

Hardback ISBN: 9781999855987
Paperback ISBN: 9781999855994

The Dome Press
23 Cecil Court
London WC2N 4EZ

www.thedomepress.com

Printed and bound in Great Britain by Clays, Elcograf S.p.A.

Typeset in Garamond by Elaine Sharples

MIX
Paper from
responsible sources
FSC® C110794

For my dad

CHAPTER 1

Murder in Mornington Crescent

London, 13ᵗʰ July 1943

Ilia Koslov's right hand nestles firmly against the comforting warm steel of the Nagant pistol concealed in the pocket of his green trench coat. Drawing on the end of a Woodbine, he exhales a bitter grey cloud of smoke and crosses Hampstead Road, hurrying towards the glossy red-tiled fortress that is Mornington Crescent tube station. Under the rim of his fedora, tilted forward to obscure his face, he glances up and down the road. It is still early and dark. Traffic is thin and most Londoners will be sleeping or eating their breakfast rations.

He ignores the wizened old guard who bids him good morning and presses the button to call the lift. He hears it creaking and cranking as the steel chamber is hauled to ground level. He pulls apart the lift gates and hesitates. The London underground is nothing more than a glorified tomb. Full of ghosts and hidden corpses; many taken by his own hand. He shudders and tries not to think about it. Once again he has a job to do and he must be swift.

As the lift lowers deep into the earth, his hand grips the pistol, pointing it forward. The steel box arrives and he slides open the gates, his eyes alert, his gun ready. The tiled corridor beyond is full of shadows, but he is confident there is no one there yet. He edges forward, glancing left then right before making his way to the agreed meeting spot on platform one.

The platform seems unusually clean. The rectangular cream tiles that line the walls, and the blue and red tube symbol, have a sheen to them. Perhaps Agent Sedova has cleaned the place to impress him. He chuckles darkly at his little joke as he walks the length of the platform, his eyes assessing every corner and every shadow.

He steps back from the platform at the rattle of an approaching train. The whoosh of cold air reeks of stale oil. He wrinkles his nose and studies his faint reflection in the windows of the train as it flies by. It feels like he is watching a live movie reel of himself. He straightens up, pushes out his chest and affects a pose like Clark Gable. Something hard presses into his back. He freezes and grips the Nagant, his pulse racing. In the windows he sees the outline of the agent behind him. He swallows and curses himself for letting his guard down and, even more, curses Clark Gable.

'Remove your hands from your pockets and put them in the air,' says Agent Sedova.

Koslov feels his spine ice over and does as he is told.

Sedova's hands search his pockets. The agent finds the Nagant and tosses it to the rail track. 'Why are you here?'

'I … I have news,' Koslov replies.

'I'm listening.'

'There has been a change of direction...' He leaves the sentence hanging, in an effort to assert some control over his predicament.

Agent Sedova pokes his back harder with the pistol.

'The British spy is dead.'

Sedova lets out a heavy sigh. 'Do not try my patience. Which spy?'

'Starling.'

He thinks it is odd that Sedova says nothing and, for a moment, he thinks the agent has disappeared. He turns to look but the pistol is thrust into his back again.

'This is not news, Koslov. Is that it? Is that all you have?'

'No. We are to find the sister. Our leaders are very interested in what she is capable of doing.'

'We?'

'You and me. We work together like an alliance.'

'But you were sent here to kill me.'

Koslov feels his stomach twisting. How did Sedova know this?

'No, no, no.'

'Liar.'

He hears a second train approaching. A distraction. 'Agent Sedova, let me explain.' He whirls around, his arms raised in a conciliatory gesture.

'I did not say you could move.' Sedova is holding a British silencer pistol, aimed at his chest. 'Move towards the edge of the platform.'

Koslov feels the blood drain from his face. 'Please, Agent Sedova. I have a family.'

The rattle of the train drowns out the phut of the silencer as a sharp pain explodes in his chest.

'So do I,' says Sedova.

Confusion fills Koslov's mind as he falls backwards, thudding hard onto the track below. He hears the train approaching and thinks he might catch it and go home to see his beloved Misha and their daughter Sasha. His eyes blink and he looks up to see Agent Sedova looking down on him with cold, hard eyes. Angry or sad he cannot tell. He opens his mouth to speak but something screeches nearby and then everything goes black.

CHAPTER 2

A Sniff of Betrayal

Chartres, France, 14ᵗʰ July 1943, the following evening

Will Starling lies on his belly, concealed under bushes and weighed down by a backpack crammed with twenty-five pounds of Nobel 808 explosive. It is a warm summer evening, his clammy face mists up the lenses of his compact, Canadian, 6x30 binoculars. He blows on them before wiping the glass with the cuff of his shirt. Adjusting the focus, he watches the blurred shades of green and grey form into lush green meadows and the sturdy steel legs of a towering pylon, an immense obelisk transmitting power from Paris through to Chartres and beyond – power the Nazis were using to their advantage. Will takes stock of the tower, sweeping the binoculars up the ugly lattice structure. It would take a lot of explosive to bring it down.

'Is it clear?' asks Emile.

Will nods. 'It's clear.'

'We should hurry, no?' whispers Claudette.

'Not just yet,' says Will. His eyes follow the sun as it sinks and disappears behind a distant forest. The sky is brushed with an amber glow and provides enough light for them to carry out the operation without attracting unwanted attention with torches.

Emile and Claudette huddle on either side of him. Despite being the leader of this mission, he can't help feeling like a spare wheel. His companions are newlyweds. Emile is athletic and handsome in a typical Gallic way and Claudette is pretty with dark hair and a wicked sense of humour that has Will laughing out loud sometimes. They are hopelessly in love, living each day as if it were their last. It is the perfect disguise for being amongst the occupying German forces, who find them innocuous and therefore ignore them.

Behind the smiles and sunny expressions, however, Emile and Claudette detest the Nazis, their feelings buried deep, emerging in the hidden meeting rooms of back-street bars and cafés where Will and other members of the Special Operations Executive and French Resistance meet to discuss the latest orders from London.

'Before we go, I have something to ask you, *mon cher*,' says Claudette.

Will hands the binoculars to Emile.

'Oui, ma cherie?' says Emile, scouring the landscape.

Claudette snorts. 'I was talking to Will.'

Like Will, Claudette has just turned eighteen. She has become like a sister to him and, despite remembering almost nothing about his real sister, he has, on occasion, had to stop himself from calling Claudette by Rose's name. He knows he should have kept his distance, but Claudette's personality, her humour and passion are just too seductive.

He often thinks about Rose and wonders if she is like Claudette. In his dreams she appears in snapshots. She seems innocent, fragile, but also stubborn – nothing unusual in any of those traits. However,

Rose was not like other girls. Will had acquired secret research papers authored by his father, which revealed a little more about his past. His father had worked for Teleken – a VIPER-funded, scientific organisation that had developed a wonder drug, which allegedly gave the user kinetic powers. Will's father had championed it and his mother had agreed to be one of the guinea pigs. However, the drug had been a failure. None of the guinea pigs had developed anything other than the need to vomit for three hours after taking it. All except Will's mother, that is. She had vomited the morning before taking the drug, unaware that she was pregnant with Rose.

Neither Will's father nor his mother could have anticipated what fate had in store for them. The drug had fed the foetus and seemingly modified Rose's genetic make-up. Will's father had no explanation as to how this could have happened. A miracle of modern science, he had concluded.

In the paper, Will's father described how, at the age of five, Rose had lost her temper and her scream had caused all the windows in the house to shatter. Reading this had stirred an uncomfortable and frightening memory for Will. He remembered his parents being confused, scared even, and recalled a terrified Rose sobbing and apologising for something she knew she had caused but had not been able to control.

In another episode they had been in a local park on a sunny afternoon. Their mother had been unpacking a picnic and an eight-year-old Rose watched on as Will and his father tried out a new cricket bat. His father had bowled a googly, catching Will off-guard. Will had whacked the ball with fervour and accidentally sent it spinning towards his mother. As he panicked and cried out, the ball suddenly stopped in mid-air and spun slowly before flying obediently into a smiling Rose's waiting hands. To his parents' horror, other people had witnessed this event. This had been the beginning of the end. Soon after that, the agents of VIPER had come for Rose and his family.

The knowledge of what followed stirs the dormant rage in Will; he feels it bubbling like lava. His parents had been murdered by the corrupt and criminal VIPER organisation. His kidnapped sister was reportedly locked up in a hidden fortress known only as the Red Tower. But two years had passed since he had learned this. Rose could be dead now for all he knew. In his fractured, unreliable mind his family appear as if they are bit-part players in snippets of a motion picture. But their love for him remains like the ghost of a tattoo on his soul.

He takes a breath and tries to focus on the job at hand.

Claudette ruffles his hair, taking him away from his sombre thoughts. Despite himself, he smiles.

'I 'ave a surprise for you.'

'I love surprises!' says Will, teasing.

'Do we 'ave to do this now?' says Emile.

Claudette ignores him. 'Will, we would love you to do us the honour of becoming godfather to our firstborn.'

Will's heart sinks. He looks incredulously from a beaming Claudette to Emile, who shrugs off his wife's eccentric, easy-going attitude. Not to mention terrible timing.

'Please say yes,' says Claudette.

Suddenly the weight of responsibility has doubled and Will feels a shadow cross his soul. He shuts his eyes and breathes slowly. Of course, he is happy for them but he is angry, too, that this news has been dropped on him now.

'Will?' she says.

'Yes, you know I will, but you should not be here. It is too dangerous … Why did you not tell me this earlier?'

'Because you would not 'ave allowed me to come! That is why. And you need my 'elp.'

'We could have managed without you!' Will replies, a little too forcefully.

Claudette's face falls. Will feels guilty as she looks to Emile for support.

'Will is right,' Emile says.

Will rests his hand on Claudette's arm. 'Emile and I will fix the explosives. You are to stay here.'

Claudette opens her mouth to speak but Will anticipates it. 'No arguments!'

Emile removes a torch from his pocket and hands it and the binoculars to Claudette. 'Stay here, *cherie*. We need a lookout. Signal to us if you see anything unusual.'

Claudette gives a sulky nod as Will heaves himself into a crouch, his shirt wet with perspiration under his backpack. Emile kisses Claudette goodbye and turns to Will.

'Ready?' asks Will.

'Oui.'

Will and Emile dart from their hiding spot and sprint across the open field; the only sound is the rustle of grass in the breeze and the thud of their feet on the soft ground. The backpack bounces on Will's back like an overweight, angry baby. For a fleeting second he worries it might explode, sending him to kingdom come before he reaches the pylon, but he pushes the thought from his mind.

The base of the pylon is immense, bigger than he expected. He wonders if they have enough explosive to bring it down.

Emile helps Will off with the backpack and carefully unbuckles the flap. A chemical, almond smell fills the air as he removes six sticks of gelignite. Will takes them from him and begins fixing them to the legs of the obelisk. When all the legs are packed, Will removes a slim, green tin cartridge from his jacket pocket. He opens it, hands four brass Time Pencils to Emile and keeps four for himself.

'Thirty minute detonation time,' instructs Will.

Emile nods.

'Use two per leg, in case one pencil fails.'

Using pliers, Will breaks the copper end of the four pencils, cracking the glass vial inside and releasing the acid. He hands the pliers to Emile, holds the detonators up to the light of the red sky and checks the vials are empty. They seem almost the same size as the cathedral spires, which stand tall on the hill where Chartres was built. He wrinkles his nose at the sulphuric smell, like rotten eggs, and is relieved to see the acid is starting to do its work, eroding the wire so that it would, in thirty minutes' time, blow the detonator and ignite the gelignite. Countdown has begun. He inserts two pencils in each explosive, conceals them with foliage and checks his wristwatch, a waterproof Timor with a brown leather strap – a gift from his secret service mentor, a brusque, Belfast man called Eoin Heaney.

It is 9.05 pm but there is still enough light.

'Claudette?' says Emile, suddenly.

Will looks up, follows Emile's gaze and sees their companion sprinting across the field towards them. Something is not right. He swallows and scans the horizon behind her, but sees nothing.

Claudette arrives, panting and out of breath. 'Soldiers. I had to come. The stupid torch would not work.'

'How far away?'

'At least a mile. They are walking in a line with their rifles out, heading in this direction.'

'They know we're here. We've been betrayed!' says Emile.

'They are not alone.'

'What do you mean?' asks Will.

'I didn't know what to make of it. There are monks with the Nazis. Four of them.'

'Monks? But there are no monasteries here,' says Emile.

Will feels his shoulders tighten. Hidden in his fractured memory is something about monks. Something he cannot reach. He tries to remember, but nothing surfaces.

'Will, do you know who they are?' asks Claudette.

He glances from Claudette to Emile and back to Claudette. 'It's probably nothing,' he says, rubbing the back of his head. 'Let's move. We have a job to do.'

His orders are to blow the pylon and head immediately to Chartres Cathedral to meet his contact, an agent with the codename Marie-Antoinette. The entire operation will be scuppered if he can't find a way to draw the soldiers away from the pylon. He glances at the backpack. There is one solitary stick of explosive remaining and one Time Pencil. A plan begins to formulate in his head. It is risky, probably crazy, but he is not going to let anything stop this mission from succeeding.

'Emile, Claudette, if we have been betrayed then it is too dangerous for us to stay here. I need you to head south, then circle round and meet me at the cathedral, as quickly as you can. Keep out of sight and stay safe.'

Emile and Claudette nod their agreement.

Claudette hugs Will warmly and kisses him on both cheeks. 'Be careful, my friend. Make sure we see you. Godfather, remember?' She pats her belly.

'I remember.' Will smiles encouragingly but has a grim sense that the outcome might not be what they hope for.

Emile grabs Claudette by the hand and they run, disappearing through the bushes and crossing a road to the fields and meadows beyond. With his friends safely out of the way, Will can concentrate. He slips his backpack on and begins sprinting north, dipping under shrubs and hiding behind trees on the outskirts of the woods.

He hears the sound of a vehicle, the unmistakable grumble of a German Kübelwagen coming from an easterly direction in the woods. There must be a track there. He hurries towards the noise, which stops suddenly. Will peeks from behind a tree and sees the dark green Kübelwagen with the black and white Balkanskreuz – the Nazi cross – painted on the side. A machine gun, a Maschinengewehr 34, is mounted at the rear. There is just one occupant, a solitary German soldier, who hops out of the vehicle and lights up a cigarette. He removes his helmet, places it on the bonnet and sweeps his fingers through his pale hair.

Will circles round the rear of the vehicle without making a sound. He picks up a stone and tosses it over the soldier's head and into the bushes on the other side of the road. The soldier jumps and takes his Luger from its belt holster.

'*Wer ist da?*' he demands, pointing the pistol at the bushes and flicking his cigarette to the ground.

Will inches behind him, picks the helmet from the bonnet. '*Guten Abend...*'

The soldier spins round as Will raises the helmet and slams it against the man's temple. The soldier's legs give way and he falls unconscious to the ground.

'...and good night.' Dragging him out of sight, Will removes his uniform and puts it on. It reeks of stale sweat and cigarette smoke. Slipping on the helmet, he drops his backpack onto the passenger seat and starts up the Kübelwagen's engine.

The car is designed to drive on rough terrain and Will steers it easily off the track and through the woods until he reaches the perimeter. He can see the other German soldiers and the monks standing around the bushes where he, Claudette and Emile had lain only twenty minutes earlier. He gets out and checks the boot, finding rope and various tools including a large spanner. Suddenly, his plan has upgraded to a new level.

Will removes the machine gun from the vehicle and places it on the ground. With the pliers he snaps the glass vial of the Time Pencil, sets it to detonate in two minutes and inserts it inside the last stick of gelignite, which he places by the driver's pedals on the floor of the car. With the engine still running, he ties the rope around the steering wheel and the brake, securing it tightly so that the wheel cannot turn. Then he wedges the spanner against the gas pedal so that it is temporarily pushed to the floor.

He releases the brake and watches the Kübelwagen drive itself out of the woods and into the field where the soldiers and monks are on the move, approximately 200 feet away. The officer in charge sees Will and shouts something Will cannot hear. All eyes are looking towards him and the Kübelwagen as it drives drunkenly towards them. Will picks up the MG 34 and fires mercilessly at the soldiers and monks. He shoots to kill and they hit the ground; most dead, some only injured.

Will ducks down just as the Kübelwagen explodes in a satisfying ball of flame. He hears cries and then gunfire.

There is little more he can do here now. He starts to run, praying that this was enough of a diversion to lead them away from the pylon.

CHAPTER 3

Rise of the Cerastes

Will sprints through the woods, his body drenched in sweat from the heavy German uniform and warm evening. He emerges into a clearing where the light from the dusking sky casts a hazy pearl sheen across the open fields and the nearby ruin of an old church. Stopping to get his bearings, he hears a ringing in the west. It's the bells of Chartres Cathedral.

He picks up his pace along the outskirts of the trees. The stillness is eerie. Something's not quite right. The hair on his neck stands up, as if he knows he is being watched. He is not alone. Glancing towards the ruin, he thinks he sees a tall, dark figure disappear into the shadows. For a moment, he thinks of his old foe, the Pastor, and shudders. But it could not be him. He had died in the crypt of St Mary le Bow two years before.

He hears a twig crack to his right and swings round. He feels something whoosh past his ear. As he crouches down, a knife shudders into the bark of the tree behind him. It seems strangely familiar. He pulls it out, turns it over in his hand and his heart begins to pound.

In the distance he glimpses the pale face of a hooded monk looking his way. Will stares, his stomach clenching. He has seen monks like him before. He knows the order.

The monk disappears into the gloom. Will holds up the knife. The shape of the grip is unmistakeable: a snake. But not any snake; it is a viper. This monk is from the Cerastes, the order of VIPER.

Will needs to find out why he's here and moves cautiously towards the run-down old church. He sees the monk looming in what was once the entrance, his face hidden in the shadow of his hood, his arms tucked into his sleeves. Will moves closer. The man is dressed in drab grey robes, tied at the waist with a thick, red, snake-like rope. A symbol of the order to which he belongs.

Will knows he is here for him and him only. But how could he have known Will was here? Where could the intelligence have come from? Was there a mole in the Secret Service?

The monk retreats into the gloom of the ruins. He is trying to draw Will closer, but Will is not going to fall for that today. Logic tells him to get the hell of there; stick with the plan. But the monk might be useful: with some persuasion, he may tell him where the Red Tower is. Clenching the snake dagger firmly in his palm, Will follows the monk.

Inside the ruined church, he stops, his eyes scanning around. He can see no one. He hears a man cry out above him and sees the monk's robed form leap from the wall. Suddenly he lands on Will's shoulders and a flash of red flies past as the monk pulls a rope towards his neck. Will blocks it with the dagger and, as the monk pulls the rope tight, Will slices through it, hurls the man off his shoulders and turns to face him.

Dropping the rope to the ground, the monk pulls two long knives from his sleeves. He raises his arms with the knife tips pointing downward like the teeth of a viper. Will has only the single dagger with which to defend himself. He does not stand a chance. As the monk runs at him, Will tears the German helmet from his head, holding it in one hand with the dagger in the other. The two men connect with a screech of metal on metal, Will thrashing the helmet against one knife and twisting the dagger against the other. The monk's strength pushes him backwards. It all seems futile and Will kicks out in despair. The kick hits the monk's stomach, winding him; he shudders but remains poised, his focus weakened just for the moment. Will wastes no time, flicks his wrist and brings the dagger down on the man's hand.

The monk drops one of his knives and steps back.

Will glances at the knife lying on the dusty ground. With it are droplets of blood and two of the man's fingers. The monk retreats, disappearing further into the ruins. Will follows and arrives at what looks like the remains of the altar, where he sees the monk with his hood pulled back. He has torn some material from it to bind his bloody hand.

'Who are you?' asks Will, taking stock of the man. His hair is shorn, his face is lean and his expression unsettlingly calm. Will notices a tattoo of a viper above his ear. The symbol of the Cerastes.

The monk does not respond. Instead, he walks towards Will, the remaining knife balanced in his good hand. Considering he has lost two fingers, he does not seem to be in much pain. Will lifts the dagger to fight but the monk is fast and slides along the ground, toppling Will over onto his back with his feet. Will hits the ground with a thud and both the dagger and helmet slip from his grip. He scrambles to his feet as the monk swipes his knife, but Will pulls back and the blade merely slices through the German jacket. The monk pushes forward, his lean face glaring at Will, his mouth twisting into a sneer, a low noise emerging, like a growl. He is strong, but Will holds his nerve and lashes his boot out at the monk's injured hand. The monk stumbles back, nursing his wounded and bloody hand. Will scoops up the dagger and runs at him, their weapons caught in a lock once more. The monk's face is inches from Will's. He whispers in his ear.

'*Tempestas rubra advenit*,' he says.

Will freezes, his mouth dries. He feels he has heard these words before.

The monk seizes the moment, pulls back and lashes his foot hard at Will's chest, knocking the wind from him and sending him spiralling back towards the altar. Down and dazed, Will is straddled by the monk, his knife arm pinned down by the man's knee. Smiling grimly, the monk raises the knife one more time. Eyes wide and mouth dry, Will thinks this is the end. His free hand searches the ground and finds only grit and debris. He scoops some in his palm and flings it at the monk's eyes. The knife plunges, but Will grabs the monk's wrist and, holding it firm, slams the knife down into the man's thigh.

The monk screams and falls to the side.

Will scrambles forward pulling the knife out of the monk's flesh, and holds the knife to the man's throat. 'Why are you here?'

The monk's eyes meet directly with Will's. '*Tempestas rubra advenit*,' he says again. And again, Will's stomach clenches. There is something in the words, something from his past, that he can't quite recall.

'What does that mean?'

The monk's jaw starts to move, his tongue darts between his teeth, but he says nothing.

'Tell me what it means,' demands Will, pushing the knife against the man's flesh, but the monk pulls away and slams the side of his face on the floor. Blood seeps from his mouth and he spits out what looks like a hollow tooth. His mouth is open, his tongue turning something over. It's a red pill. A poison capsule.

Will swears and steps back. The monk's body begins to shake violently. He seems to be choking, the whites of his eyes turn scarlet and a gruesome red froth gathers in his mouth. He is taking a long time to die but there is nothing Will can do.

What on earth could cause that reaction?

As the monk finally stills, Will tries to piece together what's going on. The Cerastes were here looking for him but it doesn't seem right to him that they'd be working with the Germans. Had VIPER and the Nazis joined forces? VIPER's influence spread far and wide – it was well known they had senior people in positions of power in all governments across the globe, including Germany's – but their goal of creating a new world order would be in direct competition with the Third Reich's ideology. There had to be a simpler explanation. The German soldiers accompanying the monks could not be Nazis – they had to be soldiers of VIPER in disguise.

Will hears voices from the woods. Picking up the helmet, he runs to the back of the ruins, hops over the remains of an old wall and runs in the opposite direction. He must get to Chartres Cathedral as quickly as possible. He cuts back into the shadows of the trees. Twigs lash at his face and hands as he sprints through the gloomy woods, but he barely notices them. He can think of nothing but the monk's words. They were a warning but not just that: they were a threat.

Tempestas rubra advenit. The Red Storm is coming.

CHAPTER 4

Codename: Marie-Antoinette

The ancient town of Chartres is built on a hill on the left bank of the Eure river. With the enforcement of the curfew the streets are quiet and full of shadows. All the shutters are closed. There are no street lights; the blackout is as well observed here as it is in London.

Will's boots echo loudly on the cobbles as he runs up a narrow street. Wiping the sweat from his brow, he stops and checks his watch. It is 9:40 pm. Five minutes past the detonation time. 'Shit!' he whispers. How could that happen? Were the Time Pencils faulty?

He turns a corner and almost collides with two armed German patrol soldiers, who reach for their weapons, but stop when they see Will's uniform. Their green collar patches and shoulder straps indicate they are privates. However, on the upper left arm of the taller of the two, is an embroidered pip, a pyramidal star marking him out as a Oberschütze, a senior private.

They seem as surprised to see him as he is them. They say nothing for a moment as they look him up and down.

'*Guten Abend.*' Will breaks the silence, with a tense smile. He fixes his helmet and buttons up his jacket.

'*Guten Abend,*' they reply, their suspicion obvious. The senior private frowns at the cuts in Will's uniform and the patches of dirt and asks, '*Wie heißen Sie?*'

Time is tight. Will glances at the cathedral spires at the top of the town. Marie-Antoinette will not hang around forever and he has Emile and Claudette to think about. He fakes a coughing fit, raising his hand to his mouth to buy time as he thinks of a name. He says the first thing that comes into his head, 'Hitler!' and regrets it immediately.

The men look at each other in disbelief, before turning back to Will.

'Hitler?' says the senior private.

Will laughs. '*Nein … nein …* Himmler! *Ich heiße* Himmler.'

They seem even more confused. 'Himmler…?' one says with a slow drawl.

Will sighs. He has had enough. His eyes dart between the two men, sizing them up and calculating that it will take no more than ten seconds to bring the two fools down. His fists curl. The senior private's eyes narrow as if he has detected a shift in Will's demeanour. Their eyes meet but, at that very second, a mighty explosion shakes the ground beneath their feet and lights the sky beyond the town where the pylon is located.

'*Schieße!*' say the soldiers, in unison.

At last.

Fearing the Allies are bombing them, the townspeople start emerging from their homes into the narrow streets. They jostle past Will and the soldiers, making it easy for Will to move away.

A second explosion fills the air and people begin running for shelter. Through the melee, the senior private calls to Will and points in the direction out of town, 'Himmler! *Kommen Sie mit!*'

Will nods, but allows the swelling crowd to grow between them. When the two soldiers are herded out of sight, he makes his way to the cathedral at the top of the town.

Will stands in the shadows in the forecourt at the west entrance to Chartres Cathedral. When he'd arrived a year before, Claudette had given him a tour of the town and told him the history of its magnificent Gothic cathedral.

'Typically Catholic and oppressive,' she had described it, with a wry smile.

He hadn't been sure what she had meant until now. Looking up at the façade with its vast, round, stained-glass window, he remembers her telling him that the west window represented the apocalypse, the Last Judgement. He thinks of VIPER. Isn't that what they want? An apocalypse of their own making? *Many must die for the world to change.* In their own twisted way they wanted to restart the world by wiping out most of its population and oppressing the rest. The thought of it sparks at his rage. He would never let that happen.

He hurries across the forecourt and up the stone steps, stopping at the three tall, heavy wooden doors. The stone eyes of Jesus and every biblical saint and sinner seem to follow him, judging and suspicious.

A third explosion blasts the night and lights up the sky.

The pylon must have fallen by now.

Will pushes the door open and steps inside, closing it behind him and breathing in the faint traces of incense. The light from the fourth blast flashes behind the stained-glass windows, throwing a blue hue across the vast interior. Chartres Cathedral is breathtaking as he walks under its immense flying buttresses towards the centre and the famous stone labyrinth carved into the floor.

Emile and Claudette are sitting together facing towards the altar. They see him and he nods, but they turn away looking worried. He remembers he is still wearing the German uniform. He takes off the helmet and jacket. His hair is thick and long on top and he sweeps it back with his fingers. When they recognise him, they are relieved. Claudette stands, but Will gestures for her to sit.

He sees the labyrinth, in the nave, and a woman kneeling at a bench, her head bowed as if in prayer. The labyrinth is faintly lit by four candles at the north, south, east and west points of the nave. There is no one else around. It must be Marie-Antoinette. Who else would risk coming here when they think they are being bombed?

He walks quickly up the aisle, stopping at the bench where she is kneeling. Glancing respectfully towards the altar, he genuflects and slides in beside her. He smells a sweet scent in the air, like a blend of exotic flowers, swathing her with an invisible cloud. Kneeling, he blesses himself and glances sideways. Her hair is brown, shaped in the pompadour style and she is wearing a pillbox hat with a black, netted veil covering a chiselled face, heavily made up. She seems older than him, perhaps by ten years or more.

Speaking the secret code words, he says, as if to himself, 'Death is nothing.'

The woman touches her forehead with a gloved hand, makes the sign of the cross and sits up. 'But to live defeated and inglorious is to die daily.' Her accent is unmistakably Parisian, as is her sense of style. She seems oddly out of place in a rustic town like Chartres. This is his contact. This woman is codename Marie-Antoinette.

'You're late,' she says.

'We ran into some trouble.'

She turns to look at him and he meets her gaze. Through the veil he sees full lips painted a deep red and large, dark, questioning eyes.

'We were betrayed.'

'By whom?'

Will has really no clue who betrayed them. He doesn't believe it was any of the local Resistance he works so closely with – they are all so passionate and determined – but he wonders if one of them has got drunk one night and let something slip. 'I don't know that yet. Besides, we have other problems now. There are monks from VIPER here.'

'The Cerastes are here?'

'Yes.'

'*Merde*!' she says.

'Do you know why?'

She bends down to pick up her purse and opens it. She takes out a slim, silver cigarette case and hands it to him. 'They are looking for this.'

'What is it?'

The case is cool to the touch. The edges are sealed with a red wax and on it is an embossed insignia of an owl.

'Inside are the plans for a powerful weapon VIPER are developing. You must take it to London, at once, without letting it fall into their hands.'

Will slips it into his trouser pocket.

'Can you swim?' she asks.

Will frowns. 'Yes…'

'Good, we must leave immediately.'

With no time to question her, Will turns and beckons to Emile and Claudette at the rear of the cathedral.

'Who are they?'

'They are my friends. The betrayal has put them in danger. They cannot stay here any longer.'

'No,' says Marie-Antoinette. 'That was not part of the deal.'

'Deal? What are you talking about?'

'We are not taking them,' she hisses.

'Yes, we are! Their association with me puts them at risk. If they are caught, VIPER will execute them.'

'It isn't my problem.'

'No, it is not. It is *our* problem.'

'No, it is not possible.'

'Claudette is with child!' says Will, through gritted teeth.

Through the veil, he sees the agent's firm expression soften. After a moment she nods. 'Very well.'

Will shakes his head, furious that he had to argue. As he turns away from the agent he notices something on the floor at the centre of the labyrinth. Pieces of a chess set have been carefully placed, but not for a game. The pieces are positioned alongside each other as if in alliance.

What on earth?

In the middle is a tight circle of pawns surrounding something red and blue and shiny. It is a solitary toy fusilier, a tin soldier brandishing a sabre as if he is running into battle. A memory slices through Will's mind. He has seen this tin soldier before. He feels dizzy and rubs the back of his head.

'Will?' says Claudette, who is now standing by his side, her hand holding his arm softly.

'I'm fine.' He crouches down and picks up the soldier. It is two inches tall, hollow, and with a split up its spine. Will's heart beats faster. He turns the soldier upside down and sees two letters scratched into the faded green paint of the toy's base.

WS

'What is that?' says Claudette.

He feels cold inside. He remembers sitting at a desk in a bedroom, a room that was new to him. Standing in the doorway was Timothy Chittlock. His face was solemn. It was six years ago when Will first went to live at Chittlock's house after the death of his parents. He had sat at that desk all night, barely able to move. His hand sore from gripping the tin fusilier. The same one he held now.

There are voices outside the cathedral. Emile hurries to the west entrance and peeks outside. 'Soldiers!'

'We must hurry,' says Marie-Antoinette.

'Who gave you the order to meet me here?' asks Will.

Marie-Antoinette turns for the north exit. 'We don't have time for this.'

'Someone knew I would be here. Who was it?'

The agent does not meet his gaze. She ignores his question and walks away. Will follows and grabs her arm. 'You know more than you are letting on. Tell me!'

The soldiers' voices are getting closer.

Marie-Antoinette pulls away from his grip and glares at him. 'I only know him as the Owl. I don't know who he is or what he looks like. That is all!'

Will searches his shrouded memory for a clue as to who this Owl could be but finds nothing. Whoever he is, he has sent a clear message: VIPER are back and they are everywhere. They are closing in and Will is at the centre of it all. Buried in his head are all of VIPER's secrets. They want him dead.

J.D. FENNELL

'Please, we must leave,' says Marie-Antoinette.

Will nods his agreement and the four of them hurry to the north exit.

Outside, in the shadows beyond the grounds, is a dark Citroën Traction Avant. Will hears the shrill barking of a small dog and sees a shadowy, rat-faced creature glaring at them from the driver's seat.

'Quiet, *cherie*. Mummy is here,' says Marie-Antoinette, in hushed tones.

The dog's barking is relentless. Will shoots a worried glance back at the cathedral, sure that the noise will attract attention.

The Parisian agent opens the boot and pulls out two blank artist's canvases.

'The girl can ride up front with me. You two in here,' she says, hiding the canvases under a bush.

Will has a bad feeling about this, but there is no alternative. There is just not time to think of another plan.

'Claudette, please try and calm that beast down,' he says.

She smiles and kisses him on the cheek.

Will climbs into the boot as Emile and Claudette embrace. Moments later, he and Emile are squeezed together in an awkward, foetal spooning position. Will would laugh if their lives were not in terrible danger.

Marie-Antoinette slams the boot closed, plunging them into darkness. Above the din of the yapping creature, he hears her footsteps and then the car's doors creaking open. The vehicle shifts as the two women get inside. The engine starts and they move off steadily. Will breathes a sigh of relief that the dog has finally calmed down.

'Will,' whispers Emile.

'Yes?'

'If anything 'appens to me. Promise me you will look after 'er.'

'Everything will be fine.' Will realises his tone is not convincing.

'Promise me.'

'I promise.'

The Citroën slows. Will hears French voices. People are returning to their homes now that they know the Allies are not bombing the occupied town. Marie-Antoinette honks the car's horn three times. Will rolls his eyes. That sound would surely attract the Germans.

The vehicle rolls slowly for another ten minutes before picking up pace. He swears he hears a German voice shout behind them, but it is lost as the car picks up speed.

'We are out of the town,' calls Claudette.

They drive for a further ten minutes then Will hears the dog growling as the Citroën slows.

'What's going on?' he asks.

'There is a checkpoint ahead,' says Claudette. 'There are monks also.'

'Those are not German soldiers,' says Will. His heart pounds as the vehicle stops. He hears Marie-Antoinette roll down her window. 'Ah, *bonsoir, Capitaine*. Nice to see you.'

'Madame,' he replies, in a curt manner.

'How can I help you?'

'Please switch off your engine.'

The dog growls and barks and Will hears two sets of heavy boots walk around the car. He feels Emile's body tighten in the small dark space of the boot and places a reassuring hand on his arm.

'Madame, it is forbidden to be out at this time of night. You must know this.'

'Ah, *oui, oui*. You see, I must take my niece…'

The captain interrupts her. 'The engine, Madame, and your papers, please.'

'Of course. I will just get my bag.'

Will hears a shuffling sound and jumps at the blast of two gunshots.

'*Merde*!' says Emile.

The Citroën's engine roars, the wheels spin violently and the car takes off. The dog is barking frantically.

Gunshots clang at the back of the car. Emile jolts against him. They are so tightly squeezed together in that small space.

'Let me make some more room,' Will says, shoving his elbow hard against the back of the rear seats. After three attempts, the back falls inwards and cool air spills into the boot. The small dog growls in his ear.

'Emile, let's get into the back seat. Quickly.'

Emile does not respond.

Will hears more bullets prang the car and smash the rear windscreen above them.

'Emile?'

But still he does not respond.

Will shakes his friend. 'Emile!'

He wants to shout out Emile's name, but he does not want to alarm Claudette. Reaching over Emile's chest, he feels warm and sticky blood. Grabbing his wrist, he feels for a pulse. There is none. His stomach lurches and he hugs his friend, pressing his face into his lifeless back.

'I need your help!' shouts Marie-Antoinette. 'Under the rear seats are pistols. Use them. Our enemies are closing in.'

Tears prick Will's eyes as he leaves Emile and edges out of the tight space.

'Emile, come out!' shouts Claudette.

'Stay down, Claudette,' calls Will, his voice hoarse. He cannot bear to look at her as he searches for the pistols.

Peeking through the broken rear window, he sees the bright headlamps of two vehicles following them, one behind the other. The front vehicle is a Kübelwagen, containing at least four soldiers. Wiping his eyes, Will shoots, but the bullets seem to go wide. A volley of return fire forces him to take cover and wait until they reload their weapons.

When the shooting stops, Will is on his knees at the rear window and with a steady hand takes out one of the headlamps. He needs to concentrate; he can see the Kübelwagen getting closer. Taking two deep breaths, he aims calmly and directly at the silhouette of the driver. With his pistol's sight locked on to its target, he can almost see the driver's grim expression as he shouts at his colleagues to hurry and reload. Will squeezes the trigger and is satisfied to see the driver's jaw explode in spray of what looks like dark ink. The Kübelwagen swerves off the road, spinning and crashing into a copse of trees and exploding in a ball of fire.

The dog whines.

Will hears Claudette call Emile, her voice, trembling.

'You must keep your head down!' says Marie-Antoinette.

The second vehicle – which seems to be a Peugeot cabriolet – is gaining ground. He can see the silhouettes of three shaved and hooded heads. Monks. One is hanging over the passenger door taking aim with a machine gun. Will wastes no time and fires two bullets. One chips the wing mirror, the other hits the man's temple. He slumps dead over the car door and drops the weapon on the road below.

Will takes aim at the headlamps. He is about to shoot, but tumbles across the back seat when Marie-Antoinette swerves the car onto a different road with rougher terrain. The dog yelps as its small frame slams against the side of the door. Will sets its trembling body on the floor.

There are tall trees on either side of them. Marie-Antoinette has switched off the lights and is driving blindly in inky darkness. She turns left, then right, slows and switches off the engine in a concealed spot off the track. Through the trees, Will hears the rumble of the monks' Peugeot moving slowly through the woods. He sees the beam of the headlamps disappear up the road they have just turned off. They are safe. For now.

His first thought is what to say Claudette. His stomach is in knots.

'This is where we part company,' says Marie-Antoinette. She is pointing across Claudette to an opening in the trees. 'Take that pathway and you will come to a clearing. He is waiting for you.'

'Who is he?'

'You will know when you see him. He will take you out of here.'

'He will take us out of here,' adds Will. He turns to Claudette. Her head is turned sideways as if she is looking out of the passenger window. Will follows her gaze but sees nothing beyond the woods and the entrance to the pathway.

'Claudette, it is time for us to leave.' He steps outside and opens her door but she doesn't move. Her pretty face is pale, her expression serene. There is a wound on her neck from which blood seeps steadily.

'No…' says Will, his voice choked and broken.

Her eyes that were once so full of mischief and humour are dull and lifeless. The walls of his throat seem to close in as he tries to stifle a sob. He kisses her forehead, which smells of the lavender soap she was so fond of.

'You must leave immediately,' says Marie-Antoinette.

But Will feels desolate, frozen and unable to budge.

'Will, listen to me. Do not let their deaths be in vain. The plans you carry are important to all of us. We are in terrible danger if you do not complete this mission.'

Will closes his eyes. He is weary of the life he has ended up with.

'Fight for them. We are not finished yet.'

Marie-Antoinette is right. He shivers and feels a familiar cold rage rise inside him, crushing his sorrow. He looks at the agent. 'Take care of them for me.'

'I promise,' she says.

Will turns and sprints up the dark pathway, mindful of who might be lurking behind the trees on either side. To his right he catches the beam of the Peugeot's headlamps slicing through the woods and then hears the sound of an unfamiliar engine starting up at the end of the path. The headlamps turn in its direction and begin to pick up speed. Will increases his pace, pounding his legs on the soft surface of the path. He emerges onto what seems to be a disused airfield. About one hundred yards away is a bi-plane with German insignia. His heart sinks. Has Marie-Antoinette betrayed them, too?

He hears the screeching of brakes and sees the Peugeot spin onto the airfield. The bi-plane is already rolling away. The pilot is beckoning him to hurry. What choice does he have? If Marie-Antoinette was a double agent, surely she would just have surrendered them at the checkpoint.

He starts sprinting towards the bi-plane which is gathering speed. Pumping his arms, he pounds the ground with his legs until he is running alongside the plane. He edges closer to the passenger seat behind the pilot and leaps into the small pit, hanging on grimly as the plane speeds up the runway and lifts off the ground.

He gasps in the cold air, the muscles in his arms screaming and his feet flailing in the air. His hands grip the worn leather seat fixed inside the cockpit and he pulls himself inside. He hears the crack of gunfire above the bi-plane's puttering engine and, looking down, sees the monks below, watching him disappear from their grasp.

Below is Chartres, his home for the past year. Beyond it, a plume of black smoke rises from the pylon, which lies burning and twisted on the meadow. At this height, it seems like a mere child's toy. The beams of headlamps speed beyond the woods: Marie-Antoinette's Citroën, inside which are the bodies of his dear friends and colleagues, Emile and Claudette, and their unborn child. He feels his soul darkening. His sorrow has left him and all he feels is the cold hard rage that has lain dormant for the past year. Embracing it like an old friend, he swears he will have his revenge and this time he will not spare the life of anyone from VIPER.

CHAPTER 5

The Acolyte

Rome

The acolyte had been surprised to be summoned so quickly to the highest office by the lady herself. Considering he was a relative newcomer and still had much to learn of their ways, it did seem an honour, albeit a dubious one. He was no fool and it had occurred to him that this could be some sort of trick and he might be going to his death, but he had come to doubt it. He knew – and the Master knew – he had much to offer them.

It was early evening and warm. A towering figure, dressed in his grey robes, the acolyte cuts through the crowds on Via Paola and crosses the Piazza, stopping at the entrance to the Ponte Sant'Angelo to admire the magnificent Castle St Angelo, the broad, round fortress glowing in shades of red and pink as the sun begins its descent. On top of the fortress, overlooking the city, is a striking, bronze statue of the archangel Michael sheathing his sword, a symbol of Pope

Gregory's sixth-century vision in which the angel had appeared to announce the end of a plague sweeping through Rome. The irony that his new master had chosen this place as the centre of operations was not lost on him.

With his hood up he crosses the bridge, offering the angel statues on either side a deferential nod. He is met by a suited, thick-set guard with an unprepossessing countenance. A so-called agent of VIPER, the man is without humour or warmth, but then again, so is the acolyte. The guard takes him up the long, dark, stone ramp leading to the first level. They are alone in the lightless space and he wonders if, at any moment, the guard might take out one or both of his weapons and shoot him dead. No one would be any the wiser. The acolyte stays close and watches the guard's every move as they ascend the ramp.

They arrive at the first level, emerge outdoors and cross the perimeter overlooking the Ponte Sant'Angelo and the Tiber river. The guard stops and knocks on a heavy, dark wooden door. Another guard appears, similar looking to the first. Bred from bloated pigs perhaps. He nods curtly at the acolyte and points to another door at the end of the corridor.

The acolyte makes his way towards the door. He can hear music, something brash and loud by Wagner, if he is not mistaken. He can also smell the acrid odour of cigarette smoke. He knocks on the door.

The music stops.

'Come!' calls Ophelia Black.

He has not met her and knows her only by her remarkable reputation. Ophelia Black was born into one of the richest families in the world; into a fortune made by spilling the blood of many. The family mined for gold, drilled for oil, manufactured cars and had recently taken over the manufacture of weapons for the war. Her adored father, a ruthless businessman, took whatever action was necessary to increase their sizeable wealth, whether it meant merely removing his opposition or committing full-scale genocide. Ophelia was following in his footsteps. She was highly educated and shared many of her father ideals – and perhaps even more of his ambition.

The acolyte enters the room, a vast space with an egregious marble floor and garish walls painted in a display of ancient Roman opulence with half-naked nymphs and cherubs. He shudders under his robes and looks out from the protection of his hood at Ophelia Black who, in a cloud of blue cigarette smoke, is closing the lid of a gramophone player. Against the wall above it, he sees a projection screen.

'Kind of you to come,' she says, without looking up.

'Good day, mistress,' he says.

She is not what he expected. She is of slender build, in her late thirties: a handsome woman with a strong jawline and blonde hair with threads of silver. She's dressed in a steel grey suit and red heels. She turns and walks behind a broad, gilded desk, where she sits down and extinguishes her cigarette. She looks at him and beckons to the chair opposite her. 'Sit, please.'

Moving towards the chair, the acolyte notices a movie projector on top of the desk and a cardboard box on the marble floor next to her chair.

With hooded, appraising eyes, she watches him approach and sit. After a moment of silence, she asks, 'How are you adjusting to your new routine?'

'It serves me well, mistress.'

The woman's face betrays no emotion, her expression is unreadable. 'Do you have any idea why you are here?'

'No, mistress.'

'I have a project for you. But first I would like you to watch this.' She reaches over to the projector and switches it on. A beam of light shoots across to the screen. Some numbers count down from five and then the image of a girl appears. She is perhaps ten or eleven years old and oddly, but not disagreeably, strapped to a steel throne. She seems to be waking up. She is talking but there is no audio with the film. He glances at the VIPER queen who regards him with interest.

'Keep watching,' she says.

The girl seems to be angry. Nothing much seems to happen for a moment until suddenly everything changes. The acolyte watches with both revulsion and excitement. How was that possible? He breaks into a sweat and feels his breathing increase. This is why he has been chosen. He swallows.

The film ends and the VIPER queen switches off the projector.

'She's quite something, isn't she?'

'Indeed, mistress.'

'That was three years ago. She's changed a bit since then.'

He is unsure what she means by this.

'In the box at your feet is a cat. It belongs to the girl in the movie. Her name is Rose. Rose Starling. I would like you to return this cat to the owner.'

'Yes, mistress.'

'She is kept in the old Pope's Apartment at the top of the tower.'

The acolyte feels a frisson of dark pleasure at what may lie ahead.

'Do not harm the cat. Keep it safe. I want you to befriend the owner. You both have a shared history that we can use to our advantage.'

'Very good, mistress.'

'Change out of those robes and wear something less intimidating. No one seems to trust the Cerastes. I can't imagine why,' she adds, dryly. She takes a shiny silver case from her jacket pocket, removes a cigarette and lights it. 'That will be all.'

'I am happy to serve, mistress.' The acolyte bends down to pick up the box. He hears a frightened meowing sound from inside and turns to leave the room. He feels a shiver of excitement as he imagines his hands round the neck of animal, squeezing the life from its wretched body.

CHAPTER 6

A Drop in the Ocean

When the plane is fully airborne, Will hears a scratching sound coming from the panel at his knees, where a small brass-mesh speaker is fixed. He hears laughter and then an older man's voice.

'Ha, ha! I say, that was a close one.'

It's the pilot. Will looks up at him, but only sees the back of his head, which is covered in a battered leather helmet.

'Can you hear me?' calls Will.

'In case you ask, I can't hear you. Only you can hear me. One-way communication, I'm afraid. Our mutual friend said you might need some convincing once you saw the Nazi insignia.'

Will wonders who the mutual friend is: the agent codenamed Marie-Antoinette, or the mysterious Owl?

The pilot continues. 'Just so you know, they are a disguise. Don't want to risk being shot down by the buggers, do we? That said, let's hope we don't fly into a squadron of Spitfires, eh?'

For some reason the pilot thinks this is hilarious and laughs a raucous, chesty, choking laugh, which does not fill Will with confidence.

'We'll fly north, skirt around Paris, swoop over Dunkirk and cross the Channel. Sit back and enjoy the flight, old man. I'll let you know when it is time to get off.' He roars with laughter again, his chesty laugh filling the small cockpit, and Will wonders exactly what he means by getting off.

It has become unbearably cold in the exposed passenger seat of the bi-plane. Will's teeth are chattering. He rubs the sides of his arms and regrets shedding the jacket he stole from the Kübelwagen driver. He checks his wristwatch, holding his trembling arm up to the stars for a clearer view. It is almost midnight. He hears the scratching sound of the speaker.

'Dunkirk below, old boy. Not long now.'

Will peers over the side and sees the long stretch of Dunkirk's famous beach below, its pale sands littered with the ghostly wreckage of war: a twisted Spitfire and a charred and shattered ship – a paddle steamer. He wonders if it is the famous *Crested Eagle* that left London on the 28th May 1940 to bring home British soldiers trapped on the beach.

The rasp of another plane draws his attention. He looks to the west and sees a second bi-plane flying nearby. It is a smart new Tiger Moth, painted cream and equipped with two sets of guns. For a moment he thinks it might engage them in battle. However, it flies alongside them and both pilots give each other the thumbs up. The Tiger Moth's pilot looks towards Will, his face obscured with large goggles, his gaze lingering long enough to make Will sit up. Despite the night's gloom, there is something familiar in the pilot's face that he cannot quite place. Before he can see any more the Tiger Moth cranks up its engines and flies off into the night, leaving them in a reeking wake of burning diesel.

Who was that?

They fly across the Channel; the dark waters sparkle dangerously under the stars. Deep in thought about his next move, Will no longer feels the cold, as if his body has adapted to the icy temperature. After a while, he hears the familiar scratching noise from the speaker followed by a guttural, chesty cough. The pilot clears his throat and says, 'Look below at nine o'clock.' Will peers down to see a boat below with a single light flashing on it.

'Hang on tight!' says the pilot. The plane picks up speed then turns wide, circling the boat below.

'Unstrap your harness now!'

Will does as he is told and gasps as the plane plummets towards the boat.

'Make sure you have everything you need!'

Will peers over the side, not at all sure that jumping into the water from this height is a good idea.

'Goodbye, son, and best of luck!'

The plane levels off.

'Sir?' shouts Will at the top of his voice. 'Is this really a good idea?'

He hears the sound of something cranking under his feet and then feels cold air sweep up his trousers. There is a gaping hole where the floor beneath his feet had been. Way below are the choppy waters of the Channel.

'What the...?'

Before he can say anything more, his seat flips down and he falls, arms waving furiously. He plummets hard and fast, feet first into the freezing water. As he sinks, the echo of a memory flashes in his mind, disorientating him. In it, he is falling helpless into the icy cold waters off Hastings. Colonel Frost has shot him in the chest. As the water closes over his head, two overbearing silhouettes of evil flash into his mind. Enclosed in their shadow are the faces of people he once knew and loved: his mother, his father, Rose, Chittlock. There are others too: faces from VIPER – faces he is not supposed to know about. He feels his rage rising, but in a split second they all disappear and there is just the ice-black sea.

Will kicks his legs, swimming to the surface.

Crashing through the surface of the water he swallows the air greedily and looks around. The bi-plane is disappearing back towards France and the chugging engine of a tugboat is approaching. A torch beam sweeps the waters and lights Will's face. Two dark figures in long heavy coats look his way. He swims towards the boat and, in the starlight, catches the boat's name and smiles: *The Outcast*. He knows this boat and once knew its owner, Skipper, the fisherman who had pulled him from the sea near Hastings after he had been shot. As he reaches the side he hears a familiar voice.

'Nice of you to drop in,' says Eoin.

Will reaches for the hull, gripping a rope fastened around a cleat. He pulls himself up and Eoin helps haul him onto the deck. As soon as he has found his feet, Eoin throws his arms around him, hugging him, not caring that Will is sodden. The Irishman steps back and looks him up and down.

'Look at you. The boy has become the man.'

Before Will can respond, the second figure, wearing a long coat tied with a belt at the waist, steps forward and smiles warmly.

'Hello, stranger,' says Anna.

CHAPTER 7

The Peace Ray

Will is alone, below deck in *The Outcast*'s cabin, where the faint, reassuring smell of sweet tobacco makes Skipper's absence all the more painful. It feels good to be here, despite the sad memories that surround it. The old man had saved his life. It had been the first real act of kindness he had experienced since losing his memory. Deep inside, he suspects it was an act of kindness he'd not experienced in a long time. Skipper had witnessed Frost's attempt to kill him and watched as Will plunged, apparently to his death, into the sea. If it hadn't been for Skipper, Will would have perished, the Stones of Fire would not have been found and London would be no more. Who knows at what stage the world and this damn war would be? For his kindness and faith in Will, Skipper had paid with his life, and it did not stop there. Violet, little Sam and many students from Beaulieu had been murdered in the pursuit of Will and his notebook. The world owed Skipper a large debt.

Will had tried to find Skipper's family but had discovered that he was a widower whose only son had been killed in action at Dunkirk. Skipper had been there too, hoping to find his boy. Sadly, that reunion never happened. However, he had saved the lives of fourteen other soldiers that day by ferrying them across the sea to the safety of home. The old man had been a hero way before Will had known him.

He sighs at the memory. The world could be a cruel and unforgiving place. He knew this all too well.

The cabin has not changed much since he rescued the boat from St Katherine's Dock two years back. The little oven is still there, along with the bed he had woken up on and Skipper's table. There is a brown leather briefcase on top, the only object that does not seem to belong here. Before leaving for France, Will had asked Eoin to look after the little boat. 'It may be useful one day,' he had said, and he had not been wrong.

From his pocket he takes out the cigarette case and the tin soldier and places them by the old sink. Removing his damp clothes, he dries his wet, salty body with a rough towel. Anna and Eoin have provided a casual, blue shirt, grey tweed trousers with braces and a navy sports jacket, all dry and neatly folded for him to put on, with some shiny black brogues alongside. The fabrics are smooth on his rough skin and feel almost foreign.

There's a knock on the door.

'Come in,' he says.

Anna and Eoin enter the small cabin and sit down. Anna discards her overcoat, revealing a smart, blue trouser suit. Her shiny, wavy brown hair reminds him of Rita Hayworth's. Her lips are full, her make-up skilfully applied to accentuate the beauty of her face. Will swallows. He has missed her. She seems different. Older, more grown up. She is very much a woman now and not a girl.

'It's really good to see you, Will,' says Eoin, smiling.

'It's good to see you, too.' He looks at Anna. 'Both of you.' Their eyes lock for a moment, before Eoin breaks in.

'Did you bring it?'

Will hands the cigarette case to Eoin, who breaks the wax seal and opens it. Inside is a small box. He opens it and Will sees a row of microfilm.

'What are they?' asks Will

'Over the past two years, VIPER have been recruiting. Their numbers have doubled, as has their power and wealth. They stole the plans for a new super-weapon, which their scientists have apparently developed.

'What kind of weapon?'

'Nikola Tesla was a US-based, Serbian scientist – a physicist and a futurist,' says Anna. 'He drew up plans for what the US press – without irony – termed the "Peace Ray".'

'It is anything but a peace ray,' says Eoin. 'It was designed to be powerful enough to stop wars. A weapon capable of destroying tanks and tearing planes from the sky. A death ray, in truth.'

'Just what the world needs. Thank you, Mr Tesla.'

Anna continues. 'In his defence, he was not a warmonger. He was an ideas man, an inventor: the archetypal mad scientist. He created plans for the "Teleforce" but he never built the weapon; it was always just a theory. However, VIPER have made the theory a reality. They have built Tesla's Death Ray.'

'This microfilm contains the plans for it,' says Eoin.

'And we need to destroy it?' asks Will, although he already knew the answer.

'Correct,' says Eoin. 'When we return to London, I will get these developed and we will work out what to do next. In the meantime, you two get some rest. I'll get us home.' Eoin gets up to leave.

'Wait. Have you heard anything about a red storm?'

Eoin wrinkles his brow. 'Doesn't ring any bells. Why do you ask?'

Will tells him about his fight with the monk and his warning.

'I'll look into it,' says Eoin.

'One more thing … is there any news about Rose?'

'I'm afraid not, Will. Sorry.'

Will sighs as Eoin shuts the door behind him. He realises finding Rose is not a priority for the Secret Service, but still he cannot help but feel resentful and disappointed.

'It's been almost a whole year since I saw you,' says Anna, when the door has closed.

'Three hundred and seventy-one days,' says Will.

'Oh? You've been counting…' She seems surprised and he wonders why she looks away.

Will reaches for her hand and she allows him to hold it for a second before freeing herself and folding her arms. She seems uncomfortable.

'There is other news that Eoin did not mention.'

The Outcast's engine chugs into life.

Anna opens the briefcase, removes a folded newspaper and hands it to him. It is a copy of *The Times*, dated 27th December 1942. The headline reads: WANDSWORTH PRISON BREAKOUT LATEST.

Will feels his stomach contract as he begins to read: 'At 6 am, on Christmas morning 1942, eight prisoners escaped from south-west London's Wandsworth Prison…'

He looks up at Anna, who gazes back with a serious expression. Will reads on, scanning the article until he finds the list of escaped prisoners. He feels his shoulders tighten when he sees two he recognises: Victor Francis Frost. Rupert Jefferson Van Horne.

The final paragraph claims the escapees had help from unknown outside sources. Will tosses the paper on the table. VIPER again.

'I'm sorry, Will.'

'Those two should have swung for what they did.'

'We will find them. I promise.'

Still raw from the deaths of Emile and Claudette, Will walks to the porthole window and stares out to sea, losing himself in the shiny, vast blackness of the water and the soporific rhythm of the boat. He feels Anna's breath close by and realises she is inches behind him. He turns to face her, but she is looking down, avoiding his gaze.

'I've thought about you every day,' he says.

'We need to talk.'

He moves closer but she steps to the side and folds her arms again.

He feels a fluttering in his stomach. 'Anna. You're not telling me something.'

She rubs her arms. 'There's someone else.'

Will steps back. He feels like he has been punched. He turns back to the porthole, wishing to be lost in the waters again. He does not know what to say or how to respond.

'You have no idea what I have been through,' she says.

Tensing, he feels his face flush and whirls round. 'What *you* have been through? Let me tell you a little bit about my day, Anna. I and my two best friends – Emile and Claudette, recently married and already expecting their first child – blew up a pylon on orders from London. VIPER knew where we were. We were betrayed and Emile, Claudette and their unborn child were murdered in cold blood…'

'I'm so sorry…'

'…just like Violet, like Skipper, like Sam: because of me – because of what is hidden up here,' he points to his head to illustrate the point.

'Will…'

'I escaped, leaving their bodies for an unreliable stranger to bury and I'm wondering: is she actually going to do it, or will she toss them onto the roadside?' He feels his eyes welling up at the thought. 'And then I'm flown across the country and dumped unceremoniously into the sea by some crazy pilot…'

'I thought you were dead!' shouts Anna.

The tension in the air between them is heavy. Will can almost feel it pushing against his chest.

'What are you talking about? I'm clearly not dead.'

'When I returned to London last year I – *we* – were all told you had been killed in action. The great Will Starling captured by the Nazis and sentenced to death by firing squad.'

'It was clearly a fabrication.'

'There were pictures, Will. Photographs.'

'How? That's just not possible.'

'I know what I saw.'

'Well, it wasn't me. As you can see. Did you see my face in those photographs?'

She shakes her head. 'I didn't believe them at first. I asked for proof and all they could say was "look at the pictures". All doors were closed to me.'

'Why didn't you speak to Eoin?'

'I did. He wouldn't deny it … because it was his lie.'

Will swallows. 'Why would he do that?'

'He did it to protect you.' Anna sits back at the table and looks at him at last. 'Yesterday he called me for a meeting: a mission I was to

47

undertake immediately. The first thing he did was apologise. When I asked what for, he told me that your death had been a cover-up. I felt sick. I didn't know what to think.'

Will sits back at the other side of the table.

'VIPER were regrouping and they had undercover agents operating in the Secret Service. Eoin had heard whispers on the grapevine that Will Starling was alive. He knew this news would reach the wrong ears and your life would be in danger again.'

Will leans on the table and rubs his face. Here he was back in the same game with the same villains. Emile and Claudette's dead faces flash in his mind but he pushes them away. The time to mourn would have to wait.

'You don't know what it did to me. I had to move on. I had to live.'

He tries to process what Anna had just told him. He knows he cannot blame her. What choice did she have? Yet the thought of her with someone else makes him go cold inside. It is better that way, he thinks. His love for her – this stupid emotion – was a distraction he could do without. The time was right to bring VIPER down and he had to be the one to do it. He is ready to start again and this time he would bring the fight to them.

'I understand,' he says.

CHAPTER 8

The Office at Puddle Dock

Will stands on the deck watching the sun rise over east London as Eoin steers *The Outcast* along the Thames and towards a wharf called Puddle Dock. A group of fishermen are selling their haul to market traders, restaurateurs and whoever else has the money to buy their catches.

'We keep an office here,' says Anna. 'It allows us to keep an eye on who is coming and going.'

Two warehouses are separated by a narrow street. The warehouse on the left has been ripped in half, its charred remains open and exposed like the toothless mouth of a corpse. The building on the right is untouched; there are four floors of tall, wide leaded windows where people are going about their jobs.

Will stares down the narrow street and sees something silver and gleaming parked at the top of it. He smiles and feels his mood lifting. It is Eoin's Embiricos.

The Irishman moors *The Outcast* and they step onto the jetty. Glancing up at the surviving warehouse, Will sees a slim, suited man looking down at them from the top floor window. He thinks he knows him. He follows Eoin and Anna across the jetty, threading through the fishermen and their lively banter, with his head down.

He hears a voice that sounds familiar.

'…and I says to him, you listen right 'ere, I says. *The Lazy Turtle* is my boat. No one else's and you ain't got no business showing your old face round here. Now clear off…'

There is a grumbling response from the men.

Will stops, his eyes focusing in on the face belonging to the voice that had grabbed his attention. The man must be in his forties, with thinning grey hair, a pot belly and blotchy skin on a pinched face with an expression carrying an air of smugness about it.

One of the fishermen speaks. 'Well, I never. What did he say to that, Ned?'

Ned! Of course. The same 'treacherous' Ned that stole Skipper's haul the morning after he saved my life.

'What is it, Will?' asks Anna.

Eoin is already at the top of the jetty and hasn't noticed that Anna and Will are lagging behind. Will scans the moored boats and sees *The Lazy Turtle*. It is a shiny, brand-new fishing boat that barely looks as if it has one day's fishing behind it.

'Anna, that man holding court. I need you to distract him for a few minutes.'

Anna looks at him questioningly.

'Trust me.'

She shrugs and walks towards the men, the hem of her coat flaring dramatically as she turns. When she gets close, she strikes up a bubbly patter, praising the men for their bravery in taking to the dangerous waters during these troubled times. Ned and his fellows seem captivated by her.

Who wouldn't be?

Will hurries towards *The Lazy Turtle*, glancing back to check that Ned isn't watching. Moments later he is walking back towards Anna and the men.

'Gentlemen?' he calls. The fishermen turn.

'Which one of you owns *The Lazy Turtle*?'

'That'll be me. She's mine,' says Ned, gruffly.

Will points across the water. 'She seems to be making a run for it.'

'What the hell?' cries Ned.

Will had started the engine and untied her from the dock. *The Lazy Turtle* is now making what seems to be a drunken reverse attempt to leave the dockside.

The fishermen roar with laughter as Ned hurries down the jetty, the blotches on his face glowing a pillar-box red. He pushes past Will to the empty spot where his boat was moored only moments back.

'Oi! Come back 'ere!'

Will is soon behind him. 'That one was from me and this one is from Skipper.' He kicks the man's backside, sending him toppling off the jetty and into the soupy brown water below.

The other fishermen roar with laughter while Will walks back up the jetty to the sound of Ned splashing in the water.

'Help, I can't swim!'

This causes the men to laugh louder and some even slap Will's back as he joins Anna.

'What was that about?'

'I'll tell you later.'

With the laughter and Ned's splashing and bleating behind them, they walk to the warehouse and take the wide concrete stairs to the top floor. As they reach the top, Will hears the tapping of fingers on typewriter keys.

The office contains just two desks, facing each other. Looming over their typewriters are two identical, red-haired, female secretaries dressed in dark green suits. They look up at Anna.

'He's in a shocking mood!' says the one on the left, rolling her eyes.

'Unbearable,' says the other. 'He just doesn't like Eoin doing his own thing,' she adds.

'Hello,' says Will.

Their attention turns to Will and their eyes roll up and over him, lingering for longer than is comfortable.

'Will, meet Daisy and Alice,' says Anna, gesturing half-heartedly so that Will is not quite sure who is who.

'Don't ask me which one is which. I have no idea.'

'State secret,' says the one on the right, who winks quickly at him.

Clearly they are twins and Will can't help but notice the outline of pistols beneath their jackets. These ladies are guards as much as they are secretaries.

'You two need a medal for what you put up with,' says Anna.

'Don't we know it,' says the one on the left.

'Go on through,' they say in unison.

'Beaulieu, Class of 1942,' whispers Anna to Will as they walk past the penetrating eyes of the secretaries. 'Both have earned their gold badges.'

He looks back and sees them both smiling sweetly at him. He smiles at them and they turn back to their typewriters without another word.

'Neither of them can type for toffee,' Anna adds. 'It's all just a front.'

There is a second office with a frosted glass door. Will hears raised voices. One is Eoin's. Anna knocks.

'Come,' calls a voice. Will recognises the tinny tone. He has met this person before.

The office behind the door is large and sparse with a filing cabinet and a mahogany desk holding just a telephone. It seems to Will that not much work happens here. Standing at the window is a slender man with a serious face and a long, hooked nose: Nicholas Morrow of MI6. His unreadable eyes linger over Will for a moment.

'So, the rumours are true then,' he says, folding his arms.

'Sorry to disappoint you,' says Will, noting the flare in Morrow's eyes at his insolence.

Eoin tosses the cigarette case onto Morrow's desk. 'I need this film developed and the pictures enlarged as soon as possible.'

Morrow looks at the insignia on the cigarette case with a sneer. 'You're a fool to trust the Owl. You paid a fortune for these and they could be pictures of anything.'

'He has never let us down.'

'As long as the price is right.'

Will is intrigued about this mysterious Owl. 'Who is he?' he asks.

'No one knows,' says Anna.

Morrow snorts. 'Owl indeed. I prefer to think thieving magpie.'

'The Owl is a rogue spy,' says Eoin. 'He is very good at his job and has no love for the Nazis or VIPER.'

'Unless they are paying more than we are,' says Morrow.

'I think he was trying to send me a message,' says Will.

'What are you talking about?' says Morrow, frowning.

Eoin's brow is furrowed too. 'Why do you think that?'

Will removes the tin soldier from his pocket. 'At the cathedral I found this.'

'A toy soldier?' Morrow shakes his head.

'Why is that important?' asks Eoin.

'Because it was mine and the last time I saw it was when I lived at Tim Chittlock's house in Pimlico.'

Eoin says nothing for a moment.

'I'd like to go back there. It might jog some memories.'

'I agree. We should go there now.' Eoin gets up immediately, clearly eager to get away. 'Tomorrow morning at the latest for those pictures, Morrow,' he calls.

As Will turns to follow, he notices that Morrow picks up the telephone.

CHAPTER 9

Morrow's Lack of Caution

The Embiricos is as shiny and glorious as it was when he last saw it two years back. Will caresses the bonnet absent-mindedly and catches Eoin watching him from the driver seat.

'She's quite something, isn't she?'

Will nods his head.

The Irishman gets out of the car, smiles and tosses the key to Will. 'You drive.'

Will catches the key in one hand, a wide grin spreading across his face.

'Wait for me!' calls a voice.

He turns to see Morrow hurrying towards them.

'What do you want?' asks an unimpressed Eoin.

'I'm coming with you.'

'Oh, that's just friggin' wonderful, so it is!' says Eoin.

Morrow's lips tighten and his eyes narrow at the Irishman.

'It might be good to have a perspective from MI6,' says Anna, clearly trying to placate both men.

'Exactly, Miss Wilder. Thank you.'

'Whatever!' says Eoin, who drops his large frame into the passenger seat and slams the door behind him.

Will hops into the driving seat as Anna and Morrow climb into the back.

'Why is he driving? This is not his car,' says Morrow.

'*He* has a name! This is my car and I decide who drives it,' Eoin replies.

'This is highly irregular!'

'Lighten up, Morrow. Will is a very competent driver, as you will see.'

Will starts the engine.

'Do you remember the way?' asks Eoin.

'I remember where Pimlico is, but I can't quite recall the house.'

'I'll direct you.'

Will reverses away from the warehouse and lets the engine roar for a moment before pressing the accelerator, perhaps a little too hard. The wheels spin and the Embiricos takes off. Will's heart leaps as he controls the steering wheel and swerves around, overtaking two other cars in front.

'I think we can slow down a little,' Eoin says.

'Yes! We don't want to draw attention to ourselves, do we?' says Morrow.

Will drives through the mid-morning London traffic, easing off the accelerator as he approaches a red light. He glances at Anna through the rear-view mirror. She is unusually quiet, her eyes down, focusing on something he can't see. He hears the clicking of metal and glances round to see her pulling apart a Walther PPK pistol made from polished steel. The barrel is engraved with beautiful feathers – a stunning piece of craftsmanship; it is both beautiful and dangerous. Just like her, he thinks.

'Is it necessary to play with that thing, here in the back of car?' says Morrow.

'I'm cleaning it,' Anna responds.

'It had better not go off!'

'If it does, I'll try to make sure it's not pointing at you.'

'That's hardly reassuring.'

'Idiot!' growls Eoin, under his breath.

'What was that?' says an indignant Morrow.

Eoin does not respond.

Will turns his thoughts to the Embiricos and wonders how someone like Eoin could own such an expensive car. Despite being well-groomed, the Irishman usually dressed in the same clothes: a grey, three-piece tweed suit, white shirt and blue tie. Hardly the garb of a rich man. Will's curiosity niggles at him; he needs to know.

'Eoin, the Embiricos. It's an expensive car.'

'Yes…'

'How did…?'

'How did someone like me come to own such a fine motorcar?' asks Eoin, finishing the question.

'That's not what I meant.'

Eoin laughs. 'Don't worry. I know what you meant.'

'If I may…' interrupts Morrow.

'I won it in a bet,' says Eoin, ignoring Morrow again.

'It used to belong to Sir Hugh Coleridge,' says Morrow, 'who happens to be our chief of staff. As it happens, I phoned him before we left. He told me he will meet us at Chittlock's house.'

'What the hell, Morrow? This is a private mission. No one is supposed to know about it.'

'Since when was it private? May I remind you we both report into him. He is your superior.'

Will hears Eoin swear under his breath. 'Well done, Morrow. You seem to forget that other people are listening in on our phone calls. It is possible your indiscretion will compromise our safety.'

Will feels a tremor of excitement in his stomach. He glances in the rear-view mirror and catches Anna's gaze. She smiles briefly and he knows she is excited too.

CHAPTER 10

The Cerastes Strike

It is almost 11 am when they arrive at Westminster. Despite the war, people are going about their business: some stand gossiping on street corners and others watch the world go by through the windows of tea rooms and cafés. Will catches admiring eyes drawn to the Embiricos's impressive styling.

Following Eoin's directions, Will navigates slowly through the bomb-damaged Pimlico streets, now a vast open space with stacks of rubble, the remains of the once grand and beautiful Regency townhouses that had stood for over a hundred years.

'This part of Westminster has recently been hit heavily by parachute mines and high explosive bombs,' says Eoin, grimly.

A harrowing sight, Will thinks. Despite the felled houses and barren streets he feels a frisson of recognition. He knows he has been to Chittlock's house. He may even have lived here for a time before his move to VIPER. Frustratingly, he just does not remember.

'Straight up, turn first right and find somewhere to park,' says Eoin.

Will drives towards an area of undamaged homes and shops and takes the first right turn into a street called Warwick Way. He pulls up at an empty space outside a beauty salon. The windows are gone, blown out by the force of recent bomb blasts, but business still goes on. There are three ladies, drinking tea and sitting under hairdryers, while another is getting her hair styled by a slender woman with silky, blonde hair curled on top of her head, and horn-rimmed spectacles dominating her face.

Eoin opens the glove compartment, takes out a black Beretta pistol and hands it to Will. 'Just in case.'

'Thank you.' It is heavy and loaded. Will slides it into the side pocket of his jacket.

Will and his passengers get out of the car. His stomach flutters with vague memories, like dreams that can't quite be grasped. He notices the stylist look in their direction. With one hand she pushes her spectacles up her nose and cranes her head at Will. A look of surprise forms on her face.

'Let's move on, Will,' says Eoin.

Will looks away and follows Eoin. He hears the tinkling of a bell. Turning, he sees the windowless door to the salon open and the stylist staring at him with one hand on her chest.

'It's really you, isn't it?' she says, her accent has a distinct South London ring to it.

Will freezes. He is in no way prepared for meeting someone who knew him in his previous life. He is at a loss for words.

'Young Will,' she says, hurrying towards him, with open arms.

Will notices Anna and Eoin reaching for their weapons and he shakes his head discreetly at them.

The woman wraps her arms tightly around him and he is engulfed in a cloud of powder and floral perfume. The scent is familiar, but he cannot place it. She pulls away from him and places her hands on his cheeks. Will smiles politely and glances above the door of the salon where it states 'Proprietress: Miss Millicent Kallender'.

'Hello Millicent,' says Will.

She stares into his eyes as if reading his soul. He wants to look away. 'You've still got those sad eyes,' she says, 'and how did you get that scar?' She runs her finger across the scar on his left cheekbone.

He shrugs and swallows. This is his first contact with anyone who knew him before he lost his memory.

'Miss Kallendar, if you don't mind, we have some important business, so we do,' says Eoin.

She glances at Eoin and nods. 'Of course you do. It's just I thought you were...'

Dead

'I'm fine.'

Her face brightens suddenly and she squeezes his shoulders and arms. 'Good. Look at you now. Not a boy any more. You're a man.'

'It's nice to see you again, Millicent.'

'Milly.'

'I'm sorry?'

'You used to call me Milly,' she says.

'Yes ... of course ... Milly.'

Her bright face slackens and she tries to smile but Will can see she is hurt.

'I better get back to my ladies,' she says.

'Bye, Milly.'

'Oh, I was so sorry to hear about your Mr Chittlock. Terrible business, especially after your fam...' She stops herself before saying any more.

'Thank you.'

'Are you visiting the old house? It's strangely busy in there today. I even saw two monks go inside.'

Will freezes, his muscle tighten. 'How long ago, Milly?'

'Only a few minutes ago, I reckon,' she says, looking across the road.

Will follows the direction of her gaze towards a tall, Regency townhouse, its yellow bricks layered with the dark soot of fire and destruction from neighbouring streets. He knows the house. It is Timothy Chittlock's.

He turns to the stylist. 'Milly, go inside and lock the doors.' He glances at the missing shop-front windows and frowns. 'Do you have somewhere you can hide?'

The stylist seems confused and looks from Will to Eoin, Anna and then Morrow.

'It's for your own safety,' says Anna.

A blast of gunshots from inside Chittlock's house kills the awkward silence. Milly pales.

'Go, Milly, and take your ladies,' says Will urgently.

'I have a shelter.'

'Perfect.'

She hurries nervously back to the salon. Despite the door having no glass she locks it anyway and turns the 'Open' sign to 'Closed'.

'We approach the house with caution,' says Eoin, removing his pistol, a Browning Hi-Power semi-automatic.

Will feels his pulse racing and nods his agreement.

'I don't have a gun,' says Morrow, nervously.

With his free hand Eoin removes a battered and old, small Walther PP from his inside pocket. 'You do now.'

Morrow regards it with a look of distaste and reluctantly accepts it.

They follow Eoin across the road, hastily ducking behind the shelter of a blue Ford 7Y parked outside Chittlock's house. Crouching with their backs to the vehicle, pistols at the ready, Will whispers 'Good luck' to Anna.

'You too.'

They hear the sound of glass breaking and a man's voice calling out in distress.

'I go in first,' says Eoin, who leaps to his feet and sprints to the front door. Will can see it is ajar. Eoin kicks it open, glances inside and then runs in brandishing his pistol. Will hurries after him with Anna and Morrow following. He stands to the side of the entrance and peers inside. Anna stays close; he can feel her breath on his neck. The hallway has a checkerboard-tiled floor and upon it are the scattered remains of pictures and frames pulled from the walls. Someone has been searching for something. There is a door to the drawing room. Eoin darts out of it, knocking over a hat stand and startling Will. Hopping over the debris, he slides into the kitchen, his gun sweeping around the space. He glances back at Will and shakes his head. They hear a groan from upstairs.

'Ready?' Eoin mouths, nodding at the stairs.

Will's pulse races.

Eoin points at Will and himself and then up the stairs. He looks at Anna with his palm out, indicating that she should stay down here, at least for the time being.

Anna nods once.

Eoin begins the countdown from three and, at one, runs at the stairs with Will sprinting beside him.

To Will's relief there is no one at the top of the stairs. Old memories of this floor flash in Will's mind, impeding his concentration for a second. Shaking out of it, he sees the landing is in a similar mess to the hall downstairs. To their left, the door to the bathroom is open and a man with dark hair, dressed in a tailored, blue suit, lies on the floor: pale, with a bloody lip. There is a broken walking stick at his feet. He is conscious and watches them, his eyes lingering with curiosity on Will. The bathroom window is broken, the glass shattered from the inside out. Eoin steps over the man and looks outside and down below. His fixed expression suggests there is no one there.

'Where are they, Hugh?' asks Eoin.

The man weakly lifts his arm and points his finger at the room behind Will. Will swallows. He knows the room. It was where he slept for the short period he had lived with Chittlock. He slides along the landing wall to the entrance of the room. Peering round the doorframe, he looks inside. He sees the single bed he used to sleep in and the wooden desk at which he used to sit. Above it, fixed to the wall, is a painting he remembers: an obscure and depressing landscape. He cannot recall the artist's name. He narrows his gaze at it, thoughtfully, but is distracted by a creaking floorboard. Through the open door, he can see a figure blocking the light of the sash window. It is a hooded monk dressed in grey robes tied at the waist with a red rope. The Cerastes. Will notices three steel globes, the size of cricket balls, hanging from the rope tied around his waist. Ether bombs?

The monk is standing at the tall sash window overlooking Warwick Way. He raises the sash.

'There is nowhere for you to run,' says Will, the Beretta pointing at the man's back.

The monk turns to face him, his arms at his side. Will's memory stirs and the room spins for the briefest of seconds.

'Everything alright up there,' calls Anna, her voice waking him from distraction.

At that same second he sees two knives leave the monk's hands and hurtle towards him. He ducks out of their path and, with relief, hears them thud into the wall behind him.

He rights himself in time to see the monk fall backwards out of the window. Will runs over to the sash and peers down, expecting to see another suicide, but the monk has landed nimbly on his feet and is sprinting up Warwick Way.

'He's on the run!' he shouts and hops down the stairs.

'I'll stay with Hugh,' calls Eoin. 'Make sure you catch him alive!' he adds.

CHAPTER 11

Death on Westminster Bridge

Anna is nowhere to be seen as Will hurtles past Morrow in the downstairs hallway.

'What's happening?' shrills Morrow.

Will only half hears him as he skids onto the pavement looking for Anna. He sees her coat flapping behind her as she pursues the monk towards Pimlico. They are already making ground despite the short head start. He looks at the Embiricos, hurries towards it, jumps into the driver seat and fires up its fierce engine. Steering out of the parking space, he slams the accelerator and speeds up Warwick Way.

The roads are thankfully clear of traffic but Anna and the monk are nowhere in sight. He swears under his breath, scans the area, then sees the tails of Anna's coat disappear over a pile of dusty rubble. He swings the car to the right and follows her, skirting the perimeter of the devastation; frustratingly he does not see either of them.

Driving slowly, eyes peeled, nerves on fire, he turns into Belgrave Road, cruising steadily as he scans the pedestrians on either side and the entrances to the ornate houses. He passes Warwick Square on his right and slows, peering at the bushes and trees. It is then he sees the dark form of the monk charging towards him. He slams the brakes and pulls out his pistol, but the monk flips over the bonnet of the Embiricos and runs up Belgrave Road.

The passenger door opens and, with relief, he sees Anna jump in, her cheeks rosy with exertion.

'You took your time.'

Will smiles. 'Nice to see you again.'

Pressing on the accelerator he pursues the monk, who is remarkably fast. Will sees him turn left into Lupus Street, narrowly avoiding a man on a bicycle who calls out in anger. The monk disappears amongst the pedestrians on Vauxhall Bridge Road.

'I can't see him,' says Anna.

Will scours the crowd but there is no sign of him. He notices the crowd's attention focused ahead and follows their gaze in time to see the monk haul the driver of a black cab from his vehicle. He punches the driver twice and throws him to ground.

'There!' says Will.

The monk is on the move, ploughing the black cab through innocent pedestrians as they cross the road. There are screams and shouts as two men fly across the bonnet and tumble on the roadside. The cab disappears down Rochester Row.

Will blares his horn and edges the Embiricos through the crowds and traffic onto Vauxhall Bridge Road. There are cries of protest and horns pressed in anger but Will ignores them.

They cross to Rochester Row, but there is no sign of the taxi. Will presses the accelerator and dodges through the morning traffic.

'I see him,' says Anna, pointing ahead.

Almost three cars ahead of them Will can see the black cab threading dangerously in and out of traffic.

'Hold on!'

Anna grips the dashboard as Will swings over to the wrong side of the road, slamming the accelerator. A red bus is heading right for them and Will registers the look of terror on the driver's face.

'Move, you fool!'

As if he has heard him, the driver swings the bus to his left, mounting the kerb and smashing a blue police box to pieces. Glancing back, Will is relieved to see no one is injured.

With his eyes fixed on the cab, Will is gaining ground. He feels cool air and sees Anna unwind the window with one hand. In the other she holds the steel Walther. She leans out the window and fires two shots at the taxi, shattering the rear window. Will steadies the wheel as Anna takes aim again, but the taxi disappears behind traffic. Will presses on but with a long line of oncoming cars is forced to return to the left side of the road. There are six cars between him and the monk and Will is forced to decrease his speed.

'Shit!' he says, his hands tightening on the wheel. He sees the taxi turn right into Great Peter Street. It drives out from the left-hand side and roars down the right forcing oncoming traffic off the road and leaving a clear trail for Will. He turns to the right and speeds after the taxi, flying past the ugly, steel North and South Rotundas, where the cabinet war rooms operate during an air raid.

Will is beginning to gain ground when the taxi swings a hard left where the road widens and the traffic seems to thin out. He slams on the accelerator and speeds past the Houses of Parliament, which seems like a great Gothic blur.

Anna hangs out of the window again. She lowers her arm and fires twice at the taxi's wheels. The right-hand tyre blows and causes the speeding taxi to swerve and collide with a post office van before slamming into a lamppost.

People instantly crowd round the vehicle obscuring the view. Will parks the Embiricos and both he and Anna jump out, moving cautiously towards the gathered onlookers. Will conceals the Beretta under his jacket and pushes his way through.

'I never seen anyfink like it,' says a man. 'Driving like a maniac, he was.'

'I know!' says a woman. 'And him a man of the cloth. The war does some queer things to people.'

Reaching the taxi, Will is dismayed to find the driver's seat empty and the monk nowhere to be seen.

'I'll see if he's close,' says Anna, but Will fears the monk may already be gone. He leaps on the taxi's bonnet, holds on to the lamppost with one hand and searches over the top of crowd towards Big Ben.

'Do you see him?' asks Anna.

'Yes!' Will spots the hooded figure hurrying towards Westminster Bridge. He takes out his gun and, ignoring the gasps from the crowd below, he aims. But the monk is in the thick of it and Will risks injuring an innocent person. Instead, he raises the Beretta in the air and fires two shots.

The crowd screams and scatters and the monk crouches, turning back to look behind him. Will jumps off the bonnet and runs with Anna towards the bridge, dodging the panicking bystanders. With pistols drawn, they arrive midway across the bridge, alongside a bus full of people who are watching intently. A breeze cools Will's hot face. What a strange sight this must be, he thinks fleetingly, him and

Anna armed and chasing what must seem like an innocent, holy man. The traffic has stopped as people duck in front of cars and cower at the side of the bridge at the sight of Will and Anna, their pistols pointing at the monk who faces them, twenty feet away. His face is obscured in the shadows of his hood, he is rolling the three ether bombs between his palms. Behind the monk, to his right, Will sees a young mother cradling her toddler, a little girl, desperate to free herself from her mother's clutches and pick up her doll, which has fallen to the pavement. Will feels a pang of anxiety.

'We need him alive,' Will whispers.

'I'll do my best,' Anna replies.

The monk begins to juggle the ether bombs as if he is some bizarre street entertainer.

'You do realise you will be dead before those things reach us,' Will tells him.

The monk seems unfazed and tosses a bomb at the upper deck of the bus. It smashes through the window causing people to cry out in shock.

'What's he doing, Will? What was that?'

'A VIPER invention. An ether bomb that will render people unconscious for a short period of time. I don't know what he is playing at.'

The monk throws the second bomb far behind him. Will hears the heavy steel globe crunch the bodywork of a car.

'What the hell is going on?' someone protests.

The monk tosses the third up and down in his palm.

'Drop it,' says Will.

Will hears screaming from the bus, his blood goes cold, but he keeps his eyes and gun focused on the monk.

'Oh Will,' cries Anna.

Will feels his heart pounding. And then he sees it. Rising behind the monk, from where the second ether bomb was thrown, is a red mist. His mouth dries. He hears more screams that make his skin crawl. The upper deck of the bus is engulfed with the same mist. The passengers howl in pain, choking, their eyes red, their mouths frothing. Blinded and disoriented, they beat against the windows in their desperation to get outside. The monk holds the final bomb: not an ether bomb but something vile and horrible.

'Anna, get off the bridge. There is nothing to be done here. Go.'

'I'm not leaving you!'

'Go!' he commands. 'Please, Anna.' He feels her retreating and is relieved. Trembling with rage, he hears the toddler cry and sees the tearful expression of horror on the mother's face. His eyes blaze at the monk whose finger hovers on the release button of the final bomb. Will squeezes the trigger. The blast of his pistol is lost in the screams of those dying on the bridge. The bullet hits the monk squarely in the chest and he falls back, lying deathly still on the road. The final bomb rolls from his hand towards the mother and toddler. The mother screams.

'No! No!' Will runs towards it, scoops it up and runs to the side of the bridge. The breeze picks up and he hears the bomb click and hiss. Had he pressed the button accidentally?

'Get out of here,' he says to the mother, who wastes no time in running away, clutching her toddler tight.

Will throws the bomb into the dark water of the Thames, inhaling what seems like the sweet odour of decaying fruit. A trail of red mist follows the bomb as it plops into the water and sinks. He turns to look for Anna, but his head begins to spin. He can see her. She is calling to him but he cannot make out what she is saying. She seems so far away. He feels his throat swell and coughs into his fist. His hand feels wet and warm. Blinking to focus, he sees blood on his palm. He groans, unsure what is happening, and then everything goes dark.

CHAPTER 12

Rose

Rome, 15th July, 1943, morning

Rose Starling stirs in her sleep. In her dream she is naked and lying on a cold steel slab in a brightly lit room. Her lips are numb, her jaw is frozen shut and she is unable to move, scream or call for help. She hears voices and rolls her eyes downward. Blinking to focus, she sees figures wearing white coats huddled around her feet.

Their voices seem familiar.

Men's voices.

Murmuring.

In the dream she is drugged, but the effects are weakening and it feels like her body is thawing. Her blood is warming and she can feel every goosebump erupt on her skin. She feels her backside shifting and her legs parting. Through half-closed eyes she sees her feet have been raised and placed in leather stirrups.

No! No! No!

She is still too weak to move and wishes the drugs would disappear from her frail body. She hears a familiar female voice. It is flat and emotionless, yet firm and authoritative. It seems to be further away, as if it is in another room.

Ophelia Black. Rose feels her stomach twisting.

The white-coats huddle closer. One of them is bending down between her legs. Frustration and shame overwhelm her and she shudders as something cold is inserted into the private place between her legs. She tries to scream, but no sound comes. Trembling inside, a rage ignites in her soul and surges through her thin, cold body.

'She's coming round!' says a man, his voice raised in alarm.

Sick with humiliation she tries to pull her knees together but she is still not strong enough.

'More ether. Quickly!' someone shouts.

Adrenalin hurtles through her body and she forces herself to lift her head. She glares at their shiny faces, half obscured by surgical masks, their eyes wide with panic and fear. She reaches her mind across the room and senses their heartbeats quicken to a gallop. There are four at her feet. Two behind. Six in the room beyond. Including *that woman.*

'Where is that bloody ether!' shouts a harsh voice.

An anaesthetist mask appears above her face. She can smell the gluey, sweet smell of ether as it spits angrily from the gaping black rubber hole. Holding it is a hand belonging to a semi-masked face with frightened eyes. She tries to warn him, but she cannot speak. Her body is weak but her mind is strong.

The mind is strong.

Focusing her thoughts she pushes against the mask with her mind. It trembles in the air above her. She pushes harder and stops when she hears the snapping of bone and a scream. She hears scuffling in the theatre and watches as the white-coats retreat clumsily.

The mind is strong.

She closes her eyes and, with her mind, caresses the heart of each man in the theatre as they clamber over each other to get out. With one merciless stroke she squeezes each beating organ until it beats no more. One by one the men drop dead to the floor.

'Rose. Stop! What have you done?' cries Ophelia Black.

She is beginning to feel movement in her legs and arms now. She pushes herself up to her elbows and lifts her feet off the stirrups. Her mouth is dry, as if it hasn't tasted water in weeks, but that's not important now. They have put something inside her. Fury envelops her and she focuses her mind across to the next room. Then she hears something clang on the floor beneath her. Looking down she sees a spherical object: an ether bomb, hissing and filling the theatre with its gluey smell. More drugs.

You cowards.

She feels herself weakening once more as the ether claims her. Curling into a foetal position, she lets the gas take her.

She has had enough.

She just wants to sleep.

CHAPTER 13

The Experiment

Rose jolts from her dream, waking to the sound of her nursemaid, Sofia, scuttling around the apartment, unbolting the shutters and throwing them open. Sunlight floods the room, sweeping away the gloom of incarceration. She blinks and lets her eyes adjust slowly to the light.

Sofia's round and kind face smiles down at her. She is wearing a black dress with a snug white apron pulled tight around her broad waist. 'Did you have the dream again, *bambina*? I heard you talking in your sleep.'

'I have it every night, Sofia. I am cursed.'

'No, *bambina*, you must not say that. You are a miracle, a gift from the Almighty.'

Rose rolls her eyes, uncurls from the foetal position she has woken in and pushes herself up into a sitting position. Sofia hurries to help, plumping pillows behind her back and kissing her on the forehead as she does so. 'I make you breakfast. Your favourite: soft boiled eggs with army.'

'Soldiers,' corrects Rose.

Sofia bellows a wheezing laugh, '*Si*, but lots of soldiers make an army, no?'

'If you say so,' replies Rose, content to humour her nursemaid, the only real friend she has in this prison.

Sofia hurries out of the bedroom, her laughter trailing to the kitchen at the other side of the small apartment.

Reliving the events in this same dream is always visceral and horrible, yet somehow, rather than breaking her, they strengthen her resolve. Not only that: something wonderful and pure has come of the whole experience. Casting her eyes downward, she rests her hands on her swollen belly and whispers good morning to the child growing strong inside her. She will be a mother any day now and the fact that it has been put there against her will, Rose knows, is not the child's fault. It's still her baby – hers alone – and she will love it and take care of it like any mother would.

The warm morning sun soothes her pale skin and she yawns, stretching her limbs. They burn at the effort, two hundred or so half-healed cuts begin to pull apart before they have had time to close. She lets out a muffled cry and slowly relaxes her arms and legs

There are no mirrors in her apartment and no glass in the windows, just empty frames with heavy duty shutters. The glass had been removed a long time ago after she had smashed it and used the sharp edges to cut her arms and legs. At first it had been an accident. One day, three years ago when she was only eleven, she had woken in a strange room, cold and numb and facing a mirrored wall. She was strapped to a steel chair as if she was some sort of mass murderer facing death by electrocution. At her feet were eight large leather medicine balls lined up in a neat row. Behind the mirrored wall lurked the ice queen and her white-coats, watching and speaking to her in silky tones through a round speaker fixed to the wall on her left.

'Rose, please try and lift one of the balls,' Ophelia had ordered.

'I'd rather not,' Rose had replied tartly. She hated Ophelia Black so much. *Evil witch.*

'Rose, dear. Please try. It is important we carry on your father's work. It is what he would have wanted.'

Rose had bristled at the mention of her father. 'My father would never have drugged me and tied me to a chair!'

Ophelia's tone had lightened then and she had spoken to Rose like a well-meaning governess. 'It's for your own good, Rose. We've talked about this. Remember?'

Rose had gritted her teeth and then caught sight of her reflection. Her heart had sunk. She had watched her mouth open in surprise as if it were not her own. There were dark rings under her eyes. She was pale and drawn with unkempt hair and wearing a dirty nightdress. How long had she been like this? She had wanted to cry but suppressed all emotion knowing the ice queen enjoyed her misery as if it somehow nourished her black soul. She had once caught her smiling as Rose wept inconsolably at the loss of her brother Will and her parents.

Ophelia had said, 'We will look after you now. Your parents left you in our care. It's what they wanted.' And so she had been taken away without attending their funerals and saying goodbye to them properly.

For almost a year after the death of her family she had felt a crippling desolation and was unable to talk with anyone. She had cried herself dry and succumbed to everything Ophelia Black asked of her. What choice did she have? She was a child and had no one else in the world. Besides, being here was, after all, what her parents had wanted.

It was just so hard.

She had thought about Will then and wondered what he would have done if he were in her position. Perhaps he would not have cried so much, or at all. He would have been sad but he would have been brave and strong. He was always so brave. How she missed him.

'Rose. Are you with us?' said a faceless white-coat.

She had still been so young then and had just wanted to sleep, not lift heavy objects. 'I'm tired. I want my pills,' she'd told them.

'You can have your pills once we finish.'

This had irked her and her hands had gripped the edge of the steel armrests.

'Rose, please try and lift one of the medicine balls.'

'No.'

She heard the murmur of their voices from the speaker and imagined them all huddled in discussion wondering what to do with her. A wicked thought had entered her mind. Through hooded eyes she had smiled at her reflection across the room, reached out and pushed it with her mind. The mirror had rippled like a millpond swallowing a pebble.

The voices in the speaker had gone quiet.

A moment passed.

'Rose, did you do that?'

She had begun to scratch the armrests.

'That was wonderful, Rose. Now could you please try and lift one of the balls?'

She had decided to play their game. They would reward her with her pills and then she would be able to go back to her apartment.

Focusing on one of the balls she had extended an invisible hand from her mind and lifted it into the air. After spinning it around she had let it thud back to the floor. She had heard an audible gasp from the speaker.

'I'd like my pills now, please.'

She recalled that the calming effects from her last dose of pills had been wearing thin and her desolation and remorse was returning.

'Can you do that again?' said the voice.

Rose had rolled her eyes.

'My pills!' she shouted.

Rose heard Ophelia's voice. 'Get out of my way! Rose!' she demanded. 'Stop being as worthless as your father. Lift the balls!'

Rose had felt her stomach twisting and her neck flushing. Two of her nails had broken against the edge of the armrest. She had never felt such rage.

One by one she had lifted the balls into the air, spinning them clockwise on either side of her.

'Good Lord!' said a voice from the speaker.

Rose had sensed the weight, shape and density of the balls as if they were part of her. She'd imagined her mind as a great octopus with eight tentacles stretching across the room controlling the balls. They zig-zagged past her flying inches from her head and face.

She'd had enough of the witch and her monkeys. Looking down at the thick leather straps around her wrists she'd lifted the buckle with her mind and yanked out the strap. She'd done the same with the second.

'Rose, you can stop now,' the faceless white-coat had said.

She had been in control. Her expression was fixed but, inside, her heart had felt as though it had been pounded by a butcher's hammer.

She'd stood up and walked towards the mirror staring at the reflection of a girl she did not recognise. The balls spun and flew behind her bending to her will. And then she'd made them stop. They'd hung vertically in the air at the back of the room, four on each side, twitching as if their work was not yet done.

'Rose, please sit down,' Ophelia had said.

Rose had closed her eyes. The loneliness, the desolation, the cold fear had returned to her like ghouls in the darkness of her mind. It was just too much. She'd screamed. The medicine balls had shot like bullets across the room and shattered the mirror. She'd heard the voices from the other room rise in alarm and the sound of chairs falling over and feet shuffling rapidly. She'd then felt a sharp pain in her right forearm. She'd opened her eyes and looked down. Her arm and hand were dripping in blood. The pain was intense.

The bitter whiff of cigarette smoke had invaded her nostrils and, looking up, she'd seen that the mirrored wall was no more: just a pile of glittering shattered glass lying on the floor. In the room beyond had been six white-coats, huddled at the back, staring back at her with a mixture of awe and horror. Ophelia Black stood in the middle of the room, arms folded, her body shrouded in a cloud of blue cigarette smoke. Beside her was a movie camera. Ophelia had grinned calmly at Rose.

'I think it is time for those pills, Rose, dear.'

The pain in Rose's arm had dominated her thoughts. She'd watched the blood drip and splash to the floor, suddenly aware that with the arrival of this physical pain and the spilling of blood, the ghouls had been released from her mind.

For two years after that she had secretly cut herself. She had no idea how she'd managed to hide it from them, but she had. And then one day all the glass and the mirrors and all the sharp objects had been removed and her drugs had been increased. She had not complained. Her limbs were now hideously ugly and the drugs kept her ghouls at bay.

That had been three years ago, although it seemed like a lifetime.

The sound of Sofia singing to herself and clanging pots and pans from the little kitchen at the other side of the apartment distracts Rose from her memories. She sighs and rubs her scarred arms. A moment later the nursemaid calls from the living room.

'Rose, I forget the bread. I lose my mind! I run quickly and be back soon. *Ciao, bella*!'

Rose hears the bolts sliding, the key turning and unlocking the apartment door. The same procedure is repeated in reverse as Sofia locks the door from the outside and hurries off to where ever she is going.

CHAPTER 14

Find Charlie

Rose pulls herself from her oversized four-poster bed and experiences an odd feeling that makes her skin prickle. The scars on her arms and legs begin to itch as they always do when she becomes anxious.

On the bedside table is a small jar of ointment. She notices the two white pills she was supposed to swallow before bed, and makes a mental note to flush them down the toilet before Sofia sees them. Opening the ointment jar, she rubs her arms and legs softly with the lemon-scented salve and shudders at the self-inflicted lines and grooves that disfigure her thin limbs.

Something feels different. What is it? She glances around the sparse bedroom looking for Charlie but does not see his shape or hear his snore.

'Charlie,' she whispers, but hears no response.

She hears Sofia come back in and begin to lay the table for her breakfast. Rose grabs the pills and hides them under her pillow. Cradling her belly, she leaves the bedroom and steps onto the cool, red tiles in the living room of her prison apartment. The room is long and sparsely furnished with an old sofa, a dining table for two people and some shelves to store books. Charlie is nowhere to be seen.

Morning sunlight floods the small but cosy space. She peers through the glassless windows to see if Charlie is on the ledge outside but the ledge is empty. In the distance she sees the gleaming dome of St Peter's Basilica and the rooftops of the Vatican City. Car horns honk across the Tiber and, closer to home, within the confines of her apartment prison, she hears the sound of men's voices barking and hollering.

'Please, *bambina*, eat,' says Sofia.

'I'm not hungry. Where's Charlie, Sofia?'

'Who knows? He'll be back, I'm sure.' Sofia's arms rest on her hips as her eyes scan the living room. 'You must be keeping up your strength, child. You are eating for two now, remember?'

'I wish you would stop saying that.'

Rose wants to lose her temper but Sofia is one of the few people who is kind to her. The men in the castle both loathe and fear her after what she did. Even the ice queen, Ophelia Black, the one person everyone fears, is wary of her. None of them understands that Rose could not stop herself. They had invaded her. She wanted to make them pay and she just couldn't stop. Her thoughts turn back to Charlie.

'Charlie?'

Rose feels her heart break into a gallop. Charlie never leaves her side. Where could he be? Her belly is so heavy her back hurts, yet she hurries out of the apartment and down the worn stones steps without a thought that this is forbidden.

'Charlie! Charlie!' she calls, her voice trembling with fear. Has something happened to him? At the bottom of steps the thick, heavy door is closed. She turns the handle and pushes it, but it does not give. It is locked. There are men's voices from the tower walkway on the other side.

What if they see Charlie and don't know who he is? What if they hurt him? Her heart begins to race and she focuses on the door. Her body is weak but her mind is not. She wills the door to open. It shudders and then begins to warp inwards and outwards, the ancient wood creaking in protest.

She hears the men's voices, raised in alarm, and pushes the door with the force of her mind. It splits into pieces, as if punched with a mighty, invisible fist. Two guards in dark blue suits stand in the walkway gaping back at her, eyes wide with astonishment. Both have their hands inside their jackets, poised to remove their pistols.

She glares at them, daring them to try, and watches with satisfaction as their olive-skinned complexions turn white. She screams at the top of her voice and both men scarper. Composing herself, Rose charges through the shattered doorway with one hand holding her belly. The heat from the afternoon sun dries her clammy face as she runs down the walkway. Her eyes dart around, searching for Charlie on the red-tiled roofs above the walkway and inside the rooms and offices. He is nowhere to be seen.

She hears a man holler a warning to his colleagues. Word is spreading that she is out but she doesn't care. She must find Charlie. He is all she has left from her old life. She runs and runs, ignoring the people who jump out of her way. She feels the scars on her arms and legs opening one by one, tears in her flesh that sting and bleed. There is warm blood on the soles of her feet that causes her to slip and almost fall. Behind her she hears Sofia's wheezing calls.

'Rose! Rose! Stop, please!'

Rose reaches the steps leading down to the Courtyard of the Angel, where Montelupo's marble sculpture of the angel Michael, with its magnificent bronze wings, watches over a gathering of people below. She sees monks, and men and women in dark suits. All at once they look up at her. She swallows and remembers that she is still in her nightdress, her scarred bloody limbs bare and exposed for all to see.

Sofia reaches her side, her face red and sweaty with exertion. 'Rose, *bambina*. Come back with me,' she says softly, removing her apron and draping it around Rose's arms.

With the cat on his lap, the acolyte sits quietly in the Courtyard of the Angel, on a stone bench under the angel Michael's watchful gaze. He has shed his robes in favour of an innocuous Catholic priest's cassock. He wears dark glasses and by his side is a white cane. To the world at large he is a blind priest, a role he has thus far relished. People defer to him, rather than recoil. They say '*Scusami, Padre*' if they walk in his path.

With this disguise comes a power that he can use to his advantage. She will take to him, the girl. She will feel sorry for him and befriend him. The cat's heart beats slowly, steadied by a small measure of opiates, which he'd administered one hour earlier.

He knows she is there. The VIPER rabble are gawping at her like frightened children. His head down, he shifts his gaze to peer up through the dark glasses. She is standing at the top of the steps: thin and pale, her arms and legs scored with a thousand cuts. A slither of pleasure ripples through his sinewy body. With one hand he softly strokes the cats back; with the other he squeezes his nails tightly into its hind legs. The creature lets out a low squeal.

Rose hears a meowing sound from the crowd below. Her eyes widen and she scans the courtyard. A man she doesn't recognise, a priest wearing fingerless gloves, is cradling her beautiful black cat, instantly recognisable with his white socks and white eye patch.

Rose feels her heart melting and, breaking away from Sofia, runs down the steps to the courtyard, ignoring the pain of her open wounds. The crowd retreats but she ignores them, her eyes focused only on Charlie. She hurries towards the priest and lifts Charlie from him. She buries her face in his fur, taking in his hot musty scent, kissing him and gently squeezing him.

'Oh sweetheart. You frightened me. Don't ever do that again.'

The acolyte watches her through the dark lenses of his spectacles. 'I think he missed you,' he says, chuckling like a kindly grandfather. He can see the girl's eyes appraising him.

'Yes. I think he probably did.'

He reaches for the cane and rests his hands upon it. 'What is his name?'

'Charlie.'

'Oh. Like Charlie Chaplin?'

The girl hesitates. He bristles inside and curses himself. What would a blind man know about Charlie Chaplin? For a moment he thinks he has lost her.

'Rose, *bambina*. Please come now,' calls the fat nurse as she scurries across the courtyard.

The girl turns to leave.

'My name is Father William.'

The girl stops and cuddles her cat. His chosen name has done the trick. 'My brother is called William,' she says, sadly.

'Oh, that's nice. Is he here too?'

'He's dead,' she replies.

'Oh, I am sorry. So, so sorry.'

'Rose, quick now,' says the nurse. '*Scusami, Padre.*'

Scusami, Padre.

'Your name is Rose? Now how about that,' he chuckles. 'What a coincidence.'

'What do you mean?' The nurse begins to usher Rose away.

'My sister was called Rose, too.'

'That is quite a coincidence. Is she dead too?'

'Rose!' admonishes the nurse.

'That's quite alright, good sister. My dear Rose died a long time ago. I still think of her every day.' His head dips and he affects a sad expression. 'She was only fourteen.'

The girl gasps. 'I'm fourteen!'

'Oh, are you now? Well, I'm sure you will live a long life.' He smiles with what he hopes is an approximation of warmth.

'Rose, we must go now,' says the nurse pulling her close. 'Come, child.'

'Thank you for my cat,' calls the girl.

'My pleasure.'

'Maybe we could have tea sometime. You can tell me about Rose and I can tell you about Will.'

'Yes, I'd like that.' The acolyte sits back and smiles to himself. He has aroused the girl's curiosity. She will be open to talking to him again and perhaps again after that. Ophelia Black had plans for her, but that was of no concern to him. He does not serve the VIPER elite, despite what they think. He is here for other reasons. He watches the girl climb the steps with her intoxicated cat lying limp in her arms. He catches the fat nursemaid frowning at him and he looks away.

That one might be a problem.

He pictures his hands around the nursemaid's neck and feels his skin prickling under his cassock.

Soon he would have the girl.

Soon.

CHAPTER 15

Return to St Ermin's

London

In his dream Will is free falling through the night. Red angry storm clouds herd through the skies spitting fire at the land below. Voices cry out as thousands of people choke and die in the midst of a bloody apocalypse. A smoking tree interrupts his fall, the crackling branches cushion his crash to the scorched ash that was once earth. He hears his name being called and pushes himself up. A cluster of people are choking to death in a cloud of red smoke on a stone road lined with the statues of angels, the kind you would see in a graveyard. At the end of the road is a tower and he sees Rose looking down from it. She is waving at him. Three shadowed figures, one woman and two men, stand imperiously behind her, watching her.

'I'm sorry, Will. I'm so sorry,' she cries as the three pull her back engulfing her in darkness.

'Rose,' he calls.

'Will!' calls Anna. He looks around the hellish scene but cannot see her.

'Anna, where are you?'

He feels a hand on his shoulder and stirs from his dream, waking to a blinding white light, his body aching, his mouth dry as if he has not drunk water in weeks.

'Will,' says Anna.

'Anna...' His voice is hoarse and weak. His eyes adjust to the light and he sees her peering down at him, her face full of worry, her hand gently squeezing his shoulder.

'You were having a nightmare.'

'Where are we?'

'In the hospital wing of St Ermin's.'

It had been two years, just after he had found the Stones of Fire, since he was last at St Ermin's, a luxury Victorian mansion-block hotel in Westminster where the Secret Intelligence Service operated under the noses of the hotel guests. His wounds had been cleaned and bandaged and it was in his room in the hotel that he had first kissed Anna. That memory alone made St Ermin's a special place for him.

'Drink this,' she says, placing a glass of cold water to his lips.

He sips it at first, then drinks it greedily and begins to feel better. 'Thank you.'

Glancing down, he sees he is fully clothed.

'Do you remember what happened?' asks Anna.

Will recalls the events that led him to the bridge. He closes his eyes. 'They were not ether bombs ... The people on Vauxhall Bridge?'

Anna shakes her head and Will feels a stabbing anger. He sits up but his head begins to throb.

'The mother and her child?' he asks.

'They got away. You saved them.'

Will closes his eyes, sighs with relief and lies back. He is happy for them but devastated for the innocents who died. He should have killed that monk the moment he laid eyes on him.

'You almost died in the process,' says Anna.

They hear the sound of approaching footsteps, leather-soled shoes echoing on a hard floor and a tapping sound, like a cane. He hears Eoin's voice and those of two other men.

There is a polite knock on the door and a bespectacled man with a shock of grey hair and wearing a white lab coat enters. Will recognises him as Doctor Jones, the doctor who had treated his wounds during his last visit: Will had thought him more a mad professor than a doctor. Eoin and the man he'd seen at Chittlock's house follow behind him, the latter leaning on a sturdy walking stick.

'Hello again,' says Doctor Jones, picking up the clipboard at the foot of his bed.

'Hello.'

Eoin gestures at the other man. 'Will, you may recall Sir Hugh Coleridge from Chittlock's house.

Will nods.

Coleridge smiles broadly at him. 'It's so good to see you again, Will, after all this time.' He grabs Will's hand and shakes it vigorously.

Aside from seeing Coleridge bruised and beaten in Chittlock's house, Will has no other memory of him.

'You and I...'

'How are you feeling?' says Eoin, interrupting the exchange.

'Like I have been hit by a truck,' says Will.

'It'll pass,' says Coleridge. 'The good doctor tells us you were not as badly affected as those poor buggers on the bus. Terrible business.'

'Will,' says Eoin, 'Anna gave us a rundown of what she saw. However, we need to understand why you were not so affected. Tell us what you remember in the seconds before you blacked out? Perhaps there is some clue there.'

The throb in Will's head increases as he tries to relive those last few moments. He recalls the monk lying dead on the surface of the bridge.

'I remember picking up the bomb and throwing it over the side of the bridge. There was an odd smell, like sour apples.'

'Was the air clear of red gas?' asks Doctor Jones.

Will's head is fuzzy. He tries to remember. 'Yes, I think it was.'

'Did you inhale any of the red toxins?' asks Doctor Jones.

'No, I don't think so. The red gas did not appear until the bomb was falling towards the Thames. I remember the bombs had two buttons: one red, the other black.'

'Both buttons must be pushed to activate the red gas,' says Coleridge, 'One must have clicked when the monk dropped it and perhaps you activated the other moments later.'

Will rubs his head and thinks that seems a plausible explanation.

'It is possible that there are two gases, both unpleasant, but not life threatening until they merge,' says Doctor Jones.

'Which means you are very lucky to be alive,' adds Coleridge.

Will's mind fritters back to entering his old bedroom at Chittlock's house where the monk had been waiting. He had noticed that something had changed but in the heat of the moment he had not seen what it was. Remembering now, he can see it clearly but he decides to keep it to himself for now.

'What happened at Timothy Chittlock's house?' he asks.

'After I received the call from Nicholas,' Coleridge answers, 'I went over to Warwick Way to meet you. When I got there the house was being ransacked. I thought it was a few local urchins but to my dismay found it was not. I fought a feeble and losing battle but, to my good fortune, you arrived just in time.'

'How did they know to go there?' asks Will.

'We don't know yet,' says Eoin. 'Perhaps someone from Baker Street intercepted Morrow's call. It could be we have another mole.'

'Did the monks find anything?'

'There was nothing on the body of the monk on the bridge. As for the one who got away, I could not say.'

'They were wasting their time, Will. There has not been anything at Tim's house for a long time,' says Eoin.

Will notices Coleridge's expression turn to a frown.

'What do you mean by that?' says Coleridge.

'I had all of Chittlock's files moved shortly after he died.'

'You did what?'

'I moved them for safekeeping, which was evidently the right thing to do if Baker Street has another mole.'

'Where are they?'

'Safe. For now.'

The exchange between Eoin and Coleridge has become tense, much to Will's surprise. They might be old friends, but there is something else – a rivalry? Anna glances at Will, her eyebrows arched.

'We'll talk about this later,' says Coleridge.

Will cannot figure out if Coleridge is angry or just disappointed.

'Please give those files to me at your earliest convenience.'

Eoin's expression is impassive. 'Of course, Hugh.'

There seems to be a lot going on that Will does not know about. His head begins to throb as he tries to absorb everything. He closes his eyes, shutting out the glare of the hospital light.

'We should let Will rest,' says Anna.

'Indeed we should,' says the doctor. He turns to Will. 'I suspect right now you feel the worst you have ever felt. I would liken it to a most terrible hangover. Some sleep will do you good.'

Will recalls his dream and the city he was free-falling into. Something in it has tapped into his lost memories. He feels his hand being squeezed by Anna and he gently returns the affection.

'Right,' says Coleridge, 'we need to look into this red gas business. Can't have monks running around the city dropping bombs everywhere!'

'I think it is called Red Storm,' says Will.

All heads turn to look at him.

'It's a gas manufactured by VIPER to wipe out factions of the world's population.'

Coleridge's cheery expression falters. 'I'm sure we can handle a few monks.'

'I think there is more to this than the Cerastes and a handful of small bombs tied around their waists.' Will says nothing more for a moment as his fractured memory tries in vain to piece together his past.

'Tell us, Will,' says Eoin eagerly.

'I'm really not sure. I had a dream. There was an apocalypse. Imagine what happened today but on a scale a thousand times bigger.'

'We need more than dreams, Will,' says Coleridge.

'Let's not discount this,' says Eoin. 'Will has VIPER intelligence hidden in his memories. It returns to him in flashbacks and dreams.'

Will is keen to get back to Chittlock's house. He is certain there is something there. A clue perhaps. He swings himself off the bed but feels his head spinning.

'You're not going anywhere just yet,' says the doctor. 'One more night's rest will do you good.'

Will tries to protest but his head begins to bang and spin faster.

'Listen to Doctor Jones,' says Anna. Bending over, she eases him back gently and he does not protest. He feels overcome with tiredness and within moments he forgets everything and is fast asleep.

CHAPTER 16

Assassin

Will wakes to the sound of something clanging outside. The door to his hospital room is slightly ajar, spilling a small measure of light from the corridor outside into the darkness. He sees his clothes folded neatly on the chair next to his bed. He has been dressed in blue and white striped pyjamas.

For a moment there is silence and then he hears a thud followed by a groan. His heart begins to race, but he tells himself he is just being paranoid. This is a safe place, isn't it? Maybe one of the other patients has fallen over? He slips out from under the covers, and is instantly relieved to discover that the dizziness is gone. From the doorway he peers up and down the corridor. The light is bright, the walls are white and bare and the floor is a pale parquet wood. He sees the nurse's desk and, standing with his back to him is Dr Jones, dressed in his white coat, his grey hair wild and sticking up. Will starts to walk towards him and stops when hears the unmistakable phut phut phut of a silencer pistol.

'Doctor Jones?'

Doctor Jones is reloading the gun as he turns around. Behind him, in a pool of blood, is a hospital porter. The porter must be a VIPER spy or assassin Will thinks, though there is something in the doctor's expression, a coldness in the eyes, that worries him. Will takes a step back, not taking his eyes off the doctor. Neither speaks. Will isn't consciously anticipating the shot but when it comes he is already diving to the floor and rolling for protection behind a stainless steel trolley. Two more shots clang off the trolley as the doctor comes towards him. Will has nowhere to go. He kicks the trolley towards the doctor, slamming it into his legs. It stops him for the moment but he manages to land deftly from a near-fall. For a man his age, Doctor Jones is certainly nimble.

Will is on his feet now, and charges him, pushing the doctor's gun hand towards the ceiling and kneeing him in the balls at the same time. The man groans and doubles over still trying to point the gun at Will. Will launches a punishing kick at the pistol, sending it spinning down the corridor. He grabs the doctor's wild hair, determined to finish him off, but the hair comes away in Will's hand. It is a wig. The man looking up at him is wearing a black hair net. He is not Doctor Jones.

For a second Will is caught off guard. The imposter seizes the moment and punches him hard in the stomach. Blunt pain stabs his abdominals. Winded, Will drops to his knees, his face close to the wall. The man is on him instantly, straddling his back. A strip of red cord passes over his head and instantly he is choking. Gasping for breath, he manages to get one hand up to his neck where a cord is tightening. He just gets his fingers under it. Will can feel the blood trapped in his head as the rope gets tighter. The man is squeezing the life from him.

He tries to pull the rope with his fingers but the lack of oxygen weakens him. Is he going to die here? Black spots appear in front of his eyes. He thinks of Anna, Emile and Claudette. He thinks of the red gas and the people trapped in the bus. *Many must die.*

But not him. Not yet. With one last desperate effort, he pushes himself up, the man still clinging to him. With his free fist he rains punches at his opponent's head and takes satisfaction at the man's pained grunting. Leaning his weight into the man, Will raises his feet and pushes them against the wall with all his strength. They tumble backwards and Will slams his elbow into the man's solar plexus. He groans as the wind expels from him. The rope loosens at last and Will pulls it from his throat feeling glorious oxygen fill his lungs. Spinning around, he sees the man remove a viper-shaped dagger from his sleeve. Will pulls back just in time, his throat inches from the blade. Without a weapon, he knows his chances are slim. He turns and runs, slipping clumsily on the blood of the unfortunate porter at the nurse's desk. It covers his hands and pyjamas as he tries to stand up. His assailant is coming. Will scrambles to his feet, sprints down the corridor and crashes through a set of double doors. On the other side is some sort of tapestry blocking his exit. He pulls it up and tumbles forward.

For a moment he is confused. It's as if he has stepped into an alternate world of luxurious decadence. There are enormous glittering chandeliers, ornate walls and ceilings painted a soft white like the icing on a cake. The floor beneath his feet is cool marble. There are people. All heads have turned to look at him, their eyes wide with disbelief. It's the lobby of the St Ermin's Hotel – and he is barefoot and dressed in bloody pyjamas.

His eyes catch those of the hotel receptionist, a West Indian gentleman, perhaps in his late twenties, who watches him impassively, over the head of an irate hotel guest, a round lady stuffed into a green suit with fox furs draped over her shoulders. Will remembers the receptionist from his last visit. His name is Joseph and he is also an MI6 operative.

Will pads towards the reception desk, ignoring the eyes that follow him.

'Hello again,' says Joseph.

The lady turns to look at Will. She gasps, and her complaints cease as her hand flies to her chest.

'Excuse me, madam,' says Will, politely, before turning to the receptionist. 'There's some trouble in the ward, Joseph.'

'I see,' replies Joseph. 'How can I assist you?'

Will turns away from the lady and makes a subtle gun signal with his hand.

Joseph's eyes flick towards the tapestry. 'Very good, sir.' From under the desk he removes a Colt 45 and hands it to Will.

The woman gasps again.

'Thank you, Joseph.' Will does not want to alarm any other guests so he tucks the Colt under his pyjama top.

'Be careful, sir. I will alert the others.'

Will is already halfway back to the tapestry. Behind him he hears Joseph addressing the lady, 'Now, Mrs Christchurch. Where were we?'

'You ... you gave him a gun.'

'It appears we have a rodent problem.'

'Oh, I see...'

More of a snake problem, thinks Will, as he lifts the tapestry. There is no one there. He slides behind it to the double doors and pulls one open a fraction. Up the corridor, he sees the dead porter and the circular pool of blood that surrounds his corpse, staining the parquet floor. He can see his own red footprints running down to the lobby – and the killer's leaving a trail in the opposite direction.

Cautiously, he scurries down the corridor, leaping over the blood and following the congealing footprints. They lead to a ward with six empty beds. He sees an office further down the corridor. The door is open and inside, slumped over his desk as if he is sleeping, is Doctor Jones. Will cannot tell if it is the real one or the imposter. He goes in with the gun pointing at the man and prods him, but there's no response. He pulls at his hair, which appears to be real. Feeling for a pulse, Will is relieved to find one and notices something small and metallic lodged in the doctor's neck. He pulls it out. It is a dart of some sort, no doubt containing a narcotic.

Leaving the office, he sees a white panelled door next to it. Despite the killer's footprints disappearing under a door marked Exit at the end of the corridor, Will pushes it open. Beyond it is an empty stairwell.

At the end of the corridor, he kicks the exit door open and stands with his back to the inside wall, out of any line of fire. Cold night air sweeps inside, a cool relief. Light from the corridor reveals a small walled yard used for storing crates and boxes. There is no one there. The footprints, now faint, stop at a back door on the wall opposite. Will tiptoes across and pulls it open. The street outside is dark, seemingly unoccupied but for several parked cars.

'Oi!' comes a stern voice.

A man in a uniform has turned the corner. His tin hat marks him out as an Air Raid Warden. Will holds the Colt 45 out of sight, behind his back.

'Turn that blimmin' light off! Don't you know there's a war on?'

'Apologies,' Will replies, hurrying back and closing the door quickly, not wanting to attract any further attention.

He walks back to his room, half disappointed his would-be assassin had escaped, half relieved. From back down the corridor, he hears the doors to the lobby opening and sees Joseph, Eoin and Anna hurry through them, armed and ready, albeit a little on the late side.

After a summary of what had happened Will and Anna watch Joseph bolt and lock the exit door where the fake Doctor Jones had escaped. Eoin is crouching down examining the bloody footprints.

'I saw Doctor Jones arrive in the hotel lobby not twenty minutes back,' says Joseph. 'He nodded hello to me and then entered the hospital wing under the tapestry. I thought it strange. As a rule we do not use that entrance because it makes our hotel guests ask questions.'

'With the real Doctor Jones in his office and the porter going about his duties there was less chance of him being challenged,' says Will.

'Correct. Poor Smith, the porter, is also the hospital guard. He must have been doing his rounds when he bumped into the fake Doctor Jones.'

Will feels the comfort of Anna's hand as it brushes close to his.

Eoin is on his feet. 'We have a meeting later this morning. We can discuss what to do next.'

'I will take care of this mess,' says Joseph.

'Thank you, Joseph,' says Will and hands back the Colt 45.

'A pity you never got to use it.'

'Yes. A pity,' Will responds, noting the coldness in his own tone. As he returns to his room to gather his things, he reflects on how different he is now compared to two years back, when he was unsure of who or what he was. His memory is still fractured, but the truth he has learned about who he is and what he has lost has only fuelled his rage and desire for retribution. This knowledge has bubbled quietly like the lava of a dormant volcano waiting for its moment to explode into the world.

CHAPTER 17

The Revelation

Rome

The following day Rose is alone in the apartment, resting on her bed. Turning over, she smiles at Charlie lying curled up on the pillow next to her. His eyes are open and he seems to be staring across the room. Rose follows his gaze, but there is nothing extraordinary, just the polished walnut dresser with her brush on top and her daily dose of pills. She nuzzles him with her face, taking in his familiar and comforting musty scent.

'What's the matter, Charlie boy?'

He lets out a weak meow, which worries her. She lifts him onto her chest and cuddles him. 'Maybe you should eat something? Keep your strength up. That's what Sofia tells me to do when I'm poorly.'

She hears a knock on the apartment door and wonders if Sofia has forgotten her key. She remembers the nursemaid locking it and waits for a moment. The knock comes again, harder this time. Rose feels a flutter in her stomach and sits up, wincing at the pain in her arms and legs. Carrying Charlie, she hobbles to the apartment door and places her ear to it. Charlie hisses.

'Hush, Charlie.' She bites her lip and wonders what to do.

'Sofia?' she calls.

But there is no answer.

She shrugs and, overcome with curiosity, stares hard at the empty keyhole and uses her mind to twist the cogs and open the lock. It makes a satisfying clicking sound. Easy stuff. She has done it many times before – before pills, that is, after which she had given up hope of ever escaping. There are two bolts built inside the door. One at the top and one at the bottom. With little effort she slides them across and then pulls the door open. For a moment she sees nothing but the dark shadowy passageway leading away down from the apartment.

'Sofia?'

As her eyes adjust to the gloom the shadows seems to merge, gather form and move towards her. She gasps and steps back squeezing Charlie a little too tight.

'Rose, is that you?'

She sees the white cane first, then the hands with fingerless gloves belonging to the blind priest, who is looming in the doorway. She is surprised at how tall he is and how powerful he seems now that she sees him on his feet.

'Father William, what are you doing here?'

'Hello, child. I was passing and thought I might drop in and say hello.'

Charlie begins to squirm in her arms.

'But it's forbidden. I am not allowed to see anyone.'

He chuckles. 'And what is so wrong with an old priest visiting one of God's children?'

Charlie's claws sink hard into her shoulder and she yelps.

'Charlie, what is the matter?' She loosens her grip letting him jump to the floor. He runs drunkenly back to the bedroom. Rose shakes her head. What has got into him?

'May I come in?' asks Father William.

'Yes, Father, do please come in. I've never had a friend visit.'

The tall priest steps into the room, clicking his cane on the stone floor, checking for obstacles or steps.

Rose closes the door. 'I'm surprised the guards let you through. They're normally so rude.'

'Guards – now is that what they were? How odd. They seemed very polite.'

Rose frowns. 'Polite? That's a first. Perhaps you worked some magic on them.'

'I was polite also. I told them I was here to do God's work.'

Rose shrugs. The guards were mostly locals who were all God fearing men, according to Sofia.

'Would you like to sit down?'

'Yes, please.'

'Shall I guide you?'

'Thank you, child.'

Rose takes his arm and leads him to the little sofa in her living room. He lowers himself, his long fingers wriggle in the air by his side searching for the arm rest.

'Would you like some tea?'

'No, thank you.'

She stiffens suddenly, blushing, as she realises her scarred arms and legs are bare and she is still wearing her nightdress. He cannot see you, you fool, she thinks and relaxes. Nevertheless she excuses herself for a moment and runs to the bedroom to pull on her pink, floral, silk dressing gown. A gift from Sofia, apparently. Rose did not believe that for one moment. Where on earth would Sofia get the money to buy such a fine garment. No, this was bought with Ophelia's money. No doubt a way to make Rose happier and more comfortable during her twenty-four hours a day, seven days a week confinement.

Tying the belt around her waist, Rose sits beside the priest on the edge of the sofa.

'I thought we would carry on where we left off,' says the Father.

'We can talk about your sister, if you like?'

'That would be nice. But I think I would like to hear about your brother.'

Father William's response catches her off guard. 'Of course. If you would like.' She pauses and tries to gather her thoughts. It is harder than she thinks. Despite thinking about him every day she struggles to form a sentence. After a few moments the words come.

'We lived with our parents in a leafy street in Highgate, London. Will was older than me by four years. He had dark hair like our mother and clear, blue eyes like our father, and he was determined like him, too. That's what mother used to say anyway. He was a typical boy, always kicking a football, climbing trees or getting into scrapes with other boys. He was fiercely competitive, which was a never-ending source of worry for Mother, but he was also kind and funny. He made all of us laugh all the time. I tried to be like him and would follow him around. I wanted to kick balls, climb trees and fight boys, too, and Will would let me.'

'He let you fight other boys?'

'Oh, no. He would sit in the garden with me and I would punch his palms like a fierce boxer.' Rose smiles at the memory and pauses.

Tears threaten to fall but she holds them back and blows her nose on a handkerchief she finds in the pocket of her dressing-gown.

Father William sits quietly and nods his head. After a moment he speaks. 'You must miss him.'

Rose casts her eyes downward. 'I do. Every day.'

She turns at the sound of someone at the apartment door.

'Rose, why is the door not locked?' says Sofia. The nursemaid stands at the entrance with a loaf of fresh bread in her hands.

Rose ignores the question. 'Sofia, look who's come to visit.' She sees the nursemaid stiffen and her face frown.

'No one allowed here. Not even you, *Padre*. I am sorry. You must leave.'

'But...' says Rose.

'That's quite alright. I must be on my way.' Father William struggles out of the sofa. He reaches for Rose's hand. She takes it and pulls him gently forward ignoring the stinging pain it causes in her arm. There is something in his palm. It feels like paper. His other hand covers hers as he surreptitiously slides the paper into her hand.

He leans towards her and whispers, 'Tell no one. These walls have eyes and they have ears.'

Rose is too surprised to know how to react or what to say. She slips the paper into her pocket and walks the padre to the door.

'Goodbye, Rose.'

'Goodbye, Father. I hope to see you soon.'

'Oh, you will. I can promise you that.'

As he disappears into the shadows Sofia closes the door and turns to Rose. 'You mustn't open the door when I am not here. You don't know what these men are like.'

'He's just a priest doing his rounds.'

Sofia bolts the door and turns the key. 'There's something about that man I don't like.'

Rose rolls her eyes. 'I'm going to my room.'

'I bring you breakfast soon.'

Rose walks quickly to her room and takes out the piece of paper. She unfolds it and reads the single line. She feels her stomach somersaulting; her head turns light and giddy.

Written across the page in neat blocked letters are the words:

YOUR BROTHER IS NOT DEAD. I KNOW WHERE HE IS.

The acolyte smiles to himself as he makes his way down the steps of the dark passageway, keeping up the guise of the blind priest. The girl had opened up to him; he had seen her emotions begin to stir as he watched her from the corner of his eye through the dark glaze of his spectacles. He had made her reminisce. It had hurt her and that pleased him immensely. The revelation in his note was a risk. If the VIPER fools discovered what he had done, they would have him killed. But they would not find out because the girl despised them. She would keep her counsel and confide only in him: he was her saviour now. The seed had been planted. He pictures her now, full of hope and desperate to be reunited with her guttersnipe brother. His work was done here.

For now.

He would keep his distance and, in time, her patience would wear thin and she would seek him out. Then, he would take her.

He hums aloud to himself, a familiar old tune, passes the guards and wishes them a good day in fluent Italian.

CHAPTER 18

Dressed to Kill

London

With the real Doctor Jones still recovering from his shock, Will discharges himself from the hospital ward. Filthy with dried blood and sweat, all he wants to do is get cleaned up and take some time to think things over. Joseph has given him the same room he stayed in two years back. Despite its grandeur and luxury it is with mixed emotions that Will stands there now. After the Stones of Fire, he and Anna had spent two days and two nights alone together. She had shared his bed and helped him forget. It was then he had fallen in love with her. All that is over now.

He showers and scrubs the blood from his hair and body. His thoughts turn to Emile and Claudette, his friends, who were alive and well less than twenty-four hours ago. He wonders if Marie-Antoinette has done the decent thing and arranged for the burial they deserved. The thought of them being ditched on the side of the road or in a pauper's grave with no stone was too much to bear.

He dries himself and tidies his hair with a comb embossed with the grand logo of St Ermin's. There is a knock on the door. Wrapping the towel around his waist he walks into the bedroom and opens the door.

'Hello again, sir,' says Joseph, who is carrying a large paper bag.

'Hello, Joseph.'

'May I come in?'

Will steps aside for Joseph who removes clothes from the bag and places them on the bed. There is a dark blue tweed blazer, a red flannel shirt, grey trousers with braces and clean underwear and socks. A pair of oxblood brown leather Derby boots are set down on the floor.

'First things first,' says Joseph. 'You have a meeting with Sir Hugh, Mr Heaney, Mr Morrow and Miss Wilder at 11 am.'

'Where will that be?'

'Somewhere in the hotel. I will confirm the venue closer to the time.'

Joseph takes out a black case and opens it. Inside is a small pistol engraved with oak leaves and finished in a high polish steel.

'A Mauser,' says Will.

'A Mauser HSc,' corrects Joseph. 'Easy to carry without being noticed.' Joseph's eyes light up. 'This one is one of a kind. A beautifully crafted pistol, quite rare and very expensive.' He hands it across. 'A gift.'

Will looks down at the weapon and can't help but admire its compact size and lovely craftsmanship. 'This must be a mistake.'

'No mistake.'

He accepts the case and runs the tips of his fingers over the cold steel. 'From whom?'

'From Mr Heaney.'

'How did he get this?' But Will suspects he might already know.

'From a card game, I believe,' says Joseph, confirming Will's suspicions.

'Did it belong to Sir Hugh, by any chance?'

Joseph shoots him a wry smile. 'It's not for me say. However your intuition serves you well, sir.'

Joseph picks up the blazer, removes a brown leather shoulder holster from the inside pocket and drops it on the bed. He holds the collar of the jacket and tries to bend it, but it seems solid.

'Concealed inside is a flexible saw that can cut through wire and steel, if time is on your side.' Turning the left sleeve cuff he points to four pen-like items secreted in the lining. 'The first one is a three-in-one multi-purpose tool containing a screwdriver, a scalpel and a lock pick; just unscrew them to get the one you require. The second is a Time Pencil with a thirty-second blast time. It's a new model and quite powerful, so do be careful. The third is a pen.'

'Just a pen?'

'Yes, and no. The top has a button that will dispense the ink into a liquid – a cocktail or cup of tea, for example. The ink will clear instantly. It is a poison that will render the drinker unconscious in minutes. Also if you write with the pen and someone touches the ink, they should suffer a reaction that will paralyze them temporarily.'

'How long for?'

'Hard to say. We've had mixed results. We're trialling this model. It has not passed our high quality standards because some of our candidates have remained conscious while others just seemed happily inebriated.'

'That's reassuring.'

'Either way, it may help you. The fourth is a torch with a small glass dome that will widen the beam.'

Joseph lifts the right hand sleeve. 'I do think you will like this one. The cuff contains a spring action pipe with two steel poison darts. Similar to VIPER's blow pipe, however, the velocity is greater: they have a range of twenty feet and will penetrate at least two layers of clothing. Quite impressive, don't you think?'

Will smiles. 'If you say so.'

'We call it the Velo-Dart.'

'Catchy.'

'To shoot a dart, simply straighten your arm, turn up your wrist and swing your arm towards the target,' Joseph demonstrates by swinging his rigid arm fast at the room's door. A dart shoots out and penetrates the wooden surface, splitting the white painted wood.

Will is impressed. 'You're right. I like it.' He pulls the dart from the door and examines it. 'A dart like this was used on Doctor Jones.'

Joseph nods grimly, 'We cannot rule out the fact that the assassin might be one of our own.'

'Hard to know who to trust in this game.'

'Quite so, sir.' Joseph points to the middle button of the blazer. 'This button is made from reinforced steel. Its thread is a thirty foot extendible and retractable wire.' Joseph demonstrates by pulling it back and forth. 'Any questions?'

'None. Thank you, Joseph. I feel ready to take on the world.' Will pulls on the red flannel shirt, which is soft and warm.

Joseph regards him thoughtfully. 'If you don't mind me mentioning something, sir ...' The receptionist-come-agent pauses, waiting for Will to respond.

'Of course.'

'Some years back I met a man: a kind man, a scholar and a scientist. We worked together briefly, just before he passed away.'

Will lifts the underwear from the folded pile of clothes and puts it on. 'I'm sorry to hear that, Joseph.'

'He told me that I reminded him of his son.'

Will pulls on the trousers and slips the braces over his shoulders.

'When I asked why, he looked at me, smiled and said, "Don't take this the wrong way. You are over-protective, impetuous and too quick to use yours fists." I explained to him it was my job to be that person. He told me he understood and that his son was just like me.'

'Sounds like he did not like his son very much.'

'Not at all. He was very proud of him, very proud.'

Will pulls on his socks and the Derby boots and ties up the laces. 'What was your job?'

'I was his guard.'

'Why did he need a guard?'

'Because his life was in danger, as were the lives of his wife, his son and his daughter.' There is a tremor in Joseph's voice.

Will stares hard at his boots and wonders how on earth a colour could be called oxblood. Wasn't all blood the same shade of red and not this brownish rust colour?

'I did all I could for them. It wasn't enough. I am sorry.'

Will puts on the shoulder holster and checks the cartridge of the pistol. It is full.

'There are more bullets in the bag.'

Will nods absentmindedly as he turns Joseph's revelations over in his head. Standing, he pulls on the blazer and feels the weight of the flexible saw around his neck, stiff but not uncomfortable.

'Sir…'

'You don't need to say any more, Joseph.'

'But I do. I feel responsible and I know your father would want me to tell you that your chosen profession is not one he would have approved of. Let others fight this fight. You are young and you have so much to live for. Walk away, before it is too late.'

Will meets Joseph's gaze. The agent's eyes are red, holding back tears, his expression pained.

'I never chose this profession, Joseph. It chose me. I am merely the sum of what others have made me. VIPER are afraid of me. I have been made an aberration, a monster, a nightmare. Not just because of what secrets I hold in my head, but because I am coming for them and they know it.'

Joseph's expression changes and Will thinks for a second he sees a flicker of fear.

'Thank you for what you did for my family.' Will picks the spare bullets from the bag and the tin soldier from his old trousers. He puts them into his jacket pocket. 'Thank you for everything, Joseph.'

'I wish you all the luck in the world.'

Will nods his thanks and turns to leave. In the corridor, he wonders where Anna could be. Before their meeting with Eoin and the others, he wants to return to Warwick Way. If he is right, then another clue has been left for him. When he stepped into the bedroom, there was something that had seemed irregular. Before he'd had a chance to figure it out he was chasing the monk across London. That was yesterday and now he was eager to get back and investigate.

CHAPTER 19

The Menin Road

Will makes his way down the marble staircase and sees Anna with a man he does not recognise talking in the lobby. Dressed in a blue pin-striped suit, he is tall and clean-shaven with sharp cheekbones and a chiselled jawline. Will wonders if he is Anna's new man. His eyes catch Will's and he leans across and says something to Anna. She turns and looks up at Will. Did the man just inform her he was on the staircase? Who is he? The man exits the hotel and Anna meets Will at the bottom of the stairs.

She has shed her coat and blue trouser suit and is wearing a dark red jacket with matching skirt and a crisp white shirt underneath. Under her arm she carries a dark leather purse that no doubt contains her Walther PPK. He swallows and tries to suppress the unwelcome desire that makes his throat dry suddenly. He is torn. He wants to spend time with her but what is the point? She is with someone else now – someone with penetrating cheekbones and a pin-stripe suit? Perhaps it is better for their working relationship. Easier to step away and become less attached.

'How are you feeling?' she asks.

'Fine. Who was that man?'

'What man?'

'That man you were just talking to.'

Anna smiles. 'Oh, him. He's just another stooge. Someone I worked with once.'

'Not your new boyfriend, then?'

Anna's eyes widen and she scoffs. 'I don't think so.'

It is so easy to mistrust anyone in their line of work that Will regrets his suspicion and thinks nothing more of the chiselled man. Anna and he had spent a year apart and she had worked on several other missions. She would know many people.

'Fancy an excursion?'

'Where are we going?'

'I'll tell you outside.'

They cross the lobby and go out into St Ermin's front courtyard where the sun is shining and the sky is a clear blue. The doorman, a stocky man dressed in a dark suit, red waistcoat and top hat, bids them good morning.

'Morning,' replies Will, noting the strap of a gun holster under the doorman's unbuttoned jacket.

'May I get you a taxi, sir?'

Will is about to say yes but decides against it. He does not want anyone to know where he is going. No one can be trusted for certain.

'We'll walk, thank you.'

'Have a good day, sir, miss.'

'You too.'

Anna loops her arm into Will's, a warm smile on her face. He can feel the heat from her body and smells an exotic fragrance that she does not usually wear. He can't help it. He wants to spend more time with her, despite her new relationship.

'Where are we going?' she asks.

Will glances behind him, ensuring they are not being followed. The doorman tips his hat and Will nods.

'Let's get out of here and I will tell you.'

They stroll casually, like two lovers, down Caxton Street, turning left towards Victoria and making their way through the locals going about the business of the day.

'What is that scent you are wearing?' asks Will.

'It's new. Do you like it?'

'Yes.'

'It's called Soir de Paris. It's what all us good girls with a "dangerous" side to their nature wear.'

Will laughs. 'I can see why that might be.'

'Why do you ask?'

'I met someone recently who was wearing it?'

'Was she beautiful and dangerous?'

Will thinks about the agent codenamed Marie-Antoinette. It had been difficult to make out her face behind the make-up and veil, but from what he remembers, she was beautiful. As for being dangerous, he reckons she was just that and more – reckless.

'I didn't really get to know her,' he says.

In reverse of the previous day's car chase, they turn down Rochester Row and Will explains about the message left for him at Chittlock's house. He does not say more than that as they cross over Vauxhall Bridge Road and on to Warwick Way. Will looks towards Milly's hairdressers and sees the shop has been boarded up and Milly's name is no longer above the door. Perhaps the sight of their guns and the news of the horrible deaths on Westminster Bridge was enough to make her leave. Who could blame her?

Chittlock's door has been bolted and locked, presumably on orders from Eoin. Will removes the multi-purpose tool from his sleeve and, using the pick, opens the lock as Anna watches the street. Moments later they are inside.

They wade through the debris that litters the floor and climb the stairs to Will's old bedroom. Standing by his desk, Will gazes at the painting, a grim oil-on-canvas depiction of a landscape from the First World War. There are trenches and bomb craters flooded with dirty rainwater and tree stumps, devoid of foliage, pointing towards an oppressive red sky full of clouds and plumes of smoke. There are two shafts of odd green sunlight that seem more like gun barrels. There is something deeply unsettling about the whole scene.

'I know that painting. I've seen it at the Hall of Remembrance,' says Anna, '*The Menin Road* by Paul Nash.'

Will had seen the picture in his flashback, though he couldn't remember the title and artist. He studies it in silence for a few moments.

'It's a copy,' he says.

'Yes, of course. The original is enormous.'

'It has been tampered with.'

Anna leans forward for a better look.

'The original does not have red sunlight or a red sky,' Will says.

'You are right!'

In the centre of the painting are two soldiers, navigating their way through the troubled scene. Will points to them. 'Look.'

The soldier on the left wears a long green coat and a helmet typical of the period, however the soldier on the right is different. He is a fusilier from the Victorian era, dressed in dark blue trousers and a red jacket, just like Will's tin soldier. He has been painted in tones sympathetic to the oil colours of the rest of the painting so that he does not stand out.

Will reaches across and runs his finger gently over the fusilier. The paint is thick and hard. He presses the soldier and frowns, 'There's something underneath.' Lifting the canvas from the wall, he uses the scalpel to cut it away from the frame. There is nothing there. Laying the canvas on the desk, he crouches down and runs his eyes across the flat surface. Anna hunches beside him and follows his gaze. The paint used for the fusilier is button-thick. The painter had done an expert job of making it seem flat.

Using the scalpel Will begins to cut gently around the shape of the fusilier, until it comes loose. He picks it up and turns it over. Concealed behind the body of soldier is a rolled-up piece of paper. He looks at Anna, his eyebrows raised.

'Bingo,' she says.

'Bingo,' he replies, with a grin. He unrolls the paper and frowns. It is blank. He turns it over and holds it up the light of the window but there is nothing. 'Could be invisible ink?'

'Give it to me,' says Anna. She sniffs the crisp paper, her eyes closed in concentration. She nods and hands it back to him. 'Hold it open, please.' She removes a small ioniser from her purse.

'Soir de Paris?' asks Will.

Anna smiles. 'Not quite. People would run a mile if I wore this on my skin.'

She stands at arm's length from the paper and sprays the surface. A sour acidic smell fills the air and Will recoils. 'You're not wrong there.'

A moment passes while nothing happens and then brown dots start appearing randomly on the paper. Within minutes four lines of symbols and hieroglyphics become visible on the page.

Will studies it and tries to make sense of it.

'Any ideas?' asks Anna.

'No. I don't recognise the code.'

'We'll try and figure it out. If we can't, I know someone who can help.'

Will folds the paper tightly, inserts it through the spine of the tin soldier and puts the soldier back inside the pocket of his blazer.

They leave the bedroom and Will stops at the entrance to the bathroom where he and Eoin had found Hugh Coleridge yesterday. It is a square room, roughly seven feet by seven feet, with a large white Edwardian bath, a toilet, a sink and rectangular white tiles on the walls. There is a pale green round rug on the floor spotted with Coleridge's blood and broken glass. Will squats down and examines a piece of the glass, curiously. Turning to the sink he sees the mirror is intact. A draught turns his attention to the broken window. Outside there is a gully below, closed in by tall walls. There is nothing out of the ordinary.

It would not have been so easy to escape over those walls. How did Eoin not see him?

'See anything?' says Anna.

Will shakes his head and checks his wristwatch. It is almost 11 am.

'I think we are running a little late.'

'Morrow will be most upset,' says Anna.

'I do hope so.'

They arrive back at St Ermin's almost twenty minutes late. Joseph is at the reception desk and he directs them to the MI6 tea room.

MI6 has its own tea room?

'Mr Morrow isn't happy,' says Joseph.

'Mr Morrow is never happy,' says Anna.

Joseph smiles. 'Isn't that the truth.'

They thank the receptionist for the warning and Will follows Anna through a grand hallway and into the Caxton Bar where several agents and customers take their mid-morning tea. He recognises Mrs Christchurch, the lady from reception who saw Joseph handing him a gun. She stiffens when she sees him and then seems to scan the floor for rodents. Will smiles politely and carries on. He feels another set of eyes watching him and looks across the tea room to see the chiselled jaw and sharp cheekbones of the 'stooge' Anna had been talking to earlier. He looks away as Will meets his gaze and nonchalantly picks up a newspaper and turns his attention towards it. There is something about him that Will cannot put his finger on.

At the end of the bar is a black door with a table for two outside it. Seated at it, sipping from cups of fine china, are Daisy and Alice, Morrow's twin red-headed guards.

'Hello, ladies,' says Anna.

Daisy, or Alice, shakes her head. 'He's not happy.'

'We know,' replies Anna.

'He's also in a spot of hot water.'

'What do you mean?'

'You'll find out. Hello Will,' Daisy and Alice say in unison, in an almost musical fashion.

'Hello Daisy … Alice.'

'You can go on through,' they say.

The door swings open before they can knock and a furious Morrow appears.

'You are twenty minutes late!'

'Sorry,' says Anna.

'It was my fault,' says Will. 'I took Anna for a stroll.'

'A stroll! We are at war and you go for a stroll!'

Anna and Morrow disappear inside. The door closes behind them.

'Daisy, Alice, who is that chap in the tea room: pin-striped suit, cheekbones, square?'

'That'll be Roland Cooper,' they say.

'And he is?'

'Handsome,' says one of twins, with a wry smile.

'US Intelligence,' says the other. 'Office of Strategic Services. They're like us, but ... American.'

'What's he doing here?'

'Lord knows. Top secret, apparently.'

'Isn't everything? Thank you, ladies.'

The door opens again and Morrow's furious face appears.

'Good Lord, Morrow, get him inside and let's crack on!' says an exasperated Coleridge.

Morrow stands aside. 'Of course, Sir Hugh. Far be it for me to delay this meeting anymore,' he says in an obsequious fashion, still glaring at Will.

The MI6 tea room is circular, with green walls and a single narrow window overlooking a small garden. There is a round dark wood table in the centre, where Eoin and Sir Hugh wait.

'Where have you two been?' asks Coleridge.

'We went...' says Anna, but is cut off by Will.

'Back to St James's Park,' says Will, who meets Anna's gaze. 'We haven't been in quite some time. We went there for a stroll to take in some air and lost track of time. It was my fault. Sorry.'

Both Eoin and Coleridge look through narrowed eyes from Will to Anna. They know he is lying, but don't press the issue.

'I hope you are feeling refreshed after yesterday's near misses,' says Coleridge.

'Very much so,' says Will.

'Are you hurt in any way?'

'No, I am not.'

'No, I am not, sir,' hisses Morrow.

'Pipe down, Nicholas. Will has narrowly survived two attempts on his life and I have no doubt there have been many in the past and will be more to come. I think we can cut him some slack.'

Morrow grumbles under his breath.

'I'm glad you are unhurt,' says Coleridge to Will. 'All in a day's work for one of our most promising spies.'

Will can feel Morrow's eyes bore into him but ignores him.

'First things first. We have a problem. A big problem, in fact,' says Coleridge, turning to Morrow.

Will looks at Morrow who seems to shrivel under the gaze of those around the table.

'Nicholas, tell us your news,' says Coleridge.

Morrow coughs and squirms in his chair. 'The plans are missing,' he says so quietly that Will has to strain to listen.

'What? How?' says Eoin.

'Someone broke into my office,' he replies.

'Jesus Christ, man! Why didn't you lock them up?'

'I did! Everything was secured. I followed all protocols.'

A flush of heat storms through Will's body. 'My friends died for those plans!'

Morrow straightens, his lips purse. 'I followed protocol,' he says again.

'Where were they?' asks Eoin.

Morrow says nothing.

'He locked them in his desk,' says Coleridge.

Eoin slams his hand on the table. 'How is that following protocol? Why didn't you just post them direct to VIPER HQ, love from Nick with a big kiss! You could have saved the thieves some bother.'

Morrow's eyes flare. 'How dare you! I warned you not to trust the Owl. Nothing good will come of anything to do with him.'

Will can see Eoin's fists balling.

'Will and Anna,' says Coleridge, 'I'd like you to look into this break in. Nicholas give them access to all areas.'

'Yes, Sir Hugh.'

'What's done is done. However there will be repercussions.'

Will notices Morrow's face drop.

'Let's move on. Next on the agenda,' says Coleridge.

Morrow holds a manila file in his hands. 'We have reason to believe VIPER spies have infiltrated the Secret Service.' Morrow glances at Will through hooded eyes and suddenly it dawns on him what Morrow's problem is. He thinks Will is the VIPER spy.

Morrow continues. 'One of our agents has been tailing a VIPER spy. Someone known to all of us: a Beaulieu alumni and resident of Wandsworth Prison, until recently.'

Will's interest is piqued. It must be Horne. Was he about to be given the chance to search for him and get his revenge for Sam?

'Rupert Van Horne was spotted in Manchester two days ago. We were alerted by the local constabulary. We sent an agent to investigate but he was murdered before he left London.'

'How was he killed?' asks Eoin.

'His car was planted with a Rolling Ticker.'

'What's a Rolling Ticker?' asks Will.

'An incendiary device fixed to a car. It kicks in when the car engine starts and blows when it stops.'

'A vile VIPER invention,' says Coleridge.

'What about Horne?' asks Anna.

'We don't know. We assume he is still in Manchester, or has moved on.'

Morrow consulted his folder again. 'It seems likely that someone within our ranks knew and either leaked the information or carried out the deed themselves. Either way, we need someone to go to Manchester immediately to see if Horne is still there.'

'I'd like to go,' says Will.

'I understand your feelings about Horne, Will, but I need you to investigate the breach of security at Nicholas's office,' says Coleridge. He looks to Eoin. 'Could you head up there, old boy?'

Will conceals his disappointment and notices Eoin seems surprised.

'Of course. I will drive up there today.'

'Thank you all. That will do for today.' With some effort, Coleridge stands and rests on his stick. He seems to be in pain. 'Report back to me, all of you, as soon as you have news.'

Everyone stands and turns to leave.

'Nicholas, please remain seated. You and I have not finished.'

Will watches Morrow's face pale.

'Yes, of course, Sir Hugh.'

CHAPTER 20

The Rolling Ticker

Outside the hotel, Eoin pulls Will and Anna to one side. 'There was something I wanted to bring up at the meeting, but Sir Hugh overruled me. He did not think it was important. I ... disagree.' Eoin looks at Will. 'My contact at Bletchley Park has acquired some intelligence that you should be aware of...' the Irishman hesitates. 'It's about your sister.'

Will feels the blood drain from his face. 'Is she dead?' he asks.

'All we know is that the Russians have despatched one of their most elite spies to find her.'

'She must be alive then.'

'One must assume they have information that we don't.'

Will feels his gut churning. 'Why do they want her? What is she to them?'

'My guess is that Rose is more valuable than any of us imagined.'

Will processes what Eoin has told him. He has worried about Rose for the past two years. He has waited and waited for news but to his frustration nothing has ever come; not one tiny bit of covert intelligence that might lead to finding her. In his darkest moments he has thought she might be dead, perhaps overcome by the demands of her oppressive captors, and therefore there was no intelligence to report. She was, after all, just a child. He feels a surge of resentment. So it seems the Russians are ahead of them and have acquired VIPER intelligence on Rose. Eoin's news both appalls and fuels him. He is relieved that she may still be alive, however, the truth is he feels completely powerless and even more anxious. Not only is she at danger from VIPER, but now from the Russians too.

'It's fair to say we are on the same side,' says Eoin. 'We're allies. However, as far as the Russians are concerned, Rose is part of VIPER. They are unaware of her history and probably wouldn't care much if they did know.'

'Do we know anything about this agent, or even where he is?' asks Anna.

'We only know him by the name Sedova. He is in the field right now but that could be anywhere, even here in London. We are looking into it. We'll find him, I promise.'

'Do you know what he looks like?' asks Will.

'We only know his second name. Nothing else. Our people are looking for whatever they can find. Hugh and I will keep you up to date.'

Will and Anna say their goodbyes to Eoin. Before he leaves he tosses something to Will. It is the key for the Embiricos.

'Look after her for me. I'm going underground and don't want her blowing my cover.'

As Will drives Anna, Daisy and Alice back to Puddle Dock and

Morrow's office, he barely notices the Embiricos or the conversation; his mind is focused on the Russian agent, Sedova. So many questions fly through his mind: why is he looking for Rose? What do the Russians want with her? Could they be working with VIPER, or like him, are they against them? The Russians may be allies yet everyone knows the Secret Service does not trust them. Whatever the answers, Will has to assume that the threat to Rose has doubled. Nothing will stop him in his efforts to bring down VIPER, but at the same time, he must do whatever it takes to find Rose before the Russians do. He doesn't know what to expect from this agent Sedova, but he has no doubt their paths will cross.

'Are you with us, Will?' asks Anna, interrupting his thoughts.

'I'm sorry. I was miles away.'

'Come back to us!' calls one of the twins. Which one, he has no idea. He glances in the rear-view mirror at the two guards.

'Daisy,' he says.

The twin sitting on the left behind Anna, looks up and smiles.

'Alice.'

'Present,' says the twin behind him.

Traffic stops at the lights and Will looks closely at the two of them. They are so alike, they are almost indistinguishable. Both faces are round and freckly, the lips thin and noses long. Daisy, however, seems to have more of an abundance of freckles around her nose.

'Morrow's really in the dog house, isn't he?' says Daisy.

'I think so,' says Will.

'It's that film Eoin brought, isn't it?' says Alice.

'Yes.'

'The Tesla Death Ray,' says Daisy.

'What's that noise?' says Alice.

'How do you know about the Tesla Death Ray?' asks Will.

'We developed the film,' says Daisy.

Will catches Alice's expression. She is frowning, clearly thinking hard about something.

Anna turns to the twins. 'Did you see the plans?'

'Of course. We studied them at length.'

'But Morrow said he locked them away,' says Will. He turns on to the Embankment and glances over at the Thames on his right side. The waters are murky and rippling from the wake of the boats going about their journeys.

'He locked away his copy. Not ours.'

'You have a copy?' asks Will.

'We weren't going to trust that idiot, boss or no boss.'

'Daisy, Alice, you are amazing! We need to see those plans.'

'We thought you'd ask. When we get back to the office we'll show you.'

Will shifts gears and presses the accelerator.

'I can still hear it,' says Alice.

'Hear what?' says Daisy.

Up ahead Will sees the traffic lights turn red.

'Listen,' says Alice.

The Embiricos purrs along the Embankment and no one says anything as they listen. There is a ticking sound. Will's throat dries and he looks at Anna. Her face is ashen. Glancing in the rear-view mirror, he sees the twins, their eyes wide with the realisation that the Embiricos has a Rolling Ticker fixed underneath.

There are many people around and the traffic slows for the lights. He beeps the horn in a vain attempt to move things along, but the traffic ahead is obstructed by a bus, which is hogging the lane.

'We have to get out of here,' says Anna.

Will knows this but does not respond. He listens carefully to the noise and swallows when he hears the ticking slow as he eases gently on the brakes to avoiding hitting the car in front.

'Don't slow!' shouts Alice. 'When the ticking stops, the car will blow.'

'We're in a bit of a jam – pardon the pun,' says Will as he focuses on the car ahead, trying to keep enough distance between them without being forced to stop. The traffic light goes green and the cars and buses begin to move.

Now is the time.

'All of you. Get out of the car. Jump!' shouts Will.

'Will…' says Anna.

'Just do it. Go. I will think of something.'

The doors fly open and Anna, Daisy and Alice scramble out as the Embiricos rolls slowly forward with the rest of the traffic. Focusing on the road ahead, with his foot resting lightly on the accelerator, Will prays the cars in front will not stop, but the sudden glare of the red traffic light makes his stomach lurch. He sees a gap in the cars on the opposite lane and swings the Embiricos across, blasting the horn and trying his best to avoid the pedestrians who leap out of his way. He crashes through the iron barrier. The bank is almost six feet below. He throws open the door mid-air, leaps from the driver's seat and falls on his hands and knees onto the wet shingle. Scrambling to his feet, he hears the Embiricos crash behind him. He hurries up the bank to get as far away as he can, but the car blows in a mighty blast that lifts him off his feet. He lands face first in the mud.

His heart pounding, he pulls himself up and looks back at the Embiricos. Fire rages inside where, only moments back, he, Anna,

Daisy and Alice had sat. He shudders. The windows have blown and flames lick and slap hungrily at the car's body, charring and blistering the fine silver paint. Smoke rises in black clouds. Once again, he has survived but he cannot help feel a pang of regret that he will never drive the extraordinary Embiricos again.

'Will?' he hears Anna call.

Anna, Daisy and Alice are looking down at him. A crowd has gathered on the pavement around them. There is rusty iron ladder fixed to the wall. He climbs up.

'Are you hurt?' asks Anna.

He is shaken, but does not say anything. In the distance he hears a police siren. 'I'm fine. The police will be here soon. We should get away.'

They push their way through the thickening crowd and hurry on foot.

'Without stating the obvious, that was rather close,' says Alice.

'Someone wants you dead,' says Daisy.

'Many people want me dead, but that bomb was not meant for us. It was for Eoin.'

'We need to warn him,' says Anna.

'He's not going to be happy when he discovers what's happened to his beautiful car,' says Alice.

'At least he's alive,' says Daisy.

'For now,' says Will. 'This is only the beginning.'

CHAPTER 21

A Nest of VIPER Spies

When they finally reach the office at Puddle Dock, Will watches Daisy and Alice pull their desks apart and unscrew a section from one of the floorboards. Underneath is a safe. Alice turns the dial and takes out folded sheets of paper the size of a book. Block letters at the top left of the paper say: TESLA PARTICLE BEAM DEATH RAY.

At the heart of the schematic is a diagram of a tall pyramidal shaft with a sphere on top. Inside both parts are various electrical circuits and some pipework. There are callouts with descriptors and numbers but none of it makes any sense.

'What do you make of it?' asks Anna.

'Alice is a bit of an electronics buff,' says Daisy. 'She's the brains; I'm the beauty.'

'I think you'll find I'm both,' says Alice, her tone playful.

'It doesn't look like a weapon,' says Will.

'I think this is only one part of a greater schematic.' She points to the base of the pyramid. 'These pipes and circuits lead on to something else.'

'What could that be?'

Alice shrugs. 'Possibly another one of these things, or perhaps the death ray itself.'

'Is this diagram of any value then?'

'Absolutely it is. We just need another pair of eyes. Obviously someone technical who understands this kind of thing.'

'I know someone,' says Anna, reaching for the phone on Alice's desk. 'I'll call him now.'

Alice takes the receiver from Anna and puts a finger to her mouth. 'All of our phones are being listened in on.'

'By who?'

'The Secret Service, of course. We trust no one. Not even our own people. Wait until we leave and use a call box.'

Will folds up the schematic. Anna takes it from him and puts it inside her purse.

'This is hot stuff, isn't it?' asks Daisy.

'Yes, it is,' says Will.

'I assume it is why Eoin's car was rigged?'

'Yes.'

The phone on Alice's desk rings suddenly. Neither Daisy nor Alice moves.

'Shouldn't you answer it?' asks Will.

Alice picks up the phone. 'Good afternoon. Minimax Fire Extinguishers,' she says in a jolly tone. 'Oh, hello, Sir Hugh … Oh my!' Alice's expression darkens. 'Mr Morrow has been arrested! Why…?'

Will and Anna exchange worried glances.

'I'm afraid I don't know where Mr Heaney is … Will and Anna…?' Alice looks to Anna and Will and Will shakes his head.

'No. They have just left … They found nothing … There's nothing here … Yes, of course, we will try and find them … I'm so sorry to hear about Mr Morrow … None of us is safe, that is true … Goodbye.'

Alice places the receiver down. 'Morrow was the VIPER mole. He's been arrested. Sir Hugh sounds in such a state. He doesn't know who to trust. He said that Puddle Dock is a high-risk location and we should leave immediately. He thinks Morrow might have other secrets hidden here.'

'I doubt that,' says Daisy. 'Yet, to be honest, I'm really surprised. I did not believe Morrow had it in him to be a double agent. Puzzling.' She walks into Morrow's office, folds her arms and looks out the window. 'They're here.'

'Who?' says Alice.

Daisy snorts. 'Four men, dressed as fishermen, wearing thick jumpers with neatly ironed trousers and brand new shoes. Amateurs! I don't recognise any of them and none of them look like they've done a day's fishing in their lives. They're watching the building.'

'VIPER,' says Will. He sidles into the office and, keeping out of sight, looks through the window. He sees the four men on the jetty. Beyond them, moored to the quay, is Skipper's boat, *The Outcast*.

'Coleridge wants us to take you in,' says Daisy.

'That won't be necessary.'

Daisy looks at him with a frown and, for a moment, Will thinks she might just try.

'Daisy,' says Anna, 'we have to leave. The Secret Service has become a nest of VIPER spies. We can trust no one.'

'Anna is right, Daisy,' says Alice. 'The best thing we can do is help Will and Anna get out of here and keep our heads down.'

Daisy shifts uneasily before nodding and rubbing her palms together. 'We must do this.'

'Good. We need a plan,' says Will. 'How are you all fixed for weapons?'

'I am a walking armoury,' says Alice.

'Me too,' says Daisy.

'Me three,' says Anna.

'Good. Is there another way out of here?'

'That might not be an option,' says Daisy. 'Two of our fishing friends are on the move. They're coming up. You two stay in here. Alice and I will take care of them.'

Daisy shuts Morrow's door behind them and Will and Anna stand on either side of it, their backs to the wall, listening. Will hears the scraping of chairs on floorboards followed by the furious fake tapping of Daisy's and Alice's fingers on their typewriters.

Then he hears the door being kicked open.

The typing stops and he hears the thudding of two bodies falling to the wooden floor. His heart sinks. He removes his Mauser from the holster and watches Anna as she retrieves the Walther from her purse.

Footsteps approach the door of Morrow's office. Will moves away from the wall and gets ready to fire.

'You can come out now,' comes a voice. It's Alice.

Will and Anna breathe a sigh of relief. Opening the door, Will sees Daisy and Alice drag the unconscious bodies of the two men away from the entrance. He wonders how they went down so quickly and then sees a steel dart lodged in one of their necks, 'Velo-Darts.'

'Life savers,' says Daisy.

Alice has found some rope and they all work together to tie the two men securely.

'They'll be out for a few hours at least,' says Alice.

'We need to hurry before the other two get suspicious,' says Will. 'Daisy and Alice, there is a boat outside called *The Outcast*. Take it and get away from here. Perhaps go to Beaulieu until we figure this out.'

'We can come with you,' says Alice.

'We need to get away from those men. It would be safer if we split up.'

Daisy and Alice agree and Will and Anna lead the way cautiously down the wide concrete steps, Mauser and Walther at the ready.

Will peers through the exit door, down towards the jetty. There is no sign of the men. Glancing to the other side, he sees it is clear. He beckons to Daisy and Alice who hurry through and run down the jetty to *The Outcast*. He watches Alice untie the boat and waits until he sees it reverse and move safely away.

'Let's go,' he says, wondering where on earth the other two men are.

They hurry up the narrow path between the ruins of the old warehouse and the building that contained Morrow's office. Glancing back, he is relieved to find they are not being followed. They turn the corner, and immediately collide with the two men, who reach under theirs jumpers for guns. Before they can aim, Will and Anna work as if on the same wavelength, delivering unforgiving kicks to each man's groin.

The men's faces contort in pain and they slump forward. Anna slams her purse down on her assailant's head. He grunts and falls to the ground, his gun slipping from his grip. She kicks it into the gutter and out of reach.

Will's assailant has managed to take out his gun but pain has made him clumsy and slow. Will grabs his arm, pointing the gun in the air. A shot rings out, followed by a second.

Anna kicks the man twice in the ribs and Will, his teeth gritted, slams his arm back with all his might until he hears a bone crunch. The man screams, dropping the gun to the ground. Will picks it up and shoots him in the chest.

'Run, Anna,' he says.

Anna runs away from warehouse and on into the centre of the road dodging the traffic and ignoring the blare of car horns. Will follows her, holding the pistol pointing down at the ground. Anna's man is hobbling after them, his face red. The traffic is thinning out and speeding up. Will sees a bus ahead of them and Anna is sprinting towards it. She leaps onto the platform and spins round, holding the post and reaching out to Will with her free hand. He grabs her hand and hauls himself onto the bus. The man is now running to catch up with them. Will raises the pistol and points it at their pursuer who is only feet away. 'You get to live today,' he shouts. 'Tell your masters I am coming for them.'

The man stops running and stands in the middle of the road, catching his breath. Will watches him get smaller as the bus gathers speed.

CHAPTER 22

Edward and Clifford

The bus takes them as far as Fleet Street, where they dismount. Anna finds a phone box and Will watches over her, his eyes profiling every passer-by, from the shadows of St Bride's Church. Anna is deep in conversation, her face turned away from view. She puts the receiver down and then picks it up and dials again.

Why is she calling someone else?

Moments later she steps out of the box and makes her way towards Will. She seems agitated and does not meet his gaze. 'He's agreed,' she says.

'Good.'

'He said he owes you. You saved his life.'

Will isn't used to praise or compliments and does not know what to say. He shrugs. 'It will be good to see him again.'

Anna flags down a black taxi and they climb inside. 'Euston Station, please.'

'Right ya be,' says the driver.

The *he* in question is Edward Simms, Will's overweight, frightened ex-room-mate and reluctant friend from Beaulieu. He had last seen him two years before when Will, Anna and Edward had escaped the terrible siege of Beaulieu, pursued by the agents of VIPER. Will's plan had been to go to London and stop the Stones of Fire decimating the capital, but, at the last minute, Edward had lost his nerve and run off into the night. But it was Edward's breaking of the code that had helped save them all.

He had seen him briefly one more time at the memorial service for the pupils and staff killed during the siege. Will had wanted to thank him for his help, but Edward had avoided him and Will recalled a haunted look on his face – was it guilt or fear? He could not discern. It didn't matter anyway. Edward did not have the mettle to be a killer, or a spy. There was no shame in that. He had other skills and they needed him more than anyone else now.

In the taxi, Will senses that Anna is distant. She is quiet, seeming to prefer to look out the window rather than talk.

'Is everything alright?'

'I'm fine,' she says, without looking at him.

The driver pulls up at Euston Station and Anna pays him. Will steps out and scours the area for signs of a threat but the station is quiet with just a handful of people around. Anna loops her arm into his and they walk towards the ticket office, smiling and casual on the outside but alert and ready to kill on the inside.

The ticket office is a stuffy, warm, square, wooden room painted a pale green and smelling of stale cigarette smoke and bleach. There is a small window with a ticket agent seated behind it and another larger window looking out on to the concourse and platform entrances.

'Two second class tickets for Bletchley,' says Will.

'Next train is noon,' the ticket agent tells them.

Anna goes to stand at the bigger window, watching the concourse outside.

'Anyone we need to watch out for?' Will says.

'It seems clear to me.'

The station clock says 11.55, so they hurry to the platform, board the train, find a quiet carriage and sit opposite each other by the window.

Anna still seems distant and preoccupied and Will does not know what to make of it. He thinks back to anything he might have said or done that was out of turn, but he can think of nothing.

The guard's whistle blows and the train begins its journey.

'Anna…'

She looks at him with a pained expression and opens her mouth to speak just as the carriage door swings open and a couple of about their age fall inside giggling to each other.

''Ere, don't mind us,' says the young woman.

Anna smiles politely and the two lovebirds sit next to her, huddled together petting and kissing.

Will leans forward. 'Anna, talk to me.'

'Not now,' she replies, head bowed and eyes down.

Will sighs heavily, sits back, folds his arms and tries to sleep. He has no idea what is going on in Anna's head and wishes he didn't care. After all, she is someone else's problem now, not his.

An hour later the train stops at Bletchley station. The young couple had left at the previous stop leaving an awkward silence between Will and Anna. He still has no clue what is troubling her.

They step onto the platform, the guard already blowing the whistle to encourage passengers to board quickly, as the train is about to leave.

At one end of the platform two men are looking back at them. One of them seems familiar.

'Will, I'm sorry. I've been a fool.'

'Anna, what's the matter?'

'He's here. At Bletchley.'

Will frowns. 'Who…? Edward?'

'No … Yes …' She sighs. 'Someone else…'

'Darling!' comes a voice.

Will turns to see one of the men hurrying towards them, his eyes only on Anna. Anna smiles and opens her arms and the man pulls her close, kissing her full on the lips. They hold each other.

Will cannot take his eyes off them. He swallows and feels himself go cold.

He takes stock of Anna's lover. He is tall, square-jawed with high cheekbones and slick blond hair. He is dressed in a smart, expensive, blue suit.

Extracting himself from Anna's embrace, the man turns to Will. 'And you must be the famous Will Starling, returned from the dead.' He extends his hand. Will hesitates and then lifts his hand slowly.

'Clifford Meadows,' Anna's man says ebulliently, shaking Will's hand. His grip is at odds with his enthusiasm. It is non-committal, his skin soft. 'So good to meet you. Anna never stops talking about you. At times I thought I would never win her heart. But I did!'

Will glances at Anna, who seems mortified.

'I do believe you know our resident genius.' Meadows tugs his hand from Will's and gestures at the other man.

'Hello, Will.'

Standing beside Meadows is a smiling Edward Simms. Not the

round, awkward sixteen-year-old; this Edward is two years older, slimmer and more confident.

Will smiles. 'Edward, I didn't recognise you.'

'I've been learning to box, and I've been running. With Cliff.'

'Clifford,' corrects Meadows. 'He's quite the sprinter. He's beaten me a few times.'

Edward beams at Meadows and blushes. 'I got lucky, Cliff ... Clifford, you know that.'

'We should get some lunch,' says Meadows, 'and you can tell us exactly why you are here.'

'We don't have much time,' says Will. 'It's Edward we need to see.'

'All in good time, old boy. Besides, I have not seen my girl in weeks and I bet she has missed me terribly.' Meadows puts his arm around Anna and leads her out of the station.

Edward watches them walk away with a sullen look on his face.

'How is life at Bletchley?' asks Will, as they follow Anna and Meadows across the road.

'Terrific. Exciting. We're doing some incredible work. Cliff is wonderful, too. Don't you think?'

'Is he?'

'He's so clever and funny. He does make me laugh. Even Alan thinks so.'

'Alan?'

'Alan Turing. He's our mentor. A great man.'

Will is keen to bring the conversation to the point.

'Edward...'

'Call me Eddie. Everyone does.'

'I thought you hated that name.'

'Cliff uses it all the time and it just stuck. Now everyone calls me that and I like it. Cliff and Eddie. It has a ring to it, don't you think? Cliff seems to think so.'

Will does not respond. His eyes follow the slick, blond hair and expensive suit of the man who has captured Anna's heart – and Edward's too, it seems.

Bletchley Park is opposite the railway station, an immense Victorian Gothic house set in almost six hundred acres of land where rows and rows of huts had been built for the encryption experts, analysts and mathematicians to work in. Meadows signs them in through the heavily secured gates and then leads the way towards the staff canteen in the main house. The interior walls are panelled in dark wood, and accusing eyes stare from the grim portraits that dominate the walls. The canteen is buzzing with activity. There is a strong aroma of meat stew and hot tea in the air.

'The place is quite something, isn't it?' says Meadows. 'Look around. Where else would you find so many boffins and debutantes in one place?'

'Is there somewhere quieter we can go?' asks Will.

Meadows gently punches Will's arm. 'I would never have put you down for such a stiff. Let's eat.'

Will has to bite his tongue. He looks at Anna, who mouths a sorry to him.

They find a table to themselves. Will and Anna have no appetite and choose a mug of tea each. Meadows and Edward tuck into the stew.

'Terrible news about Morrow, eh?' says Meadows, slurping his food, 'and the Irishman. What's his name?'

Will sits up, his stomach tightening.

'Eoin Heaney?' says Anna.

'That's the fella.'

'What about him?' asks Will.

'He came a cropper this morning. Someone planted a Rolling Ticker in his car. Terrible waste…'

Will and Anna exchange glances but say nothing.

'…I always liked that car,' adds Meadows, with a snorting laugh.

'Cliff!' says Anna. 'Eoin was our friend.'

Will grits his teeth, stares at Meadows' throat and imagines planting his fist in it, right here and now.

Meadows raises his arms in an apologetic gesture. 'Bad taste, I know. I'm sorry.'

An awkward silence hangs over the table for the remainder of lunch. Eventually Meadows breaks it. 'Let's go to my office. We can discuss what you need there.'

Leaving the canteen, Meadows and Edward guide them through the wooden huts and cabins where the code breakers work. Meadows' office sits among a block of huts at the rear of the main house. Inside, it is sparse and neat, containing a small desk with a stack of worn notebooks. There is a map of Europe on the wall and a window overlooking a gravel path.

Meadows sits down at the desk, leans back and rests his feet on the desktop. 'Now, how can we be of assistance?'

Will thrusts his hands in his pockets and curls his fists. There is something about Meadows he doesn't like. Is he jealous?

'Could we speak to Edward? Alone?'

'Sorry, old man. Eddie is my responsibility. There are no secrets between us,' he replies, winking at Edward, who blushes in response.

Will hesitates. He really wants to tell Meadows to clear off but doesn't want to risk upsetting Anna or Edward. Besides, they need answers quickly.

As if sensing his reluctance, Anna says, 'Will, you can trust Clifford.'

Will meets Meadows' gaze and for a second sees his eyes flare. Perhaps Will's hesitation has offended him. All eyes look towards Will and after a moment he relents. He takes out the schematic and unfolds it on the desk.

They all crowd around it.

'This is a diagram for the Tesla Death Ray,' says Will.

'Very interesting,' says Edward. 'Is it operational?'

'We don't know.'

'Where did you get this?' says Meadows.

'That's not important,' replies Will.

'What can you tell us about it?' Anna asks Cliff and Edward.

Meadows and Edward pore over the schematic. Edward keeps having to push his spectacles up as they slip down his nose.

'What exactly do you want to know?' asks Meadows.

'How does it work? Are there any weak points? Can we destroy it?'

Meadows snorts. 'There is very little here to go by.'

'I don't know,' says Edward. 'It would be helpful to see the actual weapon, however, what we have here is arguably more useful.' Edward says nothing for a moment as he studies the schematic.

Will leans in, hungry for information. 'Tell us, Edward.'

Edward places his finger on the pyramidal base. 'This is the link between the weapon and the power source. The power is somehow contained in the sphere. Destroy the pyramid and you break the link. Destroy the sphere and you destroy not just the weapon but much more. That is my assumption. What do you think, Clifford?'

Meadows looks at the diagram through lidded eyes. 'It's possible,' he mumbles.

'What can power something like this?' asks Will.

'There may be some sort of generator, which would need to be immense. That suggests to me the weapon is not transportable but is at a fixed spot.'

Will feels a surge of excitement. 'So, if the weapon is operational then all we need to do is find the power source and destroy it somehow?'

'Is there any clue about how we might do that?' Anna asks.

'There's nothing obvious from the diagram. I will need time to study it a bit more. However, this is an unconventional weapon and I have no doubt it will be very difficult to disable never mind destroy.'

'How much time do you need?'

'A day, maybe less.'

'Can you do it quicker?'

'I'll try … Oh, I have something for you.' Edward removes a photograph from his jacket pocket and gives it to Will. 'Eoin sent me this. It's a close up of the serial code from one of the gas bombs on Westminster Bridge.'

'You never mentioned this!' says Meadows, clearly rattled.

'It was information given out on a need to know basis. If something happened to Eoin then I was to tell Will or Anna. Those were his orders. He asked me to find out what I could about the serial code. From my research I was able to determine that the bomb was manufactured in a plant situated in the Swiss Alps.' He points to the schematic on the desk. 'Look, the same number is on the bottom right here.'

Meadows takes out a silver case and lights up a cigarette. Smoke surrounds him, filling the air.

'The plant is owned by the Teleken Black Corporation,' says Edward.

'It's owned by the Black family,' says Anna, 'one of the richest families in the world. They manufacture all sorts of weapons. The war has made them even more powerful and wealthy than they were before.'

'Teleken are also funded by VIPER. I think we have our strongest lead yet. Great work, Edward,' says Will.

Edward smiles and shrugs.

Will takes out the paper from his blazer pocket and gives it to Edward. 'There's something else. I need you to decode this.'

Edward studies it and Meadows stands over him, his brow furrowed, smoke streaming from his flared nostrils.

'We have a new super-machine. It's called Colossus. I can run it through that. What do you think, Cliff ... ord?'

'Where did this come from?' asks Meadows, ignoring Edward.

'I can't tell you that,' says Will.

Meadows scratches an eyebrow and smiles a hard smile. Will can feel the distance between them growing wider, but doesn't care. It might be jealousy. Or it might be something more. He can't be sure.

'Clifford, I can run to Colossus and sort this out,' says Edward.

Meadows smiles. 'Of course. We're all here to do our bit for the war. You run ahead, Eddie, and I'll look after our guests. I'll make a quick call to the Machine Room and tell them you're coming.'

'Thanks, Cliff,' says Edward.

'Clifford!'

'Erm ... sorry,' he says, turning to leave.

'One more thing,' says Will, taking Edward to one side and out of earshot. 'Did Eoin mention anything about a Russian agent called Sedova?'

'Yes. He asked me to find out whatever I could about him.'

'What did you discover?'

'Not as much as I'd like. His name is Pyotr Sedova. He worked for the Russian secret police. He was married to Inga and they had two daughters – Anastasiya and Elena. One day his family were sent to a gulag. No one knows why. They spent two months doing hard labour and then suddenly they were released. After that, Pyotr went missing. It's possible he negotiated their freedom in exchange for doing the Russian government's dirty work.'

'I don't suppose we have a description?'

'I'm afraid not.'

'What are you two chatting about?' asks Anna.

'I'll tell you later,' says Will, aware that Meadows is leaning across his desk and trying to listen in.

Meadows looks at Anna. 'Darling, why don't you and Will wait outside and get some air. I'll be with you in a second.' He kisses Anna brusquely on the cheek.

Will and Anna follow Edward out and stand outside watching him hurry off to the Machine Room. Will glances through the office window and sees Meadows putting down the phone receiver.

'I'm sorry about Cliff. He can be a bit territorial. What do you think of him?' asks Anna.

Before Will can answer Meadows appears and seems in happier mood. 'I left a message for Edward telling him to meet us at the Eight Bells.'

'I'd rather stay here and wait,' says Will.

'Let's go have a pint and get to know one another. I fear we may have got off on the wrong foot.'

'That's a nice idea, darling,' says Anna. 'Come on, Will. I could do with a drink after what we have been through.'

'Come on, old man,' says Meadows. 'I'll drive us and I'm paying!'

Will shrugs and agrees for Anna's sake.

'Eddie can meet us there, once he's decoded the cipher.'

Meadows' car is a striking red Alfa Romeo sports car with four seats. He winds down the roof and offers Will the front passenger seat. 'Let's talk as I drive.'

Will frowns at Anna who shrugs and climbs into the back.

Meadows starts up the car, spinning the wheels too fast, and flies out of Bletchley and through the security gates. 'A lovely mover, the Alfa Romeo, but not a patch on the Embiricos. I had my eye on that for a while. Damn shame.'

Will wonders what he means by that, but doesn't press it.

They drive through the country roads, the sun beating down their faces, the wind blowing through their hair. Will is actually enjoying the ride. Meadows slows as they approach a junction. Looking for traffic on either side, he moves forward to the centre of the junction but the engine cuts out.

'Bloody thing!' says Meadows. He hops out and tries to open the bonnet.

'Will, could you turn the engine over when I say so?'

Meadows lifts the bonnet. 'Darling, could you hold this open for me while I try and fix this blasted thing.'

Anna gets out and holds open the bonnet.

'Turn her over now!' calls Meadows.

Will leans across and turns the ignition key, but nothing sparks.

'Keep turning!' calls Meadows.

The engine is churning and choking and making quite a racket. Above the din, Will hears Anna call his name. There is something about the tone of her voice that makes him sit up straight. She is screaming at the car. In his peripheral vision is a large shadow. He turns. Hurtling towards him is another car. He thinks he sees a hooded figure at the wheel, the face almost visible. He lifts his arms to protect his head as the car smashes into the side of Alfa Romeo.

Everything goes black.

CHAPTER 23

The Red Storm is Coming

Will wakes to a blinding headache and aching ribs and muscles. Groaning, he blinks open his eyes and shuts them quickly as bright light dazzles them, doubling the pain in his head. He is lying cheek down on cold dusty wooden floorboards in a strange room. His hands and feet are tied, secured with some sort of rough cord. He tugs and pulls but the cord is tight. His blazer has been removed and he cannot feel the comfort of the Mauser strapped to his chest. He is helpless. He recalls the last few moments before everything went blank: Meadows' car breaking down at the junction, another car speeding towards them. A hooded figure. A face…

He takes a few deep breaths and lets his eyes adjust to the light. The room is small, square in shape, with low ceilings: a room in a cottage. It seems soulless and devoid of any human touches, as if no one lives here. There is a window with the curtains drawn and a table where his and Anna's pistols and jackets lie. Lying on the floor next to the table is Anna. She is staring at him, her eyes wide with concern.

'Are you hurt?' he mouths.

She shakes her head and he is relieved she is unharmed. He hears voices and twists his head to look in their direction. The door is partially open and he can see a hooded monk, dressed in black robes with a red trim on the cuff of his sleeves. A memory stirs: a name. He has seen those robes before. The man underneath them is no ordinary monk. He is the head of the Cerastes. Proatheris! His name is Proatheris and he is holding the schematic and talking to someone. Will sits up to get a better view, ignoring the stabbing pain in his head and his protesting bruised muscles. He sees the monk pointing aggressively at Meadows' chest. Meadows is nodding.

'If I had a lot of money I would have gambled all of it on you being a treacherous VIPER swine,' Will shouts.

Proatheris and Meadows turn to look at him. Will narrows his gaze at the shadowy hood and tries to pick out the face but Meadows frowns and shuts the door. He wonders if he imagined seeing the monk's face before he blacked out, as he cannot, for the life of him, remember who it was he saw.

The two men walk further away and Will hears a door open and close. Then, outside, a car door opens then closes too. An engine starts up and he hears the sound of the car driving away.

Another door closes, which he guesses is the front door of the cottage. There are footsteps in the hallway. The door to the room swings opens and Meadows stands for a moment, framed in the doorway. Then he approaches Will, crouches down, reaches across and pulls Will's hair up so that their faces are inches apart.

Will grits his teeth.

'I now have the great privilege of torturing you to find out what you know and who you have spoken to. Both of you,' he adds, glancing at Anna. 'Sorry, darling. This is not quite what I had in mind for us, but hey ho – plans change all the time, do they not?'

Anna glares at him but before she can speak Meadows raises his hand. 'Don't answer that. It's rhetorical.'

Will hears Anna muffle a reply.

'We know nothing,' says Will. 'You'll be wasting your time.'

'You know more than you should already, thanks to that zealous little queer, Simms.'

'Where is Edward?'

'He'll be here soon with whatever he has decoded from Colossus.'

'Then what? Are you going to torture him too.'

'I've thought about it many times. Fantasised in fact. I'll probably just kill him and pin his death on you. One less of his sort in the world can only be a good thing, don't you think?'

Will hears the sound of a different car pulling up outside.

'Talk of the devil,' says Meadows, with a wicked grin.

There is a frantic knock on the door. Meadows removes a handkerchief from his pocket and ties it tightly around Will's mouth, gagging him. He leaves the room, shutting the door behind him.

Will tries to wrestle free of his bonds and sees Anna doing the same. He hears Edward.

'Oh, Cliff. I got your message and then I saw your car! I was so worried.'

'Nothing to worry about, old son. Come in. Will and Anna will be delighted to see you.'

'Where are they?'

'They're a little tied up at the moment. Did you crack the code?'

'Can I see them?'

'If you must…'

And then Will hears something heavy fall to the floor. His heart sinks. He feels sorry for Edward and continues to pull at his bonds until the door swings open. Looking up he can't quite believe his eyes. Edward is staring down at him. *How can this be?* Edward hurries towards him and, with a penknife, cuts his gag.

'What did you do?'

'I punched him in the temple. I don't think he was expecting it.'

'Cut the bonds on my wrists,' says Will.

Edward reaches behind Will and begins cutting, but Will hears a roar as Meadows rushes in and pulls Edward away from Will by the collar. The knife slips from Edward's grip and Will catches it with his fingers. Deftly he turns it over and begins sawing at the cord. Edward stumbles and falls on his back and Meadows rains his fists down hard on him.

'You think you are so clever, you duplicitous shit.'

That's rich. Will cuts through the cord and turns the knife towards the bonds on his ankles, but now Meadows sees what he's doing and scrambles from Edward to the table, reaching for the guns on top. Anna slides forward and kicks him with both legs and Meadows falls forward, smashing his nose on the edge of the table. Blood sprays onto the floor.

Free of the bonds, Will leaps to his feet and runs at Meadows who is pulling the Mauser from its holster while Anna continues to kick at his shins. Will wraps one arm around Meadows' throat and grabs the hand holding the pistol. He slams Meadows' hand several times on the table – a bullet fires, blowing a hole in the plaster on the wall. Will squeezes Meadows' neck tighter and the Mauser falls to floor. Meadows makes a choking noise and moments later Will feels his body go limp. He tosses him to the floor in disgust and picks up the Mauser.

Will cuts Anna's bonds; her wrists are red raw.

'I'm so sorry, Will,' she says. 'I trusted him. I feel such a fool.'

Without thinking, he rubs Anna's wrists. 'We're fine. That's the important thing.'

'Edward...' she says.

Edward is on his knees nursing a bleeding nose and one rapidly swelling eye with one hand and putting his twisted spectacles on with the other.

'Edward, you're a bloody hero,' says Will. 'Where did you learn to fight?'

'I told you I'd been boxing,' he says.

Meadows begins to stir, so Will checks his body and pockets for hidden weapons. There is nothing. Will and Anna put on their holsters and jackets as he comes round.

'Get up!' says Will, the Mauser pointing firmly at Meadows' chest.

Meadows pushes himself up and glares viciously at Edward. 'You little bastard. You tricked me.'

'I'm afraid so. I spent a year at Beaulieu and learnt more than just code-breaking, you know. I trained to be a spy. I am a spy. I might not be at Will and Anna's level but I am a spy, nevertheless. We've suspected you for quite some time now. You think you're so clever. I was playing you, getting to know you. Did you not think I could see through your pathetic act?'

Will is quite impressed. 'You fooled me too.'

Edward looks at Anna. 'I'm sorry I couldn't tell you, Anna. Those were my orders.'

'I understand, Edward,' says Anna, brushing the dust from her jacket, her eyes downcast. Will can see she is hurt. It's a double blow: not only was Meadows lying to her, but so were her close colleagues and friends. She stands in front of Meadows.

'How about a tumble for old times' sake?' he says, sneeringly.

What happens next is almost a blur as Anna swings her fist at his face. The force of it lifts him of his feet and he falls back against the wall and slides down to the floor.

'That'll be a no, then,' he mumbles.

Anna rubs her fist and looks at Will. 'We need to lock this vermin away.'

'We can take him to security at Bletchley,' says Edward.

Will grabs Meadows' collar and hauls him up, digging the Mauser into his ribs.

Meadows snorts. 'Why bother? You might as well finish me now. We're all going to die very soon, anyway.'

Will frowns. 'What do you mean?'

'It's coming.'

Will pushes him into the hallway. 'What's coming?'

Meadows looks at him and laughs.

Anna leads the way outside where Edward's car, a green Mosquito Morris Minor is parked. The cottage is isolated, somewhere deep in the countryside. There is a road at the end of the driveway that leads up to the cottage. Will sees a blue car slow and the window wind down. It is dark inside the vehicle. Suddenly rapid gunfire explodes from inside. Edward and Anna are behind the Morris Minor. Anna fires her Walther at the vehicle. Shielded by Meadows, Will fires the Mauser at the blue car but it speeds off and disappears from view. Meadows slumps to the ground, with two bullet wounds in his chest, his breathing laboured.

'You're all going to die,' he mumbles. 'It's coming.'

Will crouches down. 'What's coming?'

'Die ... you're all going to die...'

'What's coming, Meadows? Tell us,' Will says urgently.

'The Red Storm…' Meadows exhales a final breath and then his eyes become glassy and lifeless.

Will feels a chill running through him.

'What does he mean?' asks Edward.

'I still don't know.' But he senses Meadows is telling the truth. Something is coming. Something evil and deadly.

'We should get out of here.'

'There's a tea room just out of town. We can talk there. I'll call security later and they can deal with Meadows,' says Edward.

Will drags Meadows' body back into the cottage.

All their eyes are focussed on the road as Edward drives them through the Buckinghamshire countryside to a sleepy village of thatched cottages with a grocer's, a post office and a café called Betty's Cosy Tea Room.

A bell rings as they enter the café. The tables are neatly laid out and aromas of tea and coffee fill the air. It's not busy. One older gentleman sits reading *The Times* while two ladies stir tea in china cups. No one pays them any unusual attention.

Edward orders three teas and takes them to a table that's quiet and out of earshot at back of the café.

'How is your eye?' Anna asks Edward.

'I'll live.' He hands the original paper with the code across to Will. 'This wasn't as difficult as I thought it might be. I almost cracked it myself, however, Colossus beat me to it.' Edward beams like a proud parent and gives Will a lined sheet of paper torn from a jotter.

Written in Edward's scrawl are four lines of different letters that don't make any sense to Will. Frowning, he looks at Edward. 'I don't understand.'

'The code was created using two different ciphers – hieroglyphics and an advanced pigpen. Let me show you.' Edward begins to sketch a grid on the paper.

'Actually, Edward, perhaps just tell us what it says.'

Edward looks from Will to Anna and back to Will. He smiles and shrugs. 'Sorry, I do get a little carried away sometimes. So, each word is an anagram.' Edward flips the paper over. On the other side are four lines of what seems to be a poem or a riddle.

> *Ares ruin lies hidden far and wide*
> *but the orphan sleeps*
> *where the fledgling knights joust and spar*
> *buried deep in a dungeon black*

'What does it mean?' asks Anna.

'I haven't had time to work that out,' says Edward.

Will turns it over in his head. Ares ruin. The fledgling knights. He knows exactly what it means. He smiles at Anna.

'You know, don't you?' she says.

'You're a bloody hero, Edward!'

Edward shrugs. 'There's just one more thing. The single hieroglyph on the fifth line.'

Will takes a closer look. 'It's a bird.'

'Not just any bird. It's an owl.'

'This message came from the Owl. I assume it is his signature.'

'That's correct. The owl in the Egyptian alphabet translates as M in the English alphabet. I'm not sure if it is important but I thought I'd mention it.'

Will is unsure of what to make of it. 'Thank you, Edward. It might well be important.' He pauses before saying, 'Edward, can we borrow your car?'

'Of course. It's not really mine anyway. It belongs to MI6.'

'I'll drop you back at Bletchley.'

They leave the café and Will gets into the driver's seat of the Morris. He takes Edward back to the front gates of Bletchley. They all get out of the car and Will embraces Edward. 'Thank you, for everything.'

'If you need me, I'll be here.'

Anna hugs Edward warmly.

'I'm sorry about Meadows,' he says.

'I'm not,' she responds, kissing him on the cheek. 'You take care.'

Will starts up the Morris Minor and honks the horn at Edward. As they drive away Will says, 'I'm sorry, too. About him. Meadows.'

'What's done is done. I'm glad it's over.'

'Do you want to continue on this … mission … quest, whatever it is?'

'Yes.'

'I'm glad.'

They say nothing for a moment until Anna changes the subject. 'Where are we going now?'

'We're going back to Beaulieu.'

CHAPTER 24

Return to Beaulieu

Will feels an unnerving sense of nostalgia – a sensation foreign to any amnesiac – at the thought of returning to Beaulieu House, one of the Government's secret residential training facilities for spies. Two years before, when he'd lost his memory, he had found himself at Beaulieu searching for answers about who he was. The masters, including Eoin, and most of the students had welcomed him and had taken him in when he had nowhere else to go. It was also where he and Anna had first met. He has a fondness for the place and in an odd way it feels like he is going home.

Will pulls up at the entrance to Beaulieu where the same old soldier of the Home Guard, Private Tom Fletcher, stands dutifully at the entrance.

'Hello there, young Starling, and Miss Wilder too. This is a nice surprise.'

'Hello, Tom. We're here to see the Major.'

'She's not expectin' any visitors today, but I'm sure she will be pleased to see you two.' Private Fletcher opens the gate.

Will and Anna wave as they drive inside and up the wide winding gravel drive to the imposing stone house, with its stained glass windows and a turret at each side.

The front door opens and a stocky woman with short curly brown hair and wearing a green tweed suits steps outside. It is the principal of the school, Miss Clews, or as she prefers to be known, the Major. She smiles warmly as Will and Anna get out of the car.

'Will Starling,' she says, grabbing his hand and squeezing it. 'I'm so pleased to see you. I had heard ... Well – we thought you were dead.'

'I'm very much alive. It's good to see you, Major.'

The Major embraces Anna and stands back to admire her. 'You look wonderful, dear. Spying clearly suits you. Come to my office, both of you, and tell me why you are here.'

They follow the Major to the Great Hall and along the familiar stone flags through hallways lit with sconces and decorated with educational pictures of aircraft bombers, rifles, pistols.

They pass a common room where several young students lounge on two large leather sofas, poring over their textbooks. They are dressed in the Beaulieu uniform of navy blue blazer with the crest of two crisscrossed pistols with a dagger running through them. All but one of the crests are bronze, which means the students are new. A silver crest is worn by a girl with a strong wiry frame and mousey brown hair cut just below the ears. She looks to be around sixteen years old. She watches Will through narrowed eyes. He slows to a stop, his stomach in knots. It is Kitty from Fenchurch Street in London, the leader of a gang of orphans who were trying to stay alive during the Blitz. Kitty and Sam had been friends and it was because of Will that Sam had been killed.

'Kitty?'

Kitty's eyes flare. She stands, gathers her books and walks out of the common room, passing him without saying a word. Will rubs the back of his head, still not quite believing she is here in Beaulieu. *How did that happen?*

Anna and the Major are at the end of the hallway, standing outside the principal's office, watching him.

'That girl,' says Will. 'How did she come to be here.'

'You mean Kitty? She found us. Just like you did. It has occurred to me that we might not be as secret as we think we are.'

Will wonders if Sam had confided anything about him and his connections to Kitty.

The Major's office is much the same as he remembers. It is a spacious room with maps pinned to the walls, a mahogany leather-topped desk and two threadbare sofas on either side of a small fireplace. On the walls are photographs of the Major driving speeding cars, flying aeroplanes and attending a garden party at the palace with the royal family, the prime minister and Hugh Coleridge. Pride of place in the centre of the wall, is the photo of the Major sitting closely, hand in hand, with a tall handsome woman. They are both smiling.

'How is Miss Davenport?' asks Will.

'She's very well, thank you. Teaching shooting out at the range today. She'll be pleased to see you.'

'I'm afraid we cannot stay very long,' says Anna.

'Oh, that is a shame. So tell me. Why are you here?'

'I need something of Eoin's. Something that once belonged to Timothy Chittlock.'

'I'm afraid Eoin isn't here. I heard this morning he was in the field somewhere.'

'Who told you?'

'I had a telephone meeting with Sir Hugh Coleridge this morning. We are in a dire situation, it seems.'

'Is Eoin in trouble?'

'I'm afraid I don't know.'

'How is Sir Hugh?' asks Anna.

'There have been two attempts on his life, but he is otherwise fine.'

'Where is he now?' asks Will.

'He's in Baker Street. Working long hours trying to put an end to this situation.'

'We should talk to him,' Will says to Anna. 'He…'

The Major looks from Will to Anna with curious eyes. 'Are you going to tell me what this is all about?'

Will and Anna exchange glances and nod an informal agreement. They both know they can trust the Major. Will tells the Major everything up to the point of receiving the decoded message from Edward.

'Well, that's quite a story. Life is never dull with you two, is it? Are you going to tell me what this hidden thing that you want from here is?'

'I can't,' says Will, 'It's just vital we find it and leave without anyone knowing that we've been here. I don't want to put you and the pupils at any risk.'

'*Does* anyone else know you are here?'

'No one. Not even Edward.'

The Major twiddles her thumbs and stares at them, deep in thought. 'I don't like it. I have a feeling that you have put us all in great danger. But you are here now and I can only do what is best for the country.' The Major sighs. 'Where is this thing?'

'It's hidden down in the dungeons.'

'Do you remember the way?'

'Yes.'

'Very well. Come with me.' The Major switches on the desk lamp, stands and draws the curtains hanging at the windows in her office. She walks to the wall where her many photographs hang and pushes a piece of wood panelling level with her waist. The wall opens inwards revealing a dark corridor behind it. A slight breeze of musty damp air cools Will's face.

'You know your way there and out again?'

'We do.'

'Please find whatever it is you need and leave quickly. It'll be dark soon. Good luck, both of you.'

They say their thanks and goodbyes to the Major as Will removes the small torch concealed inside his sleeve and flicks it on. For something so small the beam is indeed wide, as Joseph had claimed. They hurry down damp stone steps and through the dark passages. Grimy cobwebs hang everywhere and brush against their faces and hair. From the other side of the walls they hear the sound of voices and laughter as they pass the various dormitories and classrooms, which invokes in Will another wave of nostalgia. He wonders what it would be like to have all his memories back. Part of him wants to know everything, to remember his family and previous life, but the other part of him wants it to remain dormant. He knows that regaining all his memories would bring grief and even more of the anger that he has since learned to tame. Two years back when he had lost his memory, he was driven by a rage that he could not quite explain. Though he had mastered it, his desire for revenge has never been so great. VIPER would pay for what they had done to his family and his friends, or he would die trying to make them. First, he had to put a stop to their plans for the Tesla Death Ray and whatever the Red Storm was.

Will leads the way into the dungeon where the air becomes significantly colder and the walls are dripping with moisture. The perfect environment to store the unstable artefact that was the fragment from the Stones of Fire

'Did you hear that?' says Anna.

'Hear what?' says Will.

Anna is looking behind her. 'I thought I heard something.'

He shines the torch behind them; it reveals an empty passage.

'Perhaps it was a mouse,' says Will.

Anna removes her Walther from the holster.

Will carries on until he sees the end of the passage and the heavy wooden cell door with its steel reinforcement bands and small barred window.

'There,' he says.

Shining the torch through the window, they peer inside. The cell is bare, as he had left it two years back. Will pushes the cell door, but it does not move. He swears under his breath. How could he be so stupid!

'What is it?' asks Anna.

'Eoin had a key to get into the cell.'

'Perhaps it's hanging up somewhere,' says Anna.

Will runs the beam around the outside of the cell door but there is no key. It was stupid even to think that it might be hanging there.

'Shit!' he says.

And then something heavy slides across the floor and hits his boots. Anna swings her gun behind her as Will peers down at the object. It is a large iron key, the same one Eoin had used to open the cell door.

'You might need that,' comes a voice.

'Stay where you are,' says Anna.

Will shines the torch down the passageway and sees the wiry frame of a Beaulieu student with her hair cut just below the ears. 'Kitty. Is that you?' he says.

The girl turns to leave.

'Kitty, wait.'

She stops.

Will steps towards her. 'How come you have the key?'

Kitty still does not look at him and hesitates before answering. 'I was given a message from Eoin.'

'What did he say? Is he alive?'

'I don't know! He said that if you showed up I was to give you the key. That's it! That's all I know.'

Kitty has not lost any of her attitude. He had always admired her for taking in all of those orphaned boys and ensuring they had a home and were fed.

'What happened to you, and to the others?'

'They were all taken away from me and rehomed, no thanks to you,' she says. 'Except for Sam, of course, who was killed.' She glares at him. 'It's because of you he is dead.'

Kitty's last statement was like a blow to Will's stomach. He feels his mouth dry. He has no words to defend himself because she is right. Will should have done more to protect Sam. But he failed. 'I'm sorry, Kitty.'

A moment passes with nothing more said and then Kitty leaves.

Will feels Anna squeeze his arm. He picks up the key and unlocks the cell door. Without wasting any more time he pulls up the flagstone in the corner of the cell where the fragment is hidden.

Underneath is a shallow hole. From it he lifts an old wooden box and sets it on the table. It looks like something a cobbler might house his tools in.

The box begins to tremble, he hears a humming sound and notices flickering movements as insects begin crawling out from the cell walls. He opens the box and the same unearthly blue light as he has seen before erupts from inside, flooding the cell and the corridor beyond. Will and Anna both raise their hands to shield their eyes from the glare. When his sight adjusts he sees the glowing shard of blue stone, about two inches long.

'It can feel our presence, our energy, our emotions.'

'How dangerous is it?' asks Anna.

'I saw it turn a table to ash in seconds.'

'But how can we use it?'

'I have no clue. Right now I need to learn how to calm it down.'

'How do you do that?'

'Soothe it and stroke it and remain calm, I think. It responds to emotions and violence.'

Will holds the stone between his thumb and index finger. Small lights like miniature fireworks begin sparkling around them, stinging him like tiny electric shocks. He takes three deep breaths and begins to calm himself down as he strokes the fragment. The lights begin to spiral and snake around his hand. They spread up his arm and around his neck and back causing his hairs to stand on end. He gasps and closes his eyes, his thumb running gently over the stone. He feels the tickling sensation subside.

'It's working,' says Anna.

Within moments the fragment has stopped shining and is no longer blue, but an unremarkable shade of grey like any other stone.

It is sleeping. Will does not know how he knows this. It is more like he feels it.

'We should go,' he says, and wonders how he will carry the stone. An idea comes to his head. He takes out the tin fusilier and unscrews the screwdriver from the multi-purpose tool concealed in his left sleeve. He wedges the flat of the tool into the spine of the tin soldier and opens it up. There is just enough room inside to house the fragment. Will places it inside and pushes the two sides of the soldiers back together again.

'Nice idea,' says Anna.

Will places the soldier into his inside breast pocket and buttons it for extra safety.

They leave the passage following a different but still familiar route to the fireplace that leads to the Great Hall. The smell of soot is choking as Will removes a brick and peers through the hole. The Great Hall is empty; the students will be in the mess hall. He pulls the metal catch above his head and the wall turns inwards.

Closing it behind him, Will and Anna hurry outside, dusting the soot from their hands. Standing by the Morris Minor is Kitty.

'Kitty, no one must know we have been here,' says Will.

'I know,' she says.

Will nods his thanks and opens the driver door.

'Make them pay for what they did,' says Kitty, her eyes locking firmly on to Will's.

'I will. I promise.'

Kitty thrusts her hands into her blazer pockets, turns and goes inside.

CHAPTER 25

Moonlight Squadron One

With his hands firmly gripping the steering wheel and his brow furrowed, Will navigates through the Buckinghamshire countryside, his mind fixed on what their next move should be. Should they go to Secret Service HQ in Baker Street or head to Manchester to seek out Eoin?

Anna can sense his agitation. 'We should call Sir Hugh. He can advise us on what to do next.' She is clearly on the same wavelength.

'You're right. Let's find a phone.'

They pass through a small town and park near a telephone box. They both squeeze inside it and Will keeps a lookout as Anna phones Baker Street.

'Hello. Sir Hugh Coleridge, please.'

Will moves his head near to the earpiece so that they can both hear.

The phone rings for a few moments, before a man's voice answers, 'Sir Hugh Coleridge's office.'

'May I speak to Sir Hugh?'

'He's not here. He's not been here in days,' the voice says dryly.

Will and Anna exchange nervous glances.

'Could you give a number or address where I might find him?'

'No. Who is this?'

Will shakes his head.

'Thank you,' says Anna, replacing the receiver. She places her thumbnail in her mouth and bites on it absentmindedly. 'The Major said Sir Hugh was spending all his time in Baker Street. Why would she lie?'

Will scans the street outside. 'I really don't know. Perhaps she didn't.'

'I'll try his home number. He told me to use it if ever we were in trouble.' Anna dials the number and they both listen. After a moment the phone is picked up.

'Hello,' says Sir Hugh's voice.

Will smiles at Anna who sighs with relief. 'Sir Hugh. Thank God.'

There is a hesitation before Coleridge answers. 'Anna?'

'Yes. It's me. It's good to hear your voice. We thought the worst.'

'Is Will with you?'

'Yes, he's here; we are both fine.'

'Marvellous. Where are you? I'll send someone to pick you up.'

'No, don't worry, we have transport. Listen, we have intelligence on VIPER.'

'What intelligence?'

'I'd rather not say on the phone.'

'My line is safe, Anna. Tell me what you know.'

Anna tells him about the schematic, Edward, Meadows and the photograph of the serial number linked to the Teleken Black manufacturing plant in the French Alps. Sir Hugh listens without interrupting.

'You should go there,' he says at last.

'But how?' asks Will.

'I will need to make some calls. Phone me back in ten minutes.'

'Will do.'

They wait outside the phone box, both deep in thought.

'I wonder if we'll need to go tonight,' says Anna.

'It's possible.'

Anna folds her arms and leans against the Morris Minor.

'Are you sure you want to do this?' asks Will.

'We started this together. We'll finish it together.'

Their eyes lock for a moment and then Anna looks away. Something is troubling her. He thinks it might be Meadows and does not press the matter.

Ten minutes later Anna redials Sir Hugh's number. The receiver is picked up and Will hears the scrunching of paper, as if a sheet is being flattened out or held up.

'Will, Anna, can you hear me?' says Sir Hugh.

'We hear you,' replies Anna.

'I've just spoken with Group Captain McFarland at the RAF base in Southend. He is leading a moon squadron into south-west France tonight. I have persuaded him to take both of you with him. He will drop you close to Lyon. Have you had parachute training?'

'Yes,' says Anna.

'Good. Teddy – Captain McFarland – will give you everything you need. How long do you think it will take you to get there?'

'Two hours possibly,' says Will.

'He leaves at midnight. You'd better hurry. Do you know the way?'

'No.'

Will hears paper shaking.

'I have a map. Take the following route…'

Anna pulls a notebook and pencil from her handbag and jots down Sir Hugh's directions.

'Try and get there as quickly as you can. Excellent work both of you and good luck.'

They say their goodbyes and get back into the Morris Minor. Will is relieved and full of renewed determination now that they have a clearer plan ahead.

On what seems like a thimble full of petrol, Will and Anna arrive at Southend airfield fifteen minutes before midnight. There is a runway with a Lockheed Hudson light bomber and two Westland Lysanders. Will pulls the car up alongside a security guard at the airfield gate and winds down the window.

'Group Captain McFarland is expecting us,' says Will, handing across their ID.

'Starling and Wilder. Yes. We were expecting you earlier.'

'This is not the easiest of places to find.'

The guard points to two men standing outside an art deco building near the runway. One is a tall man in a blue pilot's uniform; the other is a dressed in overalls and holding a clipboard. They are deep in discussion.

'Group Captain McFarland in uniform,' says the guard.

'Thank you.'

The guard opens the gate and Will drives the car through, under the watchful gaze of the pilot.

Will gets out of the car and introduces himself and Anna to Group Captain McFarland, a handsome man in his thirties, clean shaven with neatly combed brown hair. 'You're a little late,' he says, frowning.

'I'm sorry, Captain McFarland. We tried to get here as quickly as we could...'

'Not easy to find. Yes, I know,' he says, his face relaxing. 'Both of you are with me tonight in the Hudson, replacing Rowden and Lefort, who are a little disappointed not to be heading to France to do their duty, I might just add. I assume you've both jumped before?'

Yes, we have,' says Anna.

'Splendid.' McFarland looks towards the art deco building. 'You'll find the ladies' and gents' changing rooms inside. There are protective jumpsuits hanging up with your papers in the breast pocket. Put the suits on and come straight out to the Hudson.'

Five minutes later, Will and Anna are walking towards the Hudson, dressed in loose-fitting khaki jumpsuits on top of their clothes. The rumble of the Hudson's and Lysanders' engines kills the silence of the night and leaves the air thick with diesel fumes.

'Nervous?' asks Will.

Anna is pulling her collar up. 'Yes. I suppose. Excited too. What about you?'

'The same.'

They say nothing more as they climb through the side door of the Hudson. The cabin is like a large steel tube painted green with two fixed metal benches under two rows of five small square windows. At the rear of cabin, six parachute backpacks are fixed securely. On the benches are two other passengers dressed in the same jumpsuits: a smiling thin-faced man and a woman in her twenties with short dark hair.

'I'm Ron,' says the thin-faced man.

'And I'm Barbara. Lovely to meet you.'

'Nice to meet you too,' says Will.

'This is our first mission. Isn't it, Ron?'

'First one, yes.'

'We're ever so nervous.'

'And excited, Barbara.'

'Yes, of course. Excited too.'

Will can see Barbara is anything but excited. This is probably her first time in an aeroplane not to mention her first jump.

'Is it your first time too?' asks Barbara.

'Not quite,' says Anna.

'Oh,' says Barbara. 'That's nice.' She rubs her thighs, smiles politely and casts her eyes to the floor.

With the pleasantries seemingly over, Will looks towards the cockpit and sees McFarland poring over a map with a man he assumes is the navigator. They finish their conversation and the map holder climbs down to the navigator cockpit. McFarland looks back and smiles.

'Me and old Pikey make a great team. We'll get you there in double time. You wouldn't mind shutting the side door for me would you, old chap?'

Will pulls it closed as McFarland addresses his passengers. 'Make yourselves comfortable, ladies and gentlemen. Moonlight Squadron One is about to hit the clouds.'

The putter of the Hudson speeds up as it rolls forward on the runway. Will settles beside Anna, facing their fellow passengers. Barbara's head is bowed, her lips moving quietly, her fingers parse through a set of rosary beads.

The Hudson's engine roars as the aircraft lifts off and begins the ascent. The cabin trembles inside as if being shaken by the hand of an invisible giant. Ron fumbles for something to grab hold of.

Moments later they are flying above the clouds with the moon lighting their way. Glancing through the windows, Will sees the Lysanders flanking the Hudson on either side. He settles down for the flight and, without thinking, he moves closer to Anna, feeling the warmth of her body. She, in turn, relaxes into him.

Two hours pass and Pikey, a small man with an eager mouse-like face, climbs from the navigator's cockpit and into the cabin. He looks at Will and Anna. 'We're approaching your drop area…' His voice is interrupted by a sudden blare like a mighty klaxon that fills the plane.

'Stone the crows! What on earth was that?' says Pikey.

A blinding flash of red light follows. Will's stomach clenches.

'Pikey! Pikey! Get up here now,' shouts McFarland.

'What's going on?' asks Anna.

'I don't know.'

Will peers behind Ron and Barbara, looking for the Lysander, but it is nowhere to be seen.

The klaxon sounds again, an unsettling and horrible noise. Will looks through the window behind him and sees the other Lysander, but then, from the clouds, a violent red streak of lightning strikes the small plane. It shatters into four pieces and falls.

'Oh my God!' says Anna.

'What the hell!' says Ron, his voice trembling, his face pale.

Barbara is sitting rigid and silent, frozen by panic.

Will gets up towards the cockpit. 'Captain McFarland, what's happening?'

'Look!' says Pikey, pointing ahead.

Will looks though the cockpit windows and swallows. Something dark is rising from the silver clouds. His first impression is that it is some sort of massive whale.

'Good Lord,' says McFarland.

Surfacing above the clouds is an enormous airship. Dwarfing the Hudson, it must be more than five hundred feet long and two hundred feet wide. It rises further, crossing their flight path, and Will can see the gondola fixed underneath at the centre of the airship's body. There are windows lighted from the inside with the silhouettes of people looking in the direction of the Hudson. Painted on the undercarriage of the airship cabin is a snake, its jaws wide open to reveal a long tongue. It is unmistakably a viper. The tongue seems to be growing, as if it is telescopic. Will sees that it's a tube, turning to point in their direction – it's some sort of cannon.

His heart rate begins to increase. *The Tesla Death Ray. They have made it.*

He turns back to his fellow passengers. 'Get your parachutes on now!' he shouts.

The klaxon sounds once more, the sky flashes and from the cannon red lightning snakes its way towards the Hudson. But McFarland has anticipated the strike and veers the plane off course causing the tail of the death ray to hit the body of the Hudson with a ferociousness that makes it shake violently.

'What the hell?' cries McFarland, battling to control the plane.

Will hears cries from the cabin and turns to see Ron on his knees and Barbara wrestling with her parachute backpack. Anna has her parachute on and tosses another to Ron. Anna seems calm but he knows, like him, she is terrified. She pulls another parachute from the cabin wall and throws it towards Will, but in that same second they hear a horrible cracking sound followed by the fast whoosh of cold wind. There's a long loud creak and, as if in slow motion, the cabin begins to split in two. With his heart in his mouth, Will reaches for Anna. And suddenly the rear of the Hudson shears and is wrenched away. It spins into the night leaving a hole gaping to the heavens through which the contents of the cabin are now being sucked out. Clinging with all his strength to the plane, Will watches as Ron and Barbara tumble, helpless and screaming, into the night, their unfixed parachutes flying ahead of them before they disappear into the clouds. It is too cold to hold on to the steel girder for much longer. He reaches for his parachute but it is whisked away before he can get close. With his free hand, the tips of his fingers reach for the strap of Anna's parachute backpack, a hair's breadth away. He hears incomprehensible shouts from McFarland and Pikey and sees Anna's feet lift off the floor, her grip on the plane loosening.

'Don't let go, Anna!' he cries.

Her eyes are wide with terror and fixed to his. He inches closer but can do nothing as her strength fades and she is sucked out into the night.

'Annaaaa!' he cries, but she is gone.

CHAPTER 26

Into the Abyss

Will hears the klaxon shake the night sky once more, announcing another blast of the cannon: enough to destroy the Hudson. He closes his eyes and exhales. There is nothing more he can do here. Opening his eyes he stares down into the abyss and swallows. He releases his grip of the girder and gives himself up to the blackness.

Tumbling through the air, he catches a brief glimpse of the Hudson as it explodes in a ball of flame and then he falls into the clouds. His life – what he remembers of it – races through his mind. He had always wondered how he would die. He'd thought he might be shot, or poisoned, or tortured to death even, but falling to his death from twenty thousand feet was never on the table. It seems odd to him that he'd never considered it as an option. He had, after all, flown quite a lot.

He clears the clouds and sees land far below, his eyes squinting in the cold, his cheeks pinched and his lips dry.

This is it. This is the end.

He looks around for signs of Anna and sees her, spreadeagled in the air, her head turned back, eyes staring in his direction. She is still holding the spare parachute. His heart begins to race. Is there still a chance? Can he reach her in time? But how? She is almost directly below him. He is the heavier of the two but she is almost two seconds ahead of him – it's not much, but there might as well be a gulf between them. He tries the only thing that he can think and flips his body, straightens it and plunges like a dart through the air. Anna turns over and faces him.

He gains speed and closes on her, but the critical time has passed: she must open her chute.

Just one more second.

Will urges his body forward, his arms reaching, hands inches from the backpack flapping about in the air. He grabs the canvas strap and Anna releases it, but the force of the wind pulls it from his grasp and it slips from his fingers and tumbles off into the night.

His heart sinks. And then he feels something tugging at his collar. Anna is pulling him towards her, straddling his lower back with her legs.

'Anna, no! It's too dangerous.'

With all her strength, she hoists him up and wraps one arm under his and around his chest. She pulls on the cord of the parachute and Will feels the sharp tug on his body as he and Anna are jerked upwards. She wraps her other arm firmly around his chest and locks her legs around his waist.

'Grab the steering line and take control. You'll have to be the legs for landing,' she shouts.

Will reaches up and takes hold of the steering line straps as he and Anna drop faster than is comfortable with a one man chute.

Above them, the clouds part and the moonlight casts a silvery sheen on the landscape below. He sees a forest to the left, thick with trees that could break their fall. Pulling on the left cord he guides the chute towards it.

'Get ready!' he calls as his feet skim the trees and they drop through the foliage, their body and faces smacked by unforgiving twigs and small branches. They stop with a jolt midway down a tree as the chute becomes entangled. The impact forces Will from Anna's grasp and he falls through the branches, tumbling as if falling down stairs. He takes a bang to the head and lands on his back on damp wet ground, his head spinning. He sits up, rubbing his head and looks up the tree. Anna has cut herself from the parachute and is climbing down. It's a miracle they have survived.

'Will, are you hurt?' she calls.

'I'm fine,' he replies as a shadow appears above them. It is the airship descending. The klaxon sounds and a prolonged blast of the cannon lights up the forest a hundred feet away, destroying six ancient trees all at once.

'Hurry, Anna!'

She jumps down and they run away from the airship and the light. They hear voices and pause for a moment to get their bearings. Peering up through a gap in the trees Will sees long ribbon like drapes – seven in total – rolling out from either side of the gondola to form what seems to be a dark curtain blazoned with the VIPER insignia. Soldiers are climbing down the ribbons, scurrying like rats, with rifles on their backs. He swears under his breath.

'Let's go! Just run,' he says.

They sprint through the shadows of the forest without knowing where they are heading.

'That was it,' says Anna, 'the Tesla Death Ray.'

Before Will can respond the klaxon blares and a streak of green lightning spirals above the treetops, twists down and scorches the ground almost two hundred feet ahead of them. Trees crack and splinter in the fire and there is almost enough light to give them away.

'This way,' says Will, turning right heading deeper into the darkness and out of sight. He hears the sounds of heavy boots behind them.

'There!' calls a voice.

A volley of gunfire ripples through the woods and Will and Anna dive for cover. The riflemen are close behind.

'We have no option but to fight,' says Will, ripping off his jumpsuit. Anna is already free of hers and she crouches behind a tree holding her Walther ready. With his back to the tree opposite, Will holds his Mauser firmly and listens for approaching footsteps. Slowly they come. Just two men, if he is correct. Anna is watching him and he holds up two fingers. She nods an acknowledgement.

Two soldiers, dressed in black uniforms with the VIPER insignia, stalk into view. Will straightens his arm and swings it up as he hears Anna's Walther fire. He feels the Velo-Dart shoot from his cuff and sees it hit the man's cheek. Both men fall forward.

Dipping behind the tree, Will looks quickly out and sees two more men approaching.

'Look!' says a voice.

Will crouches down and fires at the soldiers. He misses his target but Anna takes hers with a shot straight to the forehead. The second man ducks behind a tree and begins firing in Anna's direction. Will circles around behind him and slams his temple with the side of the Mauser. The man crumples to the ground and Will takes his rifle.

He hears more boots running towards them and begins shooting at random. Anna has picked up the rifle from the other VIPER soldier and together they fire at the approaching men.

Then Will hears the sound of more voices behind them. He turns and sees shadowy figures moving through the woods. They are trapped.

'Anna! Behind us!'

The figures behind them close in and Will looks around desperately for an escape route, but they are surrounded. There is no way out.

CHAPTER 27

Reunion

Will hears the stomping of boots and turns to see the figure of a large man running towards them. He roars; his voice is deep and guttural. Will points the Mauser but the man, eyes dark and angry, sprints past them. He charges like a bull, a pistol raised in each hand, and shoots the VIPER soldiers one by one. From the darkness two soldiers leap on him and try to wrestle him to the ground, but he is too strong. He slams one of them against the tree. The soldier slumps to his knees, arms wrapped around his ribs as the big man up-ends the second soldier and smashes him head first into the ground, crunching his neck. The big man spins round to the first man, who is now raising his pistol to fire at him, but Will has the soldier's chest in the sight of the Mauser. He squeezes the trigger and the VIPER soldier falls backwards with a look of horror on his pale face. The big man looks at Will with a wary expression.

Will hears yet more footsteps behind him and sees more armed people emerging from the shadows. He pulls Anna behind a tree and prepares to defend himself but the new arrivals ignore them and begin shooting at the VIPER soldiers surrounding them. A small battle begins, with Will and Anna lying low in the crossfire.

In the near distance Will hears the rumble of the airship. The shooting quietens and Will hears voices shouting beyond the trees. There is no sign of any more VIPER soldiers. The large man from the woods approaches and with him are the other figures from the shadows. They are not VIPER soldiers but men and women, young and middle-aged, dressed in casual civilian tweeds and flannel shirts, typical of rural France. He thinks of Emile and Claudette. Like his much-missed, departed friends, these must be French Resistance. Pointing their rifles at Will and Anna, they rally around the big man, who seems to be their leader. Will takes stock of him. He is a grizzly bear of a man who wears a heavy shooting jacket with a matted fur collar. His face is as broad as a football, adorned with a large grey moustache curled at the ends.

'Who are you?' the man says gruffly in English, his accent French; his voice deep.

'We are British agents,' says Will.

'Prove it!'

'I can vouch for them, Sebastian,' comes a familiar voice.

'Eoin?' says Anna.

And emerging from the trees, wearing a cap and looking every bit the French Resistance fighter is Eoin, smiling. '*Bonjour, mes amis.*'

The Resistance fighters redirect their weapons to the surrounding woods.

'How is it possible you are here?' asks Will.

Eoin laughs. 'Well, I'm very pleased to see you too.'

'I'm sorry I didn't mean it like that.'

Anna embraces Eoin. 'I can't believe it's you. We thought the worst.'

'It'll take a lot to bring me down. Anna, I'm sorry about Meadows.'

'You knew?'

'We had a suspicion.'

The sound of rasping static and a tinny voice from a radio receiver interrupts their exchange. 'Red Leader, this is V Command. What is your status?' All heads turn to look in its direction. The radio's owner is the soldier Sebastian up-ended. The receiver lies beside his body. 'Repeat. Red Leader, what is your status?'

Eoin picks up the radio. 'Come in V Command. Red Leader is down. Repeat Red Leader is down. We have lost several men and taken out most of the Resistance.'

'Excellent! What news of the parachutist from the plane?'

'Dead,' says Eoin.

'Good work. Head back to the ship. We are returning to base.'

'On my way,' he replies and switches off the radio. Then Eoin cuts the wire of the radio, killing the communications and the static.

'How did you know we would be here?' asks Will.

'I'll explain all later. In the meantime you two need to get out of here and head to Lyon to meet your contact.' Eoin pulls out a folded sheet of paper from his jacket pocket. 'This will help get you out of the forest and into Lyon.' He points behind him. 'Follow that trail. If you keep heading east you should get to Lyon by morning. Look for a place called Café Parisien. It's marked out on the map. Wait there and your contact will be in touch.'

'But what about you?'

'We have unfinished business to take care of. Another drop to pick up. I will look for you sometime tomorrow. Now go.'

'Eoin, the Tesla Death Ray…'

'I know. Things are worse than I expected.'

'How?' asks Anna.

'I will explain everything when I see you tomorrow. Good luck both of you and stay out of trouble. A lot to ask, I know,' he adds, squeezing a shoulder of each.

'Same to you,' says Anna.

They watch as Eoin, Sebastian and the other Resistance fighters disappear into the gloom of the woods.

Anna and Will follow the trail as directed, stopping occasionally to look at the map using the torch from Will's sleeve.

The sun rises early, the sky is a clear aqua blue and in the distance, almost two miles, away they can see the historic city of Lyon.

'We should make sure we don't look like we've just dropped from the sky and been walking through the countryside all night,' says Anna.

'You're right,' says Will, brushing down his sleeves and running his hands through his hair. 'How do I look?'

Anna tilts her head and arches her eyebrows. 'I've seen you look worse.' She reaches across and fixes his hair, combing it with her fingers on top and on the sides.

She bends over, shaking out her own hair and running her fingers through it before standing up again and straightening her dark red suit, which is still intact – and eye-catching.

'How do I look?' she asks.

'Stunning,' says Will.

She rolls her eyes. 'I doubt that.'

'We should separate,' says Will.

Anna looks at him quizzically.

'It will be safer. If we are stopped as a couple there is a risk we could both be arrested as strangers, suspected of being spies. There's less chance of that if we make our way to the café at different times.'

'You're right.'

They look at the Lyon street map and memorise the route to the Café Parisien. Will leaves the map with Anna and goes first, making his way up the pathway that runs along the Rhone. The locals are up and about and occasionally cast fleeting suspicious glances his way. Lyon is occupied by Nazis and every now and then a Kübelwagen with an officer or a soldier in it drives by. They observe him, but Will ignores them and walks casually along the river with a confident air, as if he has lived in Lyon all his life.

CHAPTER 28

Madeleine

16ᵗʰ July 1943, morning

Will turns right into Rue de Bonnel and sees the small coffee shop called Café Parisien. There are a few scattered tables and chairs outside with an old woman nursing what must be her grandchild. She glances at Will as he approaches, *'Bonjour,'* she says, tending to her baby.

'Bonjour.' He hesitates for a moment, waiting for her to say something else. Could she be his contact? She says nothing and Will moves on quickly, making his way inside where the smell of hot coffee and freshly baked bread makes his stomach rumble. He's not entirely sure of the last time he ate.

Café Parisien is small and pleasantly rustic, with a bar, and well-worn wooden chairs and tables stained with the rings from red wine glasses. It reminds him of the places he had frequented with Emile and Claudette during his year in Chartres. His hands ball into fists and he pushes the thoughts from his mind. Sitting at corner table near the window he orders a coffee and a bread roll with cheese from the waitress, a roundish woman with pleasant face.

Almost twenty minutes pass and he is still alone. He glances at the clock above the bar. It is 10 am. Where is Anna? He peers outside and is relieved to see her walking towards the café. She enters without looking at him and sits at a table by the wall on the other side of the room.

The waitress appears. '*Bonjour, Mademoiselle.*'

'*Bonjour. Un café, s'il vous plait.*'

The waitress nods and disappears behind the bar to pour the coffee.

Will hears the sound of men's voices approaching. German! He freezes and looks down into his coffee.

Two men enter the café talking and laughing loudly. He looks up for long enough to see that their black collar patches bear the SS insignia. Black shoulder straps and double-striped arrows on their sleeves mark them out as Rottenführers – corporals of the Waffen-SS. They are young men, perhaps in their early twenties. Both are tanned. One wears his cap over dark hair; the other removes his cap to reveal a full head of Aryan blond hair that would make Hitler himself stand to attention. Their talk stops as they look from Anna to Will.

Will nods at them. '*Bonjour.*'

They do not reply and sit at a table in the centre of the café resting their feet on the tabletop.

The soldier with the blond hair looks over at Anna and wolf whistles.

'*Bonjour, Mademoiselle,*' he says in a thick German accent.

Anna says nothing for a moment before replying, '*Bonjour,*' quietly and without looking at them.

189

Will feels his muscles tense.

The one with cap leans across and pokes Anna's arm. '*Parlez-vous allemand?*'

Anna shakes her head and Will can see her back straightening.

The waitress appears from behind the bar.

Anna stands and drops some coins on the table. '*Merci,*' she says to the waitress.

'*Au revoir,*' says the waitress.

'*Au revoir,*' the soldiers mimic in unison, before bursting into laughter.

Anna's eyes find Will's and she nods at the door as the soldiers order coffee. This might be the best time to leave. Will stands as Anna opens the door.

'*Attend!*' says a voice. It is the Aryan corporal.

Anna hesitates at the door and Will levels his gaze at the corporal. Which one of them was he talking to?

'Mademoiselle, you may leave,' he says to Anna, without taking his eyes from Will. The corporal with the cap turns his attention to him. The blond one appraises him with a frown and talks to his friend in German, '*Ich mag sein Gesicht nicht.*' *I don't like his face.* Will understands every word. He remains calm but can feel the shard tremble slightly in the confines of the fusilier tucked inside his blazer pocket.

The blond corporal approaches Will and his colleague swings around to watch the exchange.

'How may I help you, Corporal?' asks Will, his French crisp and fluent.

'Your papers,' the German says, in his thick accent. 'Show me them.'

Will searches his inside pocket and cannot find his papers. He had placed them with the map and given them to Anna. He curses his bad luck and glances through the window where Anna is standing pretending to wait for someone.

Will smiles at the corporal and wonders if he is too close for a Velo-Dart.

The corporal frowns and Will sees his hand inching towards the Luger strapped to his waist.

Suddenly, the door flies open and someone shouts, '*Cherie*!' at the top of her voice. Before Will can turn to see who it is, the arms of a young woman are wrapped around his neck and he is being kissed full on the lips.

'Darling, I can't believe you are here at last!' She kisses him more, pushing her tongue deep into his mouth and hugging him, urging him to respond. With nothing to lose, he hugs her and lets her kiss him. Then he buries his face in her neck, which is pleasantly fragranced with Soir de Paris. She pulls back and looks at him, her face beaming. She looks to be in her early twenties with dark wavy hair, full cherry-red lips, olive skin and brown eyes with glittering flecks of green. She is quite beautiful and wears a fashionable green trouser suit that would not look out of place in Paris.

She turns to the corporal. 'Hello Franz. I see you two have met. That is so nice.'

The corporal remains tight-lipped and greets her informally. 'Good morning, Madeleine. It is nice to see you. I have asked the gentleman for his papers and he appears not to have any.'

Will notices the corporal's eyes rolling hungrily over Madeleine's body.

Madeleine turns to Will with a teasing frown. '*Cherie*, have you not checked your pockets?'

She reaches inside his blazer and takes out a wallet that is not his. Will is impressed with her sleight of hand. She hands it to the corporal, who checks the papers and hands them back, seemingly satisfied. He looks at Will with hooded eyes; Will can tell he is not quite convinced.

Madeleine wraps her arm around Will's waist and through the corner of his eye he sees Anna sitting outside, furtively looking in at the scene.

'Please tell me you are coming to the garden party tonight, Corporal?' says Madeleine.

'I am afraid I have other important business.'

'Oh, I am sorry to hear that.' Madeleine sounds quite convincing.

The corporal nods formally, replaces his cap and bids her goodbye.

'*Au revoir*, Corporal,' she says and sits down at Will's table. They watch the two soldiers leave and Madeleine waves and blows kisses at them. When their backs are turned her expression turns to stone.

'Thank you,' says Will.

She shrugs and smiles. 'Thank you for the kiss.'

There is something familiar about Madeleine. 'Have we met before?' he asks.

'No, I don't believe we have.'

'My name is Will.' Will hears the door to the café open and a shadow appears over the table. It's Anna.

'Two coffees,' says Madeleine, without looking up.

Will looks from Madeleine to Anna and back again. 'Madeleine, this is Anna.'

Madeleine glances at Anna and merely says, 'Please bring sugar.'

Not looking very pleased, Anna walks to the bar and orders the coffees.

'Who is she?' whispers Madeleine.

'She's an agent, like me.'

Madeleine rolls her large dark eyes, pouts and folds her arms. 'I was expecting only one person.'

Anna pulls up a chair and sits at the table. Madeleine forces a smile. 'I apologise. I thought you worked here.'

Anna remains tight-lipped.

'It must be your outfit,' adds Madeleine.

Will feels the air between the two women ice over. The waitress appears with coffees and Will is glad of the distraction.

'Madeleine, we are pleased to meet you, and thank you for getting me out of that difficult spot. We need to get out of here, away from any more prying Nazi eyes.'

'You are safe with me. For the time being.' Will wonders what she means by that. 'We will take my car to my uncle's house. He is the mayor and he is hosting a garden party for a very special guest. That is where we will need your help.'

'To do what?'

'To kill the very special guest.'

CHAPTER 29

The Resistance

Madeleine's car is a sporty red Mercedes Benz 770, parked on the roadside by the Rhone. There are only two seats so Will and Anna squeeze into the front together, with Will sitting in the middle. Madeleine turns the engine over and drives them away from the river.

'The Gestapo headquarters is on the Avenue Berthelot, which is five minutes from here,' says Madeleine, switching to English. 'The soldiers mostly stay around that area. It was unlucky those two showed up at the same time.' She glances at Will, with a wry smile. 'I hope you are not always this unlucky.' Her spoken English seems flawless and he wonders if she has ever lived in England.

'Luck is not something I've ever been blessed with,' says Will.

'Correct. You have been blessed with much more. You are a fighter, a survivor.'

Will shoots a quizzical stare at Madeleine and ignores the snorting from Anna.

'You are wondering how I know this, no?'

'It had crossed my mind.'

'The Irishman talks about you with great fondness.'

'How do you know Eoin?' asks Anna.

Madeleine leans across to Will. 'I do not understand her accent. What did she say?'

Will feels Anna tensing. 'Anna was wondering how you know Eoin.'

'We have worked together before,' she says, nonchalantly.

They skirt past the gated entrance to the Parc de la Tête d'Or where two red swastika flags flutter in the morning breeze. Madeleine curses under her breath and speeds past heading north-west to a wide bridge over the Rhone and on through narrow streets lined with tall ornate French townhouses and ancient squares. For a moment Will gets lost in the atmosphere and colour of the city until he catches sight of the grey uniforms and jack boots of the occupying Nazi forces, threading their way through the streets and crowds like vermin.

The mayor's house is on the outskirts of the city, in one of Lyon's most affluent communes, Saint-Didier-au-Mont-d'Or. Madeleine drives through a large double gate and into the grounds of a stone mansion house set within beautifully kept French gardens, where decorators and gardeners are at work preparing for the party tonight.

'This is my uncle's private residence. You will be safe here until tomorrow when you will have to leave.'

'Madeleine, we cannot stay. We have to make our way to the Swiss Alps as soon as we can.'

Before Madeleine can respond, the front doors open and Sebastian, the burly resistance fighter with the thick moustache appears looking very different from how he did in the forest. His hair and moustache are combed neatly, his grizzly cheeks are clean shaven and his flak jacket has been replaced with a smart brown suit. 'Madeleine. *Cherie,*' he calls. He opens his arms, his face beaming at Madeleine and pulls her gently to his broad chest.

So Sebastian is her uncle – and the mayor.

Will sees Eoin appear behind Madeleine's uncle, dressed casually with his sleeves rolled up.

'Good to see you made it without any hitches.'

Sebastian turns his attention to Will and Anna. *'Bonjour, mes amis.* I am pleased see you again.'

Will extends his hand. *'Bonjour,* Sebastian. Thank you again for rescuing us,' he says. The mayor's hand is hard and thick with calluses.

'Think nothing of it.' Sebastian smiles warmly. 'Come inside. Everyone. We have much to discuss. But first we eat.'

The interior of Sebastian's house seems a strange setting for the rough and ready strongman who had mercilessly killed half a dozen VIPER soldiers only hours earlier. The hallway is laid with smooth sandstone tiles, the walls are painted an elegant white and adorned with four oil paintings depicting French rural life. Sebastian takes them to a dining room where his housekeeper, a brittle and grey lady, is laying silverware and napkins on a glossy oak table in preparation for lunch. There are tall and wide French windows leading out to the garden where carpenters are sawing wood and banging nails. The ceiling is high, with ornate coving and hanging chandeliers that glitter in the morning sun.

'Please sit wherever you like,' he says.

Will and Anna sit opposite Eoin and Madeleine. Sebastian sits at the head of the table.

'Edward tells me you have had quite the adventure,' says Eoin.

'He was very helpful,' says Will.

'He's quite the wizard with communications. He was listening in on radio transmissions and heard you two were at Southend making the drop to Lyon. If it wasn't for him, we wouldn't have been there for you.'

'We assumed Sir Hugh had been in touch with you,' says Anna.

'I'm afraid Sir Hugh did not make it.'

'Oh no,' says Anna.

'What happened?' asks Will.

'A VIPER spy murdered him.'

'I'm sorry. I know you two were old friends,' says Will.

The Irishman sighs and seems lost in thought for a moment. 'I will miss him.'

The silence is broken by the housekeeper who returns with a younger assistant, carrying trays of food and drink. Lunch is fresh bread, cheese, ham, artichokes and red wine. Simple but delicious. When the eating is done, the housekeeper clears up, serves strong coffee and then leaves.

Will takes this moment to tell them what he has learned. 'Eoin, Sebastian, we have intelligence that VIPER has a manufacturing plant in the Swiss Alps. The airship you saw yesterday – that weapon – it was made there. This morning we all heard the radio receiver. The airship captain said he was returning to headquarters. I believe the manufacturing plant and the headquarters are the same place. We need to go there as soon as possible and destroy that place and the weapon.'

No one says anything for what seems like a long time, until Eoin speaks.

'This is going to sound odd, Will, but VIPER are not our priority for the time being.'

197

'But why?' says Anna. 'They have never been so dangerous. You saw what that weapon did in the forest. You must have seen what it did to the aeroplane that was flying us here?'

'We were given orders from Sir Hugh just before he died,' says Eoin.

'But…'

'There is a war on,' says Sebastian. 'My country is under Nazi occupation and our people are starving and dying.'

'We know that,' Will cuts in, 'but there are dark forces at work here. This isn't just about that weapon. Something worse is coming.' Will notices that Madeleine is watching and listening to him intently. But she says nothing.

'What exactly is coming?' asks Sebastian.

'They call it the Red Storm.'

'They?' asks Sebastian.

'VIPER.'

'And what is this Red Storm?'

'I am not sure. They have grenades that carry a deadly red gas.'

'If they come to us with those grenades, then we will kill them. But before that we have a man to get rid of.'

'Uncle,' interrupts Madeleine, 'perhaps I can take Will to the Swiss Alps?'

'No, I forbid it. We are all needed here.'

'But…'

'Madeleine, I said no.'

'Why is this visitor so important?' asks Will.

Sebastian leans forward, his elbows on the table, his fingers interlaced. 'Hans Krüger is an Obergruppenführer, a senior ranking officer in the SS. He is man without a soul. A man with the blood of

198

thousands of innocent men, women and children on his hands. A creator of death camps and destroyer of families, livelihoods and dreams. He is coming here to Lyon, to my home, for a party to celebrate his illustrious career. It will be the last visit he makes before we send him to Hell.

'We owe it to all the people who have died because of him to carry out this mission. This assassination will be a blow for the Nazis and a major win for the Allies.'

'What do you expect from us?' asks Will.

'Let me show you,' says Sebastian. He stands, gesturing for them to follow him, walks towards the French windows and looks outside. 'They are building a platform, a stage if you like. At 8 pm this evening there will be a break in the party and Krüger will take to the stage to be applauded and revered by his Nazi colleagues. Except Krüger will not make it to the party.'

'What do you mean?' asks Will.

'I expect by 7 pm you will have killed him, Monsieur Starling.'

'Me?'

Eoin speaks. 'Will, there is something else about Krüger. Something very important. He is also a key figure in VIPER's military wing. He has worked on many of their weapons programs, including the Teleken project your father worked on.'

Will feels a clawing at his throat. 'He knew my father?'

'He betrayed your father. His treachery led directly to your parents' deaths and Rose's kidnapping.'

Will feels a cold hollowness inside.

'Eoin and me,' says Sebastian, 'we are old-fashioned men. We believe in revenge. Killing Krüger will help your head.' He taps his own temple to emphasise his point. 'So, two birds with one stone, no?'

'Sebastian has used his influence with the local soldiers to throw a party in Krüger's honour. We were going to kill him ourselves tonight, however, when we heard you were coming I put the suggestion to my friend, the mayor, that you would be a better choice and he was agreeable. What about it Will?'

'I will do it,' Will says, without hesitation.

Sebastian smiles. 'I am very pleased to hear that.'

Will watches the men outside, building the stage. It reminds him of a hangman's gallows.

'You are special, Will. I know you can do this. I am aware of your reputation. Your history, your exploits in London and more recently in my beloved country, are well known.'

Will hates the idea that he has been discussed and analysed by people he does not know. He shoots a sideways glance at Eoin, his brow furrowed.

'Uncle, that is enough, I think,' says Madeleine.

'You are right, my dear. Forgive me, Will. But please, do not blame Eoin for these indiscretions.'

'Who I should I blame?' asks Will.

'We have another mutual friend. You may know him as the Owl.'

'The man with a thousand faces,' says Anna.

'You know him?' asks Will.

'No one has ever met him,' says Anna. 'He's a rogue spy who cannot be trusted.'

'No spy can be trusted, my dear. They are all skilled in the art of deception,' says Madeleine.

'The Owl has no morals. He works for whoever has the biggest wallet.'

'Everyone has their price,' says Madeleine.

Anna looks icily at Madeleine. 'Really? What's yours?'

Will catches Madeleine's eyes flaring. She folds her arms.

Sebastian speaks. 'Please, let us deal with the matter at hand. Will, you will work with Madeleine tonight. She knows the area and can help you. Like you, she has much experience. It pains me to bring it up but she has had as difficult a life as both of you. I think you three have much in common.'

Anna and Madeleine snort almost at the same time.

'My niece will sort you out with suitable attire for tonight's party. In the meantime, Eoin has something to show you and I have much to prepare for this evening.'

'Come with me, both of you,' says Eoin.

Eoin takes them back into the hallway and through a door under the staircase where there are more stairs leading down to a cellar.

At the bottom of the steps Eoin flicks a switch and the room lights up. The cellar is cold with damp air and contains rows of wine racks. 'This is Sebastian's pride and joy,' he says.

There is also a bench and a table where an open suitcase containing a Whaddon Mark VII radio transmitter lies. On the floor are two khaki green trunks. Eoin flips the lids open. One of them contains six Lanchester submachine guns and boxes of ammunition while the second contains a dozen or so gas masks. 'This was our unfinished business this morning. After finding you we had another drop to pick up. I had Edward despatch these masks for me. Sebastian was expecting more weapons and was not very pleased. He is dangerously indifferent to the VIPER threat despite what happened this morning.'

'The death ray, on the airship, is more powerful than I ever imagined,' says Will. 'It tore our plane apart in seconds.'

'For VIPER it is a magnificent addition to their arsenal. I fear we have only seen half of what it can do.'

'Do you know how we can destroy it?' says Anna.

'I'm afraid not. I have asked Edward to try and remember as much as he can about the schematic we had, and lost. He is sketching it from memory. I'm hoping he'll come up with something soon; we don't have a lot of time.'

Will sits down heavily on the bench. His limbs still ache from the fall and his body feels battered and bruised.

'You two have had a long night. You should get some rest. The housekeeper has prepared rooms for you. Get some sleep and we'll talk more later.'

Will lies, with his eyes closed, on a soft bed on the first floor of the mayor's house. The curtains are closed, the room dark and warm, yet sleep is impossible amid the relentless hammering of nails into wood. Nevertheless he feels oddly calm. The shard is warm and pulsates quietly like a snoozing puppy on his chest. He feels himself drifting off, the hammering becomes a distant memory and he seems to float in a swirl of blue light.

Am I dreaming?

His body tingles and his eyes flicker open. The room is bathed in an unearthly blue luminescence. Small blue lights, like miniature fireworks, fly from his face and body and penetrate every fibre of his flesh and bone. Writhing on the bed he feels an extraordinary power that is not of this world and he doesn't know whether to laugh or cry. His body feels hot and clammy and he feels a howl deep within his soul. He opens his mouth to cry out but his voice is silent. His heart burns as the dormant emotions of sorrow, pain and rage shatter the blue lights like fragments of glass. The room trembles as if there is a storm. The curtains rise and flap noisily, pictures fall from the walls and a wind whirls around the room like an angry spirit. The shard trembles, rattling in the confines of the tin soldier. Will places his palm over it and soon it quietens down, resuming its slumber.

He hears knocking on the bedroom door. The handle cranks open and Madeleine and Anna rush in.

'Will! What happened?' says Anna.

Will swings his legs round and sits on the edge of the bed. 'I think I know how we can destroy the death ray.'

CHAPTER 30

Les Collègues

In a bathroom at the end of the hallway, two rooms down from his bedroom, Will dries himself after a warm shower and shave. Wrapping the towel around his waist he heads back up the hallway to the bedroom. The curtains are closed, but a line of sunlight slices through a chink in the curtains and casts a golden glow over the bed.

His clothes have been tossed carelessly on top of it. Lying next to them is a clean, freshly pressed tuxedo, a white shirt, a black tie and some socks. Resting on the floor is a shiny pair of black brogues. A surge of anxiety scratches at his spine; someone has been in the room. He curses his carelessness and searches the inside pocket of his blazer. The tin soldier is still there. He takes it out, peers through the gap and relaxes when he sees the shard still lodged inside. He places it upright on the dresser and unfurls his towel, dropping it on the floor.

'I hope everything fits you,' says a voice. It's Madeleine's.

He can't quite determine why he is not surprised. He turns to see her standing in the shadows watching him. She steps forward wearing a low-cut black dress with a lace trim on the chest and shoulders. Shimmering from the hem and around her waist and ribs are a thousand silver sequins sewn into the shape of a roaring dragon. A diamond necklace sparkles dangerously around her neck.

'I'm sorry if I startled you.'

Will glances at the tin soldier. 'What are you doing here?'

'I wanted to drop by and give you your clothes for this evening. I saw you were not here, so I decided to wait.'

'Considerate of you.'

She smiles. 'Most Englishmen blush when they are naked in front of a lady.'

'I am not "*most Englishmen*".' He lifts the shirt from the bed and pulls it across his back. Madeleine moves towards him, standing inches from him so that he can feel the heat from her body. She begins to button his shirt, starting from the top and working her way down. Her breath is warm and sweet, her full lips, glossy, red and smiling. Stopping at his navel, she meets his gaze and with the palm of her hands slowly brushes his chest and fixes the shirt. He feels his blood warming and rushing to his loins. She steps back, appraises her work and unashamedly glances at the hemline of his shirt.

'Just perfect,' she says.

There is an element of danger to Madeleine's brazen attention that fires up desires he has not felt in a long time. His feelings for Anna are still there but they had to change when she confessed to having taken another lover. Meadows had been a traitorous VIPER swine, now deceased, but things are no longer the same between them. He pulls on the trousers and watches Madeleine watching him.

'She is your lover?' asks Madeleine.

Will hesitates, thrown by the question. 'At one time.'

'Do you love her?'

Sitting on the edge of the bed, Will puts on the socks and shoes, his eyes focused on the shiny leather. He does not respond.

'She still likes you.'

'I'm not sure she does.'

'I can see it. Women know these things.'

'We're colleagues now. Nothing more.'

'Are you?'

'Yes.' He picks up the tie and wraps it around his collar.

'Let me,' says Madeleine, taking hold of it. She ties it gently. '*Les collègues*,' she says, in a mocking fashion.

'*Oui. Les collègues.*'

'*D'accord.*' Madeleine finishes tying the bow tie.

'Tonight you will be my partner at the party. The Nazis will think you are my lover. It is the perfect cover for you. Because of this, some of them may resent you, however, my uncle's position in this town keeps them at arm's length. That will all change tonight.'

'What about Anna?'

'Who?'

Will arches his eyebrows at Madeleine.

'Oh. Is that her name? Do not worry about her. I have made sure she has the perfect dress.'

'I'm glad to hear that.'

'You must excuse me. I have some last-minute party arrangements to take care of. We will meet in the dining room for the final briefing in ten minutes.'

Will pulls on his shoulder holster. '*D'accord.*'

She pauses before opening the door and looks back. 'Thank you for helping us.'

He nods and Madeleine smiles and leaves the room, shutting the door behind her.

He checks the Mauser, which feels lighter than it should. Sliding out the magazine he sees it is short of bullets. There are spares in his blazer and he pops them one by one into the magazine.

The hammering has stopped at last. Walking to the window Will peers through the curtains and looks down at the garden. The carpenters have finished building the stage and are in the process of dressing the backdrop with a Nazi flag. There are two long tables covered in white cloths on either side of the garden. The mayor's staff are laying out bottles of wine, jugs of water, bread, cheeses, hams and cakes. In times of rationing there is nothing but the best for the master race.

His eyes look beyond the stage where he sees Madeleine walking towards what look like a small gîte. Narrowing his gaze he sees a paint-splattered easel leaning against the wall outside. Madeleine looks behind her before disappearing inside.

Curious.

CHAPTER 31

Kill Krüger

It is almost ten minutes later when Will slides the Mauser into the holster and pulls on his tuxedo. It is a snug fit with just enough room to stop the Mauser's outline from being visible. Combing his hair back with his hands he hurries down to the dining room and hears the voices of Eoin, Sebastian and Madeleine inside. He is about to knock when he hears Anna's voice behind him.

'What are you wearing?' she says.

Will turns, expecting to see her dressed in a beautiful gown.

'Oh…' he says.

Anna is wearing a loose fitting and unflattering black and white maid's outfit. He bites his lip in an effort not to smile – or laugh for that matter.

'The housekeeper brought this to my room. This is *her* doing, isn't it?'

Will is on the verge of bursting into laughter and coughs to hide it. 'I'm sure there must be something else you can wear.'

Anna's face turns red with anger. 'Oh forget it!' she says marching past him and into the dining room, where Eoin, Sebastian and Madeleine are sitting around the table. The room goes quiet and all heads turn to look as they walk in. Eoin and Sebastian's eyes widen as they gaze at Anna's outfit.

'My dear, why are you dressed like a maid?' asks Madeleine.

'I have been asking myself the same question.'

'It must be the housekeeper. Perhaps she misunderstood my request.'

'I'm sure she understood every word.'

'I must say, you make a very convincing maid,' says Madeleine, 'The Nazis will never suspect you.'

Anna does not respond. Instead she sits down and looks to Eoin and Sebastian. 'I'm ready.'

'Superb,' says Sebastian.

Will sits down next to Anna as Sebastian slides a sheet of paper across the table. It contains a roughly sketched layout of the garden with the stage and two banqueting tables. Around the tables are dozens of circles representing people. In between the two tables and in front of the stage are more small circles with swastikas inside. Sebastian points to the middle where the swastikas are.

'At 8 am the officers will gather here to listen to Krüger. Before then word will get out that he has not arrived. It is not possible that they will know he has been assassinated. If so, all hell may break loose. If that happens we will assemble at the tables. Hidden under both banqueting tables are the Lanchester submachine guns: two at each table. Will and Madeleine, if you make it back in time, you will take the table on the right. Eoin and Anna will take the table on the left. I will organise my people to pick out the strays.'

'What happens if they do not make it back in time?' asks Eoin.

'Two of my men will take their place. Keep your eyes on me and the clock above the stage and also ensure your watches have the correct time. Just in case.'

Will glances outside at the clock on the stage. It is almost thirty minutes past six. He checks his Timor wristwatch, which is two minutes slow, and adjusts it. He hears the sound of vehicles approaching; among them is a car blaring its horn like a trumpet, as if announcing their arrival.

Sebastian's face darkens. *'Merde,'* he mutters. 'They are early.'

Will feels his arm being squeezed.

'We should go,' says Madeleine. 'I will brief you on the way.'

'Thank you, Madeleine,' says Sebastian. 'Does anyone have any questions?'

'None from me,' says Will.

'Nor me,' say the others in turn.

'Very well. I will greet our guests. *Bon courage!*'

Will, Anna, Madeleine and Eoin leave through the French windows.

'Anna,' says Will.

She turns to look at him with a concerned expression.

'Be careful tonight.'

Eoin and Madeleine are out of earshot. 'I'm not sure about this, Will. Something feels wrong.'

'What do you mean?'

'It's just a feeling. I can't put my finger on it. It just seems so convenient that we are all here at the same place and unable to move on to the most important place in our mission.'

'I know. But this is such a good opportunity.'

'For what – revenge?'

'Will!' calls Madeleine.

'We will leave tonight. I promise.' He hurries after Madeleine who takes him to a gate at the rear of the garden where a black Citroën is parked. He sits in the passenger seat as Madeleine drives them out of town and along an isolated tree-lined country road. Anna's words echo in his head, but he pushes them away as the thought of confronting Krüger releases a spark of adrenaline that begins to surge through his body.

Almost twenty minutes later Madeleine eases on the brakes and stops the car in the middle of a road.

'There are two Lanchester submachine guns hidden under the back seat,' says Madeleine. 'Krüger will be coming along this route. He will not be alone; he will be guarded.'

'I don't doubt that.'

Will hides behind the trees at the side of the road, with a Lanchester machine gun in one hand and binoculars in the other. Madeleine is peering under the bonnet of the Citroën, which blocks the narrow road. To a casual onlooker, she might appear to be a driver with no idea of how to fix her broken vehicle – a damsel in distress. She is anything but that, Will thinks. Only moments ago she had casually and confidently taken out the machine guns and tossed one to him without a thought. The way she held hers, feeling its weight, extracting the magazine and checking the contents revealed a little more about the mystery of this French Resistance spy. Will had no doubt this kind of mission was not new to her. She knew precisely what she was doing. On the surface she appeared to be spoiled and rude, to Anna certainly. She was also brazen, courageous and definitely dangerous. He is intrigued by her. She reminds him of someone and he smiles to himself as he realises who it is. Two years ago he and Anna had gone to watch *Gone with the Wind* at the Empire in Leicester Square. In many ways Madeleine was like Scarlett O'Hara, the over-privileged and seemingly immoral heroine who overcomes war and poverty with her courage, intelligence and grit.

He sweeps the area with binoculars. The rolling hills and meadows are serene and glow in the simmering red evening sun. For a moment he is overcome with a sense of peace before the rumble of a car engine tears through the country calm. Through the lenses he sees a shiny black six-wheel Daimler-Benz with two small red Nazi flags flapping above each of the headlamps. It is an impressive vehicle designed for military officers who require comfort and space, and this one belonged to Obergruppenführer Hans Krüger. He would be here in minutes.

Will catches Madeleine's dark eyes. She nods once. He dips into the cover of the trees and watches the Daimler slow behind Madeleine's car. The driver is frowning, clearly unhappy at being slowed down. Krüger sits in the rear of the vehicle, his attention focused on the driver. The two men exchange words. Madeleine is smiling sweetly, beckoning the driver to help her. The driver says something to Krüger who nods and folds his arms. The driver gets out. Madeleine smiles a wicked smile.

Will walks out of the woods, the machine gun fixed on the man who betrayed his father and whose actions caused his parents' murders and his sister's kidnapping. He hears the driver's pitiful broken French as he tries to question Madeleine about her car.

Krüger is rounder than he expected and is squeezed into full uniform with several medals and ridiculous Nazi symbols. With an eager audience waiting, he was intending to put on a show tonight. *Shame.*

Will sees his own reflection appear in the windows of the car like a dark spectre of death, an unwelcome vision of the future he was turning towards. He hesitates as an overwhelming sense of unease prickles his skin. Joseph's words stab at his conscience. '*...I know your father would want me to tell you that your chosen profession is not one he would have approved of.*'

Frozen, he stares blankly at the man whose actions devastated his life.

Krüger looks up and sees him. His pudgy jowls frame confusion. He calls to the driver but it is too late. Madeleine's machine gun rattles and the driver cries out in fear.

'Will. Do it!' cries Madeleine.

Krüger's expression contorts in anger, sparking Will's desolation and rage. There is no going back now. Gritting his teeth, he squeezes the Lanchester's trigger and sprays the car with several rounds of bullets.

A strange smoke fills the air before him.

The smoke clears and he looks at the car waiting for that unspoken sense of achievement, but all he feels is cold inside. Krüger is nowhere to be seen. Will imagines him lying bloody and dead on the back seat of the car, but something is not right. There are no holes in the car nor is the glass broken. He sees Krüger sitting up, his face deathly white and clammy with shock. *Why is he not dead?*

Madeleine is looking his way, frowning.

'The bullets are blanks. We've been betrayed. Again!' he says. He sees that the driver is on the ground, unharmed and reaching for the Luger at his belt, but Madeleine runs at him. Will is distracted by goading laughter and sees Krüger pointing a pistol at him. A bullet cracks through the window narrowly missing Will's shoulder. Dropping the Lanchester, Will spins around, pulls out the Mauser from its holster and, through the rear window, shoots Krüger in the side of head. Blood sprays the interior of the car. Madeleine is beating the hapless driver half to death with the Lanchester. The man is unconscious.

'What the hell is going on?' she cries.

Before Will can answer, the thunderous klaxon sounds from the skies shaking the ground beneath their feet. Above them, the VIPER airship – like an enormous blood-red cigar – flies towards the town.

'The Resistance! The party! My uncle! We've been betrayed!'

'Get into the car!' shouts Will, taking the driver seat. The skies flash with a horrible red lightning that scorches the ground ahead. He knows it and Madeleine does too. The target is the mayor's party. His heart sinks as he thinks of Anna and Eoin left alone to defend themselves with machine guns that are as much use as water pistols. He prays that they are both safe.

CHAPTER 32

Poison Cyclone

The airship flies across the sky with all the stealth of a shark as Will skids the Citroën to a stop outside Sebastian's home. Mercifully the house is still standing. Beyond it in the distance is a wall of black smoke. He hears gunfire. His heart sinks. A battle is underway. If all the ammunition is made up of blanks then the Resistance are horribly ill-equipped.

'*Merde!*' cries Madeleine as she runs towards the house.

'Madeleine, wait!' But she does not listen.

Sprinting after her, Will takes out his Mauser and watches the airship as it circles around, casting a shadow and blocking out the sun. Long red drapes unfurl from the gondola's base and flutter together to reveal the blood red VIPER flag with the image of the black snake curled around the planet.

He sees Madeleine peeking around the side of the house at the rear garden. The battle seems to have stopped. There are a dozen bloodied bodies scattered on the grass, including the carpenters who built the stage, Sebastian's old housekeeper and several other French civilians he does not recognise. Most of the Nazis are alive and are gathered at the stage in a circle, facing out with their Lugers ready. There is no sign of Anna, Eoin or Sebastian.

The airship blares its terrible klaxon again and begins to descend. A red flash blinds him for a second as the Tesla Death Ray cuts through the air and scorches across the ground like a giant crooked scythe. Trees split and explode and the Nazis scream and scatter like mice to avoid the beam that slices through their circle. Two soldiers are caught as they run past Will and Madeleine. Will pulls Madeleine to him as the bodies of the two men light up and sizzle and, in seconds, become clouds of ash and dust. Will coughs as the dusty remains fill his nostrils and coat his face.

The ray cuts through the right side of the mayor's house like a knife through butter. The brickwork begins to crumble, falling around them and exposing the inside. Will tries to pull Madeleine away but she sprints across the garden dodging the death ray and its lights which have split into a dozen separate blades of death.

'Madeleine, stop!' he cries, but she does not listen. *What is she thinking? It's a bloody suicide run.* She is making for the artist's studio at the end of the garden.

'Will!' comes a voice. His heart skips. It's Anna.

There is a break in the firing of the death ray. Eoin, Anna and four members of the Resistance are hauling two black trunks from the front of the house. Will hurries towards them. He is relieved to see Anna and he can see from her smile she feels the same way too.

'Where's Madeleine?' asks Eoin.

'She ran to the artist's studio.'

'There is stash of hidden weapons inside it. Sebastian is there too.'

Eoin opens the black trunks. Inside is an array of old rifles and pistols.

'Look!' says Anna, pointing upward.

Red dust clouds are emerging from beneath the gondola and are falling towards the house. A sickening sensation grips Will's stomach as he recalls the poison he almost succumbed to on Westminster Bridge.

From the viewing balcony of the gondola, the acolyte watches the battle unfold. The slaughter intoxicates him. He is moments from being there among them and is hungry to open flesh and spill blood. As the airship descends, the soldiers on either side of him kick out the rolls of thick material that unfurl beneath. They fasten their gas masks and begin the drop to the garden.

He puts on his gas mask and kicks out the red roll of material at his feet.

He is ready.

He is his old self.

Gone is his priest's cassock, the white cane and the dark glasses. In their place, a long dark coat and a fedora. He prays he will find the Starling swine and carve the life from him once and for all. The thought of it arouses him and he swallows.

And when he is done with him, he will take the sister. She is an abomination; a daughter of the devil himself. Without mercy he will do God's work, squeeze the life from her and her unborn spawn and send them back to Hell.

'The gas masks are in the basement!' cries Eoin.

Will runs into the house with Anna close behind him, past a gaping hole cut by the death ray. In the basement they grip one end of the trunk each and clamber back outside.

The base of the gondola has four large fans, which are spinning, pushing out the dust clouds to form them into a gruesome deadly red cyclone. At the same time, armed soldiers in gas masks are hanging from the drapes waiting for the ship to reach a safe distance so they can drop to the ground. Will thinks of Madeleine and Sebastian. They have no masks. He straps on his, securing it tight to his face. Grabbing two spares, he runs, his rapid breathing resonating through the rubber mask. The door to the artist's studio is open and Madeleine and her uncle are loading the magazines of two Beretta submachine guns.

'Madeleine! Sebastian!' he calls, but his voice is muffled. Sebastian sees him and swings the Beretta in his direction. He doesn't know who he is behind the mask. Will freezes, his arms in the air, and – thank God – Madeleine realises it's him and pushes Sebastian's gun down.

Will hands across the masks, pointing at the sky. A look of horror crosses Madeleine's face and she tosses the machine gun to Will.

'No blanks,' she says, pulling on her mask. Will scans the studio and pauses at an oil painting of a battlefield lying against the wall. Will has seen it before. One of them is a very talented painter.

He watches Madeleine as she crouches at an open trapdoor in the floor and reaches down, pulling out rifles, pistols, grenades and another submachine gun.

'Hurry!' shouts Will, pointing to the front of the house. 'We need to join the others.'

Madeleine and Sebastian nod their agreement.

Will steps outside cautiously looking up at the approaching red storm. He sprays bullets blindly through the billowing clouds hoping to take out some of the soldiers climbing down the drapes. With satisfaction he watches two of them fall dead to the ground as Madeleine and Sebastian run to the front of the house.

The cloud swirls around his head and shoulders. Daylight diminishes as the thick red dust envelops the garden and the house. Will hears feet thudding onto the grass. The VIPER soldiers are here. Overhead the airship's engines kick into gear as it begins its ascent, the fans' steady whirling spreads the dust far and wide.

Will moves forward blindly, heading in what he thinks is the direction of the front of the house, and collides with a dark figure. Through the churning red mist he makes out a VIPER soldier dressed in black combats. The mask makes him look even more sinister. The man raises his pistol but Will swipes the butt of his machine gun knocking the pistol from his hand. He then rams his elbow into the man's windpipe and the soldier falls to his knees clutching his throat.

Gunfire sounds from all directions. The battle has resumed.

Suddenly he feels an arm around his neck and a hand attempting to prise off his mask. Dropping the Beretta, Will tries to pull the hand and arm away but they are too strong. Gasping, he reaches behind him and wraps both his arms around his assailant's neck. Using all his strength, he pulls him up and flips him over his shoulder. As the man tumbles through the air Will rips the mask from his face. He lands on his back, his arms clawing at Will begging for the mask. His body trembles violently, his eyes desperate, the blood already beginning to fill them. Will tosses the mask away just as the first man runs at him with a knife. Swiftly he grabs the man's wrist, twisting his arm to straighten it before slamming a fist hard into the man's elbow, forcing it inwards. Above the din, he can just about hear the snapping of bone and the muffled howl of pain from beneath the soldier's rubber mask. Still holding the man's wrist, Will slams the knife point into the man's chest. As his victim falls, Will scrambles forward feeling across the ground for the machine gun. To his great relief, his fingers find it.

There is a movement on the edge of his peripheral vision. He shivers as if someone has walked over his grave. Through the red cloud he sees a tall slim figure wearing a fedora and a long dark coat that flaps behind him like the wings of the angel of death. Something long and sharp glimmers in his hand. Will feels the hairs on his neck stand on end. The figure disappears among the billowing red clouds.

Who is that?

There is humming. Someone is humming a tune, a hymn he has heard before. The shard trembles against his chest. Something in him has triggered it. Or was it the man who just walked by? Will scans the area but the man has gone. Perhaps he saw a ghost, but logic bucks that thought from his mind. Perhaps he imagined him, yet still he is gripped with a strange uncertainty.

With the blood pounding in his ears and the machine gun pointing ahead Will heads in the same direction, cautiously navigating through the swirling poisoned clouds and across the garden, stepping on and over the corpses of the dead. The man is nowhere to be seen. Pushing on, he nears the house, its side now open to the air. Two soldiers are shooting at the front of the house where Eoin and Anna were moments before. Will squeezes the trigger and takes them down.

The red dust is still falling thick and fast. The drone of the airship is distant but still the poison cyclone swirls. *Is there no end to it?*

CHAPTER 33

The Man in the Fedora and the Long Dark Coat

The shard is trembling harder now against Will's chest. It begins to spark and a hole burns blue in his tuxedo. He shivers as a blue light snakes across his chest, down his arm and onto his hand. Sparks pop from his fingers and around them the red dust begins to disperse.

What on earth?

He waves his hand and, in wonder, watches the red poison dissipate as if he has cast a magical spell. He takes out the tin soldier which is oddly scorched yet cold to the touch. He prises it open, pulls out the shard and drops the soldier to the ground. The shard is glowing its familiar unearthly blue but it seems to be getting fainter. Soon the blue light fades and the red dust gathers again around the shard and his hand.

No!

He recalls the first time Eoin showed him the shard and demonstrated its power. The Irishman had placed it on a table and slammed the butt of his pistol onto the stone causing it to ignite and burn the table to ash. He had never seen anything like it before. He stares at it, wondering.

Is it possible?

Placing the shard on the path, he lifts a rock from the rubble of the house and smashes it down hard. A booming sound like a thunderclap roars through the air and the ground shakes beneath his feet. The house wobbles and the glass in the windows shatters. Will ducks to avoid the flying fragments. The shard begins to shake angrily. Like a firework, it fizzles a blue flame that grows to eye level, shining so bright he has to stave off the glare with his hand. Lights begin to shoot from the shard in all directions, eating through the red dust and clearing the air. Behind him he sees Madeleine and Anna shooting at three VIPER soldiers at the other side of the stage. Will fires off a few rounds from his magazine killing one of the soldiers. Realising they are exposed, the soldiers run behind the stage but Madeleine and Anna are already ahead of them and pump them full of bullets. He sees Sebastian snapping the neck of another soldier and wonders where Eoin could be.

Looking up, he sees the airship wobbling precariously as the shard's blue lights snake around the gondola searching for more poison to consume. However, it seems they are not enough to bring the ship down. Instead, it retreats. *Until next time.*

The red dust has cleared but Will keeps his mask on in case the air is not yet clean. He senses someone beside him and turns. Madeleine's black curls frame her mask. In her hands is the tin soldier and she is pushing the shard back inside the spine. She shoves it into his hand and he feels its satisfying weight. He frowns at her. How did she know? But already she has gone to help Sebastian and Anna.

With the soldiers at the rear of the house dead and his friends safe, Will makes his way across the rubble, eyes fixed ahead, machine gun ready. He sees a soldier sitting up and leaning against the rocks, blood seeping from a bullet wound in his chest. The man sees Will and reaches for his pistol, which lies at his feet, but he is too weak to get to it. He can't have long to go, thinks Will. He reaches down and pulls off the man's mask. He is dark-haired with olive skin, Italian perhaps. His face is gaunt, pale and glistening with sweat. He looks at Will with a pained expression.

'Kill me,' he croaks.

Satisfied the red poison has cleared, Will pulls off his own mask and crouches down, levelling his gaze at the man. 'Where is the airship going to?'

The man frowns and coughs. 'Kill me … please.'

'Tell me where the airship is going.'

Will places the machine gun on the ground. The soldier begins to sob. Will holds his gaze like a seasoned poker player. After a moment the soldier lifts his arm and points into his chest. Will reaches across, unbuttons his jacket and sees a map tucked inside. He unfolds it and lays it out. The soldier points to a location in the Swiss Alps.

'Schöllenen Gorge?'

The soldier nods, his face contorted with pain.

A memory flashes in Will's mind. He is cold and climbing up a sheer rocky cliff face. Around him are snow-capped mountains. He hears a voice barking commands. It is Frost. Will feels dizzy. He swallows and puts his hand on the rubble to steady himself.

'Please,' says the soldier.

Taking two deep breaths, Will stands, removes the Mauser from its holster and points it at the man's chest. He recalls his dark spectre-like reflection in the windows of Krüger's car. There is no going back now. This path has been chosen for him and he must follow it.

'Blessed Virgin, forgive me,' says the man, speaking in Italian.

'I'm sorry,' Will says and, stepping back, he puts a bullet into the man's heart. The Italian's body jerks and sags as the life leaves it forever.

Will regards him pityingly and thinks about Schöllenen Gorge. He has clearly been there, but why, when and for how long he has no idea. This information is hidden somewhere in his fractured memory.

'Will!' comes a voice.

Will turns to see Eoin carrying a rifle in one arm and waving with the other. He smiles, relieved to see the Irishman is fine. Placing the Mauser back in its holster he notices the bodies of three of Sebastian's men lying on the front path. The oxygen tubes on their gas masks have been cut in two with a knife. *Strange.*

A shadow appears at the corner of his eye. He sees the man in the fedora and long dark coat glide towards the Irishman as if weightless. Will feels his spine icing over. *It can't be.*

'Eoin … stop … no!'

The Irishman looks at him quizzically and smiles. At the same time the man in the fedora swings his arm up and points a pistol at Eoin's back.

Will feels his stomach lurch and sees Eoin frowning, an expression of not quite understanding. A single shot shatters the air and Eoin's face contorts in agony as a bloody hole appears on his chest.

'No!' cries Will, desperately reaching for his Mauser.

The man in the fedora looks up. A small tongue darts out of his mouth and wets his lips. His one remaining eye blinks three times. The other is a scarred empty socket.

It's the Pastor. Returned from the grave.

Will fires the Mauser, torn by grief, rage and fear as Eoin crumples to the ground. His bullets go wide, his aim and concentration rocked by his emotions. The Pastor is nimble and darts to the gated entrance laughing maniacally. Will tries to focus and fires four more times in succession but all he does is chip the gatepost as the Pastor disappears behind it.

When Will gets to the gate, the Pastor has gone.

He runs back and kneels by Eoin's side. The Irishman is trembling and trying to talk. Blood seeps from his wound. Will presses down on it and hears rapid footfalls on the grass. Anna, Madeleine, Sebastian and two of his men arrive by his side.

'Get some towels and fetch the doctor!' he hears Sebastian barking at someone.

Will looks down at the man who had taken him under his wing two years ago. This man who believed in him and became a mentor and replacement father. His face is grey, his lips dry, moving as if he is trying to speak.

'I'm sorry. I'm sorry,' says Will.

Eoin looks up at Will and, smiling weakly, says, 'I'm not gone yet.'

CHAPTER 34

Aftermath

Later, while Sebastian's remaining men gather the bodies of the dead, Will stands over Eoin's bed as the newly arrived doctor cleans and patches up his wound. Having briefed the Irishman on what happened, he watches on as guilt begins to prickle his inner voice. If only he'd acted sooner Eoin might be in a better state. To make matters worse there are no painkillers – only whisky – and the Irishman flinches as the doctor stitches his flesh.

'You're lucky to be alive, Monsieur.'

'This is not what I call *alive*,' croaks Eoin, wincing as he reaches for the whisky, his brow sweaty with the pain.

'You must go easy on that,' says the doctor. 'It will thin your blood.'

'I have work to do, Doc. The only way I will get through it is to numb the pain.'

'The bullet went straight through you, Monsieur Heaney. Bed rest for you, nothing else. Understand?'

Eoin swears under his breath.

'The doctor is right, Eoin,' says Will.

'I will come by tomorrow,' says the doctor, as he walks towards the door. 'Take care of yourself. *Au revoir.*'

'Thank you,' says Will.

Eoin tries to sit up. 'The feckin' Pastor. How can he still be alive?' He swigs back a generous helping of whisky.

Will recalls the last time he saw the Pastor. It was two years back when they fought at the hidden crypt below St Mary le Bow. The German bombs had fallen and destroyed the little church. Will and Anna had escaped and he'd really thought the Pastor – already half-blinded in their earlier fight – was dead and buried in the rubble. He was clearly wrong.

'The truth is I never actually saw him die.'

'He's as slippery as an eel that one.'

'I have no idea how he escaped the crypt. He must have found another gap to the surface. But why is he here and why now?'

'VIPER can be very persuasive. I can only imagine the offer of employment includes first choice on killing off his old enemies. You and Anna must watch your backs.' Eoin's eyes begin to flicker and close. He is tired.

'We'll be careful.'

'Make sure you are.' The Irishman takes another slug of whisky and winces. 'I see you brought the shard. Good thinking. At least we now have a way of killing the red gas. As for that bloody death ray – Christ knows how we can destroy it.'

'There is a way. But I – we – need to go to Schöllenen Gorge. Tonight.'

The Irishman frowns, shakes his head slowly and fights to keep his eyes open.

Will continues, 'I've been there before. I think it's a VIPER military base and it must also be where the Teleken-Black manufacturing plant is based.'

'But…' Eoin's voice grows fainter, '…but how can you destroy the weapon?'

'I don't know the finer details yet. I'll work it out.'

The whisky bottle slips from the Irishman's grasp. Will takes it from him and places it on the bedside table.

'Good work today,' mumbles Eoin. 'Now disappear. I need to rest.'

Will turns to leave and stops at the door. 'I'm sorry I didn't stop him … the Pastor that is.'

But the Irishman's eyes are closed and he is already fast asleep. Will leaves and closes the door quietly behind him.

In the landing outside his own bedroom he pauses to look at the night-time panorama of French countryside through the immense hole created by VIPER's death ray. The weapon was so powerful. How on earth could it be destroyed? He really has no clue. *I'll work something out.*

The sound of Madeleine's Citroën springs into life and distracts him from his thoughts. He wonders where she could be going. Perhaps to get some supplies for the wounded: he had overheard earlier they were short of medicine and bandages.

He changes out of his tuxedo and pulls on his red flannel shirt and dark grey trousers with braces. Sitting on the edge of the bed he laces up his Derby boots and then stands to pull on his MI6 jacket. He hears a knock on the door.

'Come in.'

Anna enters.

'We were betrayed again!' spits Will.

'I know.'

'Eoin said Sir Hugh died sending us the intelligence on Krüger's visit. VIPER must have intercepted the call for more guns and sent us those duds. This whole scenario with Sebastian's party and Krüger's visit was a set-up. They knew we were here.'

'We have a VIPER mole in London. Someone with influence who can pull strings.'

'Who could it be? Morrow is out of the picture and Coleridge is dead.'

'There are others. I will get in touch with Edward using Eoin's transmitter. See if he has heard anything.'

'Good idea. Thank him from me. Without those masks we would be dead, too.'

There is something different about Anna, Will thinks. He looks at her, up and down, trying to work out what it is. She looks more confident, taller. He thinks it must be the clothes: high-waisted blue trousers with a matching jacket. It is stylish – like something Madeleine would wear.

'You look … different,' he says.

'Her ladyship warmed to me and gave me some of her very expensive French *haute couture*.'

'She has good taste.'

'I'll take that as a compliment, I think.'

'I'm sorry, I didn't mean it like that.'

'It's not important.'

After a moment, they sit on the edge of the bed and Anna says, 'I just spoke to Sebastian. He told me you are going to Schöllenen Gorge.'

Will has deliberately not discussed this with her. He stares at the hardwood floor unsure what to say. 'He is gathering his remaining arsenal. He and his men are going also.' Will reaches across and takes her hand.

'When were you going to tell me?'

'Anna … I want you to go back to London.' He feels her stiffen.

'Why?' she asks, curtly. But before he can respond she goes on, 'You think I am incapable of seeing this through.'

'No! It's just dangerous. Now the Pastor is back from the dead, I have no doubt you and I are high on his kill list.'

'And?' she replies, standing.

The words take moments to form in his mouth. 'I've lost everyone Anna. Everyone. We almost lost Eoin. I … I can't lose you too.'

'You don't get to make that choice, Will. Neither of us does. This is our job. It is what we do.'

Will gets up from the bed. He'd known it was futile to ask and that Anna would not take it well, but still, he'd had to try.

'Very well. We leave tonight.'

Will and Anna look for Sebastian in the hive of quiet activity in the gardens. The corpses are gone, the bodies of the Nazis and VIPER soldiers have been covered with sheets and laid respectfully in a row underneath the stage: despite who they represented, they were still human beings and – Will thought – had been acting under orders, just as he, Anna and Eoin were.

Passing by the open side of the mayor's house, he sees the deceased Resistance members laid out on the table in the dining room, where they had sat that afternoon. The fingers of the dead are interlaced as if in prayer. Standing over them is a priest, shaking holy water from a vial and saying a prayer aloud. Will thinks of Emile and Claudette, their deaths still so raw in his heart. The dead lying on the table are strangers to him yet he feels a choking sensation in his throat and looks away.

Sebastian appears by his side as a truck drives through the gateway.

'We'll travel in that tonight,' he says. 'It contains enough weapons to blow them from the face of the planet, the bastards!'

'I'm glad to hear that,' says Will, coldly.

The truck is large and green with the Nazi cross painted on the side doors. A large canvas covers the rear.

'We acquired it from our German friends,' says Sebastian. 'I knew it would come in useful one day.'

The driver gets out. Will recognises him as one of the carpenters. He is tall, fair-haired and unshaven. A cigarette hangs from his mouth.

Sebastian beckons to him. 'Luca!'

Luca takes the last draw from his cigarette, throws it down and exhales as he approaches.

'Luca is half French, half Swiss. He grew up as a shepherd in the Alps before moving to Lyon to follow the love of his life, Sabine, who'll be with us too. He knows the area around the gorge and how to get there.'

Will shakes his hand. 'Can you speak German?'

'*Ja*,' replies Luca, 'but I am told I have a slight French accent.' He nods politely at Anna.

'I am fluent and will ride up front with you.'

'As you wish.'

'Let's look inside. Luca, do you have that inventory?'

Luca removes some folded sheets of paper from his jacket pocket and hands them across to Sebastian as they walk back to the truck.

Inside are trunks of rifles and explosives, some German and some from the Allied forces. There are two long green metal containers with an American star on them. Inside each one is a portable rocket launcher.

'Bazookas! How did you get these?' asks Will.

'I have friends,' replies Sebastian and leaves it at that.

'If we get close enough, we can destroy the airship.'

'Exactly my thoughts.'

Buoyed by this unexpected addition to their armoury, Will asks, 'How many Resistance fighters are coming with us?'

'We are low on numbers, I'm afraid. There is just me and Luca, Thierry and Sabine.'

Will frowns. 'Madeleine?'

Sebastian shakes his head. 'She has gone.'

'Typical,' mutters Anna.

'But why?' asks Will.

'Do not worry about my niece.'

Will can't help but feel horribly disappointed. How could she leave now when they needed her skills more than ever? No matter. They would have to do without her.

'We should take three of the German uniforms. One each for me and Luca. Sebastian, you can wear the other one. This should keep us free from prying Nazi eyes until we reach the Swiss border. Thierry, Anna and Sabine can pose as captured Resistance spies.'

'I think that might just work,' says Sebastian. 'The Swiss borders are heavily guarded. Luca, however, knows a back route. He has a cousin in Lauterbrunnen, which is close to Schöllenen Gorge.'

'It's our best and only option,' says Will. 'Let's get to it.'

CHAPTER 35

Trouble on the Road to Switzerland

They leave at four in the morning. The night sky is a charred black and the air is cool and fresh. Luca is driving and Will is sitting in the passenger seat wearing a Nazi officer's cap and jacket. Sitting in the back of the truck is Sebastian, squeezed uncomfortably into the biggest uniform they could find. Opposite him is Thierry, a tall gentlemen of mixed race: African and French, Will guesses. Beside him are Anna and Sabine, who is a quiet cat-like woman with dark hair. They each wear makeshift bonds and sit patiently, with their weapons concealed under their jackets. Hidden under the benches are trunks of weapons including guns, bazookas and explosives. Will feels a surge of excitement. They are bringing the battle to VIPER and he will have his revenge.

They drive out of Lyon, heading east into the countryside as the darkness fades and the summer sun rises and warms Will's face. They pass local folk who look away at the sight of a German truck navigating its way through their towns and villages. On occasion another German truck, or a Kübelwagen or two, pass them by, their passengers offering a nod or a salute. As they drive deeper into the countryside Will begins to feel a small sense of achievement. At last they are making progress and getting closer to VIPER.

On the journey so far, Luca has been a man of few words, preferring to drive quietly and not indulge in small talk. That suits Will. Only after several hours does Luca finally speak.

'We are almost one hour from the border,' he says. His accent is unusual – mostly French with a trace of Swiss from where he spent the first half of his life. 'We will take the next turning and head into the mountains.'

'That sounds good.'

'There are no Germans there. We will pass through an unmanned border that is known only to a few.'

The countryside expands into miles of rolling hills and fields like a wonderful green ocean with the Alps floating on air in the distance. Will feels a sense of remoteness that he has never felt before. It makes him feel oddly safe.

As Luca turns left, heading up the narrowest of roads, Will sees a black car driving towards them. It flashes its lights. His stomach begins to clench. 'Slow down,' he says to Luca.

The car is a Peugeot 202 with French registration. Inside are what seem to be three male civilians: two in the front, one in the back. They are casually dressed as if on a day trip but there is something about them that makes him nervous. Three men. As they get close, he sees that the two in the front are young, perhaps in their early twenties, with cautious and humourless expressions. Will zones in on the passenger in the rear, but cannot make out his face.

'There are three men inside the car. They look like military to me,' he says.

The car stops ahead of the truck and the two men in front get out. They stretch their legs and light up cigarettes. The rear door opens and the man in the back seat steps out. He is thin, tanned and Aryan blond. Will freezes. He knows this man. It is the German corporal who asked for his papers in the café. The one Madeleine had called Franz. So this is why he could not make the mayor's party.

'They could be Swiss Army,' says Luca.

'Or German spies watching over the Swiss.'

Surreptitiously Will pulls his cap lower over his forehead.

The corporal nods in a formal manner, reaches back inside the car and takes out his jacket. Doing up the buttons he reaches in for his cap and fixes it on his head, checking his reflection in side mirror. Will unbuttons the Luger that came with his borrowed uniform from the holster at his waist.

The corporal approaches the truck and indicates for Luca to wind down the window. The man has an officious air about him.

'*Guten Tag*,' says Luca, in his not-so-perfect accent.

The corporal frowns.

'*Guten Tag*, Rottenführer,' says Will, deflecting attention from Luca.

The major's eyes slide across to Will and blink a few times as if he is trying to place his face. After a moment he says, 'Where do you think you are going on this road?' The man clearly likes to be in control.

'We are delivering three French Resistance spies.'

The corporal frowns. 'To where?'

Will swallows. *Good question.*

'To L'Étournel,' says Luca.

The corporal glances from Will to Luca with narrowed eyes. 'This road leads to Switzerland. L'Étournel is the opposite direction.'

Will slaps Luca on the arm. '*Dummkopf!* I told you we took the wrong turning.'

Luca swears under his breath, laughs and shakes his head.

'We'll reverse back,' says Will. 'Thank you!'

Luca turns the ignition; the cabin trembles as the engine fires up.

'Wait!' commands the corporal. 'I want to see these spies.'

Will grits his teeth and smiles. 'Of course, Rottenführer.'

The other two German soldiers watch on with a trace of amusement. Through the driver-side mirror, Will can see Franz is already walking along the side of the truck inspecting it closely with his hands behind his back.

What on earth is he doing?

'Get ready for those two. If it comes to it, take no prisoners,' says Will, quietly. 'I will take care of our officious friend.'

Luca smiles at the two men. 'I am ready,' he says.

Will hops out of the truck and walks to the rear where he meets the corporal. He hears the driver door opening and Luca stepping down to the path.

'Do you have a light?' Luca asks the two men.

The corporal looks at Will again, with a frown, as if he trying to place his face.

Will smiles. 'Hello again, Franz,' he says in English.

The corporal's eyes flare and he reaches for the Luger at his waist but Will is fast and launches his fist at the man's face, knocking him back against the truck. Sebastian appears from behind the green canvas with a thick piece of cord, which he loops around the man's neck, choking him. As his face turns purple Will hears the blast of gunfire and sees Luca putting a bullet into the chest of one of the soldiers. The second is unarmed and making a run for it across the fields.

Will aims the Luger but its unfamiliarity makes him clumsy. His first shot misses but the second hits the man's thigh. The soldier cries out, stumbles but limps on. He turns at the sound of Luca's rapid and heavy footsteps and sees the Resistance fighter pointing his stolen Luger at him.

The soldier hops to a stop and raises his arms. 'I surrender! I surrender!' he cries in German, his voice desperate.

Take no prisoners, Will had instructed. Luca shoots him in the head. The force of the bullet propels him backwards and he lies deathly still on the green grass. Will feels his mouth drying. He turns away and slips his Luger back into its holster, clipping it shut as he scans the area for a place to conceal the bodies.

Working together, it takes them almost ten minutes to hide the corpses.

'We can take this car. It might be useful,' says Will. 'It's best we ditch the Nazi uniforms in case we bump into the Swiss Army. Removing his stolen jacket he retrieves his Mauser, MI6 blazer and civilian clothes from under the seat of the truck and puts them on.

'Sabine and I both know the way to my cousin in Lauterbrunnen. I can drive the car and she can drive the truck. If we meet any more obstacles and are forced to part company, then at least we have a better chance of getting both parties to safety.'

'Good plan,' says Will.

'We should stay on this trail for another hour or so,' says Luca.

'At some point we will need to ditch this truck. The Swiss Army will not take kindly to a Nazi truck in their country,' says Sebastian.

'Some might. There are many Nazi sympathizers in Switzerland,' says Luca.

'How far away are we from Schöllenen Gorge?' asks Anna.

'Perhaps two hours. We'll stop at Lauterbrunnen first and meet my cousin, Max. He can hide the truck and perhaps provide an alternative.'

As Luca explains the plan to Sabine, Will and Anna find themselves alone, standing by the Peugeot.

'How're you doing?' asks Anna.

'I'm doing alright.'

Anna pauses. 'Since you came back from France, you seem different.'

He wonders what she means and looks at her questioningly.

'When you killed that wounded soldier at the house…'

'He was dying.'

Anna folds her arms. 'You killed him without hesitation.'

He mulls over her point for a moment. 'He asked me to. I wanted something from him and he wanted something from me. This is our job, Anna. These people are our enemies.'

She shifts uneasily and averts her eyes. 'You just don't seem yourself.'

'They have taken everything from me, Anna. And along the way they have murdered hundreds, if not thousands, of innocent people, robbing families of their loved ones; and it is only going to get worse. They have to be stopped. I have to stop them.'

'I understand that. I just don't want you to be consumed by your need to destroy them. We should be cautious and methodical.'

'Eoin said that two years ago. I agreed to do it his way and look where it got him. I acted under his and bloody MI6's orders. I gave him that promise and nothing happened the way it should have. For two years we've been caught up in this stupid war and what have we achieved? We killed a few Nazis. Great! We blew up their trains, their cars and we brought down a French pylon here and there. Good for us! And what has happened in that time? VIPER have grown. They have an airship with a super weapon and a red gas capable of wiping out lives in any village, town or city, horribly and quickly. And what about Rose? She could be dead for all I know.' Will feels himself trembling inside. 'We've been played. Someone in the Secret Service wanted us out of the way and I have no idea who. Morrow and Coleridge are dead. Eoin is lucky to be alive. We are alone, Anna. Alone.'

Anna leans against the car and tilts her head back. 'We really are.'

'This time we will do it my way.'

'Our way. We are in this together.'

Leaning on the car next to her, Will breathes. 'Our way,' he concedes. Despite asking Anna to return to London, he knows he needs her.

'I just want you to know I am here for you. Always.'

He shoots her a sideways glance and sees her looking across the rolling hills, her eyes misty.

'Thank you,' he whispers. He wonders if he should mention his brief memory of Frost and Schöllenen Gorge, but decides not to. There is nothing concrete to tell.

CHAPTER 36

Rose's Mistake

Rose has not seen Father William since he left her the note with the surprise revelation about her adored brother Will. She has not slept with the excitement of knowing he was out there alive and well. She wonders what he is doing. Does he still live at their old house? What a thrill that gives her, the thought of being back in her own bed. Rose wants answers, but the blind priest is gone as fast as he appeared.

For two days she has demanded a meeting with Ophelia Black, but typically the ice queen has ignored her requests. Rose has thrown tantrum after tantrum and been horrible to Sofia, which she bitterly regrets. She has threatened to leave her apartment and march straight down to Ophelia's office, stopping hearts and pushing open doors and walls if she has to, but the truth is she is feeling tired and weak and does not have the strength to venture anywhere. Her baby is due any day now and, despite the fact that *they* put it inside her, it is still hers. It is part of her – her child – and she wants it.

But this morning Sofia comes back with the breakfast loaves and the news that Ophelia will be here at the apartment very soon. For a moment Rose thinks to cancel. She was not expecting this. Flustered, she gets dressed and washes her hot face with cool water.

Sofia serves breakfast at the little table by the window but Rose has no appetite. 'I can't eat.'

'You must. You are…'

'…eating for two. I know.' From the corner of her eye Rose sees something move and looking outside sees a man on the terracotta-tiled roof opposite. He looks away when her head turns, and she thinks no more of it. No one ever looks at her; they are all too terrified.

Sofia sits beside Rose and places a soft chubby hand on top of hers. 'Why do you want to see that woman? She will do you no good.'

'I only want to talk to Father William. Just once more.'

Sofia tuts. 'I ask around about this blind priest and no one has heard of him. I tell you I no trust him.'

'Priest or no priest, Sofia, he told me a secret.' Rose trembles with excitement at the memory.

'What secret?'

'I can't tell you. Not yet.'

There is a knock at the door.

'Is it eleven already?' says Rose, who is both nervous and excited. Soon she will be able to speak to Father William and learn where Will is and perhaps run away with the baby to be with him.

Sofia opens the door and Ophelia Black walks in with smoke streaming through her nostrils. She drops her cigarette to the floor and kills the flame with the toe of her pointed shoe. She folds her arms and looks at Rose. 'What is it?'

Rose bristles but stands up. 'I want to speak to Father William.'

'Why?'

'That's none of your business.'

'Tell me what you want to say and I'll pass it on.'

'No. I want to talk to him in private.'

'That won't be possible.'

'Why not?'

'He's not here.'

'Where is he?'

'I don't know.'

Rose grits her teeth. 'You're lying.'

Ophelia sighs and rolls her eyes.

Rose's eyes flare, her fuse is lit. With her mind she pushes out at Ophelia. The ice queen trembles and frowns. Blood begins to pour from her nostrils, rolling over her glossy red lips and dripping on to her white silk blouse.

'Rose, stop!' says Sofia, with a quiver in her voice.

Rose pictures snapping Ophelia's neck. The thought excites her and she grins.

Ophelia can barely move but she is looking beyond Rose's shoulder and out the window. She manages a slight nod.

Rose feels her skin prickle. She turns to look out the window and sees the man on the roof aiming a rifle at her. All she can think about is her baby. She makes to run out of the way but a sharp pain cuts into her arm and she feels coldness race through her veins.

'Catch her before she falls and damages that child!' yells Ophelia.

Rose sways, her head is swimming.

'Rose! *Bambina*!' cries Sofia pulling her into her warm soft arms.

Rose falls into them and feels herself almost floating to the ground. Blinking she looks up to see Ophelia looking down at her. The blood on her nose makes her face almost clown-like. Rose wants to laugh but tears prick at her eyes.

'You can't be trusted, Rose. From now until that baby is born this is how you will be. You're a danger to that child. I will not let you…'

The sound of her voice trails off as Rose's eyes grow heavier. All she wants to do is sleep.

CHAPTER 37

Lauterbrunnen

Will sits in the front beside Luca as he navigates the Peugeot through the mountainous roads of the Alps. Lying across the back seat, an exhausted Anna tries to sleep.

It is a warm sunny afternoon. They wind down the windows and breathe in the gloriously clean mountain air. Through the rear-view mirror he sees Sebastian and Thierry, free of their too-snug Nazi uniforms, scanning the countryside carefully as Sabine concentrates on driving the heavy German truck on the trail of the Peugeot.

It is almost one hour later when they clear a narrow mountain pass that opens out into a valley between steep lusciously green hills scattered with chalets and lodges. He sees a tall white church spire amongst them.

'Lauterbrunnen is a thriving municipality here in the Alps,' Luca tells them as he drives down towards the small town. 'Do you hear that?' He points to the right where a giant waterfall roars down a rocky cliffside. 'The Staubbach Falls,' he says.

Lauterbrunnen seems like a green and peaceful paradise. Will cannot help but be bowled over by the beauty of the place.

'We're here,' says Luca, as he steers off the road towards a lodge-style house. Beside it is a large barn with a farmer's lorry parked outside. 'And there is Max and his family!' On the hillside running up from the house a man with dark hair, a blonde woman and three children – two boys and a girl – rake hay in the mid-afternoon sun. Luca honks the car horn three times for their attention and waves out the window.

The family turn to look in their direction.

'Uncle Luca!' cries the smallest of the children, a golden-haired girl of around six years old, holding a rake twice her height. She smiles and waves as Luca eases the Peugeot to a stop at the bottom of the hill.

'Maria, my beautiful girl!'

She drops the rake and runs down the hill towards the car.

'Maria!' scolds the deep voice of the man, but she ignores him and runs with her arms open. The others follow her down. Luca gets out of the car and embraces the girl. 'Your father has you working hard, I see.' He tickles her and she giggles and then runs to embrace Sabine.

The man called Max wears a white collarless shirt and a threadbare brown waistcoat. He embraces Luca and Sabine and, when the introductions are over, all except the father and Maria return to their chores on the hillside. Max seems pleased to see them but his eyes keep being drawn back to the Nazi truck and when the others are out of earshot he asks, 'Luca, what have you brought here?'

'Max, we need your help.'

Max looks suspiciously at Will, Anna, Sebastian and Thierry.

'These are my friends, Max.'

Maria leans against her father and watches Will. He smiles at her and she beams back revealing two missing front teeth.

'We don't want any trouble here,' says Max.

'Max, hear us out. We are all of us in great danger.'

'This is not our war, Luca. Switzerland is neutral, remember?'

'It's not just about the war, Max. There are others worse than the Nazis. They have an airship with weapons that can kill thousands.'

'It is true, Max,' says Will. 'There are powerful people who will stop at nothing to get what they want.'

'And what might that be?'

'Power. Control. Oppression. They will control people with their weapons and with fear.'

'I have seen the airship,' says a little voice.

Will and the others had forgotten Maria was still there.

'Maria, go to your mother!' says Max.

'But, Papa!'

'Now!' he scolds.

Her face drops and tears threaten to fall, but she spins around and stomps up the hillside.

'You've seen the airship?' says Will.

Max sighs. 'Come inside and please hide that truck in the barn before someone sees it.'

As Sabine and Thierry sort out the truck, Will and the others follow Max into his home where the aroma of wood smoke, coffee and spice welcomes them. Max's kitchen is neat and well-kept with tall windows on all sides opening on to the views and the farmland.

'Please sit,' says Max, gesturing to a long wooden table. 'We can talk without interruption.'

Will, Sebastian and Anna sit as Max and Luca prepare coffee and talk in hushed tones. Will can hear Max explaining the events of yesterday evening. Max shakes his head, his expression grim. Will hopes their presence doesn't threaten him and his family.

When they each have a hot cup of coffee, Will begins, 'Max, we will not stay long. I … we don't want to put you and your family in danger – but you must believe me when I say these people must be stopped. They intend to kill us all.'

Max cradles his coffee and seems to consider Will's words.

'We have seen their ship,' he says. 'It flies overhead sometimes. The children chase after it. They dream of one day flying in it.' He looks outside at his family raking the hay on the hillside. 'I have heard talk,' he says. 'There are whispers in the village.'

'What sort of whispers?' asks Will.

'People have gone missing. There have been "accidents", or at least that is what the factory say.'

'Which factory?'

'The Teleken-Black plant in Schöllenen Gorge. They make weapons of all kinds, including chemical ones. They employ local people but sometimes there are accidents and workers die in mysterious circumstances. The rumours are that the chemicals are dangerous. Families have lost fathers, mothers, sons and daughters.'

'Why does no one involve the police?' asks Anna.

'Because Teleken-Black are very rich. They pay the police off. They pay the families off too and no one says anything.'

'How do you know all of this?'

'They go to all the towns and villages looking for workers. They employ local people to do their dirty work. They pay well and people need money.'

'Can't the Swiss government intervene?' asks Anna.

'In return for setting up a "peaceful" hidden factory in the Alps, Teleken-Black give the government a generous rental. They turn a blind eye to any complaints of people who die there.'

'Have they asked you to work there?' asks Luca.

'Yes. My wife too. But we refused. They were not happy. They told us they would return.' Max looks outside at his family hard at work on the hillside. 'I do not trust them. I fear that one day it will be impossible for us to turn them down. And, if we don't return, who will take care of our children?' Max slumps into an armchair, head hanging down.

'We will not let that happen. I promise,' says Will.

'In that truck we have a lot of explosives,' says Sebastian.

'We are going to wipe that place from the Alps, Max,' says Luca.

'How do these workers get to Schöllenen Gorge?' asks Anna.

'There is a bus that takes them there and takes them home again. The plant operates twenty-four hours a day. The next bus is due to pick up the night shift workers at 6 pm.'

'Where from?' asks Will.

'The pick-up point is in a place called Lochbrücke on the other side of town.'

'This could be our way into the gorge. Max, can you show us where Lochbrücke is?'

'Of course.'

'Luca, do you know the way to Schöllenen Gorge?' asks Will.

'I do.'

'Good. Then you will take over as the bus driver. So, let's figure out what we do from here.'

'You will need passes to get inside the plant,' says Max.

Will looks at Max and mulls this over. 'We'll cross that bridge when we get to it. Thank you, Max.'

Later, with the plan in place, Will and Anna take the transistor radio from the truck to the highest point at the top of the hill. Their plan is to send a broadcast to Edward telling him about Eoin's injury, the airship and the operation of the death ray and the red gas in the hope that, if he picks it up, he might relay it to the military. Anna takes over the controls and with the headphones fixed to her ears she begins transmitting.

Two hours pass with no response. Anna shakes her head and drops the headphones.

'We've done all we can,' says Will. 'Besides, technology is different these days. Perhaps one of Edward's super-machines will pick up the transmission and keep it for him.'

'Let's hope he gets it in time. We're going straight into the nest of vipers.'

Despite himself, Will laughs. 'I like that pun: the nest of vipers.'

By 8 pm that evening a fine mist has descended over Lochbrücke making visibility poor. This could work to our advantage, thinks Will, as he, Anna and the others wait at the pick-up point. Parked nearby, and out of sight, is Max in his van into which they have transferred the haul of weapons.

They hear an engine approaching and two headlamps appear like giant cat's eyes in the mist. The bus pulls over. Will counts the silhouettes of seven passengers. Max believed that the local workers lived in fear and mostly hated working at the Teleken plant. They would do anything to stay out of trouble, he had told them.

The driver, a surly man with olive skin and a dark cap, opens the door.

'*Guten Abend!*' says Will. 'Please can you help me with my bags?'

The driver growls something impenetrable and gets out. Will

249

retreats into the mist, drawing him away from the eyes of his passengers.

'*Scheiße*! Where are you?' snarls the driver.

'I am behind you,' replies Will, and pulling the man's head back he squirts a solution of poison ink from his pen into the man's mouth. The driver struggles for a moment before his body weakens and slips to the ground.

Luca removes the man's jacket and puts on his driver's cap.

Will boards the bus with his Mauser to hand. The passengers comprise two women in headscarves and four men. One is wearing a dark brown fedora. Two of the men have backpacks and one of the women holds a large bag. They each carry a gas mask box hanging from string around their shoulders. They glance at him and then quickly look away.

Speaking in German, Will says, 'Leave your passes and your bags, get off the bus and go to your homes. Do not speak of this to anyone. Do I make myself clear?'

Without hesitation they mumble agreement, drop their bags and hand their passes to Will as they get up and leave the bus. Will places a hand on the chest of the gentlemen in the fedora. The man's head dips.

'Do not be alarmed. Your hat, please.'

The man pulls off his hat without question, hands it across and slides quickly past Will and off the bus.

As the passengers hurry down the misty road, Will helps the others load the weapons inside and under the seats. No more than ten minutes later, they say their goodbyes to Max and continue towards Schöllenen Gorge.

CHAPTER 38

Schöllenen Gorge

The road leading into Schöllenen Gorge is narrow. The sheer granite looms high as they descend into what seems like a rocky hell. At this height they are still above the mist and visibility is good.

Will stands at the front as Luca steers the bus around a corner. He sees a line of buses below them in the distance driving towards an old stone bridge.

'Teufelsbrücke – Devil's Bridge,' says Luca.

Will has the sense they are going deeper into the earth and thinks the bridge is aptly named. They are soon joining the other buses and behind them are four more. Luca drives them across Devil's Bridge and into a dark tunnel where Will takes a seat next to Anna.

'Checkpoint ahead!' Luca warns.

Will and Anna stand to get a better look. There are two buses ahead of them at the tunnel exit where VIPER guards, dressed in black, man the checkpoint.

It takes approximately four minutes to check passes and get each bus through.

'*Schnell!*' calls a guard to the bus in front, waving it through with the beam of a torch.

With the guards distracted as they usher the bus forward, Will begins the first phase of their plan. 'Now Luca!' he says, removing Joseph's Time Pencil from his sleeve. He snaps the copper end of the pencil cracking the glass vial inside. The acid releases and countdown begins.

Luca pulls the lever and opens the bus door. Cold night air sweeps inside. Will hangs down at ground level and tosses the Time Pencil back up the road and under the bus behind them. Slipping back inside, he sits beside Anna and puts on the fedora, tilting it slightly so that it covers his face. Turning to look at her in the gloom he sees her breath steaming.

'Cold for the time of year,' she says.

'Not long now.'

Anna smiles wanly. 'I must admit defeat and say these fashionable threads of Madeleine's are not suitable apparel for an excursion to the Alps.'

Will meets her gaze and covers her hand with his. 'Good luck and stay safe.'

'You too.'

The bus eases to a stop and the guard boards, shining the torch in their faces. 'Passes!' he commands. As he walks to back of the bus to check Sebastian's pass first, Will notices he wears a thick utility belt with a pistol attached and a knife and gas mask hanging from it.

'*Guten Abend,*' says Sebastian, handing him his pass.

The guard ignores him and checks his pass under torchlight before examining the others one by one. He comes to stand by Will, his gloved hand extended.

'*Guten Abend,*' says Will, handing across the pass. He wonders about the Time Pencil. It should have detonated by now.

The guard grunts and shines his torch on the paper. He looks at Will for longer that is comfortable and frowns. 'I know your face,' he says.

Will's stomach clenches. Is it possible his face was on some kind of VIPER Wanted list? Will smiles politely. 'I work here.'

The guard breathes heavily through his nose. 'Which division?'

Before Will can respond there is an explosion far bigger than Will had anticipated from the Time Pencil.

'What the hell?'

The base of the bus behind them is engulfed in flames. Thankfully the door is open and all the passengers are able to escape.

The guard hurries out of the bus and waves at Luca, '*Schnell! Schnell!*' Luca wastes no time in driving through the checkpoint. The guards have their rifles raised, stopping anyone from leaving the tunnel. In seconds the engine of the bus is on fire and it explodes in a ball of flame. Abandoning protocol, the guards and the passengers run through the exit together.

Joseph was not wrong about the Time Pencil being powerful. Will can't quite believe he has been carrying that thing around. What if there had been an accident while he was wearing it? He pushes the thought from his mind. It's bad enough carrying the shard, which on its own makes him a potential weapon of destruction. It occurs to him he has not felt a pulse from the shard since they left France. He rests his palm on his breast pocket and feels the reassuring outline of the tin soldier. It is still there inside the fusilier. Sleeping.

Luca drives them quickly through a car park where dozen of buses are parked and the occupants gather in droves to watch the scene at the checkpoint. Will and the others sit at the front of the bus taking in their first view of Schöllenen Gorge.

Will feels his throat drying. There is an unsettling familiarity to this place. He has clearly been here before. The gorge is vast, like a valley fit for the gods, with stunning and oppressive granite rock faces that stretch high into the sky. A long and steep stairwell runs from the car park and leads almost a quarter of a mile up to a stark three-storey building built into the side of the rock face. The Teleken-Black weapons plant.

'*Merde*! It is much bigger than I expected,' says Sebastian.

'The length of four football pitches,' says Will.

He feels the eyes of his companions rest on him curiously and pretends not to notice.

Carved in stone at the centre of the building is the ominous Teleken-Black logo: a T overlapping a B with a viper coiled through the letters. There are twenty-four small windows on each level, however on the top floor at the far end is a large window with a balcony overlooking the gorge. He swallows and his pulse races.

I know that place. But how? I have stood there. Once before. No, more often than that.

He shakes the thought from his head. With no time for retrieving lost memories, he looks beyond the plant at the bottom of the gorge where there is a vast flat landing pad, big enough to hold an airship.

Their plan had been to split into two teams, one led by Will, the other by Sebastian. The goal of Will's team, comprising Anna and Thierry, was to attack the factory from within. Sebastian's team of Luca and Sabine was to find a secluded spot where they could fire the bazooka rocket launchers at the airship and factory.

But there was no airship to be seen.

'*Merde*! Where is the airship?' says Luca.

'Damn it,' says Will. 'Sebastian, we need to adjust our plan.'

CHAPTER 39

Bon Courage

With the airship absent Will has to think fast. 'Sebastian, you'll have to use the rocket launchers on the factory. We may not get the opportunity to get to the first and second floors so aim for the top two floors if you can.'

'That is a good plan but I would suggest holding back with the rockets in case the airship returns,' says Sebastian.

'Agreed. Remember everyone, this mission is about sabotage and subversion. This is our best chance of blowing this place from the face of the earth. If by any chance the airship appears then be my guest and take it from the sky.'

'Our pleasure,' says Sebastian.

'Will, the workers are heading into the factory,' says Anna.

Will looks out to see the Teleken-Black employees making the climb up the stone steps with their gas mask boxes. 'We need to go.'

Thierry and Will take a backpack each. Anna takes the bag.

'Good luck everyone,' says Will, 'Remember, there will be a mass evacuation. If all goes well, and if, by some miracle, we achieve this without being caught or hurt, then I hope to see you back on the other side of the tunnel. Stay in the crowd and keep out of sight.'

'*Bon courage, mes amis,*' says Sebastian.

'*Bon courage,*' Will and the others reply, shaking each other's hands.

Will can't help but feel guilty. These people are risking their lives to join him on what might be a suicide mission. He feels a strong warmth and kinship like none he can remember. He can't thank them enough but now is not the time. Perhaps in another life, if there is one.

Will, Anna and Thierry leave the bus and melt in with the crowd trudging up the stone steps. Turning back he sees the fire has been tamed in the tunnel and there are a dozen or so guards investigating the scene. Some are questioning the civilian workers at gunpoint. Swallowing, he looks at the entrance to the factory in the distance. It is arched, with two ornamental spikes pointing towards the ground. They are walking into a viper's mouth.

Guards on either side of the entrance are making random security checks. His stomach knots and he keeps his head down, only looking occasionally from under the rim of the fedora. Thierry is three people ahead of him and has cleared the entrance without being checked. Will feels a surge of excitement. Anna is next.

'*Guten Abend!*' she says in a jolly tone.

The guard, a young man with a ferret-like face, whistles his approval at Anna.

Anna smiles at him and with this distraction Will hurries by, but the young guard has moved forward to speak to Anna and collides with Will.

'*Entschuldigung,*' says Will.

The guard does not seem in the mood for accepting apologies. '*Dummkopf*!' he shouts, poking Will's chest.

Under the shade of the fedora Will rolls his eyes. '*Entschuldigung*,' he repeats, and tries to bypass the man, but the guard grabs his arm.

'What is in your bag?' he asks, as people file past.

Will looks up and sees the guard smiling quickly at Anna. This show of authority is clearly for her benefit. He grits his teeth as the guard squeezes his arm and shakes it.

'Your bag!' he commands.

Cursing his luck, Will glances to the side. The other guard is caught up with his own security checks and is unaware of what is going on with his colleague. Will wonders how he can solve the problem of this irritant without attracting attention. He levels his gaze at the guard. The man's ferrety eyes take in his face and focus on the scar on Will's left cheekbone. For a second he seems confused and then he steps back, reaching clumsily for the pistol on his utility belt. But before Will can spring into action he hears a nearly inaudible whoosh. The guard stiffens, eyes wide. Will sees something small and metallic lodged in the guard's neck. A Velo-Dart. He turns to see Anna's arm drop to her waist.

The guard falls back and Will eases him to the wall leaning his stiff body against it. Will furtively snatches the dart from his neck, tosses it to the floor and joins Anna. They merge with the crowd.

'Reassuring to know that France's finest *haute couture* comes equipped with the latest in Velo-Dart technology,' says Will.

'I must admit, I did make a few adjustments before leaving France. A girl is just not safe in these troubled times.'

'I like your style.'

'What's our next move?'

Will is loath to admit he really does not know. Their intelligence on Teleken-Black's factory is next to nothing.

'Still trying to work that one out.'

'Is it possible you have been here before?'

'I can't be sure. Some things seem to resonate but I haven't any details.'

Looking around him none of it seems familiar. The ground floor lobby of the building is immense, with tall ceilings and functional grey concrete walls, and four lifts that lead up to the upper floors. Queues of people wait patiently by the doors.

'Look,' says Anna, nodding at the wall opposite the lifts.

Will sees Thierry looking at a diagram on the wall. It's a layout of the building. He feels his adrenalin pulsing. They thread their way through the crowd and join him.

The ground floor is marked in three coloured zones: white, yellow and grey. The white zone is a weapons building facility – rifles; the yellow zone is pistols; and the grey contains an lightening symbol. Pointing to it Thierry says, 'The power generator.'

The first floor is split into a blue zone – Teleken research – and a red zone marked with a skull and crossbones, the symbol for toxic substances. Will's hands ball into fists. So that is where they manufacture it. He sees what looks like two staircases on either side of the plant, each with a 'Restricted' sign.

The second floor is a green zone comprising offices, meeting rooms, classrooms and training facilities. His memory stirs and his mind spins. Unsteady on his feet, he leans against the map.

'Will, you have been here before, haven't you?' asks Anna.

He nods. 'Yes, I believe so. This is the main training facility.'

'Are you feeling alright?'

He takes a few breaths and feels better. 'I'm fine.'

'I can take the ground floor and blow the generator,' says Anna.

'First thing we need to do is evacuate the building,' says Will. Looking up he sees red alarm bells dotted around the walls. 'I'll set off the alarms when you two are out of sight.'

'I can take the first floor,' says Thierry.

'Good, but be careful there. It is inevitable the red gas will be released, so make sure you both keep your masks close. Set your explosives to detonate at 11 pm.'

To lessen his load, Will removes the mask from the box and straps it to his backpack as Thierry wastes no time and runs to the open doors of the lift, jumping the queue, much to the consternation of those before him.

As they part company Anna reaches for Will's arm. She pulls him close and kisses him warmly on the lips. 'For luck,' she murmurs and then turns quickly and disappears into the crowd before he can say anything to her.

'Good luck,' he whispers, his stomach fluttering.

CHAPTER 40

The Training Ground

Hearing raised voices back at the entrance, Will sees some new guards milling around their stiff, unconscious colleague who has slid to the floor on his back.

The queues for the lifts are still three people deep, the doors firmly closed as the latest batch of workers ascend to their respective floors.

According to the map, further along the lobby is a corridor with a staircase, where he catches the glow of a light as a door opens. A stern-faced woman dressed in a grey suit with a Teleken-Black badge emerges clutching a batch of manila folders. Behind her he sees the staircase. As she walks away he hurries towards the door noting the sign written in German on the outside: 'Teleken-Black badged personnel only.'

A risk worth taking, he thinks, and slips through before it closes. The steps are concrete, painted a clinical white like the walls. There are two flights of stairs per floor. He hurries up the first one two steps at a time until he reaches the landing and the entrance to the top floor. On the wall next to the door is an alarm activator.

Slinging off his backpack he crouches down and begins to undo the straps to get his mask. So far so good, he thinks, opening the flap of the backpack, but at that moment he hears men's voices. The door swings open. He swallows and looks up to see three guards frowning down at him. The door closes behind them.

'Hello!' says Will, in a disarming tone.

'What are you doing here?' says the guard on his right, a broad man, the largest of the three.

Will stands to face them, smiling politely, his hands raised in an appeasing gesture. 'I'm sorry. I wandered up here by mistake.'

'Your pass. Show it to me now!'

Will's eyes slide to the guard on his left who is leaning across and looking down at the contents of his backpack on the floor behind him.

'What is in the bag?' he asks.

Will smiles and shrugs. 'Explosives.'

The first guard snorts and glances at his colleagues in what seems like the longest of seconds. Will can sense their next move and feels his hybrid martial arts training and survival instincts switch into gear. He lunges his fist at the throat of the large guard to his right. The man topples back against the wall behind him.

The second guard is canny. Growling, he swings his fist at Will's face, but Will leans back, narrowly missing the blow. Pain sears his ribs as the third guard hits him hard. The second guard swings a fist at Will's stomach winding him and forcing him back, his feet knocking the backpack of explosives.

Holding his ribs and stomach he smiles at the guards. 'You'll have to do better than that.'

They run at him and, pushing back from the wall, Will deflects their fists with skilful Aikido hand-blocks that confuse his opponents. The first guard quickly edges behind Will and locks his arm around his throat. Leaning back Will swings his feet onto the second guard's shoulders. The man drives forward unwittingly giving Will the power to propel himself head over heels behind the first guard. Landing on his feet Will picks the guard up by the belt and tosses him over the bannister. He scrambles at the bannister rail but misses and cries out as he plunges to the concrete steps below. The large guard has made a recovery and, despite still clutching his throat, has removed a knife from his utility belt. The second guard has unfastened his pistol and raises it. Will grabs the second man's arm and swings his pistol at the first. The gun fires twice, shooting the large guard who drops the knife and tumbles down the white stairs in a bloody mess.

Will slams the second guard's hand on the bannister, cracking his bones until he releases the pistol and it clatters onto the stairs below. The guard is strong and with his other hand claws at Will's eyes and mouth, pushing him against the bannister and forcing him over with all his might. Grunting, Will feels his feet slipping beneath him. He cannot escape this. The guard forces him harder. Will's feet lift off the ground. He wraps his arms tight around the guard's neck, pulls the man to him and together they flip over the bannister. With a keen sense of what is around him, Will twists his body over the guard so that he is on top as the two of them fall through the air to the steps below. The guard slams and crunches on the steps, cushioning Will's fall. They slide down the flight of stairs like a man on a bobsleigh, making a stop beside the first guard, whose neck is twisted in a gruesome way. The bobsleigh is verging on unconsciousness, breathing erratically and groaning.

'What the hell!' Will hears from the landing above. A pair of boots begins to tread carefully down the steps. Will pulls out his Mauser and ducks out of sight.

'Hello?' calls a voice.

'Help me,' Will responds in a weak voice.

Standing out of sight, he waits for the new guard to show. A moment later a figure in black combats appears with a rifle pointing before him. As he examines his groaning colleague Will shoots him in the chest. He topples down the stairs and Will darts past him up to the landing and the bag of explosives. Pulling on his gas mask as a disguise, he smashes the alarm glass with the butt of his Mauser. One by one alarms begin ringing across all floors in the plant.

People flood into the stairwell below. Will steps into a corridor lit only by the flashing of red warning lights. Teleken-Black employees are still emerging, their faces terrified, fumbling with their gas masks and pushing their way past each other. The red gas takes no prisoners, thinks Will, not even those who create it, process it, bottle it and ship it.

He sees men in white lab coats hurry from a doorway like frightened mice. In the room they have left are rows and rows of glass cabinets containing jars and bottles of chemicals. He has no idea what is inside but reckons they might boost the effect of his explosives. He takes the first batch from his backpack and places them carefully behind one of the cabinets.

Checking his watch he sees it is twelve minutes to eleven. He has precious little time. He sets the timer for eleven and hurries out of the room. The crowd in the corridor has thinned to a trickle of masked people moving towards the stairs. Will is drawn towards the far right of the building, though he is not sure why. His mind swirls and he hears voices from another time. Among them is Colonel Frost's barking orders. Will remembers men in training gear running down this same hall. He can't quite recall what is down there. Taking off his mask, he goes down the hallway where there are large green double doors.

He opens them.

The smell of stale sweat fills his nostrils, evoking old memories of sparring and gruelling workouts. Inside is an enormous, brightly lit gymnasium with a shiny hardwood floor, French windows and a balcony overlooking the gorge. Around the walls are weights, duelling daggers, chains, nunchucks, swords, gymnast hoops, climbing bars. At one end is a boxing ring and a martial arts floor. He feels the hairs on his neck stand up. This space had been his training ground. He has spilled blood here, his own and that of others. He takes out the remaining explosives. Hearing gunshots outside, he goes to the window, wondering if Sebastian, Luca and Sabine are in trouble. Opening the glass doors he steps onto the balcony. The cold night air prickles his hot face. The car park has been lit with flood lamps and the floor of the gorge resembles a giant runway. The car park is full of people and he is too far away to pick out any individuals. The base of the landing pad has been lit and, as he watches, a great shadow appears blocking out the night sky. It is the airship.

His heart racing, he scans the area for any sign of Sebastian and his team but is distracted by the rasp of a second engine. To his right, beyond the tunnel, a bi-plane flies towards him and sweeps over the car park. It is a cream Tiger Moth. He has seen it before. Could it be the same one that flew past him on the way to his drop-off point over the Channel?

The guards fire at the plane but it dives quickly, spinning and dodging and shooting off several unforgiving rounds in their direction. The Moth loops over the car park and across the factory, passing close to Will on the balcony. The pilot smiles as she pulls upwards, all guns raging at the gondola of the descending airship. It is Madeleine. He laughs. He thinks back to when he flew from Chartres to deliver the microfilm. Was she the pilot who flew alongside him?

As he sets the timer on the explosives a glance at his watch shows he has three minutes left. *Shit!*

CHAPTER 41

Frost

Picking up his mask, Will hurries out of the gymnasium, runs up the hallway of flashing lights and ringing bells and down the stairs, leaping over the still bodies of the four guards. As he reaches the second floor he stops at the unsettling blare of the death ray's klaxon. Red light flashes through the small windows as the scorching blast roars and people scream in terror. He thinks of Madeleine and his stomach clenches. Has the death ray just finished her off?

On the ground floor he runs towards the exit, shouting to the crowds, 'Get out of here! Run for your lives!'

The airship hovers high above the landing pad. There is no sign of the Tiger Moth. His heart sinks. Search beams on both sides of the gondola sweep through the skies. The beams swing down to scan the crowds below. One stops on Will. He raises his hand against the glare and then hears the buzz of the Moth as it swoops up from behind and spins like a corkscrew in the air firing at the gondola, killing the lights and plunging him into darkness. Two bodies drop from the gondola to the rocky surface below.

The cannon spins around searching for the little plane. The klaxon blares and the death ray whips through the night sky lashing angrily at the Tiger Moth.

Around him people watch in wonder as the plane loops and dives, dodging the murderous ray, which misses and slashes the surface of a nearby cliff skimming off a flurry of rocks and dust. The cannon tracks the plane as it flies over the car park, across the landing pad and up the gorge

Will feels his heart pounding. *Get out of here, Madeleine. It will take a miracle for you to survive this attack.*

The klaxon blares and the cannon fires. The red ray spirals through the air. Madeleine steers the Tiger Moth close to the granite walls of the gorge, darting from one side to the other like a mouse being pursued by a snake. The heat ray hits the surface, missing the little plane by inches as it disappears over the gorge.

Will starts to move, scanning the tops of heads for any sign of Anna or the others, but there are too many people. 'Anna!' he calls, but there is no answer.

Suddenly a thunderous roar bellows through the gorge as the plant blows in six simultaneous explosions. Debris flies through the air as people scream and swarm towards the tunnel. Will reaches a bus. Using it as cover, he watches the Teleken-Black building crumble in on itself. He feels a surge of adrenalin; a grim smile creases his face.

He hears Anna's voice. 'Will!'

She is running towards him, pushing her way through the panicking people.

'Anna!' Without thinking, he embraces her and feels relief wash over him. 'Thank God, you're safe.'

'I saw Thierry run ahead of me from the plant. Have you seen him?'

'No. Perhaps he's with Sebastian and the others. We have to find them. I want those missiles to blast that airship from the sky.'

'Look!' says Anna, pointing beyond him.

Will turns to see six or more VIPER soldiers shooting in the direction of a pathway cut into the granite and leading to the landing pad. Halfway along, poorly protected by some rocks, are Sebastian and Thierry trying to provide cover for Luca and Sabine as they run the gauntlet towards the landing pad with the bazookas.

Will takes out his Mauser. 'We're not finished yet.'

The buzz of the Tiger Moth has not returned. He hopes Madeleine is safe.

A second search beam from somewhere at the top of the factory sweeps downward and picks out Sabine and Luca. They shoulder the bazookas and lift them towards the airship as the blare of the klaxon sounds. Will sees the cannon below the gondola swing around and point downwards. The VIPER soldiers turn from their battle with the mayor and Thierry and begin to scatter.

'No!' says Will, grabbing Anna's arm.

Luca! Sabine!' he screams pointlessly.

And then it comes. The flash of red light, whipping like a glowing tentacle as it lashes at Sabine and Luca.

It is too late. The two Resistance fighters and the bazookas light up and explode in a cloud of grey dust and ash.

'Oh Will,' says Anna, her voice trembling.

Boots stomp behind and around them. They swing around, their guns ready, but there are too many VIPER guards surrounding them. They are trapped.

'Remove their guns,' says a familiar voice that makes Will go cold. It is Colonel Victor Frost, the man who was his VIPER trainer and leader for four years; the same man who murdered his parents and kidnapped his sister. Will had last seen him two years ago when he was captured by Eoin, just before he was sent to jail.

One of the guards snatches Will's Mauser and Anna's Walther and cuffs them both.

Then Frost makes his way from behind the VIPER guards. Will's hands curl into fists as the muscular figure comes near.

'The prodigal son returns,' says Frost. 'I would say welcome home, William, but there is nothing left of it. You've made quite a mess here, haven't you?'

'It's the first of many home improvements I intend to make.'

Frost smiles wanly at Will, then assesses him. 'Look at you. All grown up and the fire in your belly is still raging. Despite our history, William, I am pleased to see you.'

'Because of our history, Vic, I am pleased that soon I will get to put a bullet between your eyes.'

Frost snorts and turns to Anna, looking her up and down. 'Have we met?'

Anna levels her gaze at Frost, her expression fixed and unafraid. He walks around her, leaning towards her and sniffing the air. 'I remember you, missy. London, May, 1941. What a rollercoaster of a night that was.'

'Fun times,' says Anna, coldly.

'Maybe when the dust settles you and I could grab a drink somewhere.'

'I'd rather go on a date with a fetid corpse.'

Will hears some of the VIPER soldiers stifle a laugh and notices Frost's nostrils flare.

'That could be arranged,' says the Colonel, glancing upward. 'For now we are all going on a little trip.'

Guards and some of the workers are making a quick job of sweeping the debris from the surface of the landing pad. Above them the airship begins its descent. The painted viper on the base of the gondola gets bigger and the cannon retracts and disappears inside the snake's mouth. The gondola is larger than it seemed, perhaps a hundred feet wide and two hundred feet long. Will can see the front window and, through it, the hooded shape of Proatheris, leader of the Cerastes, looking his way.

Who are you?

'It's time for you to atone for your sins, William,' says Frost.

CHAPTER 42

Proatheris

The airship hovers unsteadily twenty feet above the landing pad. The engines chug relentlessly, the cooling fans swirl and expel mini tornadoes of warm air, raising dust and pushing it into the faces of everyone below. Will squints and watches as a rope falls from the centre of the gondola and is grabbed by several guards who hold it firmly, tethering the ship to *terra firma*.

A hatch opens from the belly of the snake and lowers to the surface of the landing pad: a walkway to and from the airship.

Frost points at two of the guards. 'You and you. Come with me.' He pushes Will and Anna towards them. 'Put a bullet in their backs if they try anything.' Frost leads them towards the airship. On either side of the pathway workers and guards watch. Will sees Sebastian, and the mayor takes a step towards him. Will shakes his head. *No, Sebastian! There is nothing you can do here.*

As if reading his thoughts, the mayor halts and jerks his head at something behind Will. Confused, Will keeps his eyes trained ahead and walks on a few paces before quickly glancing back to see what Sebastian was trying to indicate. A familiar face is shaded by the visor of a guard's helmet. Thierry! The Frenchman shoves him in the back. 'Move!' he orders, and Will stumbles forward, hiding a smile inside.

Up the ramp, all Will can see is a rectangular bright white light. The ramp wobbles as the guards fight to control the tethering rope.

'Faster,' snaps Frost.

With Anna beside him, Will steps onto the unsteady ramp and ascends into the gondola, sandwiched between Frost and Thierry and another armed guard.

A line of armed VIPER soldiers awaits them at the top of the ramp. It leads to what seems to be the deck, which is more than ten feet tall and almost thirty feet wide. As well as being the access and exit point for the airship it also seems to be a storage area. Stacked high along the walls are dozens of yellow barrels marked with a skull and crossbones. The red gas.

'Raise the ramp,' calls Frost.

As the ramp is pulled up the engines accelerate and Will feels a lurch in his stomach as the airship rises. Frost walks ahead to the front of the ship. The two guards shove Will and Anna, urging them to follow the Colonel.

The inside of the ship is a hive of activity filled with maintenance people, soldiers, guards and engineers with grease-covered skin. Will notices two sliding windows that run from floor to ceiling on either side of the deck. Beyond both are slatted balconies with angled windows overlooking the world below. At the base of each window are the red rolls of material that together combine to make the VIPER flag, and which are used by the soldiers to climb down to the ground.

Frost leads them to a steel door where two grim-faced guards stand like sentinels. Passing through, he is greeted by a warm blast of steam hitting his face from two giant fans in the ceiling above them. There is no floor, only a narrow steel lattice bridge, wide enough for two people. Steam rises around and through it and below it he sees the Tesla cannon, hidden from the outside world, like a sleeping dragon. Around it men in heavy overalls spray water from hoses to cool it down.

Crossing through a flurry of steam Will steals a glance at Anna, who surreptitiously nods to her left. Will follows her gaze and sees a walkway from the bridge leading to what looks like a bank of machines the like of which might be used at Bletchley. Operators turn dials, flick switches and write notes on clipboards. They make him think of Edward and he imagines his pal would love the opportunity to play with this equipment. A steel pipe runs under the walkway and connects to the cannon. *The power source. Does the machine control it all?*

'Move!' says the guard behind him, prodding him with the barrel of his gun.

At the end of the bridge there is a white door, which slides open to reveal a dimly lit navigation room. Two uniformed men stand with their backs to him at a control panel with a wooden steering wheel. Curved front windows run from floor to ceiling to enable them to navigate the ship.

He sees a familiar face. Tall, with pale pockmarked skin, thin lips and oiled red hair: Rupert Van Horne looking every inch the model of smug superiority.

'Child killer,' spits Will, through gritted teeth.

A smile appears like a scar on Horne's face.

And then he hears Anna say, in a bewildered voice, '*Sir Hugh?*'

Horne is standing beside a brown Chesterfield sofa. Seated upon it, with a cane resting by his leg, is Sir Hugh Coleridge. His hair is ruffled, he looks pale and gaunt with dark rings under his eyes. He does not seem to notice them. Behind him is a guard holding a pair of hair clippers. Gently he tilts the chief's head back and begins to shave his dark hair right down to the skull. Coleridge says nothing and lets the barber get on with it.

Has he been drugged?

Moments later, Coleridge's hair has fallen to the floor where it lies by his feet in small wisps and tufts. Prisoner-like stubble is all that remains on his head. But there is something else. A shadow beneath the stubble, like a tattoo of something Will can't quite make out.

Anna turns to Frost. 'Why are you doing this? Hasn't he suffered enough?'

Frost does not respond.

Will glances at Horne, whose eyes have never left him since he walked into the navigation room.

The guard lifts a bowl from behind the sofa and begins to lather Coleridge's head with soap and water. With a shaving blade he begins skilfully to cleave through the stubble, leaving streaks of bare white skin and revealing the tattoo. Will feels his stomach fluttering. The tattoo is a viper rising from the base of his skull – the symbol of the Cerastes, the Order of VIPER. He glances at Anna who watches, frowning in confusion. The barber finishes and pats Coleridge's head with a towel. Coleridge blinks, rubs his eyes and looks from Anna to Will.

'We thought you were dead,' says Anna. 'Perhaps it's a shame you are not.'

Coleridge smiles grimly and sits up. 'Sir Hugh Coleridge is long gone, my dear,' he says, as the cane slides away from the sofa and falls to the floor. Rolling up his trouser leg to the knee, he reveals his wooden leg. Will can now see three silver clips running up the calf. Coleridge undoes them one by one and pulls the wooden limb apart, revealing his real leg underneath.

'*You're* the mole!' says Will.

'Deception is king in our line of work, Will. Ten points to you, although I'm deducting eight for not working it out sooner.' The MI6 Chief of Staff stands, his eyes levelling with Will's. He wobbles for a moment before emitting a low hoarse laugh. 'Forgive my theatrics. I can't help myself sometimes.'

Horne lets out a sycophantic cackle. Coleridge gives him a disdainful look and Horne's face drops, his cheeks flushing a deep red.

Coleridge lifts what looks like a black blanket resting on the back of the sofa and pulls it around him. But it is no blanket. It is a monk's robe with a red trim around the hood and cuff. It is the robe of Proatheris – the leader of the Cerastes.

'You are Proatheris?' The parts of the jigsaw begin to fall into place. Coleridge had fooled them all.

'You have cost us quite dearly today, Will.'

'It's been you all along. That night in the hospital, it was you who tried to kill me.'

Coleridge pulls a platted red rope around the waist of his robe. 'Regrettably, I did not succeed.'

'You framed Morrow. You planted the Rolling Ticker under the Embiricos. You employed Clifford Meadows to spy on Anna and Edward. You sent us to France on a plane that you shot down.' Will glances at Horne, who smiles coldly from the shadows. 'You freed that treacherous child killer and sent a murderer after your best friend! You betrayed him. You betrayed us and you betrayed your country!'

'It was all necessary for the greater goal. Besides, as detestable as Horne is, he is my nephew and I made a promise to look after him.'

'So many people have died because of you!'

Coleridge smiles. 'I'll take that as a compliment. Thank you.'

'You disgust me.'

'And you disappoint me. I thought you were better than this. I really believed my time was up when we met at Chittlock's house. Dear sad old Nicholas mentioned that the hairdresser told you two monks had entered the house, but only one had left it. You went back and did not even find the hidden robe. You're not as bright as Eoin thought you were.'

Will steps forward, his face inches from Coleridge's. 'You treacherous scum!'

A punch hits his ear and Will falls to his knees, nursing the burning ear with his cuffed hands.

'Watch your mouth!' says Frost.

'Try not to damage the goods, Frost. She wants him in one piece, remember.'

'Let's just kill him now, Uncle. She doesn't have to know. Let me do it!'

'Be quiet, Rupert!' bellows Coleridge.

Will pushes himself up. 'Who is *she*?'

'She is the *Lady*. You will meet her. Soon enough.'

'Where is my sister?'

'In cloud cuckoo land!' laughs Horne, almost deranged.

Will's fingers dig into his palms. He looks from Horne to Coleridge. 'What does that mean?'

Coleridge ignores the question and whispers something to Horne. Horne's face pales. 'Yes, Uncle,' he says and immediately leaves the navigation room.

'Captain Smythe, are we on course?' asks Coleridge.

'Yes, sir. The winds are on our side. We may arrive thirty minutes early.'

'Not a minute less, Smythe.'

'Yes, sir.'

Will steps towards Coleridge, but is held back by Frost.

'Just what are you expecting to achieve with this bloated flying contraption? Do you really think one airship with a fancy gun and some red gas is enough against the Spitfires and Messerschmitts of the world?'

Coleridge folds his arms inside his sleeves. He hesitates and then smiles slyly. 'If it were up to me you would be dead with a bullet between your eyes. But there is a reason you are still alive.'

'Because you are an incompetent idiot who can't seem to kill me?'

Frost raises his fist, but Coleridge gestures at him and shakes his head. Turning to Will he says, 'You have something we want.'

The shard.

'In Lyon, something destroyed the red gas. Something extraordinary. Something blue.'

'I don't know what you are talking about.'

'The Stones of Fire were allegedly destroyed. But a fragment of them still exists and I think you have it.'

Will does not know what to say to that. It seems futile to deny it considering he is carrying the shard in his blazer.

'Search them,' says Coleridge.

Frost uncuffs Will and Anna and nods to the guards. Acting out the role Thierry manhandles Will, copying what the other guard does to Anna, who does her best to ignore the indignity. They wrench out the Velo-Darts and toss them to a nearby bin. Thierry checks the collar of Will's blazer where the flexible saw is kept.

'Check the sleeves. There are all sorts concealed there,' says Frost.

Ignoring the saw, Thierry moves to the cuffs and removes the tools. Will knows he has to do this and lets him get on with it. Thierry begins to empty his pockets finding only a packet of bullets, some coins and, of course, the tin soldier. Will pulls back when Thierry's fingers brush the soldier. The Frenchman reads the signal and pulls his hand away.

'Wait!' says Frost.

He pushes Thierry out of the way, reaches into Will's pocket and pulls out the tin soldier. He glares at Thierry. 'Eyes open, private! Leave no stone unturned.'

'Yes, sir. Sorry, sir,' replies Thierry.

Frowning, Coleridge takes the fusilier from Frost and studies it. He shakes the tin soldier and smiles at the rattling sound. 'That was easier than I thought.'

Behind his stony expression Will tries to conceal his fury. He glances at Anna, her eyes linger on his. He wants to reassure her, but he can't. VIPER will now own the shard. Lord knows what they might be able to do with it.

Coleridge prises open the spine of the fusilier, takes out the stone inside and holds it up in the light, his expression full of awe. 'Is this really a piece of the Stones?'

It is now Will's turn to frown. The stone that Coleridge is holding is not the shard. It is a long piece of gravel. Just like the gravel on Sebastian's drive.

CHAPTER 43

The Owl

Coleridge's expression turns sour. 'This is not a piece of the Stones of Fire!' He throws the gravel to the floor and crushes it with his boot. 'Where is it?'

'I have no idea what you are talking about.'

Coleridge exhales. 'Very well. Frost, kill the girl.'

'Pleasure, sir,' says Frost, raising his pistol and pointing it at Anna's head. The colour drains from her face.

'Wait!' cries Will.

'Shoot!' says Coleridge.

With his heart in his mouth, Will springs at Frost and pushes the pistol away. 'Wait, I'll tell you!'

'Let's hear what he has to say, Colonel Frost,' says Coleridge.

The Colonel shrugs and slips the gun back into its holster.

'Don't tell them, Will,' says Anna.

Will looks desperately from Anna to Coleridge. The truth is, he has no idea where the shard is.

'On the count of five I want the answer or she dies. Five, four, three, two…'

'I had it! I did. It was in my pocket concealed inside the tin soldier but now it's not and I don't know why. I swear to you!'

'You'll have to do better than that.'

Will tries to think, recalling the battle at Sebastian's house. 'I last saw it at the mayor's house. The red gas was everywhere. I used the shard. The gas dissipated. Madeleine was there. She picked it up and gave it back to me.' He feels his stomach churning.

'Ah, the wily Madeleine. Always two steps ahead of the game. Impossible not to admire her,' says Coleridge.

'How do you know Madeleine?' asks Will.

'I know everything about everyone and Madeleine is no exception. What you don't know is that before Chittlock coerced you into joining his crusade, there was someone else. Another protegé. You were not his first.'

'What do you mean?'

'Madeleine was Chittlock's first experiment. He was a friend of her family and, after her parents met with a fatal accident – regrettably, caused by us – he offered her a way to exact revenge. He recruited her and trained her to be a spy.'

Will is finding it hard to swallow what Coleridge has just told him. But what did he have to gain by lying? Besides, Madeleine's story was almost the same as his. He wonders why she never mentioned it.

Coleridge continues. 'As time went by, Tim started getting involved with all sorts of weird and wonderful things. The Stones of Fire was his pet project. Madeleine, however, betrayed him and sold his research and precious notebook to the Fellowship of Fire. Ultimately, that led to his death. So you could say Madeleine killed him.'

'You killed Timothy Chittlock. You and your ridiculous organisation.'

'Well, yes. But thanks to Madeleine…'

'You'll never get the shard now,' interrupts Will.

'I wouldn't be so sure about that. She is following us right now in that little bi-plane of hers. She thinks we don't know but we do. Our scanners are keeping track of her. It is my guess that she will bring along the shard with the absurd notion that it will help defeat us. Except we will be waiting.'

'She's smarter than you think,' says Will.

'Is she?' Coleridge responds, dryly.

Coleridge turns and walks towards the navigation desk, making it clear he has finished with them. 'Colonel, take them to a holding cell for now. Miss Black can deal with them when we reach Rome.'

'Yes, sir.' Frost marches them back through the machine room.

Will looks at Anna with concern. She nods quietly, indicating she is fine, but he expects she is not. Even if you are trained to be shot at on a daily basis it is another matter to be defenceless and have a gun pointed at your head by an unpredictable psychopath acting under the orders of another unpredictable psychopath. They cross the bridge and the deck in silence and reach a small windowless cell at the rear of the ship.

They sit down on the only bit of furnishing: a hardwood bench. Will's head reels with the revelations about Madeleine. 'Always two steps ahead of the game,' Coleridge had said, and he was right.

'Are you thinking about Madeleine?' asks Anna, interrupting his thoughts.

'Is it that obvious?'

'She's quite something. I'll give her that.'

281

'Yes. She is.'

'She has her price like all rogue spies.'

'Does she?' asks Will, sceptically.

Anna looks at him with a quizzical expression. 'She stole the shard from you and has probably sold it to the highest bidder like she did with the Stones of Fire notebook.'

'She's not interested in money. Her parents left her with plenty.'

'It's because of her Timothy Chittlock is dead.'

'Maybe, but that was something she could not have foreseen.'

'What do you mean?'

Will is lost in thought for a moment and thinks back over the past few days. Standing up, he begins to pace the cell. 'I can see it now.'

'See what?'

'Madeleine has been two steps ahead of the game. That's what Coleridge said and he is right. Damn it. Why did I not see it before?' Will continues pacing as he remembers. He laughs and shakes his head.

'Will, you're worrying me!'

Sitting down he turns to Anna. 'A few days ago at Chartres Cathedral I met a liaison to pick up the microfilm. Her codename was Marie-Antoinette and she had been set up by the Owl to make the drop.'

'I know this. What is your point?'

'Indulge me. We escaped in Marie-Antoinette's car. Emile and I hid in the boot. There were painter's canvases inside. Emile...' He stops for a moment, sighs and closes his eyes. He recalls Emile's body jolting against his as he was shot and the image of Claudette in the passenger seat, her eye's lifeless and her neck pouring with blood. 'We didn't all make it.' He takes a deep breath and continues. 'Flying across the channel we were overtaken by a Tiger Moth. The same one that attacked this airship tonight.'

'I'm still confused.'

'Remember when we went to Chittlock's house alone?'

'Yes.'

'The painting on the wall of my bedroom – *The Menin Road* – with the red fusilier from another century painted on top and concealing the coded message underneath.'

'Are you saying she painted it?

'She has a studio in Sebastian's garden, where she also stores weapons.'

Will thinks of Milly, from the hairdresser's opposite Chittlock's. She had seemed familiar to him. Had Madeleine disguised herself as Milly? Of course! 'Things are becoming clear to me now, Anna. Marie-Antoinette, the pilot in the Tiger Moth, Milly from the beauty salon: they were all Madeleine.'

'That's ridiculous.'

'Is it?

Anna furrows her brow, clearly doubting her own statement. 'Sounds like she's competing for the Owl's reputation as the man with a thousand faces.'

'How do we know the Owl is a man?' says Will.

'You can't be serious!'

'The Owl's signature is an Egyptian owl. Edward told us it translates to M in the English alphabet. M for Marie-Antoinette. M for Milly. M for Madeleine. She has the perfect front already. Spoiled attention-seeking rich girl.'

'That's an understatement.'

'It's an act, Anna. Madeleine has had her parents taken from her in the most terrible of circumstances. She wants revenge, just like we do.'

'You seem quite taken with her.'

Will looks away. 'She's following us and she has the shard. There's still a chance we can win this.'

'And what then? If we destroy this ship what's to stop them building another?'

'I don't know the answer to that.'

They sit in silence for a few moments listening to the sound of the engine's rhythmic chugging.

'We should try and get some sleep. We'll need all our strength tomorrow,' says Anna. 'This is far from over.'

Will rests his head against the wall and closes his eyes. He tries to zone out, to think of other things, but all he can think about is the Tiger Moth out there, dipping in and out of the clouds and following them.

CHAPTER 44

The Hangman's Noose

Will does not sleep. He sits with his eyes closed, mulling over the revelations and their current captured state. Any thoughts of breaking for freedom seem futile. Even if they could disarm the guards and find parachutes, escaping from an airship with a particle beam death ray and killer red gas is unlikely to be a resounding success. After two hours or so the cell door rattles. Both he and Anna sit up.

Frost's broad silhouette appears in the doorway. He is carrying a pistol. Will shifts uneasily seeing the barrel pointing directly at him but, in spite of it, he is not frightened.

'Morning, Colonel. Must be odd being the jailer and not the prisoner. By the way how was your little sabbatical at His Majesty's pleasure? Did you have fun?'

'Shut up,' snarls Frost.

'I thought you might at least have sent a postcard.'

'Get up. Both of you.'

'It's a little early for breakfast. But that's fine. Bacon, eggs and hot buttered toast? Yum. I could do with a hot bath too. Could you arrange that? I'll make sure you get a generous tip.'

Will can see his old foe gritting his teeth but, to his disappointment, Frost holds back and gestures for them to leave the cell. Will can smell whisky as he passes the colonel. A guard is waiting outside but there's no sign of Thierry. Will has an uneasy feeling and wonders where he could be. Glancing at his watch, he sees it is just after 3 am. Frost orders them forward, through the gloom of the deck: the only light is from the moon and stars glittering from the viewing gallery outside. They walk through the grey doors and over the lattice bridge. A cold breeze pinches his skin. Beneath them he sees the slumbering Tesla Death Ray cannon.

From across the walkway, by the cannon's power source, a woman in horn-rimmed spectacles and a lab coat, looks up nervously.

'Get on with your work and say nothing about this to anyone,' barks Frost, with a slur in his voice.

The woman pales, quickly picks up her clipboard and turns back to the machine.

Will feels his shoulders tightening and glances at Anna, who is frowning back at him.

'Down there,' says Frost, pointing to a wooden stepladder at the right side of the bridge.

'What's going on, Frost?' says Will.

'You'll find out. Get going!'

Will goes down first, followed closely by Anna. They are in a side passage within touching distance of the cannon. The cold breeze is stronger here, as if powerful fans are pushing wind over the cannon. Looking around he sees no fans other than the two above the machine room which turn slowly. Anna rubs her arms to keep warm.

'I don't like this, Will. He's drunk and is up to something,' she whispers.

'Agreed. If something happens I will take care of him. Can you deal with the other guard?'

As Frost climbs down the ladder, Anna nods a confirmation.

Will looks at the cannon. He reaches across and places his fingers upon it. The cold mottled steel reminds him of scales, like dragon skin, he imagines.

Frost prods him with his pistol and nods towards the front of gondola. 'Down there, towards the light.'

White light is coming from an open door at the end of the passage. He and Anna make their way towards it. He wonders if he can destroy the death ray using the power source. Maybe the only way would be to destroy the entire ship from the inside … planting timed explosives maybe? His stomach flutters at the thought. He has no idea.

As he approaches the doorway the wind intensifies and he begins to understand why. He glances at Anna and swallows.

'Move!' barks Frost.

Will stands at the doorway. The room contains the airship's tethering rope wound around an enormous metal pulley. At the centre of the room is a waist-high safety rail surrounding a hatch in the floor. The hatch is open to the cold night air. Gripping the rail is Horne who smiles grimly at Will. 'Do come in,' he says.

Will notices Horne's knuckles are caked in dried blood. It is not his. Lying on his chest, bruised, shirtless, inches from the edge of the hatch is Thierry. His hands are bound behind his back and he looks up at Will through eyes swollen like a boxer's, his nose and mouth bloody and almost unrecognisable. Will hears Anna let out a sharp gasp but keeps his face blank. The Frenchman shivers, coughs and spits blood from his mouth.

'Disgusting,' says Horne, his face contorting.

Frost shoves Will and Anna forward until they are both at the rail looking down at the vast darkness below.

'Somehow it doesn't seem out of character for you to beat up a defenceless man, Horne. Even one of your own. Bravo,' says Will.

Horne's thin lips distort into a sneer. 'Except, he's not one of ours. Is he?'

Will blinks. 'I don't know what you are talking about.'

'I found him snooping around,' says Frost. 'Looking for you two, I believe.'

'I have no idea who this man is,' says Will.

'He's French for a start,' slurs Frost. 'We don't have many of them here. And he doesn't seem to know his rank or section. I believe that makes him an imposter, Starling, a stowaway – and a guilty one at that.'

Will swallows.

'He must pay the price,' says Horne.

'You want to kill your own men, that is fine by me.' Pierced with guilt, Will glances down at Thierry who looks back up at him, a desperate expression on his badly beaten face.

'I'm a fair man, Starling,' says Horne. 'You might not think it, but I do wholeheartedly believe in giving people a choice.' Horne crouches down and hauls Thierry to his knees, so that he's facing over the open hatch.

Will holds his tongue.

Horne beckons at Anna. 'Come here, Anna, dear.'

'Why?'

Horne's face flushes with anger. 'Because I said so!' he screams.

'Move,' says Frost, nudging her along with his pistol.

Will feels his spine icing over. He inches back and feels the second guard's pistol in the small of his back. Just where I want you, he thinks.

Frost stands to the side of Thierry, his pistol trained on the Frenchman.

'What are you playing at Horne?' says Will.

Horne stands behind Anna and raises his hands to her shoulders. Glancing at Will, he moves his face to the side of her head, burying his face in her hair. He inhales slowly. 'I always enjoyed your scent, Anna. It's such a pity you made the wrong choice.'

Anna shrugs him off but Horne pushes her gently down so that she is kneeling next to Thierry at the edge of the trapdoor. She looks up at Will and does not seem in any way frightened. If anything, she is angry.

With a flourish, Horne waves his arm above Anna and Thierry. 'You get to choose, Starling.'

Will feels his pulse racing. In his mind he is calculating how he can take out the guard behind him, and Frost too, without risking a bullet hitting Anna or Thierry.

Horne reaches behind him and lifts the end of the tethering rope. Will's stomach clenches. The rope has been tied into a hangman's noose.

'You get to choose who swings tonight.'

'You cannot be serious!' Will glances at Frost who is laughing at Horne, but at the same time seems unsteady on his feet. Thierry has shot him a sideways glance and notices also.

'Oh yes, I am,' says Horne. 'Who's it going to be?' He swings the noose over Anna. 'Your girlfriend,' he holds it over Thierry, 'or the Frenchie?'

Will frowns. 'I told you I don't know who he is.'

'Liar. Liar!' Horne swings the rope back and forth over their heads.

'Stop it, Horne. I want to talk to your uncle. Immediately!'

'Who's it going to be, Starling? You better choose quick or they both get it!'

'Stop it!'

'Choose, damn you!' screams Horne.

Will sees the muscles on Thierry's bare shoulders tightening. He is looking at Will and nodding at Frost. He's going to go for him. Not yet, thinks Will. It's too soon.

'Choose!'

'The Frenchman! I choose the Frenchman.'

Thierry looks up at him in shock at hearing those words. A pang of guilt stabs at Will.

'Of course you choose him, but it is the wrong choice,' says Horne. He places the noose over Anna's head. Will nods at Thierry who lunges at Frost. The colonel's whisky-addled brains have slowed his responses and give Thierry an temporary advantage. Will feels the second guard's gun move from his back but, before the guard can shoot Thierry, Will reels around and snaps his wrist. The guard cries out in pain and the pistol falls to floor sliding through the hatch and out into the night. Will launches two punches to the man's ribs and finishes him off with a hard uppercut. The guard stumbles backward and falls to the floor.

Horne is trying his best to tip Anna over the edge of the rail. She fights back, punching and kicking him but his eyes are wide, his expression deranged, and he does not seem to feel her blows.

Will wraps his arms around Horne's neck and pulls him away. His nose wrinkles at the musty smell of unwashed hair forever marinated in stale oil. He crushes Horne's windpipe and, after a moment, feels his grip on Anna weakening. Thierry is raining kicks on the colonel who has not yet managed to get up though he seems to be rallying. Will feels Horne's body going limp. His head drops forward as he loses consciousness and Will is relieved to see Anna get into a safer position. Relaxing his hold on Horne, Will reaches for Anna. But something's not quite right. Horne is still standing. Will hears him laugh as he lunges forward and shoves Anna. Crying out, she topples over the rail and falls through the hatch.

'Anna!' shouts Will, but Horne cuts him off, slamming his elbow into his solar plexus. Will gasps and crumples to the floor, his heart sinking. Horne begins to kick him and stamp at him, but the thought of Anna, her neck broken, body swinging below the ship fills him with a burning fury. He grabs Horne's foot as it swings towards his face. Holding it firm by the toe and heel Will uses all his strength to twist the ankle. Horne cries out and yanks his foot away. Will jumps to his feet and launches a kick Horne's chest. He spirals backwards with the force and tumbles over the pulley. Will sees the guard has gone. He will return with back-up in minutes, no doubt.

His heart pumping, Will crouches down, peers under the rail and through the hatch where he sees Anna clinging on to the edge by her fingers. Dawn is breaking and sunlight climbs over the horizon, lighting up green countryside scattered with houses below.

'I'm slipping,' she calls, her face pale and terrified.

Will uses all his strength to pull her up hauling her on to the floor. As Anna pulls the noose from her neck he sees Horne scramble from the pulley towards Frost's Browning, which has fallen to the floor behind Thierry.

'Behind you, Thierry!' calls Will.

The Frenchman's head turns around, but Horne already has the pistol. Grinning, he fires twice at Thierry's broad back.

Two large holes seem to explode on Thierry's upper back. His face contorts and his legs wobble as he slumps forward falling on top of Frost.

Will dives at Horne as the pistol turns towards him. He grabs his wrist with one hand, wrapping his other arm around Horne's head, gripping his ear and yanking it to the side. Horne lets out a muffled cry. Biting Will's sleeved arm, Horne squeezes the trigger, firing off several shots as Will battles to control his gun hand. Anna dives to the ground. Will pulls Horne's arm to the right. More shots explode. Out of the corner of his eye Will sees Frost rising. He slides his arm over Horne's eyes and swings the pistol in Frost's direction. The colonel's face is red with anger but his eyes widen at the gun barrel pointing his way. Will holds Horne's arms firm as he squeezes the trigger and pumps four bullets into the colonel's chest.

'That's it, Horne. Keep pressing the trigger,' says Will, sliding his arm away from Horne's eyes.

Horne lets out a shrill cry as Frost stumbles backward, toppling over Thierry's body and falling dead to the floor. Will feels Horne trembling and slams his gun hand on the rail three times, breaking the bones until he eventually drops it. The Browning falls through the hatch and disappears. Will pushes Horne forward against the rail. Breathing heavily he recalls the moment he discovered what he was and what his destiny was to be.

Sleeper

'Anna, give me the rope,' he calls.

She picks it up, the noose dangling from her hands, and frowns at him.

'What are you going to do?' she asks.

Liberator

'Give me the rope, Anna.'

He snatches it from her and puts the noose over Horne's head, pulling it tight over his neck.

Executioner

Horne struggles to pull the rope off but Will slams a fierce punch to his kidney.

'Aaaahh!' cries Horne, lurching and trembling.

'Will, stop! Don't do this. You're not like them,' says Anna.

Will hesitates briefly but his rage feels so absolute.

'This is for Sam, the boy you murdered two years ago. This is for Thierry – a French hero you tied up and beat with your filthy paws and then shot in the back. This is for all the people you oppressed and bullied, you coward.'

Horne begins to howl and cry. 'Please no. I don't want to die. I'm sorry for everything. I won't do it again.'

'No, you won't,' says Will, tipping him feet first over the rail.

Horne cries out as he falls but grabs the leg of the rail clinging half in and half out of the airship.

'Enough!' comes a voice. Standing at the doorway and dressed in a black suit, black shirt and tie, is the bald and tattooed Coleridge. Beside him are four armed guards, including the one who had escaped earlier. Coleridge scans the room, taking in the bodies of Frost and Thierry.

'Uncle! At last. Help me.'

'Move away from my nephew, Starling,' says Coleridge.

Will hesitates, but there are four guns pointing at him. He steps away from Horne. Coleridge walks into the room and crouches down, his arms reaching for Horne.

'Take hold of my hands.'

'Thank you, Uncle. Thank you.' Horne reaches across with one hand and then another. Coleridge grips his wrists. He stares hard into his nephew's eyes.

Horne's brow furrows. 'Pull me up, Uncle.'

'You are as weak and as stupid as your father,' spits Coleridge.

Horne shakes his head. 'Uncle, I'm sorry. I just wanted to teach them a lesson.'

'I have done all I can for you.'

Anna gasps as Coleridge releases the hold on his nephew. Horne barely has time to frown in confusion before he disappears through the hatch, screaming until the tethering rope goes taut and there is silence. The only sounds are the airship's engine, the breeze from the hatch and creak of the pulley as the rope swings back and forth.

Coleridge stands and turns to Will, who shifts uneasily.

'Come with me,' he says, 'both of you.'

Will and Anna exchange confused glances.

Coleridge addresses one of the guards. 'Have my nephew's body prepared for a full honours ceremony.'

Full honours for being a bully and a murderer. Such is the VIPER way. Will recalls Anna's words: *You're not like them.* He shudders. But I am like them. I was about to kill Horne in the most brutal of ways. He follows Coleridge and Anna with the guns of the three other guards pointing at their backs. Climbing the ladder and crossing the bridge they enter the navigation room again. The captain is steering at the wheel and his second is manning the controls.

'We taught you well, Will. I have to tell you I do admire you, you know.'

'As much as you admired your nephew?'

'I wish he had been more like you.'

Will narrows his eyes at Coleridge. His sudden flattery unnerves him. 'What do you want from me?'

'Very soon, you will be meeting the lady herself.' Coleridge pauses.

'And?' asks Will.

'You should consider where your true allegiances lie.'

Will laughs. 'Are you offering me a job?'

'Does that surprise you?'

'No. Nothing about VIPER surprises me.'

'We have a lot in common.'

Will shakes his head. 'I despise you. All of you.'

'Do you? Really? I'm not sure I believe that.'

'You killed my parents. You kidnapped my sister. You murdered my friends.'

'That's all in the past. It's history. You need to think about your future.'

'All I can think about is killing you and wiping VIPER from the face of the planet.'

Coleridge gazes deeply into his eyes. 'The fire in your belly and the drive you have is quite remarkable. I see that now. We are making the world a better place, Will. A safer place. You could be part of that.'

Will says nothing, too astonished and disbelieving to form words.

'Ironically, Will, you are one of our great success stories. Not only did we make you what you are, but you have something others don't. You survive against all the odds. We could use your skills. Think of what you could bring to the new world.'

'Sir. It is almost time,' interrupts the captain.

'Come to the window,' says Coleridge. 'I do think you will enjoy this.'

As they draw closer, framed in the navigator's window Will sees a city rise up before them. It is a city steeped in history, with ancient ruins standing majestic among the red roofs of its houses: Rome, Italy's capital city. Was this their destination? Will has no memory of having been here before, no signals or memories flash in his mind. His knowledge of the city is what he has read in books and seen in pictures. He recognises the Colosseum, the immense amphitheatre that was once the home to gladiatorial battles almost two thousand years ago. He sees the dome of the Pantheon and the grand piazzas of the city. He has an unsettling feeling about this. It is bad enough being prisoners of VIPER but to be taken to the capital city of a country which has firmly aligned itself with the Nazis is another thing altogether.

'A magnificent city, is it not?' asks Coleridge.

Will does not respond.

The ship flies over the Tiber and turns towards the Vatican City, the smallest country in the world. Unlike Italy – and like Switzerland – the Vatican City, governed by Pope Pius XII, has remained neutral, refusing to align with either the Allies or Hitler, in order, the Pope says, to prevent the city being bombed.

The undamaged dome of St Peter's Basilica looms over the city and Will is surprised by how close they are to it. The airship turns again and flies over St Peter's Square with its one hundred and forty statues of obscure saints.

'What are we doing here?' asks Will.

'Just a demonstration,' replies Coleridge.

'Of what exactly?'

But before Coleridge can answer Will feels his mouth dry. Dotted across the blue sky over Rome are dozens of airships with VIPER flags blowing in the wind beneath their gondolas. His eyes dart over them counting: eight, twelve, eighteen, twenty. More appear overhead and join the others in formation. Three sets of twelve: thirty-six airships. Will feels Anna move close to him. He can sense her fear.

'Behold my fleet. Behold the Red Storm,' says Coleridge.

CHAPTER 45

The Red Tower

'You were correct, William. One airship might not fare well against an attack from Spitfires or Messerschmitts. However, a fleet of airships, each equipped with a particle beam death ray and red gas is quite another matter,' says Coleridge.

'Why do this?' says Anna. 'Why do you want to kill innocent people? The world is suffering enough with this damn war!'

'There is no question about that, Miss Wilder. Our cause has benefited enormously from the war and will continue to do so.'

'Your cause? You make it sound like some holy crusade,' says Anna.

'You might call it that. There is definitely something biblical and pure about genocide. Don't you think?'

'You're mad. All of you.'

Coleridge laughs to himself. 'Really? This is the second world war I have witnessed, Miss Wilder and, once again, I have seen ordinary men rise to become megalomaniacs and cause untold destruction. I have no doubt this will not be the last world war in my lifetime. The

Germans and the Americans are already developing atomic bombs. Either this war, or the next one, will see the end of the world. We cannot allow that to happen. The population of the world must reset itself. Many must die for the world to change.'

'And what then? VIPER take over?' asks Will.

'VIPER, as we know it, will disband. A new world order will be established. The world will become a utopia once more.'

'Why not use your power and influence to work with world leaders and make a change for the better?' says Anna.

Coleridge snorts. 'And you have the nerve to call me mad.'

'One fleet against the rest of the world? What delusions of grandeur you have!' says Will.

'Sir,' interrupts the captain, 'we are ready for Castle St Angelo.'

Coleridge does not respond to Will's comment. Instead he turns to the captain. 'Take her down, Captain Smythe.'

'Yes, sir.'

The airship begins its descent towards a vast round tower surrounded by a wall, with a turret in each corner. There are men on the tower's expansive terrace signalling to the navigator under the watchful gaze of a large bronze statue of an angel sheathing his sword. Will feels Coleridge's eyes upon him.

'There is a rather charming story associated with that statue of the Archangel Michael. Legend has it that in 590 AD Michael appeared on that very spot sheathing his sword as a sign that the plague was over. Many people died and the world changed. And here we are at the eve of a new dawn. I love the irony of it. That's why I chose this place.'

Will is only half listening. His mind is reeling as the terms *genocide*, *plague*, *atomic bombs* and *biblical* echo in his head.

'Take them to the deck,' Coleridge says to the guards.

As they turn to leave Will hears a voice from the communication speaker on the dashboard. 'VA1, you are clear to drop the ramp when ready.'

'Thank you, Red Tower. We'll be with you in five minutes.'

'Roger that.'

Will feels his heart race. Glancing at Anna, he can see she has understood the significance of what they have just heard.

The castle below is the Red Tower. Somewhere inside it is his sister, Rose.

CHAPTER 46

Ophelia's Proposition

Will watches the ramp as it is lowered slowly to the roof terrace of Castle St Angelo. The morning is bright and balmy and warm air caresses his face. Down on the terrace half a dozen men pull on the tethering rope, unaware that less than thirty minutes earlier the same rope had choked the life from the treacherous Rupert Van Horne. They hold it firmly as the base of the ramp comes to rest on the terrace floor.

Will follows Coleridge down the ramp. Anna is behind him, with Coleridge's personal guards watching their backs. He looks up at the statue of the Archangel Michael. It is immense, much larger than it seemed from the airship. Despite not having any religious affiliations, he cannot help but offer up some sort of prayer. *If you did, in some way, put an end to the plague, then I could really do with some divine intervention to prevent a bloody disaster. Please.*

His thoughts turn to Madeleine and he wonders if she made it alive or if her plane was destroyed by one of the other airships. He hopes not. Looking up, he sees the other ships leave Rome's air space in almost single file. He wonders where they are going; they can't fly all the time. He approaches the end of the ramp.

'Is my sister here?' he asks.

After a moment's hesitation, Coleridge replies, 'Yes.'

'I want to see her.'

'You will.'

'When?'

'Soon.'

They leave the terrace and enter a narrow dark stone staircase that takes them down to a balcony that runs all the way around the outer wall of the castle. They arrive at the steps to a courtyard containing another statue of an angel with bronze wings. Will has an odd sensation of being watched and looks up to an open window with two wispy white curtains. He squints but can see no one.

'What is it?' asks Anna.

'I'm not sure. Just an odd feeling.'

'Are you alright?'

He nods and they carry on. Passing the angel statue, they enter a hallway with a wide well-trodden staircase that leads down to darkness.

'I'm afraid, Miss Wilder, this is where you leave us,' says Coleridge.

'No!' says Will. 'She stays with me.'

'Miss Wilder will be in no danger. I can promise you that,' says Coleridge.

'I'll be fine, Will.'

'Where are you taking her?'

'To a suite of rooms we reserve for all our prisoners. The dungeons.'

Will feels helpless as two of the guards usher Anna away at gunpoint.

'Come this way, Will, please.'

Will watches until Anna disappears in the darkness. He is taken through a warren of corridors and rooms, some containing tall machines manned by boffin types, others with rows of desk where suited men and women work diligently. They emerge outdoors and cross a perimeter overlooking the Tiber and a bridge lined with statues of angels. Coleridge knocks upon a heavy wooden door. A guard appears and stands to attention when he recognises Coleridge. Will hears opera coming from somewhere behind the guard. It is thunderous and dramatic and seems to be coming from behind a gilded door at the end of a short corridor. The smell of cigarettes tickles his nostrils. Coleridge knocks the golden door and enters, leaving Will and the two guards outside. Moments later he returns and beckons them inside.

The room behind the door is a vast space with a glistening marble floor and walls painted with half-naked nymphs, cherubs and Roman generals. The walls must be thirty feet high with a vaulted ceiling covered in ornate golden plaster carvings surrounding several different frescoes and murals.

At the far left of the room is a gramophone player with a large brass flower-shaped horn. Morning sun pours through the open window and a golden desk is engulfed in a cloud of blue cigarette smoke. Lurking within it is a woman with blonde hair, wearing a grey suit. She inhales on a cigarette, shoots two jets of smoke from her nose and stares out the window, seemingly lost in the music. Will shifts uneasily as a scene from his past rolls like a movie reel in his mind. But it's not easy to see. It's like looking through a shattered mirror. He concentrates harder through the broken glass.

He can see her. She is there. He knows her. He has seen her before.

Ophelia Black.

Will is standing in the rain amongst a sea of khaki green foot soldiers, agents and monks looking up at the landing bay at Schöllenen Gorge. It is a stage with speakers and a microphone. He sees Proatheris, Frost and faceless shadowy figures lurking in the dark behind Ophelia Black who is bellowing at the crowd and using a fist to emphasise her points. Her audience cheers. They love her. They believe in her. They want what she wants. She is their queen. She is both beautiful and dangerous: a toxic combination.

Queen Ophelia, leader of the new world.

Will rubs the side of his head and blinks twice. The music has stopped.

'Are you having a turn?' says Ophelia Black, sharply.

It takes a moment for Will to gather himself.

Ophelia is standing by the gramophone player watching him through a haze of blue smoke.

'Where is my sister?' he asks, ignoring her question.

'The question you should be asking, Mr Starling, is why are you here?' The VIPER queen stands up, extinguishes her cigarette and immediately lights another. She walks from behind the desk and approaches him slowly, arms folded, red heels clicking on the marble. She stands an arm's length from him and studies his face as smoke engulfs him like an out of body spirit. Caught within her blue fog, he takes stock of her. Her straight blonde hair is flecked with grey streaks and is cut below the ears. Her eyes are ice blue with crow's feet that reach beyond her temples. She wears no make-up other than a slash of red lipstick to match her long nails and shoes.

'I had a son once. Took his own life. He was only sixteen. He had everything he could possibly want.' She draws on her cigarette and walks around him looking him up and down. 'Suicide is a curse among the men of my family. It claimed my grandfather, my father, my brother … my son.'

'It's hard to lose those you love to suicide, murder or kidnapping,' says Will.

'Quite so, Mr Starling. But you adapt. You learn to live with that loss. You move on.'

'Do you?'

Black points her cigarette at him. 'Let me ask you this. Your parents, your sister, do you miss them?'

Will blinks and turns away from her gaze.

'I thought not.'

Will feels his muscles tightening. 'Of course I miss them,' he snaps.

'But how could you? You don't remember them. You are an amnesiac, Mr Starling. You have no memory of your parents or your sister. So let me ask that question again: why are you here?'

Will can feel the heat rising inside him. He glances at Coleridge who watches him closely with a half grin.

Sleeper. Liberator. Executioner.

Not only had VIPER taken his family away from him, they were also responsible for his amnesia. Deep inside, he never wanted to admit to himself that his memories of his parents and sister were next to none. They were shadows in his mind, ghosts, strangers, really. But for all that he couldn't see or remember, he could still feel; he knew what love was. He knew that his family had loved him and he had loved them. The raw emotion still existed inside him and, despite his being unable to equate it with memories like anyone else, he could still feel their presence and their loss. There was something beautiful about that, but also something terrible and sad. It drove him. It spurred him on.

Will answers her question. 'I'm here to destroy you. To bring down VIPER. To prevent genocide. To bring my sister home. To avenge my family, my friends.'

'Pipe dreams, Mr Starling.'

'Not for much longer.'

Ophelia smiles drily, drops her cigarette to the floor and stabs the flame with the point of her red heel.

'Let me tell you why you are here.'

She returns to her desk to retrieve and light another cigarette.

'You came here for answers. You want to understand who you are and what your purpose is…'

Sleeper. Liberator. Executioner.

'I can help you with that, Mr Starling. I can provide you with a purpose that would make your parents and your sister proud.'

'Let me guess. You'd like me to join you?'

Her red lips part in a wide humourless smile and expel smoke at the same time.

'You were one of us before, albeit not on our side. You were an exemplary student. A leader. The youngest of your group and as tough as the older men and women you trained with.'

She is wasting her time. Will feels nothing but contempt for her, Coleridge and everything they represent.

'We are on the verge of creating a new world. You could be part of that. You could lead an army. You could become admiral of my fleet. You can have your own country. Somewhere hot, perhaps? We … *I* … need people like you.' She smiles in an almost matriarchal and caring fashion, which he does not swallow.

'Give it some thought.' She turns to Coleridge. 'Is there any news of the French spy?'

'Her plane was spotted just outside Rome. She should be here soon.'

'I want that shard,' says Ophelia.

'I will make it happen, ma'am.'

'See that you do.' Turning back to Will, she says, 'The ladies are all chasing after you, it seems, Mr Starling. Join us and I will spare the lives of your two women. Don't say I am not generous considering what you have cost us already.'

Before Will can respond, there is a knock on the door.

Ophelia smiles darkly at Will. 'I forgot to mention. We have a visitor for you. Someone who can perhaps persuade you.'

'Come in, Sofia,' she calls.

The door opens slowly inward and Will sees the back of a short round woman dressed in rustic clothes. She looks round, catches Ophelia's gazes and blanches.

'*Ciao, scusa,*' she says, nodding in a deferential manner. She eases something gently through the door – a battered wooden wheelchair with large black wheels. Someone is sitting on it. He can see long dark hair, neatly combed in a middle parting. Will feels his skin erupt in goose bumps. The woman called Sofia turns the wheelchair around to face them.

Will swallows. Sitting on the chair, dressed in a simple white dressing gown, is his sister.

An image slices through his mind, unsteadying him. He is in the park with Rose and a cricket ball is spinning in the air feet from his mother's head. Other people in the park are watching it and asking questions. His parents quickly gather up the picnic and Will takes Rose by the hand and hurries away. Their lives had changed from that moment onward.

He blinks and takes stock of her. She looks different. She is thin, pale and … heavily pregnant.

'Rose … how?' Her swollen belly is a shock to him. His throat clenches and his eyes begin to sting. He presses his palm over his mouth and trembles inside. He stares at her for the longest time. How long he cannot be sure.

'Doesn't she look well?' Ophelia's words seem far away and hang in the air like a bad smell.

Rose does not seem to be aware he is here. She stares straight ahead, at nothing. Her mouth opens and drool dribbles from the side and runs down her chin. Sofia crouches by her side and wipes it away with her apron.

'*Bambina*,' she coos, fussing with Rose's dressing gown and fixing her hair.

'Sofia is her nurse and her handmaiden. She looks after her. Gives her everything she needs. Can't have any children of your own, isn't that right, Sofia?' says Ophelia.

Sofia nods once without looking at Ophelia, '*Si, Signora*,' she says quietly, her expression like stone.

'What have you done to her?' Will says at last, his voice cracking.

'We've kept her alive,' says Coleridge.

'She's a danger to herself,' says Ophelia.

'She's … she's *pregnant*!' Will can barely bring himself to say it. How could this have happened. Who could have done this to her?

He goes to crouch beside her and looks into her eyes. An image flashes in his mind. Rose with her kitten, Charlie, sitting beside him in the garden laughing. A happy time. Her eyes are blue, like his – but they seem older than her fourteen years. Much older.

'Rose. It's me … Will …' His throat feels parched, as if it has not been moistened in weeks. 'I found you at last.'

She does not respond.

He recalls the family photograph of him and Rose that Eoin had revealed two years back when he discovered the truth about his sister. In the picture Will looked to be around twelve years old, which would have made Rose eight. She had been smiling up at him and holding his hand with a firm grip. He takes her hand now, squeezing it gently.

'Rose, I've come for you. We can go home soon.'

But still she does not respond.

'Rose.'

She blinks once and a bubble of spittle appears in her mouth.

Will bows his head and wipes tears from his eyes.

'We can help her get better,' says Ophelia.

'Help her? She's fucking pregnant!' he roars.

Ophelia's cigarette glows a fierce red as she sucks the nicotine into her bony body. 'If it eases your mind she is quite chaste and has not laid with any men. At least, not to my knowledge.'

Will takes a moment to gather himself and stands up. 'What have you done to her?'

'We … artificially inseminated her.'

Will shakes his head in disbelief. 'Why would you do that?'

'We want more like her. A new world is coming, Mr Starling.'

Will exhales a deep breath and looks upward, his eyes roll unseeing over the frescoes and gold cornicing.

'She is sedated. Nothing more. It helps her sleep.'

'Why do this to her?'

'She is dangerous,' says Coleridge.

Will's voice rises. 'How can she be dangerous? She is fourteen years old and she's pregnant!'

'She, like you, is another one of our success stories,' says Coleridge.

'Rose is powerful. More so than any of us every expected,' says Ophelia.

Will looks from Ophelia to Coleridge. 'This is not about me, is it? It's about Rose. You are using me to manipulate her.'

'It's about both of you,' says Ophelia, 'but, more importantly, it is about the child she is carrying.'

Will glances at Rose's pale face. 'What about it?'

'The seed is from another, just like her. The father was a remarkable but difficult young man. He could start fires by thinking about them. His power consumed him in the end and we lost control of him.'

'You killed him?'

'We did what we had to do. Regrettably he was a danger to himself and to us. Like Rose, he was the first generation of the Teleken Kinetic experiment. Sadly for him, his body was not equipped to deal with the power he was born with. The next generation will be different. Rose's baby will evolve. She will give birth to a god. A messiah for the new world.'

'You're mad! All of you.'

'I can assure you, Mr Starling. We are anything but mad.'

'What about Rose? What happens to her?'

'She is frail. However, assuming she survives the birth she will join us and help mother the child, until a more suitable replacement can be found.'

A cold terror overwhelms Will. Rose is expendable. It's her child that is important to VIPER. Not Rose. Who else realised this?

'Why are the Russians looking for my sister?'

Ophelia snorts. 'Oh yes. They tried to buy her from us and now apparently they have sent a spy to steal her from us. Quite laughable, don't you think?'

'Hilarious,' bites Will.

'Understand this, Mr Starling. We are preserving this world. We are taking it away from those who would destroy it. A new world. A new utopia.'

Will crouches down beside Rose. His heart feels crushed at the thought he might lose her so soon after finding her.

'Join us, Will,' says Ophelia, using his first name as a means to soften him.

'No! You will never have me or my sister.'

Ophelia meets his gaze for a few long moments. 'I am not sure you have quite thought this through.'

Will leans across and kisses Rose on the cheek. 'Don't give up on me, Rose,' he whispers.

'I'll ask you one more time,' says Ophelia.

'No.'

'As you wish.' She turns to the nurse. 'Take the rest of the day off, Sofia.'

The nurse shakes her head, rests her hand on her bosom and gestures at Rose with the other, '*Scusa, Signora ...* Rose...?'

'...will be just fine. Please go home,' demands Ophelia.

Sofia hesitates and nods reluctantly. She then bends down to kiss Rose on the top of her head and scurries out of the room.

'We're ready for you now,' Ophelia calls and, at the same time, Will sees Coleridge gesture at the guards and hears the opening of a door. At the top end of the room is a door he had not noticed before, hidden within a mural depicting two large men carrying something on a stairwell. A figure emerges from the shadows behind it. Will feels the hairs on his neck stand on end. Gliding towards them like a dark spectre is the Pastor.

Will's muscle tighten, his hands curl into fists and he makes to run at the Pastor but the guards deliver two swift punches to his ribs and twist his arms behind his back. Crippled with pain, Will struggles to free himself but they are too strong.

The Pastor looks at him greedily with his one eye. His small tongue darts out and moistens his dry lips.

'Take her to her rooms, Pastor,' says Ophelia.

'Yes, mistress.'

'And be gentle with her.'

'Of course, mistress.'

Will feels his stomach lurch. 'What are you thinking? You cannot leave her alone with that madman!'

The Pastor wheels Rose out of the room as Will struggles against the guards.

'Stop!'

'Take him to the dungeons,' says Coleridge.

'Wait!' he calls as the guards drag him to the door.

'You had your chance, Mr Starling,' says Ophelia.

A third guard appears and pushes his way past. 'Ma'am,' he says breathlessly.

'Now is not a good time.'

'I'm sorry, ma'am. This is important. We have reports of an Allied airstrike heading to Rome.'

'How credible is this report?'

'Confirmed by our agents on the inside.'

Will is dragged down the corridor before he can hear any more. He struggles to break free but two more guards grab his legs. There are too many. He thinks of Rose with the Pastor and his heart sinks, but his rage thunders through and he lets it simmer. They have not killed him yet.

CHAPTER 47

Prisoners

Will is carried down flights of dark cavernous stone stairs and tossed into a small cell secured with a heavy iron gate. One of the guards, an unshaven, thin faced, cross-eyed fellow, locks it with a rusty old key, deposits it in his jacket pocket and leaves with the other three. The cell is nothing but bare stone with a filthy cot for a bed.

'Will, is that you?' says Anna's voice.

Looking through the bars he makes out a similar cell opposite with Anna inside. 'Yes. How are you?'

'I'm fine. What about you?'

He says nothing for a moment. 'She's here, Anna. I saw her.'

'Rose?'

Will leans his forehead on the bars. 'Yes. They've done terrible things to her.'

'Did you talk to her?'

'They've drugged her. She wasn't even aware I was there ... and she's pregnant, Anna. They...' but he cannot finish his words.

'I'm so sorry, Will.'

He shakes his head, his rage simmering inside. 'We have to get out of here.'

'I've tried forcing this lock, but it's too strong. They took all my tools on the airship.'

'Mine too. Except for one.' Will lifts the collar of his jacket and slips out the flexible saw that runs the length of it.

'Clever you!' says Anna.

'Thank you, Thierry,' he whispers, then, 'Anna, keep an eye on the stairwell while I try and cut through this lock.'

'Right.'

With one hand outside and one inside the bars, Will begins to saw back and forth against the bolt. The teeth are jagged and sharp and seem to be sawing through. Twenty minutes later, his fingers are raw and his brow is coated in sweat. He removes his jacket and hears Anna call his name.

'Someone's coming,' she says.

He hears footsteps approaching. Quickly, he hides the saw under the mattress and lies on top of it with his hands behind his head, affecting a relaxed look. His eyes narrow in on the floor beneath the lock. There is a small pile of dust, the remains of the half-sawn bolt. He swallows and looks up as the cross-eyed guard appears looking in on him with a suspicious stare.

'Good afternoon,' says Will, politely.

The guard growls something incomprehensible and turns towards Anna's cell. She is perched on the edge of the bed and rubs her arms. 'Hello. It's very chilly in here. May I borrow your jacket?' she says, silkily, with a warm smile.

The guard hesitates, removes his helmet and sweeps back his thinning dark hair. Was he considering her offer? Anna bites her lip and cocks her head.

Will watches, hoping and praying that her ruse works. Once the guard sets foot inside that cell it will be the last thing he does. He moves closer. Will sits up, his eyes widening.

'Mario!' comes a voice.

The guard curses under his breath and places his helmet back on his head. He seems unsure what to do and lingers near Anna's gate.

'MARIO! calls the voice, once more.

'*Merda*!' says Mario as he turns to leave.

'*Ciao*, Mario,' says Anna, softly.

He stops to look back at her and waves delicately with his fingers. '*Ciao, bella.*'

Anna looks at Will and shrugs. 'It was worth a try.'

Will continues sawing at the bolt, putting everything he has into cutting through the thick iron lock. An hour passes and sweat drips down his brow and over his nose, but he is making progress; the lock is weakening.

'Someone's coming,' says Anna again.

'Shit!' says Will under his breath. He is so close. He blows the grainy dust from around the bars and leans against the wall with his arms folded.

The guard called Mario arrives with a friend in tow, another guard, a large man with jowly cheeks and greasy skin. Mario shoots a withering look at Will before turning his attention to Anna. '*Ciao, bella,*' he says, removing his helmet.

Will rolls his eyes.

'*Ciao*, Mario,' says Anna, glancing at Will. She offers them a welcome smile and they move closer to her cell gate jabbering to each other in Italian that is too fast to comprehend.

Anna keeps the guards occupied with flirtation and flattery. As the men grow louder and start to compete for Anna's attention, Will decides to take a risk. He starts to saw slowly at the lock, his eyes never leaving the two men. Anna laughs loudly at every joke and inane comment, drowning out the noise of the slow strokes. The jowly guard reaches through the gate and tries to touch her. She bats his hand away softly and teasingly, but the mood changes. Will frowns as the man starts to rattle the gate.

Mario shoves his friend's arm. '*Arresto*, Lorenzo!' But Lorenzo shoves him to the floor, pulls a key from his jacket pocket and begins to unlock Anna's gate.

'Lorenzo!' cries Mario.

Will begins to saw faster. He is almost all the way through; the bolt is weakened and he begins to push at the gate. After the third attempt the gate gives way and he storms towards a confused-looking Mario who is rising from the floor. With one swift hard punch, Will knocks him unconscious.

'You took your time,' says Anna. She is standing at the gate of her cell, arms folded. The jowly Lorenzo is lying in a heap, face down, half on, half off her cot. Like his friend, Mario, he is unconscious.

'He didn't get very far,' says Will.

'The big ones are always the easiest to topple.'

'We can use their uniforms as disguises. A small blessing.'

An alarm begins to clang, echoing loudly throughout the castle.

'That can't be because of us, can it?' asks Anna.

Will looks around for signs of something that might have raised the alarm: a broken wire, a hidden microphone, anything. But there is nothing.

Anna hurries to the steps and looks out. 'There are lots of people running around like headless chickens,' she reports.

Will pulls Lorenzo off the bed, removes his helmet and begins to unbutton his jacket. 'There's something else going on. Just before I was brought here I heard a guard tell Coleridge that an Allied airstrike was on its way to Rome.'

'So, this might be an evacuation?'

'Or a call to arms.'

Anna removes Mario's jacket, puts it on over her clothes and tucks her hair inside his helmet.

'We have to find Rose,' says Will.

Anna nods, pulling the visor of her helmet down slightly to maximise her disguise. 'Top priority.'

They pull the two guards into Anna's cell, lock it and toss the key into the shadows of Will's. Side by side they hurry up the vaulted stone steps, passing monks and guards who do not give them a second glance. As they reach the top of the stairs Ophelia Black's voice fills the air from speakers dotted along the hallways to the left and right. Everyone stops to listen.

'War is upon us. The enemy approaches. This is the eve of the new world!'

A cheer erupts around the castle from the guards and monks.

'We have been preparing for this for ten years. Our time has come. Your time has come. Evacuate the Red Tower and go to your designated ships. Destroy the enemy and bring down Rome!' Ophelia raises her voice. 'MANY MUST DIE FOR THE WORLD TO CHANGE!'

The crowd cheers once more but their voices are soon drowned out by a siren that fills the air. From outside, Will can hear the drone of bombers and fighter planes. He meets Anna's gaze.

'Here we go again,' she says.

'Fun times.'

'We should split up. We can cover more ground.'

'Good idea,' says Will. 'Stay safe.'

'You too.'

Anna takes the left turn and runs off into the crowd. Will goes right and quickly threads his own way through the throng.

CHAPTER 48

Rose and the Pastor

Will sees the figure of a roundish woman pushing her way against the tide of people. It's Rose's nurse, Sofia. She isn't leaving the castle; she must be going for Rose.

'Sofia!' he calls, but she does not hear. He pushes through the crowd and calls again. 'Sofia, wait!'

The woman stops and turns, her eyes searching the crowd. Will waves his arms and she sees him. Her face drops and she turns and runs ducking into the crowd.

'Damn it!' He is wearing the helmet. But then, if he wasn't, would she trust him? He fights his way after her through the rising tide of evacuees, recognising the dark narrow stairwell leading up to the courtyard of the angel with the bronze wings. The bright blue afternoon sky is dotted with several airships, floating in a predatory circle.

A guard hurries past and Will grabs him by the neck, pulling him behind the angel's plinth. He struggles but Will slams his fist into his stomach. 'Rose Starling. Where is she?' he says.

The guard reaches for the pistol at his belt but Will snatches it and shoves the gun into the man's mouth, chipping his front teeth. 'Where is she?' he shouts, forcing the barrel down his throat. The man's eyes begin to water and he starts to choke. He lifts his arms in a conciliatory gesture. Will pulls out the barrel but keeps it firmly pointed at his head. The guard catches his breath and points upward. Will sees only the walls of the castle beyond the statue. Overhead he hears the rattle of Spitfire guns. He pulls the guard out into the centre of the courtyard. 'Show me!'

The guard points to a window where two white curtains are drawn. Will had noticed it that morning on his way to see Ophelia. Was Rose behind those curtains? He looks at the guard who seems terrified and eager to get away. A rare sense of mercy grips Will and he motions for the man to leave. The guard's eyes widen in surprise. He raises his arms and steps back.

Will turns towards the steps leading away from the courtyard however, out of the corner of his eye, he sees a movement and, looking around, sees a knife spinning towards him, thrown by the treacherous guard. He ducks and it clangs off the wall to his left. The guard turns to run but Will has already squeezed the trigger and a bullet explodes in the man's neck.

Regretting his mercy, Will does not hang around. He hurries up the steps and halts at the roar of a klaxon overhead. Above, the oppressive shadow of an airship falls as it unleashes a red death ray which lashes across the sky and slices through two Spitfires. The planes break apart, collide and explode. Their remains tumble through the air and into the Tiber below.

With his heart in his mouth, Will runs up the steps taking two at a time. He races through a doorway and up a stairwell. At the top is the door to what looks like an apartment. There are two dead guards lying on the floor – one has been shot in the head, the other's throat has been sliced open. It seems this could be the recognisable work of his old enemy, the Pastor, or the Russian agent, Pyotr Sedova.

With a firm grip on his pistol, Will steps cautiously into the room. It's a small lounge with a sofa and a wooden table. Oddly, there are glassless windows overlooking the city. He sees plumes of black smoke rising above the rooftops and turns at the sound of whimpering, coming from a half-open door.

'Rose?'

Peering round the door, he sees Rose's wheelchair, overturned, the rattan seat twisted and broken on the floor. Pushing the door open he sees a bed at the top of the room. Sitting on the floor, and crying into her hands, is Sofia. Will takes off the helmet. There is no sign of Rose anywhere.

'Sofia,' he calls softly.

The nurse looks up slowly. Her lip is swollen and cut, her face is puffy, her eyes red and filled with tears.

'Where is Rose?' he asks in Italian.

Her bottom lip quivers and she seems confused about who he is. He crouches down in front of her. 'Rose is my sister, Sofia. I only want to help her.'

The woman seems terrified but after a moment she points towards the ceiling.

'The roof terrace?'

The nursemaid nods. 'Please help her,' she says gripping his arm.

'I will. Thank you, Sofia.' He races out of the bedroom, hops over the dead guards and takes the steps leading to the terrace. Outside,

321

the heat smacks his face and the smell of cordite invades his nostrils. A war is raging in the sky. The Allied strike force is outnumbered by the VIPER airships and is losing the battle.

Will sees the Pastor standing with his arm raised, a blade held tightly in his hand. Backing away from him on unsteady feet is Rose. Barefoot and dressed in a white nightdress, she cradles her belly with one hand and holds a limp and lifeless cat in the other.

Charlie.

Rose is staring at the Pastor intently, her teeth clenched, her long dark hair wet and hanging like curtains over her pale face. The Pastor cannot move. He is trying but she is preventing him, keeping him at bay with the force of her mind.

'Rose,' says Will.

Her eyes flicker for a moment and she turns slowly to look in his direction.

Will feels a tightening in his throat as their eyes meet.

Rose's eyes widen. Her lips begin to move. She tries to speak, but her voice is hoarse. Reading her lips he can see she is saying his name.

'Yes. It's me. Will.'

Her face contorts in pain suddenly and she doubles over. Will hears a splashing sound as her waters break and pool around her bare feet. At that same moment her hold on the Pastor loosens and his glittering knife sweeps towards her.

'No!' cries Will. Swinging the pistol, he fires at the Pastor as his knife slices Rose's shoulder. Through the sight of the pistol, Will sees the Pastor fall as the bullet skims the back of his head, spraying blood over the terrace floor. He stumbles to the ground, trembling.

Will runs to Rose whose breathing has become shallow and rapid. His heart pounds with fear and he catches her as she falls. Laying her on the cool tiles, he places his pistol down and wipes her hair from her hot brow.

'Will, is it really you?'

'Yes. I've come for you at last.'

'I don't understand.'

'Don't try to. We have to get you out of here.'

'My baby, Will. Look after it for me.'

Will shudders. 'Don't talk like that, Rose.' He straightens his back and slips his hands underneath her, preparing to lift her up, but she cries out as a contraction hits her. He lays her down. 'Rose…' but before he finishes he is wrenched back by the hair and a savage punch is launched at his kidney. He gasps and falls to the ground. Looming over him is the pale one-eyed face of the Pastor.

He kicks Will in the ribs and stamps on his hips. Will tries to roll away but is weakened by the holy man's brutality. The Pastor crouches down to pick something up. Smiling he holds up the cut-throat razor. He kneels behind Will's head and pulls his chin up, exposing his neck. Will tries to wiggle away but he is weak. He sees the hungry grin and madness in the holy man's one remaining eye.

The blade comes down.

Will tries to break free but suddenly the Pastor disappears as if sucked away by a vacuum. He hears the crunch of bone and looks back to see the Pastor lying face down by the terrace wall. Rose is standing now and staring with ferocious concentration. She looks towards the statue of the Archangel Michael. Will watches in awe as the bronze sword arm of the statue turns its blade outwards. Rose looks to the Pastor and he begins to tremble. Within seconds his body flies across the terrace and impales itself on the sword. The Pastor screams as he looks down at the sword sticking out from his chest.

Blood fills his mouth and his body goes limp as his cruel and evil life ends.

Rose stumbles forward and Will rushes to her side.

'Will,' calls Anna.

He looks up to see Anna and Sofia standing at the terrace doorway.

'Help me,' he calls.

'*Bambina*!' shouts Sofia, rushing across the terrace and performing the sign of the cross.

The three of them carry Rose down the steps.

'Ophelia is still here,' says Anna.

'How do you know?'

'I overheard her guards talking. She's sent a search party for Rose and is planning to board her airship in the next fifteen minutes.'

'She'll be leaving from the top of the castle.'

'That's my guess.'

'We have to get Rose out of here.' An idea forms in Will's head. He turns to the nurse. 'Sofia, is there a way to get Rose out of here without being seen by Ophelia and her guards.

'*Si*,' she replies, nodding her head.

'Then please take her.'

'*Si, Signore.*'

'Anna, go with them and protect them.'

Anna nods. 'What about you?'

Will hands the pistol across to Anna. 'I'm not finished here and someone needs to look after Rose.'

'I understand.'

Rose's body shudders and she cries out again.

'She needs a doctor.'

Anna takes Will by the arm, leans across and kisses him softly on the lips. She sweeps his hair back and looks at him closely in the eyes. 'I'm sorry,' she says.

'For what?'

She looks away and does not respond, then takes one of Rose's arms, helping her down the stairs.

Will watches them leave, confused by Anna's parting words. Sorry for what? Clifford Meadows? He doesn't quite understand.

CHAPTER 49

Carpe Diem

Will returns to Rose's apartment, picks up the helmet and hurries back down towards the courtyard of the angel. As he reaches the top steps he hears Ophelia's voice and dips out of sight behind a corner wall.

'Keep looking. She can't be far, for heaven's sake!'

He sees her marching up the steps with plumes of blue cigarette smoke following her. Caught within the smoke are Coleridge, two guards and two monks. A shadow appears over the courtyard. Ophelia's airship descends towards the roof terrace. The mouth of the viper is open and the cannon has been released and primed.

As they hurry towards the terrace Will emerges from the corner but pulls back when he sees a hooded monk appear from the entrance below the steps of the courtyard. He seems shorter than most other monks and is carrying a shoulder bag and looking up towards the airship. He begins to sprint up the steps running towards the terrace. As he passes, Will gets a whiff of something familiar, something …

exotic. He catches up with the monk and walks alongside him. The monk slows and glances sideways.

'Is it common practice for the Cerastes to spray themselves with Soir de Paris?' asks Will.

The monk stops and looks at him under the cover of the hood. 'Hello, stranger,' says Madeleine.

'Have you joined the Cerastes?'

She pulls her hood back slightly so that only he can see her face. 'Not quite.' She smiles. 'I am so pleased to see you. I thought you were dead.'

'I'm still here.'

'Did you find your sister?'

'Yes. She's in good hands.'

'I am so happy for you, Will.'

'Are you going where I think you are going?' He nods upwards at the airship.

'Yes,' she says, her smile fading. 'You should leave while you still can.'

'What's in the bag?'

'Gelignite.'

'And the shard?'

Madeleine loosens the buttons on her robe and pulls out the stone, which is wrapped in copper wire attached to a gold chain around her neck.

'Good. Let's go,' he says, hurrying up the steps.

'Wait. You cannot go.'

'Why?'

'Because I expect when I go up I will never come back. This is a suicide mission.'

'I realise that.'

'So go home. Have a nice life.'

'Why don't you give me the explosives and the shard and then you go home and have a nice life? Go help your uncle. He needs you.'

Madeleine exhales quickly. 'He's still alive then?'

'Very much so.'

Madeleine smiles and sighs. 'Thank God. I was so worried.'

'So go home. Help him. The war is not over yet.'

Madeleine shakes her head. 'No. Too many of my friends and family have died because of VIPER. I must finish this.'

'As you know, they have taken almost everything from me. Two heads are better than one. We do this together, Madeleine. If we both die, so be it.'

She meets his gaze and smiles. 'Carpe diem.'

'Carpe diem.'

'For France.'

'For humanity,' says Will.

'For humanity.' Madeleine pulls up her hood and together they hurry up the steps.

'What's your plan?' asks Will.

'Not quite sure of that yet.'

'I have something in mind.

'Good.'

CHAPTER 50

Countdown

Will and Madeleine reach the terrace and see the guards and monks hurrying up the airship's ramp behind Coleridge and Ophelia.

Will quickens his pace and as he steps on to the ramp, he glances back at the limp corpse of the Pastor impaled and bloody on the Archangel Michael's sword. The irony was not lost on him. In the Bible, Michael leads God's army against the forces of evil. If he was a superstitious man he would see the Pastor's death as some sort of sign. But he is not. He carries on and keeps his head down, avoiding the eyes of any that might recognise him.

As he reaches the deck he hears a guard shout, 'Raise the ramp!' The ramp is pulled up, and Will and Madeleine line up side by side with the other guards and monks as Ophelia and Coleridge walk towards the navigation room.

Ophelia is angry. 'I don't care that you have not found her. Radio whoever is down there and have them search every corner and turn over every stone. If Starling has her they won't get far. He will take her to hospital rather than risk the journey out of the city. If the Russians have her, then that's the end of that!'

Coleridge responds but they are already out of earshot.

The guards and monks begin to disperse. Will shoots a look at Madeleine and signals across the deck at the yellow barrels of gas. Glancing around, he checks no one is watching them with suspicion. Everyone is going about their duties. Will makes his way across with Madeleine following. Behind the barrels and out of sight, he points at the grey doors with the two sentinel monks.

'That's where we need to get to. The power source is there and beyond it is the navigation room. We just have to get past those two guards.'

'Take one of these,' says Madeleine, handing across a Beretta pistol.

Will takes it and slides it under his belt in the small of his back. 'Thank you. But I was thinking of something more subtle.'

The grey door opens and a machine operator walks through to the deck. It is the woman in the horn-rimmed spectacles and lab coat. She is carrying four large files with both hands.

'I think we've found our ticket inside. Follow me.' Will hurries after the machine operator. 'Can I help you with those?'

She looks at him suspiciously, but he smiles sweetly. The woman relaxes, nods her head and hands them across. 'Thank you. They are rather heavy.' She leads him out of the deck and into a corridor with views over the city. 'I must powder my nose. Would you mind?'

'Not at all. I'll wait.'

She disappears into the ladies' room followed moments later by Madeleine.

The gondola shudders as the airship rises and turns. Will sees the city below veiled in billowing clouds of black smoke and its people running for shelter from the apocalyptic skies above.

Madeleine appears at the entrance to the ladies room. Her dark hair is swept back and she is wearing the lab coat and horn-rimmed spectacles. She beckons him across and takes one of the files from him. She removes the printouts from inside and shoves them into a bin by the toilet door, replacing them with six sticks of gelignite.

'Ready?' says Will.

She nods and they make their way back across the deck towards the grey doors.

An alarm begins to sound and red lights fixed to the ceiling begin to flash. Will's muscles tighten and Madeleine looks worried. Have they been caught out?

A voice comes over the tannoy. 'Cannon engaged. Five-minute countdown. Ensure you are all at your stations.'

Will relaxes and follows Madeleine to the grey doors. The sentinels watch them as they approach. Madeleine begins to babble. 'Hurry,' she says to Will, in a shrill loud voice. 'We only have five minutes and the machine room need these printouts.'

The sentinel on the right steps in front of the door blocking their path. 'I don't recognise you,' he says to Madeleine.

'She's a science officer on loan from another ship,' says Will.

'And?'

Madeleine interjects, 'Please remove yourself from the doorway. We must deliver these printouts immediately. The machine operators need these codes before the cannon is fired.'

'Show me your papers.'

'We are at war, minutes from firing the cannon without the correct codes and you wish to see my papers?' She pushes her face up to his. 'Ophelia Black personally selected me for this ship. Just consider how angry she will be when the cannon fires with the wrong codes. It may strike one of our own airships. How will you explain that to her?'

The sentinel's brows knit together briefly as he considers his options. After a moment he steps aside to let them through. Madeleine glares at him as he opens the grey doors. Passing through Will feels the familiar warm blast of steam on his face and hears the mechanical whooshing from two giant fans in the ceiling above them. They make their way across the steel bridge.

'How did you know about the codes?' he asks.

'I made a copy of the microfilm I gave you.'

'Ah yes, the uptight Parisian agent codenamed Marie-Antoinette.'

She regards him with a wry smile. 'Of course. After leaving London I travelled to Lyon where Eoin and I worked hard to interpret the schematic. We were in constant touch with your friend, Edward.'

'Good old Edward.' The mention of Chartres turns his thoughts to his friends. 'Madeleine, my friends, Emile and Claudette…' Will lets the sentence hang. The painful reminder of his dead friends scuppers his train of thought.

'I took them to the local priest. He will see that they get the burial they deserve.'

'Thank you.'

'You do realise we only have one shard and enough explosive to blow *this* ship.'

'Yes, I do. However, I have seen what the shard is capable of. If we do this properly we might just take out more than one.'

'How?'

'I don't know yet.'

Midway across the bridge Will hears voices but there seems to be no one in the machine room. Looking down he sees the Tesla cannon surrounded by men in dirty overalls shouting at each other as they prepare the weapon for battle. Turning left, he follows Madeleine across the walkway and up the steps to the bank of machines and the tall pyramidal shaft with its glowing glass sphere on top. A man writing on a clipboard appears from behind it. He frowns. 'Who are you?'

Will hears the unmistakable *phut* of a silencer pistol. The man topples forward. Madeleine catches him and eases him to the floor. Will glances around hoping no prying eyes have suddenly appeared. His heart racing, he helps Madeleine drag the man behind the machines and out of sight.

The tannoy crackles. 'Three minutes!' a voice calls. Will looks down and sees the men under the bridge working faster around the cannon.

'We have to hurry,' he says.

Madeleine slips behind the power source. Will joins her with the gelignite, watching as she undoes the catches of a panel. She places it on the floor and a blast of scorching heat and blinding green light assaults their faces and eyes. Madeleine takes the explosives and retrieves a Time Pencil from her pocket. She removes the shard from around her neck and ties it with the chain around the explosives. Blue sparks surround her hand. The shard can feel the Tesla power source.

'Three minutes?' she asks, her face pale.

Will nods his agreement.

Cautiously she cracks the glass vial releasing the Time Pencil's acid and inserts it into the soft gelignite. She then places the explosive inside the power source and fixes the panel back on.

'Now what?' she asks.

'This is Ophelia's ship. Arguably the most important. We need it to go rogue.'

'How?'

'We need control of the navigation room first. We do whatever it takes to get that.'

The tannoy crackles once more. 'One minute.'

As they hurry down the steps Will notices the men are no longer by the cannon. Running over the bridge they slow as the navigation room door slides open and Coleridge walks through. Will can see Ophelia standing with the captain watching the war in the skies outside.

'Frith!' calls Coleridge. 'What the hell is keeping those figures?'

Will dips his head as Coleridge approaches.

'Mr Frith!' Coleridge steps onto the bridge and walks down towards the machine room.

Madeleine eases past him. Beneath the bridge the bottom doors of the gondola open. Cool air rushes in. Will can feel Coleridge's eyes on him.

'One moment,' says Coleridge. His hand reaches across to Will pushing up his chin. Their eyes meet.

'Starling!' he hisses angrily.

CHAPTER 51

The Rogue Airship

Will launches a punch at Coleridge's face, but it's deflected, and Coleridge tries to push Will over the rail. 'Guards!' he calls, his hands clawing at Will's face.

Will turns away from the raking fingers and gasps at the long drop to the Vatican City and St Peter's Basilica below. Madeleine is engaged in a gun battle with the captain and his second. Ophelia is nowhere to be seen. Will pushes harder and clenching his teeth he kicks at Coleridge's shins. The older man shifts his leg and Will is able to slam his knee into his balls. Will feels his body shuddering. Taking his chance, Will head butts Coleridge in the nose. It makes sickening crunch and blood explodes across his face. Coleridge is finished. Will grabs the lapels of his suit and flips him over the rail. Coleridge's eyes and mouth widen in disbelief as he plunges, arms and legs flailing, towards the ground.

'Hurry, Will,' says Madeleine.

Looking up, Will sees the captain lying dead and his second nursing a bloody wound in his stomach. Madeleine is thankfully unhurt. The sound of the klaxon reverberates around the bridge forcing them both to cover their ears. They hurry to the navigation room and find Ophelia waiting. She is clutching Will's Mauser with one trembling hand and in the other is a cigarette, which she sucks at greedily.

Out of the corner of his eye Will sees Madeleine raise her pistol.

'You are too late,' says Ophelia. 'We are many. We…'

Madeleine squeezes the trigger. The shot blows a hole in the VIPER queen's scrawny throat. Her eyes widen and her jaw begins to moves up and down, as if she is trying to finish her statement. Blood and smoke ooze from the hole and then she collapses, her eyes dead, her twisted life gone forever.

'VA1, this is VA12. What are your orders?' a voice comes over the speaker.

Will picks up the receiver. 'All ships. Ophelia Black is dead. VA1 is going rogue. Destroy VA1 immediately. Repeat, destroy VA1.'

Will stares at the large red button on the navigator's control panel. He slams his palm on it. The cannon fires. The beam lashes wildly across the sky and connects with an airship. The ship erupts instantly in a blinding ball of flames.

'What the hell?' shouts a voice over the radio. 'VA1, what is going on?'

'Stand back,' says Will. Taking out his pistol he fires it at the button, blowing it from the control panel. He looks at Madeleine. 'Time for us to abandon ship.'

'But how? Lifeboats are hardly an option.'

'There's still hope. Come on.' Will sprints out of the navigation room with Madeleine behind him. Below them, the cannon lashes its fiery green death ray across the skies. They run through the grey doors and past the sentinels. Midway across the deck Will glances behind him. The sentinels are checking through the doors.

'Quick!' he shouts, heading towards one of the sliding windows that run from floor to ceiling on either side of the deck. He pulls it across and steps out onto the slatted wooden balcony with the angled windows that overlook the world below. At the base of each window is a red roll of material – the ribbons that, together, combine to make the VIPER flag.

From the balcony Will can see the airship passing over St Peter's Basilica and the dome below. He looks at Madeleine. 'Ready?'

She nods. 'Let's do it.'

Will opens the window and pushes a red roll outside. It is heavy, the material thick and strong. It tumbles through the air and flutters in the wind below the airship. Madeleine climbs out first, followed by Will. They scurry down the red ribbon as the airship rises above St Peter's. He sees the dome approaching but the ribbon does not stretch quite far enough.

'Now!' he shouts as the ribbon floats above the immense dome. There is perhaps a ten foot drop. But the airship continues to rise. 'Drop now!'

Madeleine lets go and falls and Will swings towards the dome. Terrified, he scrambles to grab on to something as his body slams the surface of the roof and slides over the dome, tumbling to the base where he flips over and manages to grab the ledge. His heart racing, his face damp with perspiration, he clings on hard. Glancing down he sees a further twenty-foot drop to the rooftop below where Madeleine lies, unconscious or dead, he cannot be sure. 'Madeleine!' he calls but she does not respond.

He sees a column to his right and, holding tight, climbs across like a monkey on a thin branch. Wrapping his legs around the column he shimmies down it and onto a rooftop with statues of saints overlooking St Peter's Square.

He kneels by Madeleine's side and leans close. She is still breathing. Her eyes flicker open and meet his. 'Did we do it?'

He looks up towards the skies. All thirty-six airships are surrounding VA1 whose cannon continues to fire indiscriminately. The sound of half a dozen klaxons fills the air around Rome. And then Will watches as Ophelia's ship is surrounded by an unearthly blue light. *The shard's power is growing.*

The other ships launch their cannon fire on Ophelia's ship, but somehow the vessel remains undamaged. *The shard is working.*

And then Ophelia's ship blows from the inside with a roaring echoing boom that makes the rooftop quake and the statues around St Peter's square tremble. A bright blue flame swirls out from the remains of the airship and spreads across the skies destroying anything and everything that flies there. Raising his hand to stave off the glare, Will watches in wonder as Ophelia's fleet, the Red Storm, is reduced to ashes, it's deadly gas neutralised by the blue shard.

'We did it,' says Madeleine, pushing herself up, with some difficulty.

'How are you feeling?'

'My head is sore. I don't think anything is broken.'

Looking up at the sky Will can't quite believe what has just happened. VIPER is finished. The Red Storm is now nothing more than ash. He wonders about the shard. Has it been destroyed? The Allied planes are gone too. Some have no doubt been destroyed in the battle; others have escaped, he hopes. The skies are quiet once more as ash falls across the city like black snow.

CHAPTER 52

Sedova

Will helps Madeleine up and she dusts herself down and fixes her thick black curls.

'I have to return to Castle St Angelo,' he says.

'Your sister?'

'Yes. Anna is watching over her but who knows what trouble they may run into. A Russian spy called Sedova is searching for her. He is here in Rome.'

'Pyotr Sedova?'

'Yes.'

'Pyotr Sedova is dead. He died in a gulag five years ago.'

Will frowns at her. 'Are you sure?'

'I am in the business of buying and selling information. I know this stuff.'

'Then who is the Russian spy searching for Rose?'

'We must hurry, Will,' says Madeleine, not meeting his gaze. 'The quickest route will be via Passetto di Borgo,' says Madeleine. 'It is a raised passage above the city designed as a fast escape route for popes whose lives were under threat. It will take us direct from the Vatican City to Castle St Angelo.'

Will feels that Madeleine knows more that she is letting on but follows her to a weathered door at the base of the dome. It is locked but fortunately also weak. He forces it open and they climb down through narrow passages and then onto a wider staircase, which they sprint down two, three steps at a time. The inside of St Peter's is immense and, in the church itself, some sort of mass seems to be happening. Below he see the congregation – a mixture of priests, nuns, lay people and German and Italian soldiers. God-fearing types driven there by the hellish battle in the heavens above them.

He follows Madeleine across to an exit on the side of the dome that leads them out onto the Vatican wall lined with its pale statues of saints.

'How do you know about this?' says Will, as they join the narrow walkway that is Passetto di Borgo.

'My parents and I spent a lot of time here when I was young. My father helped restore some of the paintings in the Basilica, including the Sistine Chapel.'

'That's who you get your painting skills from?'

She glances at him with a wry smile, but does not say anything.

They sprint across the elevated passage. The passage is less than half a mile in length and they reach the castle within minutes. Inside the rooms are empty and the silence is loud.

'Rose! Anna!' Will calls, but there is no response. He hurries through the castle shouting their names at the top of his voice. Madeleine does the same. They split up, searching through the rooms in each of the corridors and making their way gradually down each level.

Then, 'Will!' cries Madeleine, 'Hurry!'

Running down the stone steps near the entrance Will sees the body of the nursemaid lying in a pool of blood. His heart sinks. 'Rose! Anna!' he calls, his throat hoarse and dry. He hears the sound of a vehicle approaching outside. He meets Madeleine's gaze and they both jump up and run down the cobbled stone steps and out through the arched doorways.

Agent Sedova had not meant to kill the nursemaid. She had been useful as a midwife enabling safe passage for the child to this godforsaken world. But she'd refused to let the baby leave. Sedova had had no choice.

Now, with the crying child held softly and firmly in one arm, and a pistol in the other, Sedova hurries away from the Red Tower, eyes blinking away the strange black snow, to cross Ponte Sant'Angelo under the watchful gaze of the angels on either side of the bridge. Sedova sees the approaching Russian agents in the stolen baker's van and then stiffens as a voice calls from behind.

It is the last voice Sedova wants to hear.

'Anna!' calls Will.

Sedova stops and closes her eyes. Shame tears at her soul and she wishes she had time to explain, but he would not understand. She has betrayed him and lied to him. But she has her reasons. Perhaps one day he will understand. He must ... she hopes. She hears his footfalls approaching and turns, swinging the pistol in his direction.

He slows, he sees her properly and the colour seeps from his face. 'Anna? What's going on?'

'So you're the Russian spy?' says Madeleine. 'You're the older daughter, I assume. Anastasiya Sedova? A Muscovite. I should have known. That explains your dress sense.'

The Frenchwoman's words mean nothing to Anna. Her eyes never leave Will's. She can feel the smallest of shakes in her gun hand and fights to steady it.

The van screeches to a stop and she hears the two agents emerge with their rifles clicking.

'Anna, don't do this. Give me the baby.'

'I can't, Will. I'm sorry.'

He shakes his head and she can see his eyes full of disbelief and hurt.

'Anna…'

But she will not be broken. 'Rose is in her apartment. There was no time to get her to a hospital. Go to her. Take her to a doctor.'

Will glances back at the Red Tower and seems uncertain about what to do.

The two Russian agents are now standing beside her, their rifles trained on Will and the Frenchwoman.

Sedova retreats to the back of the van and climbs inside to sit among the empty wooden crates where flour is scattered and the smell of fresh bread lingers. It makes her think of home and she strokes the child's head and tries not to think about Will. She has turned a corner and there is no going back. Her stomach twists and she feels something die inside her. She has always known this day would come and that it would be hard. She hadn't realised just how hard.

CHAPTER 53

A Tiny Voice

Will's hands cup the sides of his head as he watches the baker's van disappear further down the Ponte Sant'Angelo and away from him and Madeleine. He can see Anna and the baby framed in the van's dirty rear window like a murky portrait of the Madonna and child.

'Anna!' he calls at the top of his voice, but the van soon disappears and she is gone. He remembers their last moments together. She had taken Will by the arm, kissed him softly on the lips, swept back his hair back and said, 'I'm sorry.' He had thought it a delayed and unnecessary apology for Meadows, but it had been something much worse.

She had been lying to him all this time.

He feels hollow inside.

'Will,' says a voice. In his confusion he turns in its direction and sees Madeleine. She takes his hand and squeezes gently. 'Let's go inside. We must find your sister.'

In that moment, despite a creeping desolation, Will comes to his senses. 'Of course.'

They leave the Ponte Sant'Angelo and run back into the tower. As they hurry inside Will stops where the body of the nursemaid lies peacefully dead. Despite working for VIPER the woman seemed kind and had doted on Rose. Was Anna responsible for her death? Had she tried to stop Anna taking the child?

'Who was she, Will?' asks Madeleine.

'Someone who cared.'

They run up to the top of the tower and Will stops outside the apartment when he hears a tiny voice call out. They hurry inside. There is no one in the living room. He dashes to the bedroom and sees Rose lying on the bed, eyes closed, sleeping soundly. The floor to the side of her bed contains bloody blankets and a bucket of bloody water. She is pale but otherwise seems fine.

'Will, look!' says Madeleine.

He follows her gaze to a chest of drawers, which has one protruding drawer at the bottom. Lying inside it, nestled in a blanket is the source of the tiny voice. It's a baby.

'Rose had twins,' he whispers.

'Ooh, poor thing,' says Madeleine crouching down to pick up the child.

'Will?'

Will turns to see Rose awake and looking up at him. She is drawn and tired.

'I can't believe it's you.' She reaches for him and he bends forward and hugs her tight.

The baby makes a gurgling sound.

'Is that my baby?'

Madeleine carries the child over and lowers her onto the bed. 'Yes it is.'

Will watches as Rose smiles lovingly at her child. 'Oh my. Look at you. Aren't you beautiful. And I thought you'd be a boy.'

Despite her poor health, Rose seems happy and Will does not want to change that. He looks at Madeleine and shakes his head furtively. She nods and he knows she understands that for now Rose must not know about the second child.

CHAPTER 54

Ana

Ana Sedova cradles the child. Holding it close to her chest, she caresses its cheek and hums an old Russian lullaby, one her beloved father used to sing to her. The journey in the back of the baker's van is bumpy; the wooden crates shake and rattle, yet despite that the child is soon fast asleep. They have driven for over an hour and Ana has been so captivated by the child that she has forgotten about Will and his sister, the mother of the child she had stolen.

It all comes back to her now, though. Her stomach turns and she closes her eyes. Not only has betrayed the only man she has ever loved but she has become someone who robs mothers of their children. Her father would never approve. She was sure of that. But he was gone and she had been left with no choice. She would do it again in a heartbeat … she shakes her head. *No, I couldn't.*

She recalls the birth and how troubled the mother had become. There had been no time to take her to the doctor so they made her comfortable in her apartment despite the war raging in the red skies outside. Ana had fetched water and towels as the labour began. The mother was in pain and had been unable to control her kinetic power. The walls had trembled and cracks had begun to appear in the floor and ceiling. The nursemaid had had no choice but to sedate her and perform the birth herself. The nursemaid pulled out the child and Ana's resolve had wavered. She had decided she could not go through with stealing the baby, despite what it would cost her.

But then, as a thunderous explosion roared outside and an unearthly blue light filled the skies, a second child came.

There were two. This was so unexpected and surely a gift – her mind had raced with possibilities. The mother was still sedated and would be none the wiser. Ana held the second child as the nursemaid placed the first one in a makeshift cot fashioned from the drawer of a dresser. As she cleaned and made the mother comfortable Ana slipped away with the child. But the nursemaid was no fool and pursued her. Regrettably, Ana had had no choice but to kill her. The truth was, the fewer the people who knew about this child, the better. The mother would wake to find her baby safe and well and Ana would be gone with a second child that no one would ever know about.

She almost laughs. That had just been wishful thinking. She leans over and kisses the baby on the nose. The child has somehow brought her an inner peace that she has not felt in a long time. Was this part of its gifts? Was this why people wanted Rose Starling's offspring?

The van drives out of Rome and into remote countryside. Ana looks up through the windscreen and recognises the meeting point.

'Stop here,' she says.

The driver pulls over and Ana gently wraps her arm around the head of the child protecting its swaddled ears. With the other hand she lifts the pistol and blows a hole in the back of each of the agent's heads. Blood and brains splatter across the windscreen, but she is past caring about such things.

She opens the back door of the van and hurries through the woods cradling the baby who has not been disturbed by the gunshots at all. She smiles down at it and feels an odd sense of protectiveness, just like she felt with her sister Elena and her mother. She wonders what they are doing now and if they ever think of her.

Twenty minutes into the woods she sees the cabin. There is an ambulance parked outside. She hurries across to it, her eyes darting from side to side.

The cabin door opens and she stops to look at the man standing at the door. Roland Cooper is dressed in his trademark blue pinstripe suit and leans against the doorframe like an old friend welcoming her to his home.

He is anything but a friend.

'Well, well. I never thought you'd actually do it. I must say I am very impressed, Agent Sedova.'

Behind him a small medical team emerges: a doctor and two nurses dressed in whites. One of the nurses tries to take the child, but Ana hesitates.

'Now, now, we had an arrangement, missy.'

Missy.

Ana holds her tongue and fights the urge to plant her fist in his smug face. She hands the baby across but it begins to cry.

'Wonderful,' says Cooper. 'I will see to it your mother and sister are taken good care of.'

'I want them to go the United States. As we agreed.'

'Yes, Agent Sedova. I plan to send them to Minnesota. It's cold and remote there. They'll love it. A home from home.'

The baby continues to cry loudly.

'Please shut it up,' says Cooper.

The medical team can't seem to calm it down. Ana takes it from them and holds it softly to her bosom. The baby coos and stops crying.

'Seems you have a knack,' says Cooper. 'Perhaps we'll extend your contract for a while longer.' Cooper stands over the child, 'Well, hello young man. And what shall we call you?'

'His name is Peter,' Ana lies, thinking of her father, Pyotr. 'The mother said if it was a boy that's what she would name him.'

Cooper nods his head. 'Then Peter it is.'

ACKNOWLEDGEMENTS

Thank you to everyone at the Dome Press. In particular the dynamo that is Emily Glenister and my ever-patient editor, Rebecca Lloyd, for bearing with me as I tried to pull the Red Storm together. But most of all, thank you David H. Headley for everything.

Sleeper

JD FENNELL

Sixteen-year-old Will Starling is pulled from the sea with no memory of his past. In his blazer is a strange notebook with a bullet lodged inside: a bullet meant for him. As London prepares for the Blitz, Will soon finds himself pursued by vicious agents and a ruthless killer known as the Pastor. All of them want Will's notebook and will do anything to get it.

As Will's memory starts to return, he realises he is no ordinary sixteen-year-old. He has skills that make him a match for any assassin. But there is something else. At his core is a deep-rooted rage that he cannot explain. Where is his family and why has no one reported him missing?

Fighting for survival with the help of MI5 agent-in-training Anna Wilder, Will follows leads across London in a race against time to find the Stones of Fire before the next air raid makes a direct hit and destroys London forever.

www.sleeperbook.com